Emmanuel Guibert

Marc Boutavant

ARIOL

The Three Donkeys

PAPERCUT Z™
New York

ARIOL Graphic Novels available from PAPERCUTZ

ARIOL graphic novels are also available digitally wherever e-books are sold.

Emmanuel Guibert
Marc Boutavant
ARIOL
Just a Donkey Like You and Me
PAPERCUTZ

Graphic Novel #1
"Just a Donkey Like You and Me"

Emmanuel Guibert
Marc Boutavant
ARIOL
Thunder Horse
PAPERCUTZ

Graphic Novel #2
"Thunder Horse"

Emmanuel Guibert
Marc Boutavant
ARIOL
Happy as a Pig...
PAPERCUTZ

Graphic Novel #3
"Happy as a Pig..."

Emmanuel Guibert
Marc Boutavant
ARIOL
A Beautiful Cow
PAPERCUTZ

Graphic Novel #4
"A Beautiful Cow"

Emmanuel Guibert
Marc Boutavant
ARIOL
Bizzbilla Hits the Bullseye
PAPERCUTZ

Graphic Novel #5
"Bizzbilla Hits the Bullseye"

ARIOL
PAPERCUTZ

Graphic Novel #6
"A Nasty Cat"

Emmanuel Guibert
Marc Boutavant
ARIOL
Top Dog
PAPERCUTZ

Graphic Novel #7
"Top Dog"

ARIOL
PAPERCUTZ

Graphic Novel #8
"The Three Donkeys"

ARIOL graphic novels are available for $12.99 only in paperback, except for "Where's Petula?" which is $9.99. The ARIOL Boxed Sets are $38.99 each. Available from booksellers everywhere. You can also order online from "http://www.papercutz.com" papercutz.com. Or call 1-800-886-1223, Monday through Friday, 9 – 5 EST. MC, Visa, and AmEx accepted. To order by mail, please add $4.00 for postage and handling for first book ordered, $1.00 for each additional book and make check payable to NBM Publishing. Send to: Papercutz, 160 Broadway, Suite 700, East Wing, New York, NY 10038. ARIOL graphic novels are also available digitally wherever e-books are sold.

Emmanuel Guibert
Marc Boutavant
ARIOL
Where's PETULA?
PAPERCUTZ

"Where's Petula?"
Graphic Novel

Emmanuel Guibert
Marc Boutavant
ARIOL
The Teeth of the Rabbit
PAPERCUTZ

COMING SOON
Graphic Novel #9
""The Teeth of the Rabbit"

PAPERCUTZ.COM

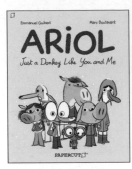

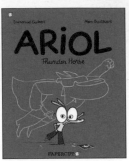

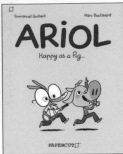

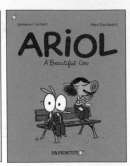

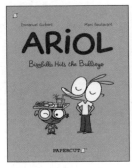

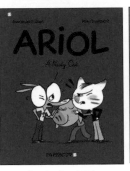

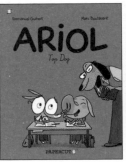

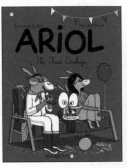

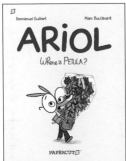

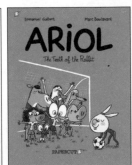

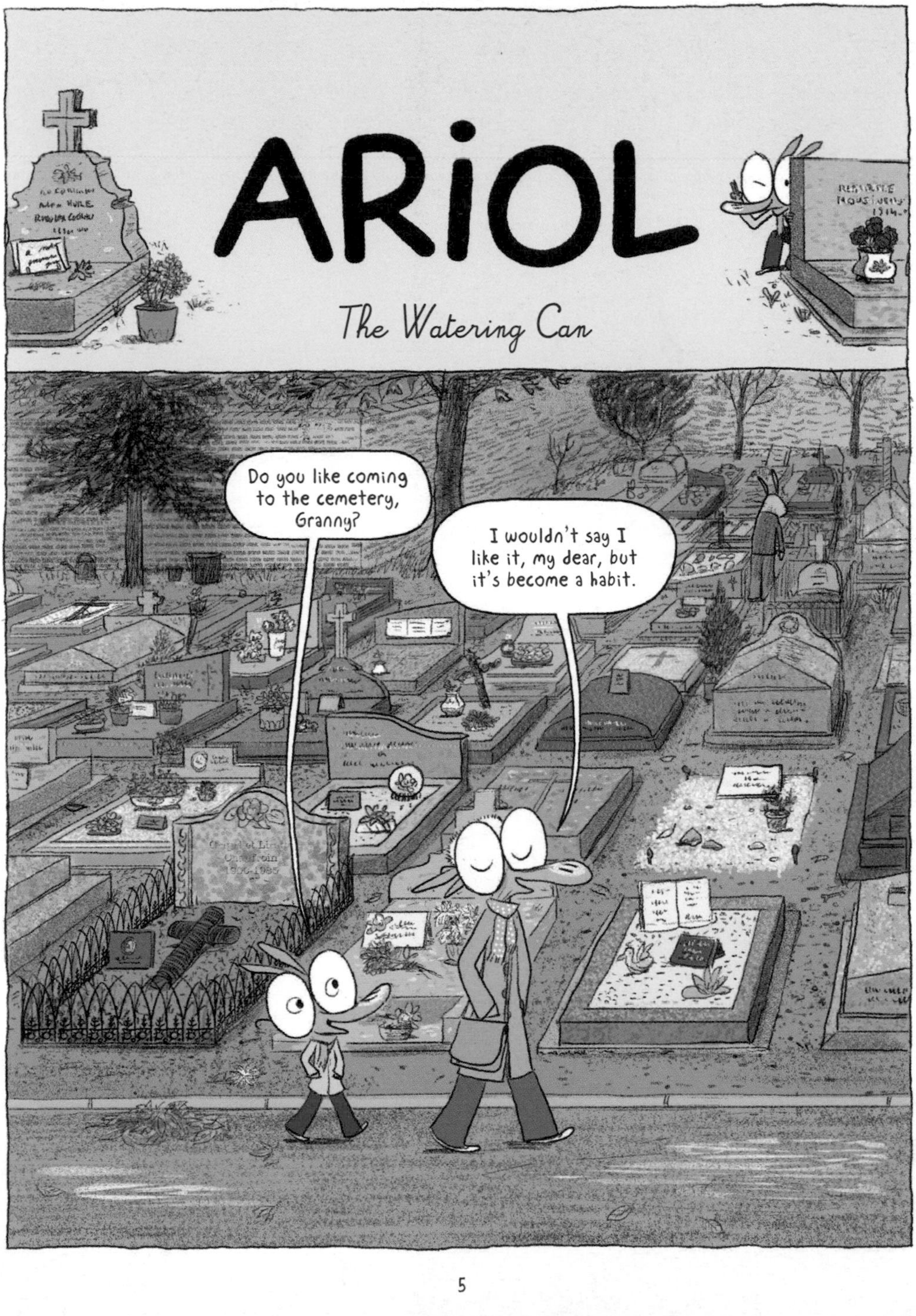
ARiOL
The Watering Can
Do you like coming to the cemetery, Granny?
I wouldn't say I like it, my dear, but it's become a habit.

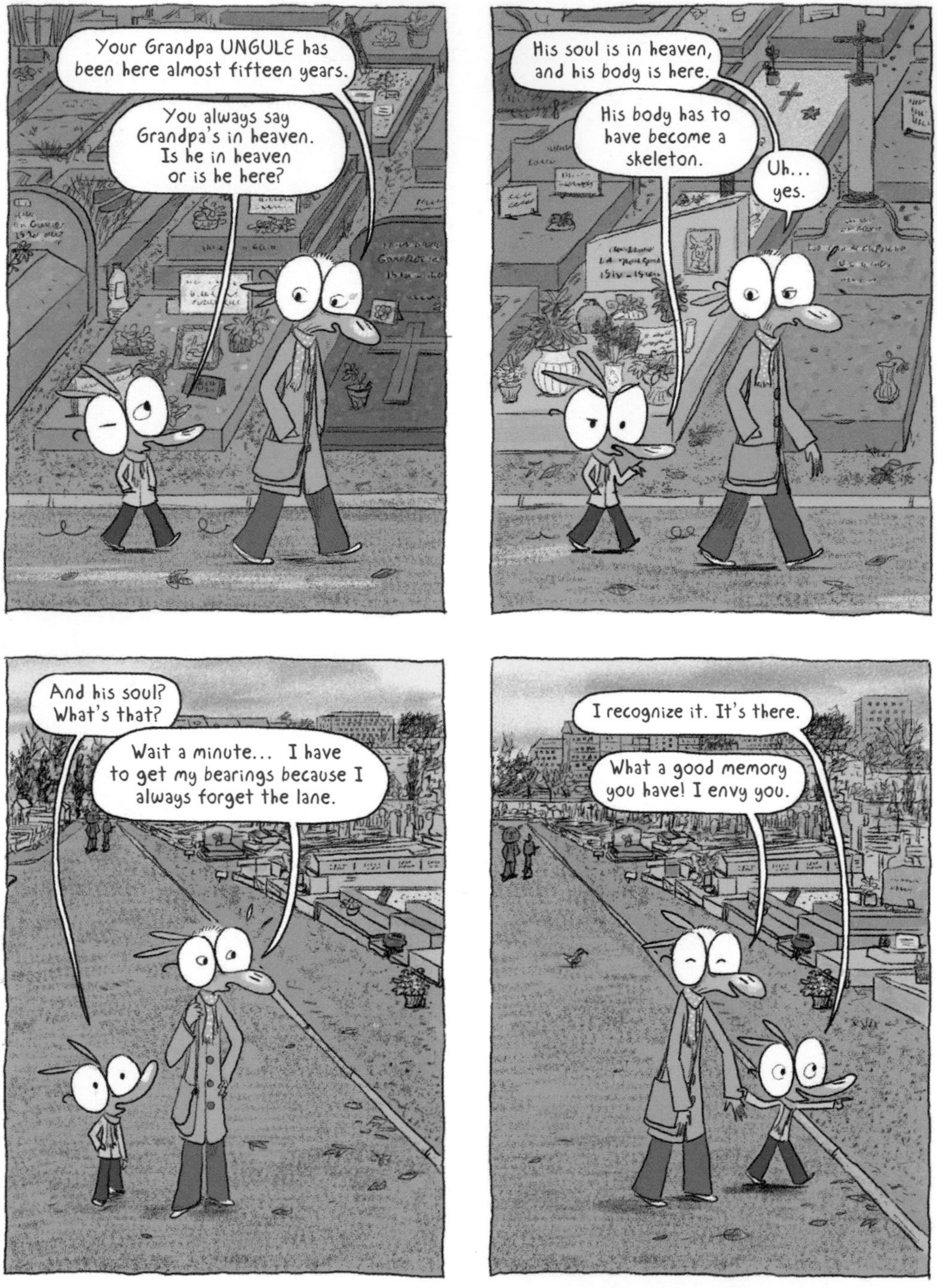
Your Grandpa UNGULE has been here almost fifteen years.
You always say Grandpa's in heaven. Is he in heaven or is he here?
His soul is in heaven, and his body is here.
His body has to have become a skeleton.
Uh... yes.
And his soul? What's that?
Wait a minute... I have to get my bearings because I always forget the lane.
I recognize it. It's there.
What a good memory you have! I envy you.

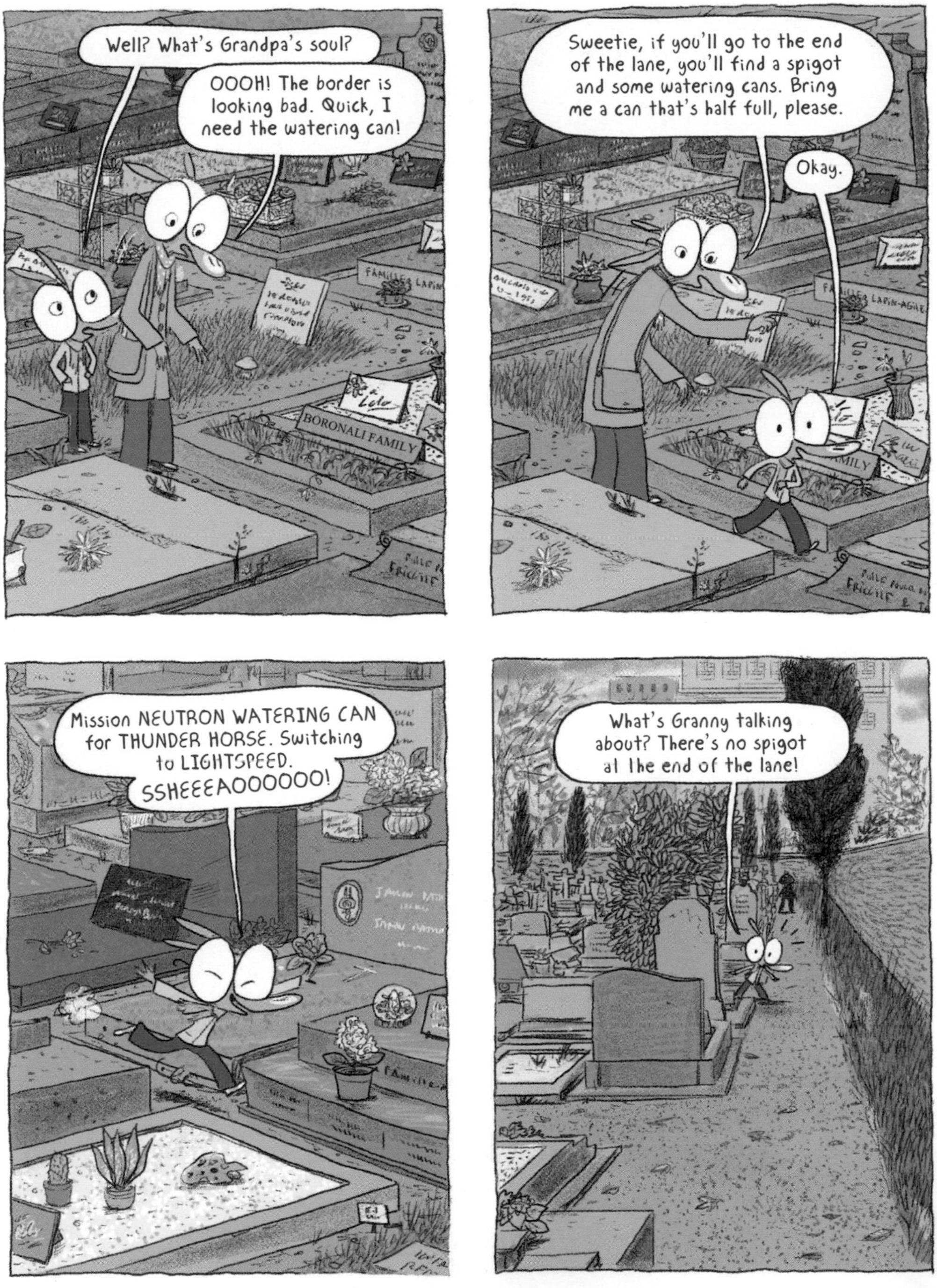
Well? What's Grandpa's soul?
OOOH! The border is looking bad. Quick, I need the watering can!
BORONALI FAMILY
Sweetie, if you'll go to the end of the lane, you'll find a spigot and some watering cans. Bring me a can that's half full, please.
Okay.
Mission NEUTRON WATERING CAN for THUNDER HORSE. Switching to LIGHTSPEED. SSHEEEAOOOOOO!
What's Granny talking about? There's no spigot at the end of the lane!

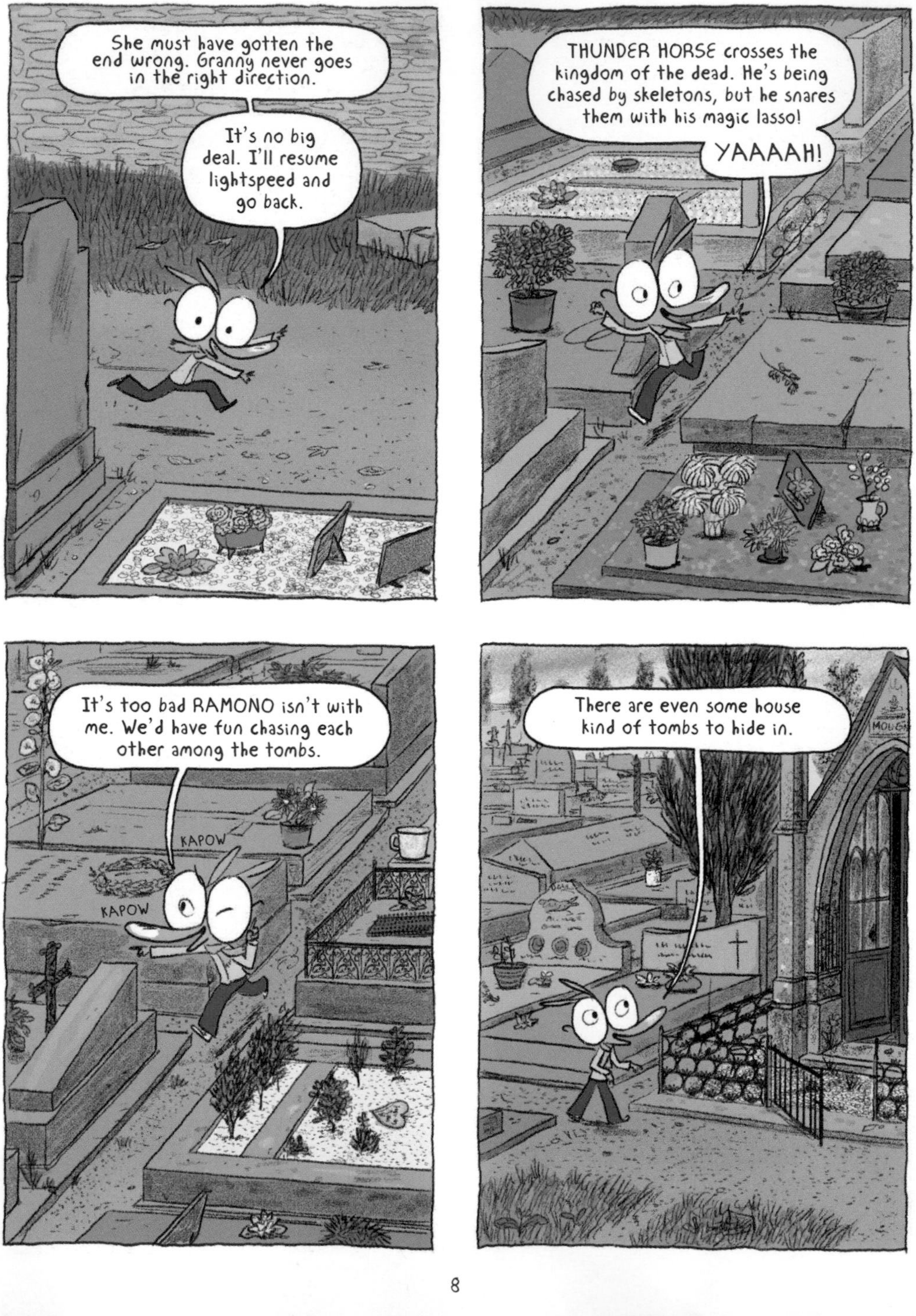
She must have gotten the end wrong. Granny never goes in the right direction.
It's no big deal. I'll resume lightspeed and go back.
THUNDER HORSE crosses the kingdom of the dead. He's being chased by skeletons, but he snares them with his magic lasso!
YAAAAH!
It's too bad RAMONO isn't with me. We'd have fun chasing each other among the tombs.
KAPOW
KAPOW
There are even some house kind of tombs to hide in.

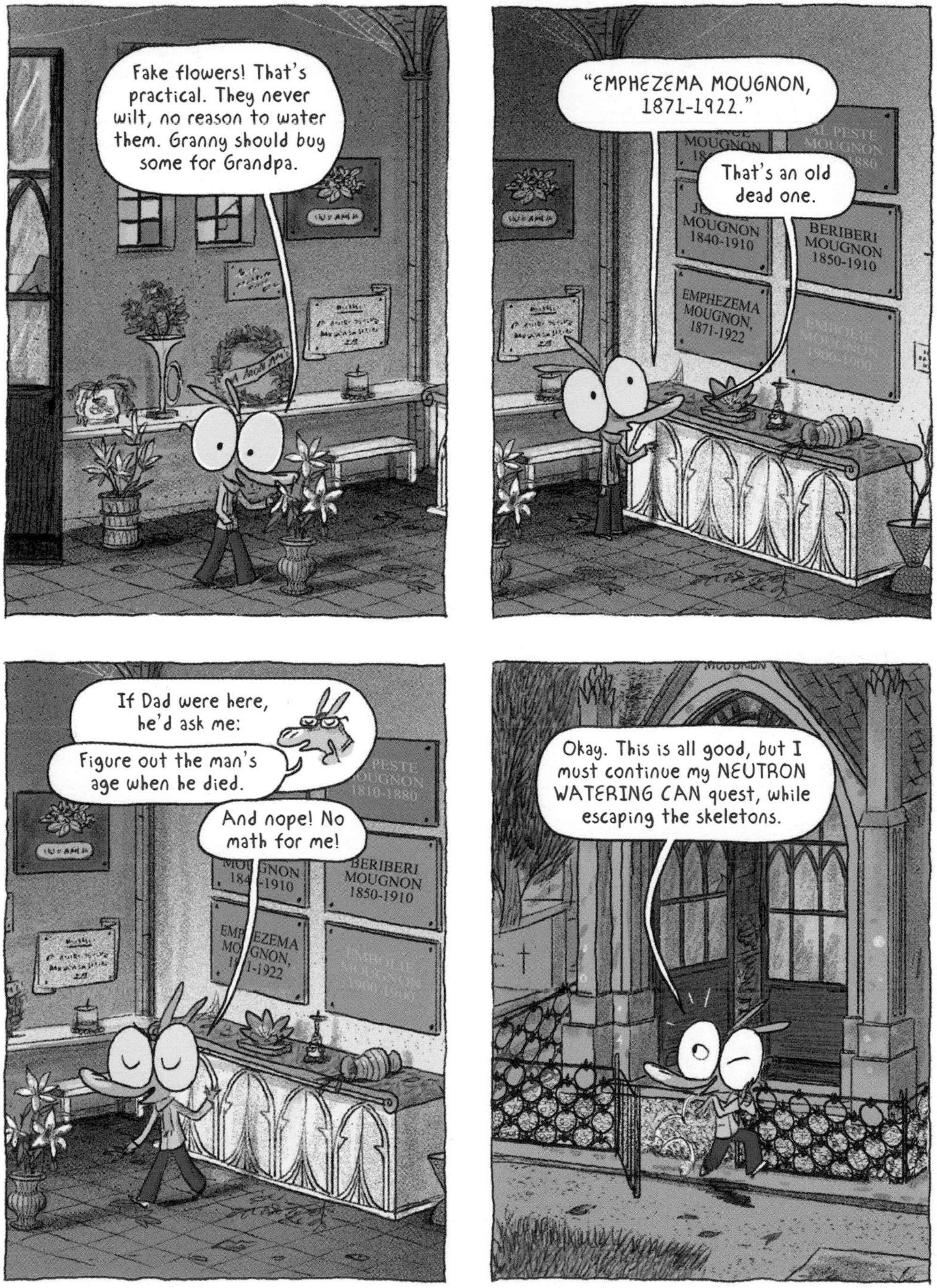
Fake flowers! That's practical. They never wilt, no reason to water them. Granny should buy some for Grandpa.
"EMPHEZEMA MOUGNON, 1871-1922."
MOUGNON 1840-1910
BERIBERI MOUGNON 1850-1910
EMPHEZEMA MOUGNON, 1871-1922
That's an old dead one.
If Dad were here, he'd ask me:
Figure out the man's age when he died.
And nope! No math for me!
Okay. This is all good, but I must continue my NEUTRON WATERING CAN quest, while escaping the skeletons.

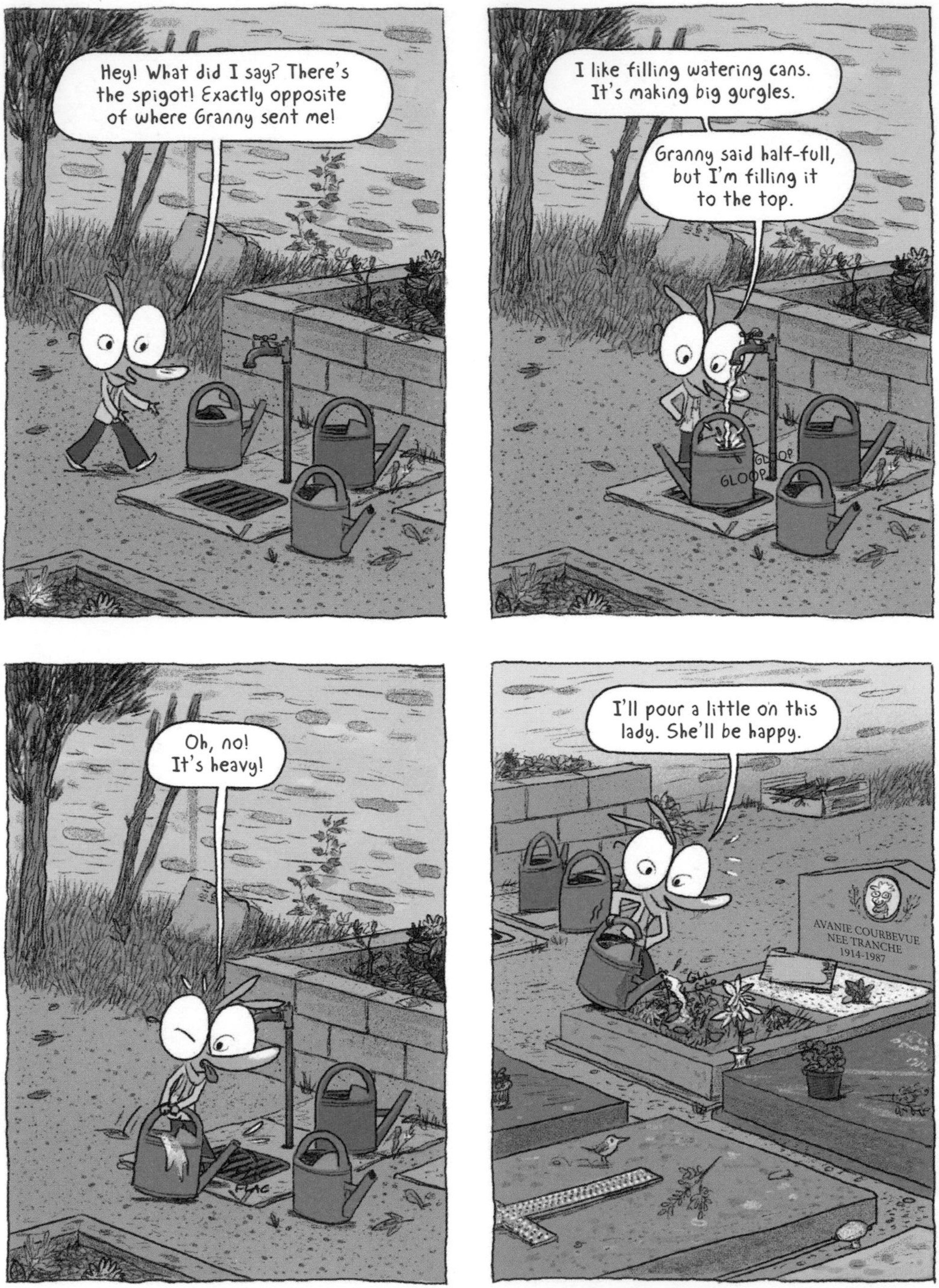
Hey! What did I say? There's the spigot! Exactly opposite of where Granny sent me!
I like filling watering cans. It's making big gurgles.
Granny said half-full, but I'm filling it to the top.
GLOOP
GLOOP
Oh, no! It's heavy!
FLAC
I'll pour a little on this lady. She'll be happy.
AVANIE COURBEVUE
NEE TRANCHE
1914-1987
GLo
GLo

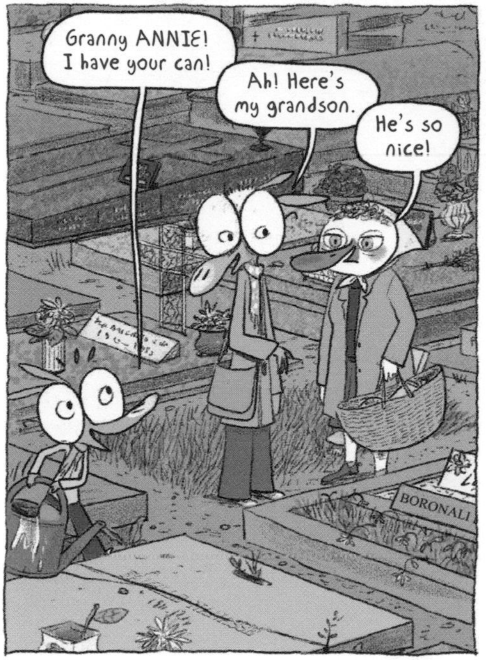
Granny ANNIE! I have your can!
Ah! Here's my grandson.
He's so nice!

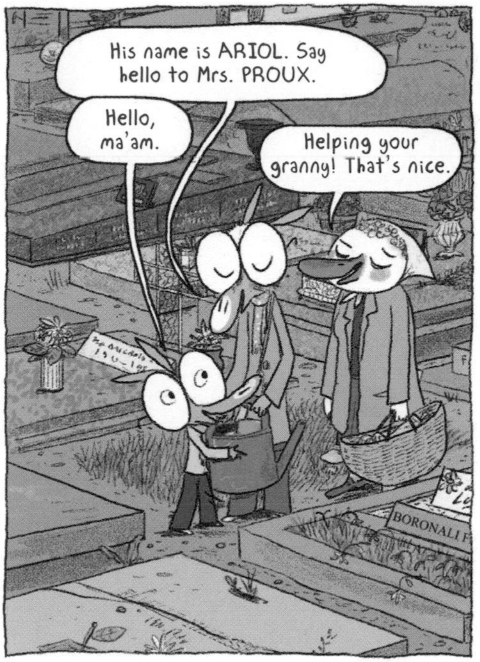
His name is ARIOL. Say hello to Mrs. PROUX.
Hello, ma'am.
Helping your granny! That's nice.
BORONALI F

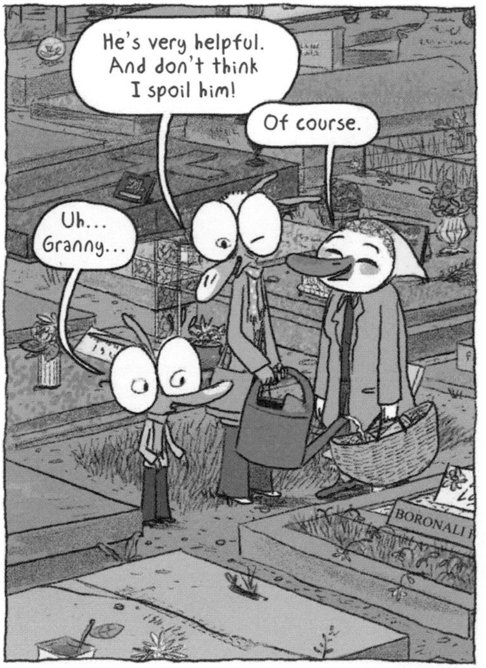
He's very helpful. And don't think I spoil him!
Of course.
Uh... Granny...
BORONALI F

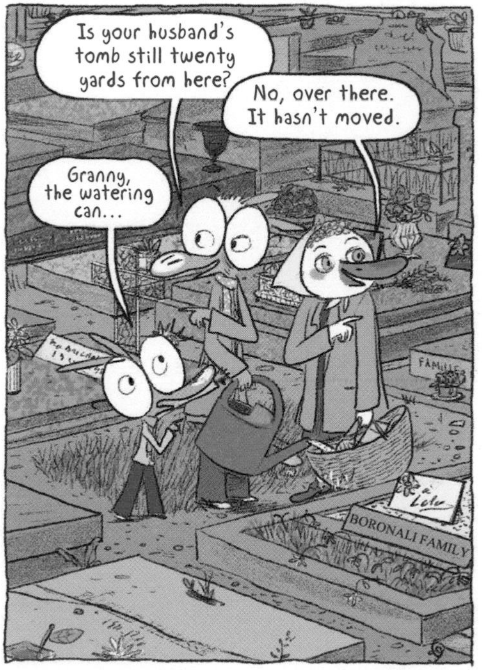
Is your husband's tomb still twenty yards from here?
No, over there. It hasn't moved.
Granny, the watering can...
BORONALI FAMILY

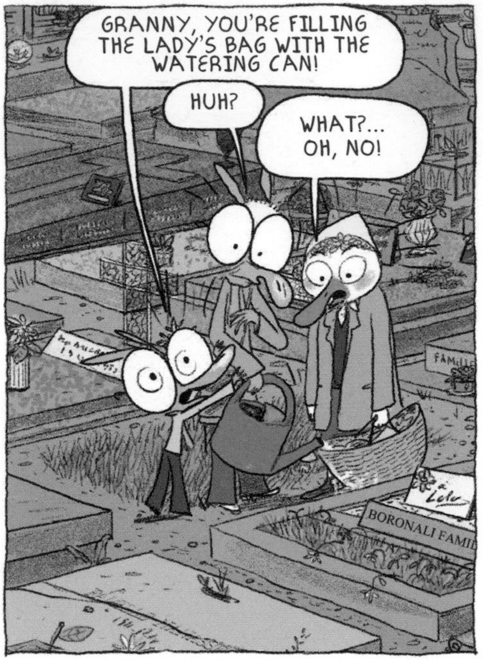
GRANNY, YOU'RE FILLING THE LADY'S BAG WITH THE WATERING CAN!
HUH?
WHAT?... OH, NO!

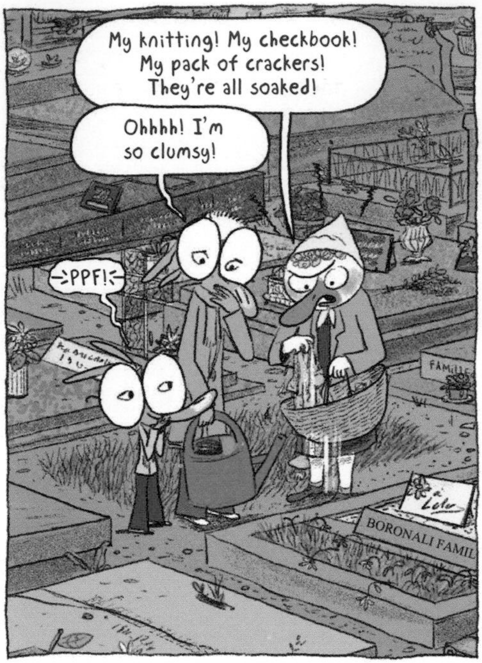
My knitting! My checkbook! My pack of crackers! They're all soaked!
Ohhhh! I'm so clumsy!
PPF!
BORONALI FAMILY

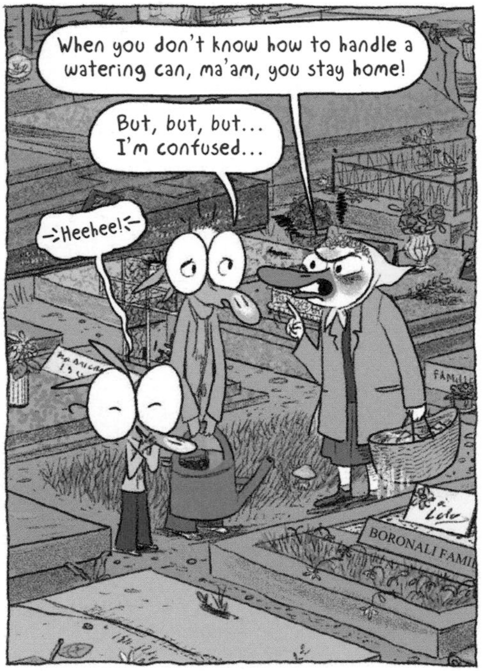
When you don't know how to handle a watering can, ma'am, you stay home!
But, but, but... I'm confused...
Heehee!

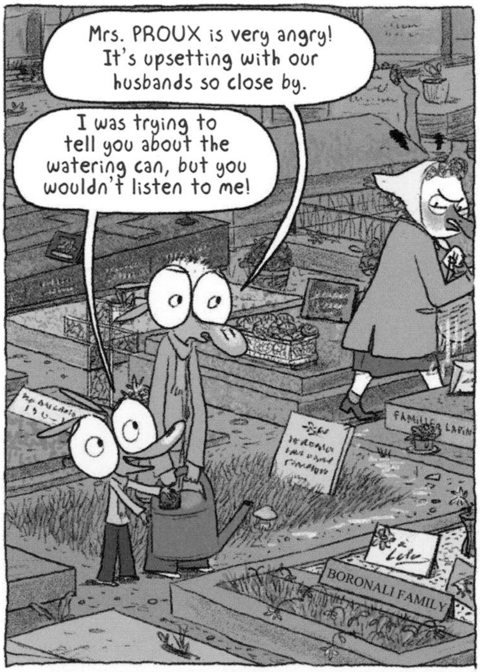
Mrs. PROUX is very angry! It's upsetting with our husbands so close by.
I was trying to tell you about the watering can, but you wouldn't listen to me!
BORONALI FAMILY

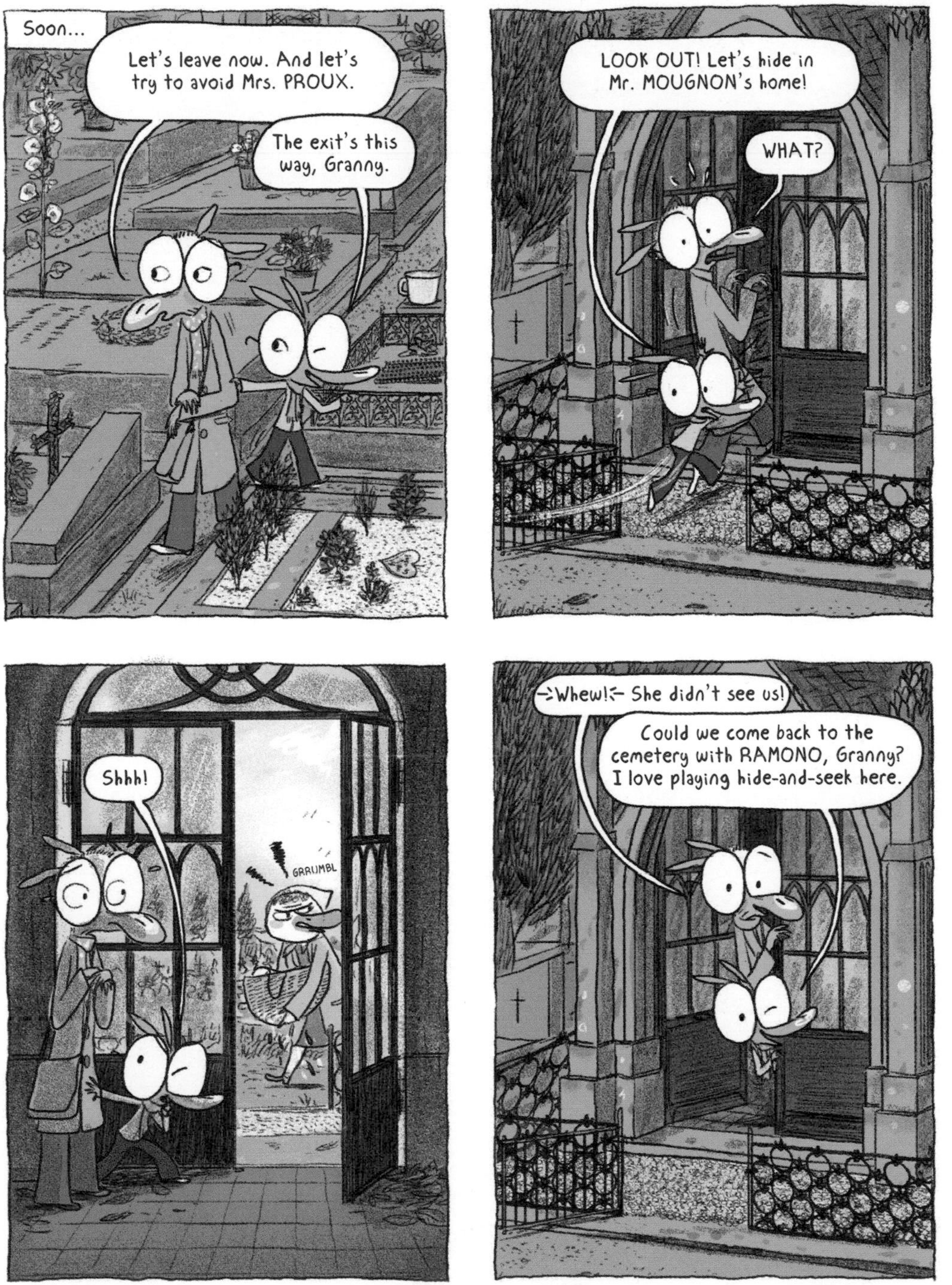
Soon...
Let's leave now. And let's try to avoid Mrs. PROUX.
The exit's this way, Granny.
LOOK OUT! Let's hide in Mr. MOUGNON's home!
WHAT?
Shhh!
GRRUMBL
Whew! She didn't see us!
Could we come back to the cemetery with RAMONO, Granny? I love playing hide-and-seek here.

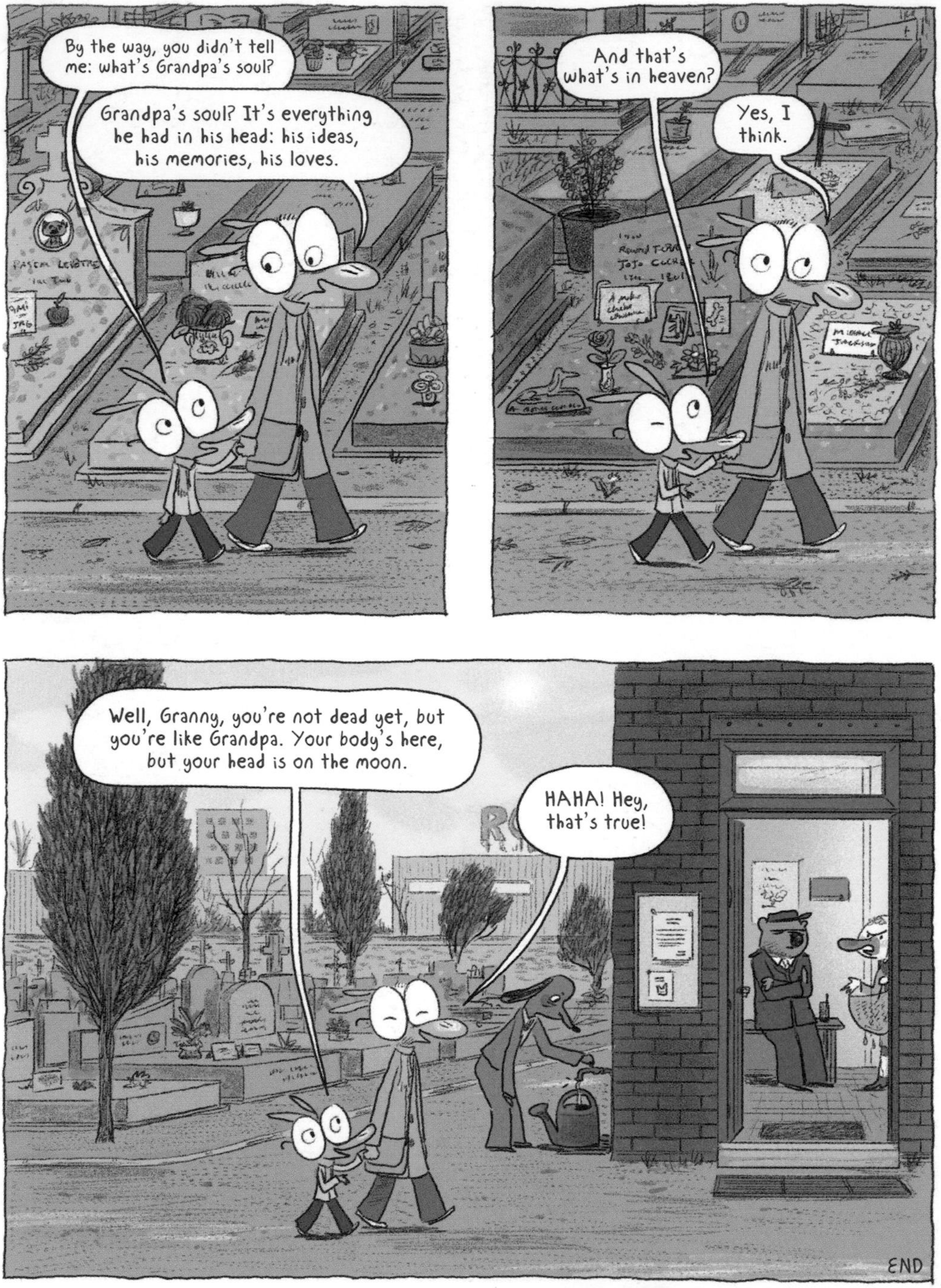

By the way, you didn't tell me: what's Grandpa's soul?
Grandpa's soul? It's everything he had in his head: his ideas, his memories, his loves.
And that's what's in heaven?
Yes, I think.
Well, Granny, you're not dead yet, but you're like Grandpa. Your body's here, but your head is on the moon.
HAHA! Hey, that's true!
END

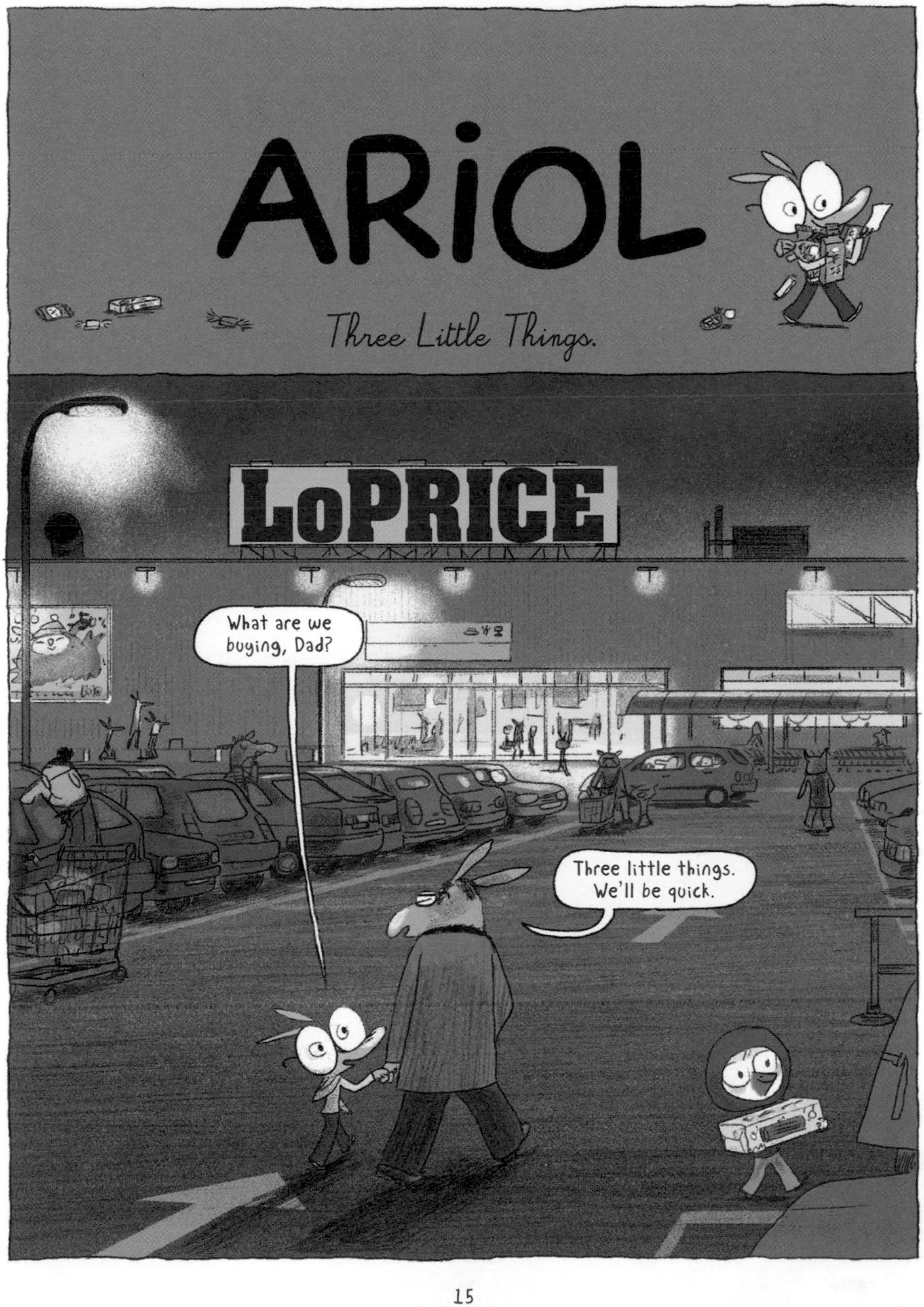
ARiOL
Three Little Things.
LoPRICE
What are we buying, Dad?
Three little things. We'll be quick.

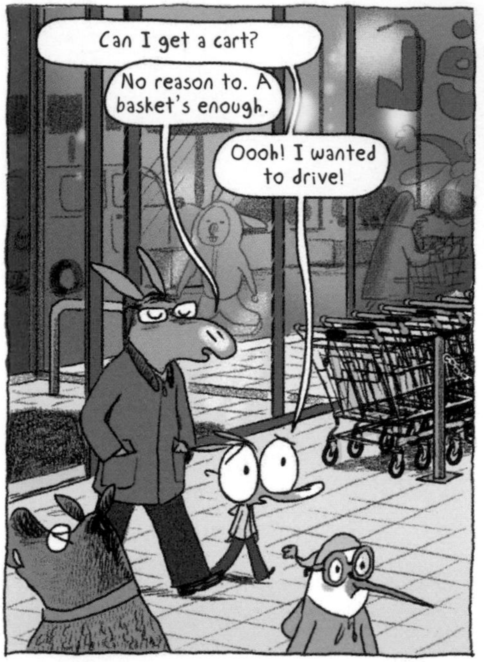
Can I get a cart?
No reason to. A basket's enough.
Oooh! I wanted to drive!
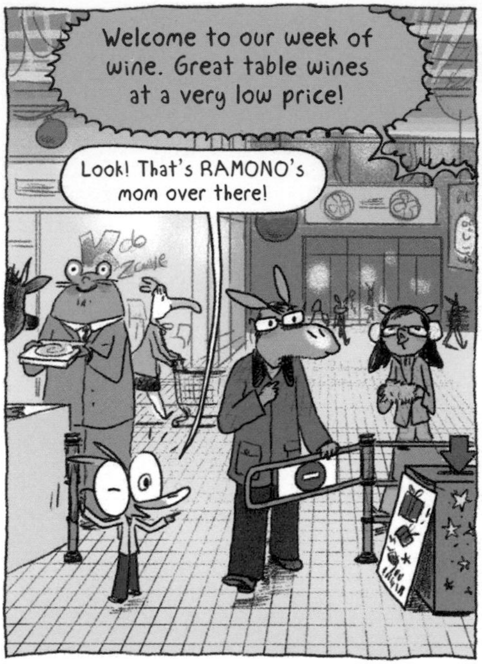
Welcome to our week of wine. Great table wines at a very low price!
Look! That's RAMONO's mom over there!
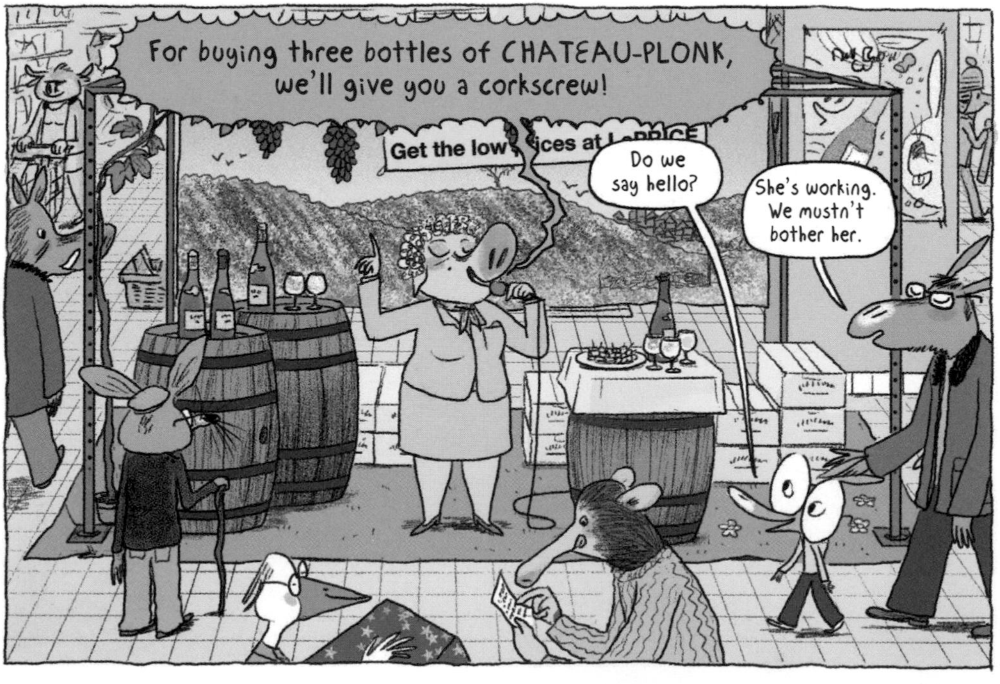
For buying three bottles of CHATEAU-PLONK, we'll give you a corkscrew!
Do we say hello?
She's working. We mustn't bother her.

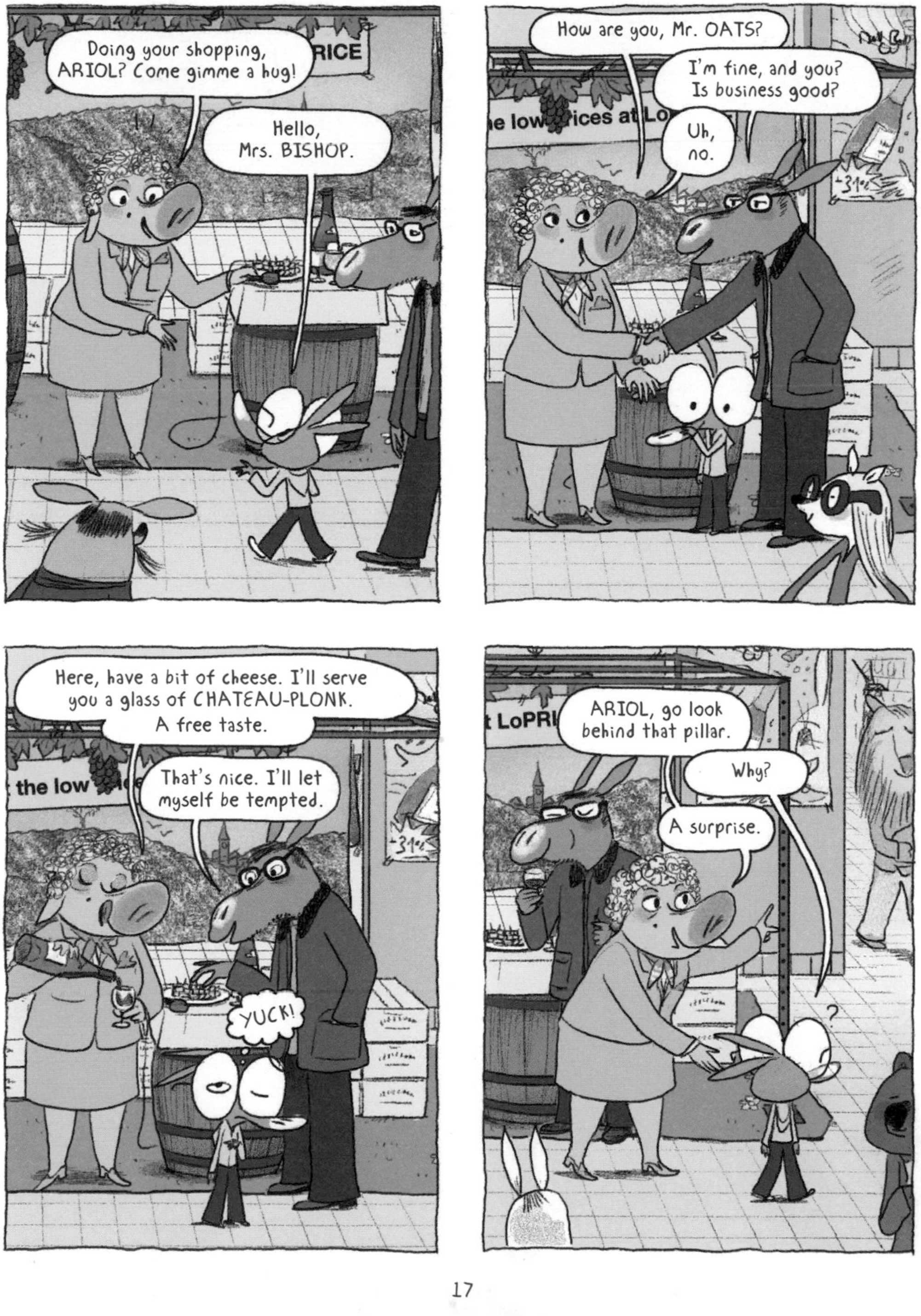
Doing your shopping, ARIOL? Come gimme a hug!
Hello, Mrs. BISHOP.
How are you, Mr. OATS?
I'm fine, and you? Is business good?
Uh, no.
Here, have a bit of cheese. I'll serve you a glass of CHATEAU-PLONK. A free taste.
That's nice. I'll let myself be tempted.
YUCK!
ARIOL, go look behind that pillar.
Why?
A surprise.
?

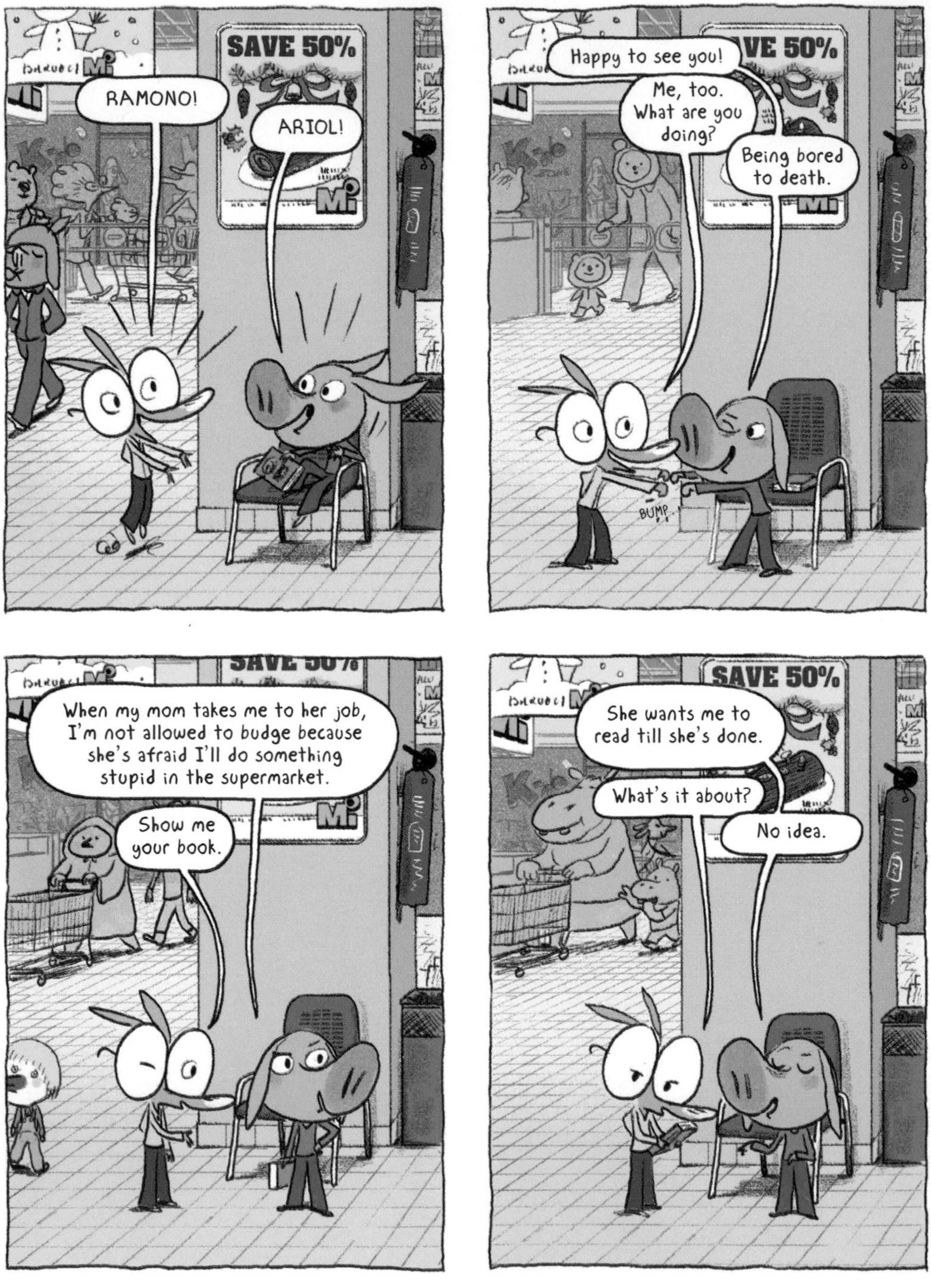
RAMONO!
ARIOL!
Happy to see you!
Me, too. What are you doing?
Being bored to death.
BUMP
When my mom takes me to her job, I'm not allowed to budge because she's afraid I'll do something stupid in the supermarket.
Show me your book.
She wants me to read till she's done.
What's it about?
No idea.

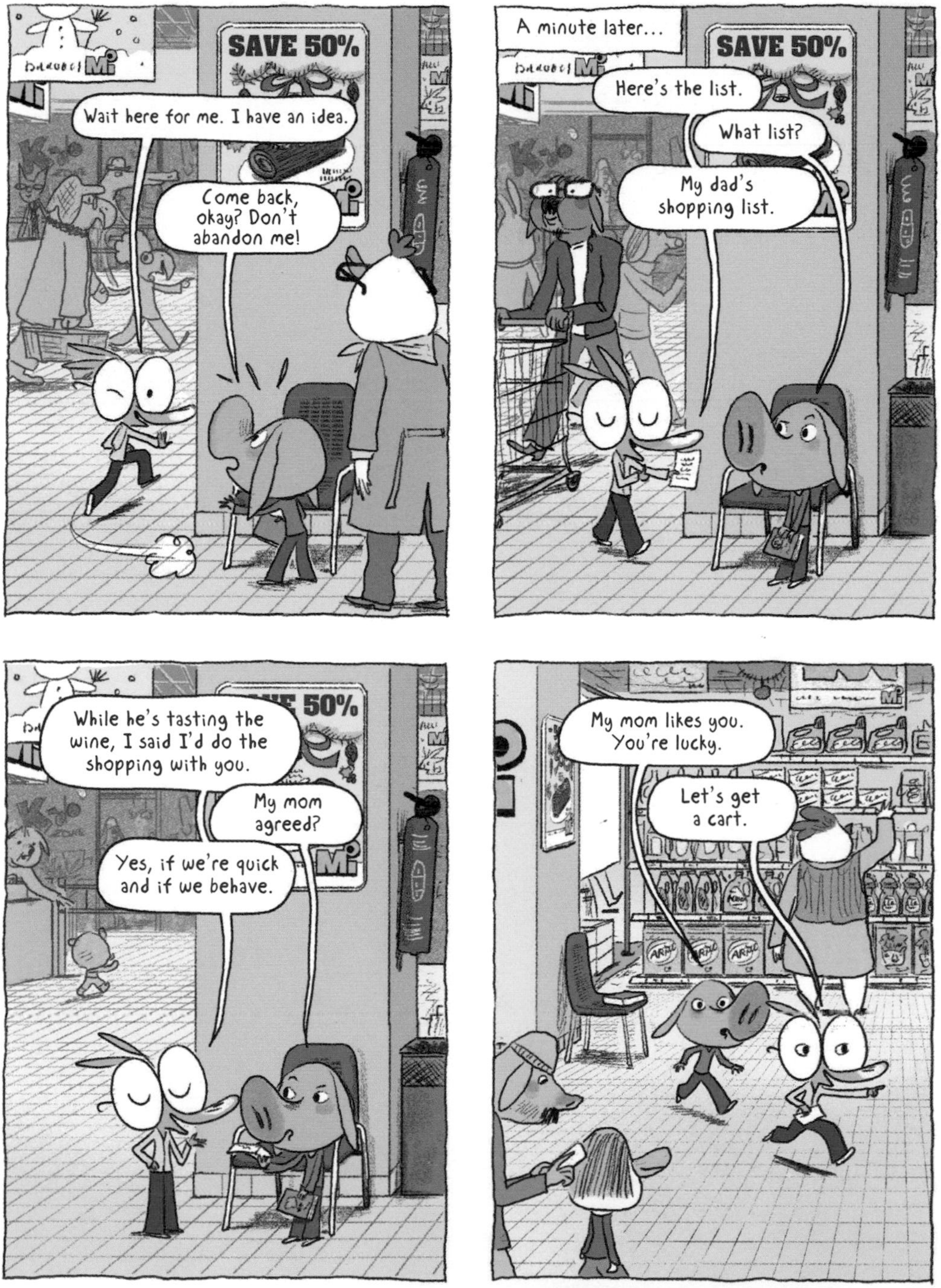
SAVE 50%
Wait here for me. I have an idea.
Come back, okay? Don't abandon me!
A minute later...
SAVE 50%
Here's the list.
What list?
My dad's shopping list.
While he's tasting the wine, I said I'd do the shopping with you.
My mom agreed?
Yes, if we're quick and if we behave.
My mom likes you. You're lucky.
Let's get a cart.

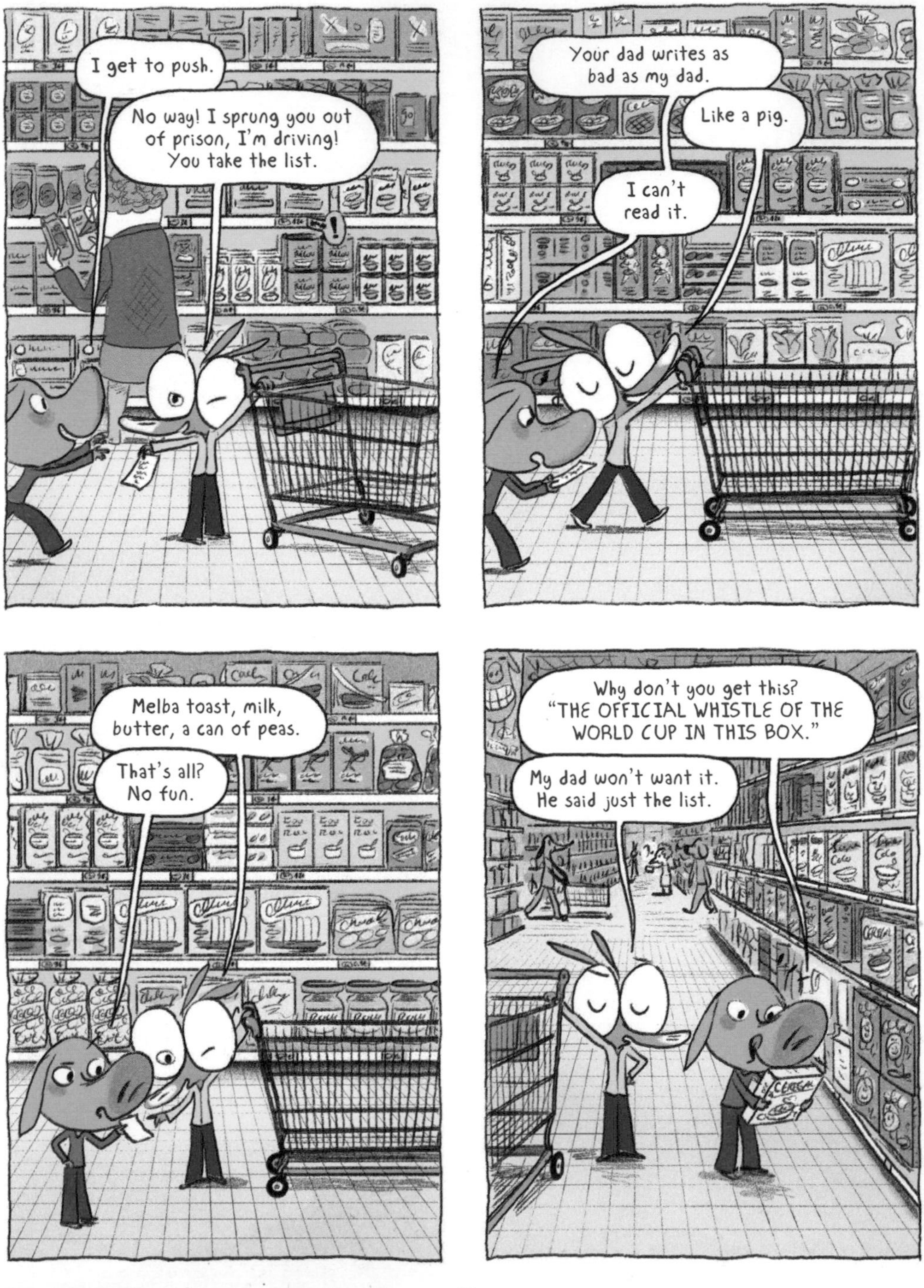
I get to push.
No way! I sprung you out of prison, I'm driving! You take the list.
Your dad writes as bad as my dad.
Like a pig.
I can't read it.
Melba toast, milk, butter, a can of peas.
That's all? No fun.
Why don't you get this? "THE OFFICIAL WHISTLE OF THE WORLD CUP IN THIS BOX."
My dad won't want it. He said just the list.

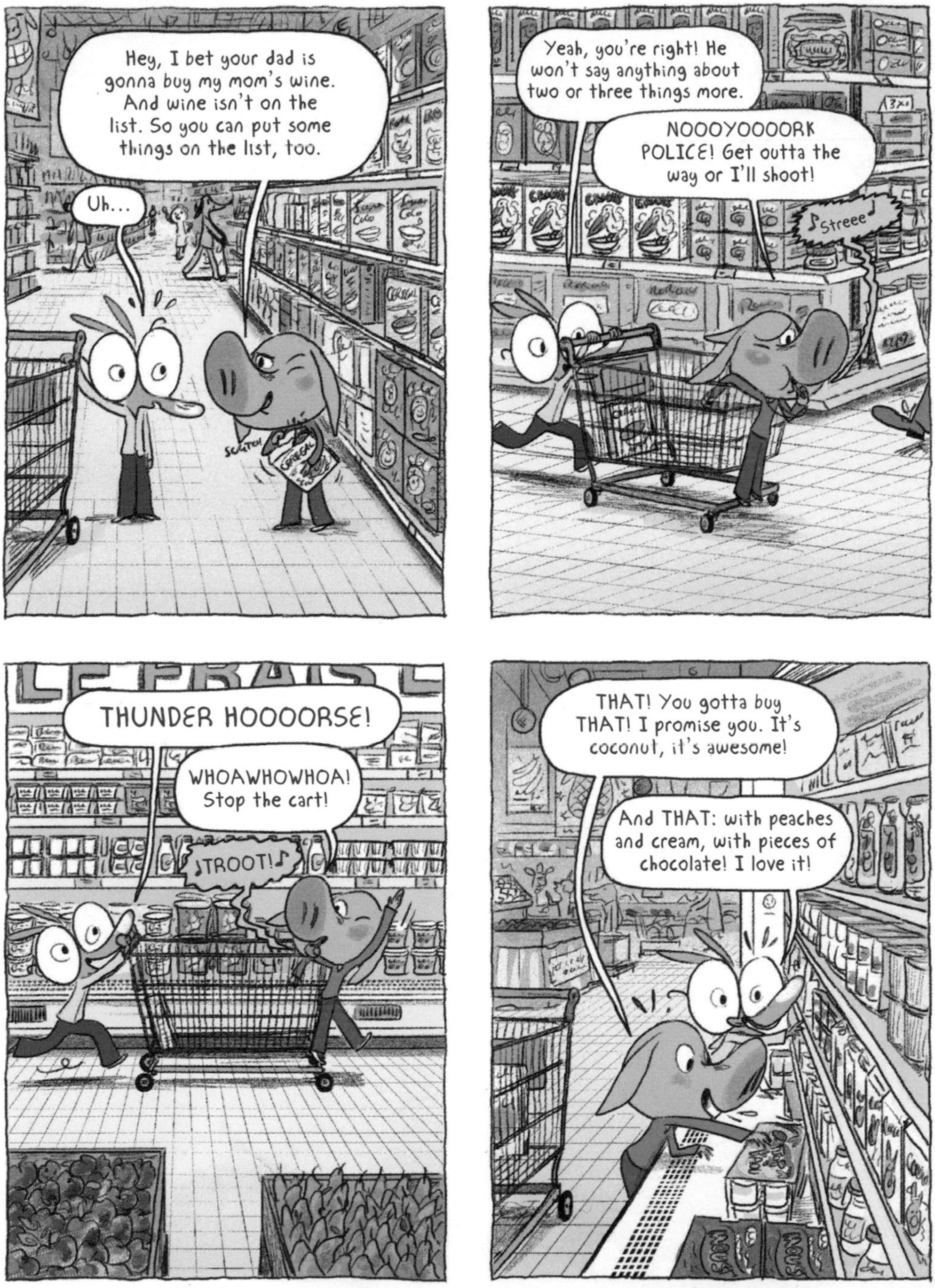
Hey, I bet your dad is gonna buy my mom's wine. And wine isn't on the list. So you can put some things on the list, too.
Uh...
SCRATCH
CEREAL
Yeah, you're right! He won't say anything about two or three things more.
NOOOYOOOORK POLICE! Get outta the way or I'll shoot!
Streee
THUNDER HOOOORSE!
WHOAWHOWHOA! Stop the cart!
TROOT!
THAT! You gotta buy THAT! I promise you. It's coconut, it's awesome!
And THAT: with peaches and cream, with pieces of chocolate! I love it!

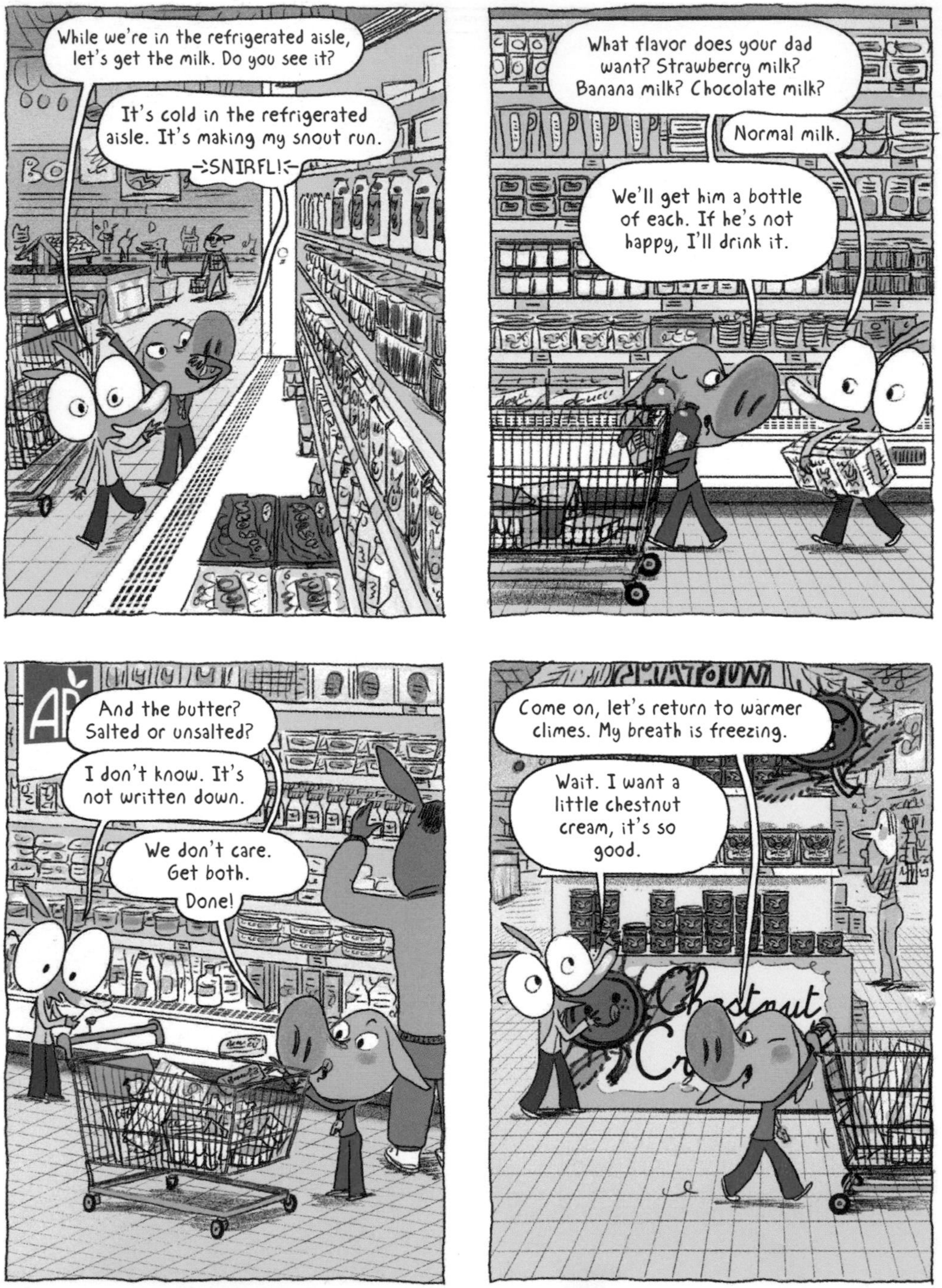
While we're in the refrigerated aisle, let's get the milk. Do you see it?
It's cold in the refrigerated aisle. It's making my snout run.
SNIRFL!
What flavor does your dad want? Strawberry milk? Banana milk? Chocolate milk?
Normal milk.
We'll get him a bottle of each. If he's not happy, I'll drink it.
And the butter? Salted or unsalted?
I don't know. It's not written down.
We don't care. Get both.
Done!
Come on, let's return to warmer climes. My breath is freezing.
Wait. I want a little chestnut cream, it's so good.
Chestnut Cr

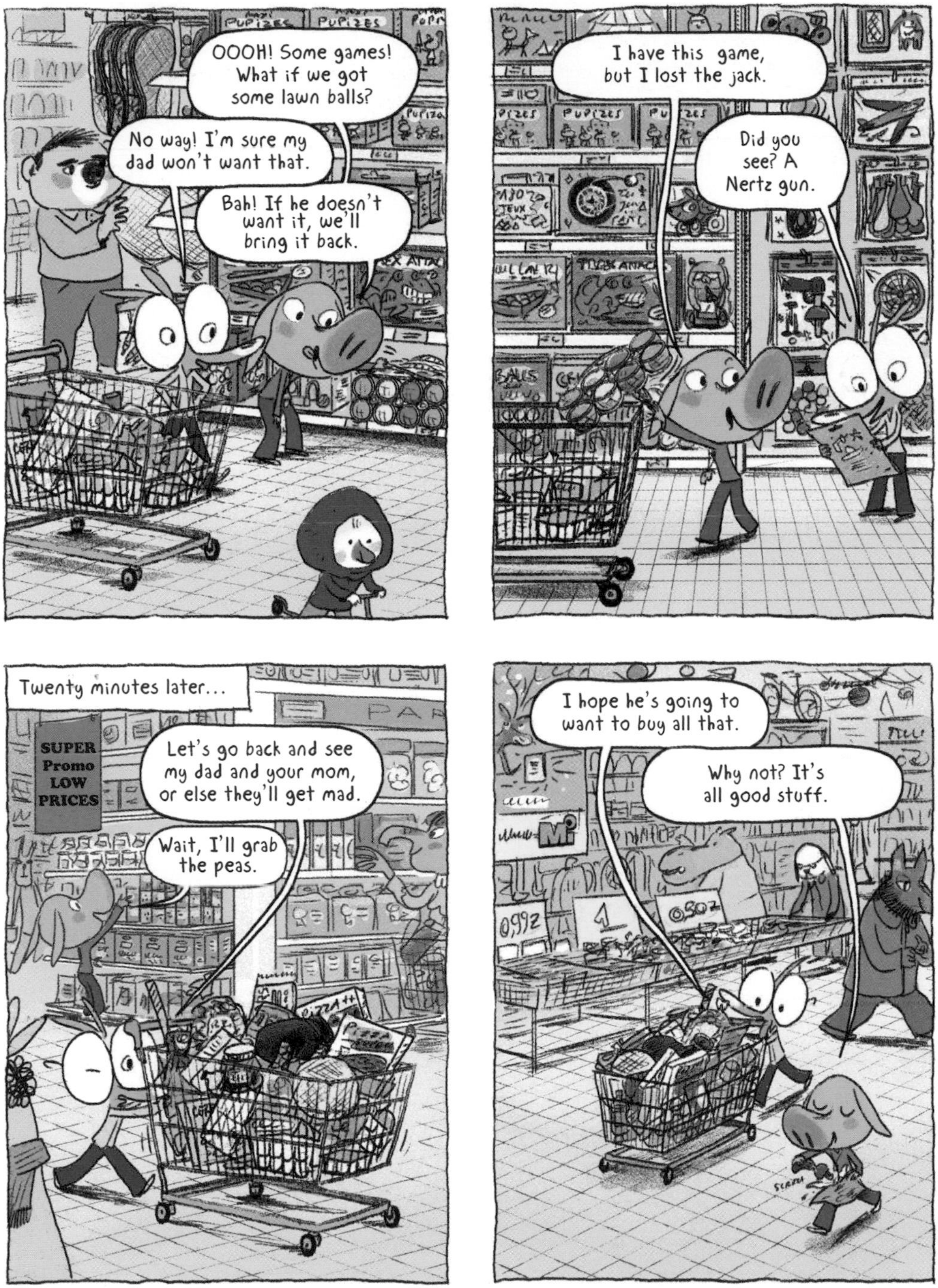
OOOH! Some games! What if we got some lawn balls?
No way! I'm sure my dad won't want that.
Bah! If he doesn't want it, we'll bring it back.
I have this game, but I lost the jack.
Did you see? A Nertz gun.
Twenty minutes later...
SUPER Promo LOW PRICES
Let's go back and see my dad and your mom, or else they'll get mad.
Wait, I'll grab the peas.
I hope he's going to want to buy all that.
Why not? It's all good stuff.

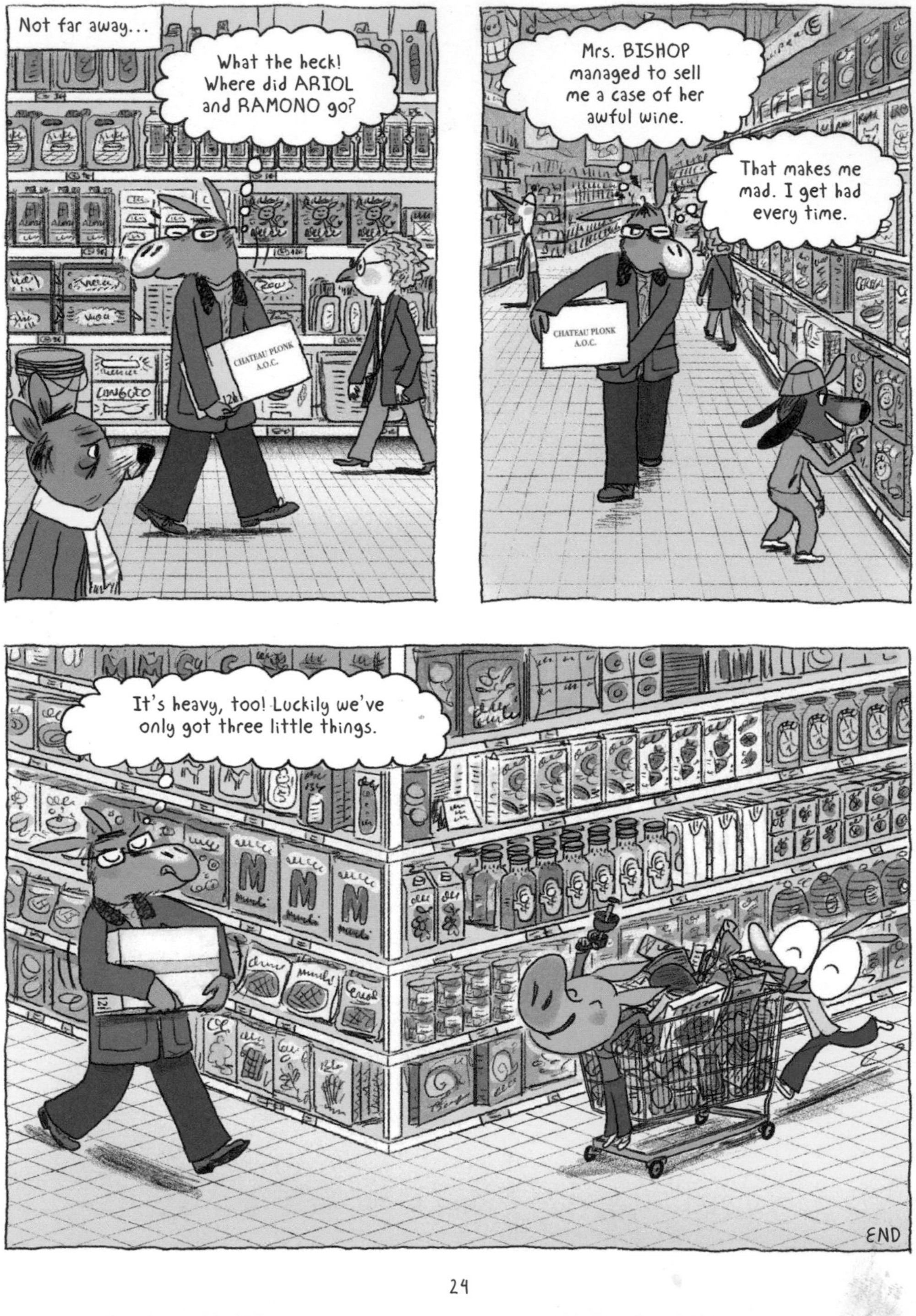
Not far away...
What the heck! Where did ARIOL and RAMONO go?
CHATEAU PLONK A.O.C.
Mrs. BISHOP managed to sell me a case of her awful wine.
That makes me mad. I get had every time.
CHATEAU PLONK A.O.C.
It's heavy, too! Luckily we've only got three little things.
END

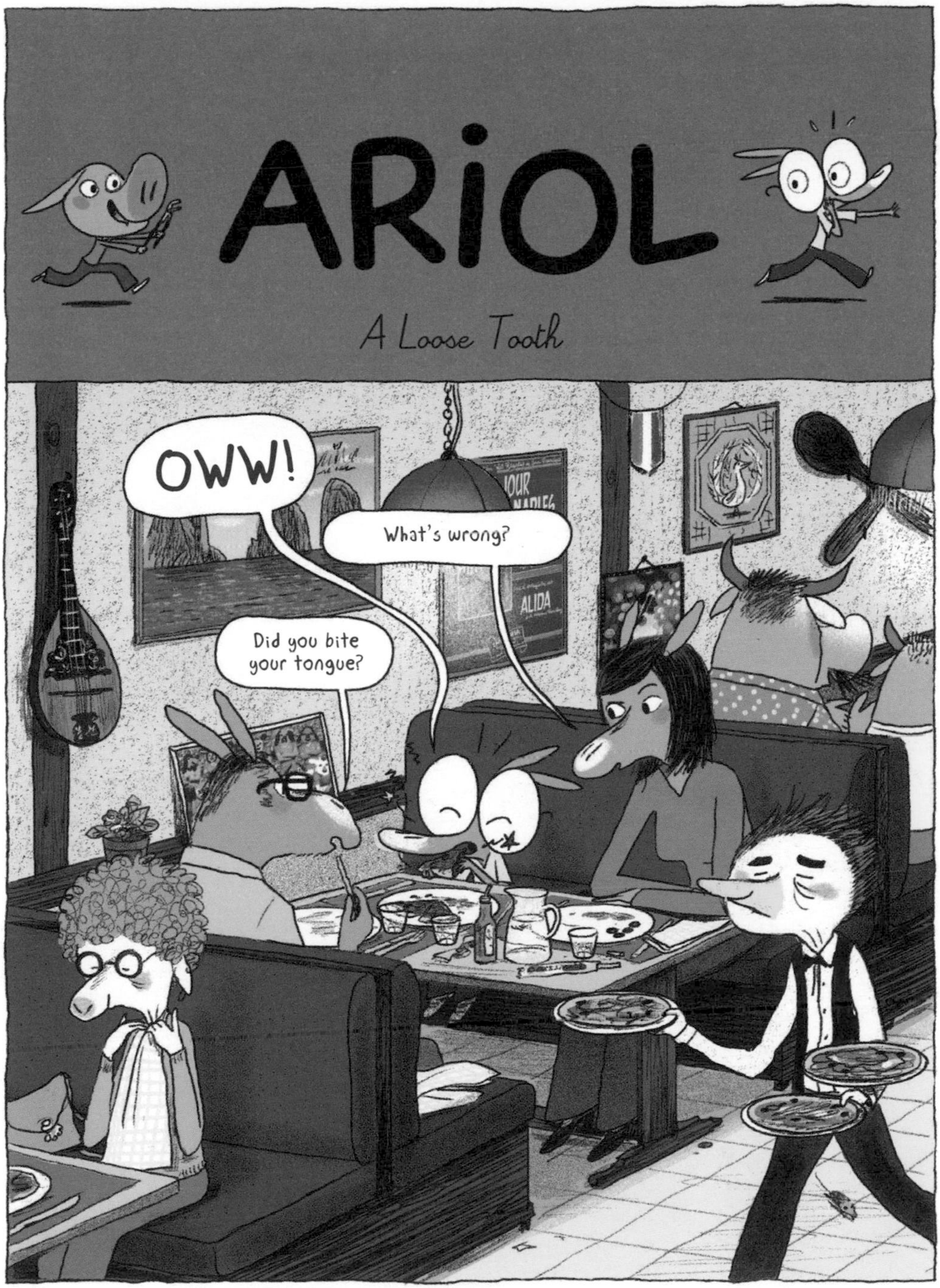
ARiOL
A Loose Tooth
OWW!
What's wrong?
Did you bite your tongue?

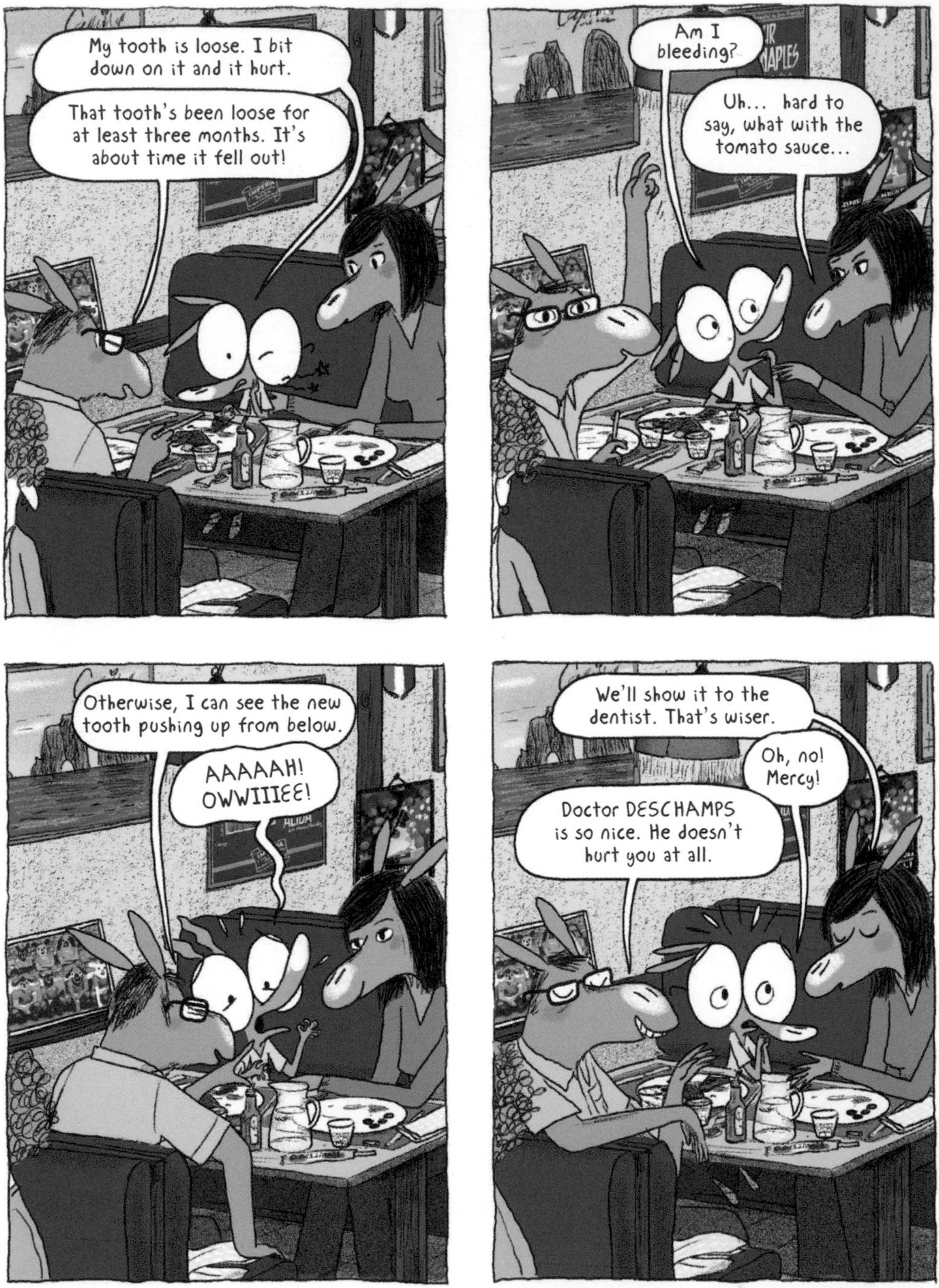
My tooth is loose. I bit down on it and it hurt.
That tooth's been loose for at least three months. It's about time it fell out!
Am I bleeding?
Uh... hard to say, what with the tomato sauce...
Otherwise, I can see the new tooth pushing up from below.
AAAAAH! OWWIIIEE!
We'll show it to the dentist. That's wiser.
Oh, no! Mercy!
Doctor DESCHAMPS is so nice. He doesn't hurt you at all.

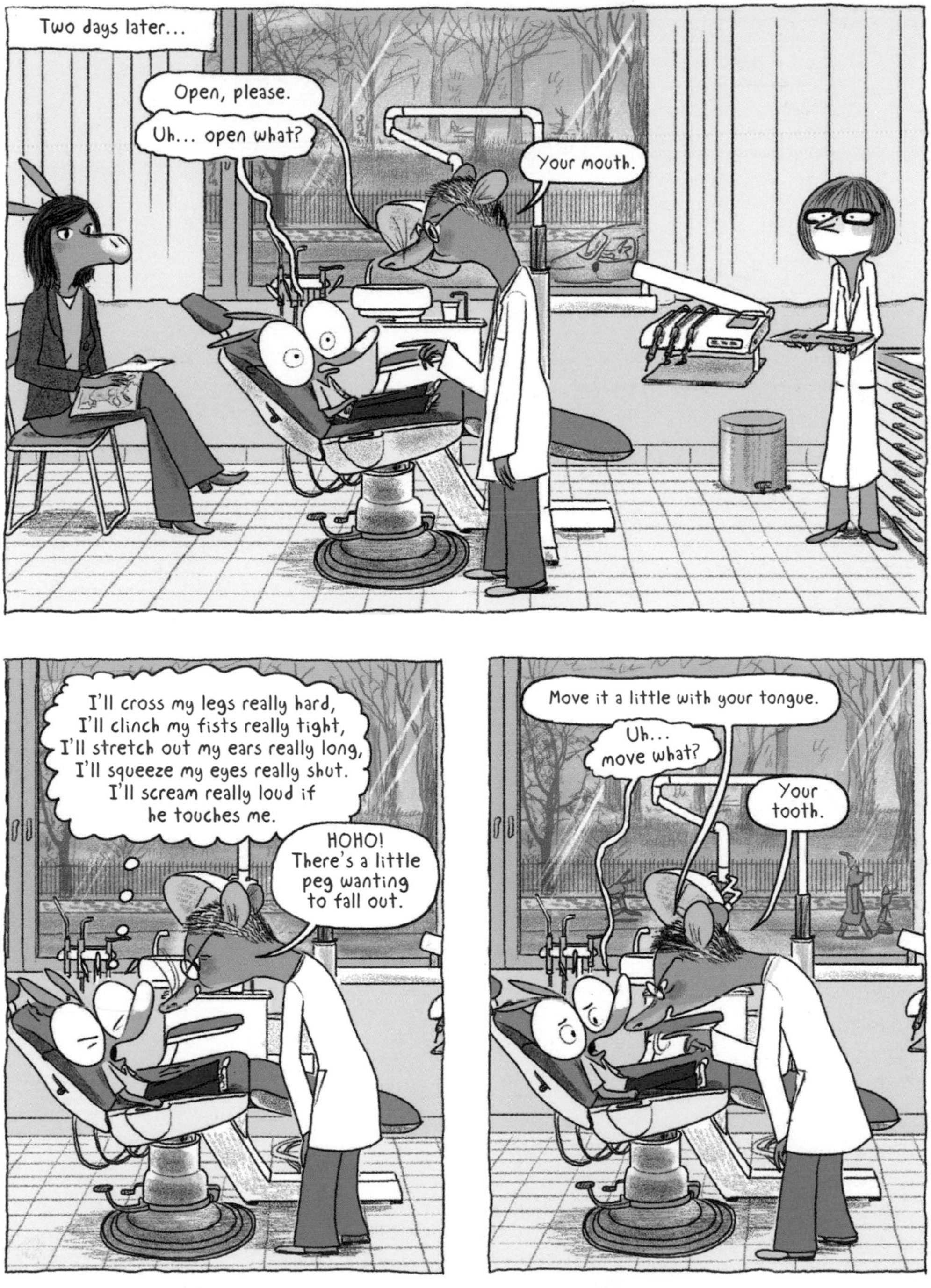
Two days later...
Open, please.
Uh... open what?
Your mouth.
I'll cross my legs really hard, I'll clinch my fists really tight, I'll stretch out my ears really long, I'll squeeze my eyes really shut. I'll scream really loud if he touches me.
HOHO! There's a little peg wanting to fall out.
Move it a little with your tongue.
Uh... move what?
Your tooth.

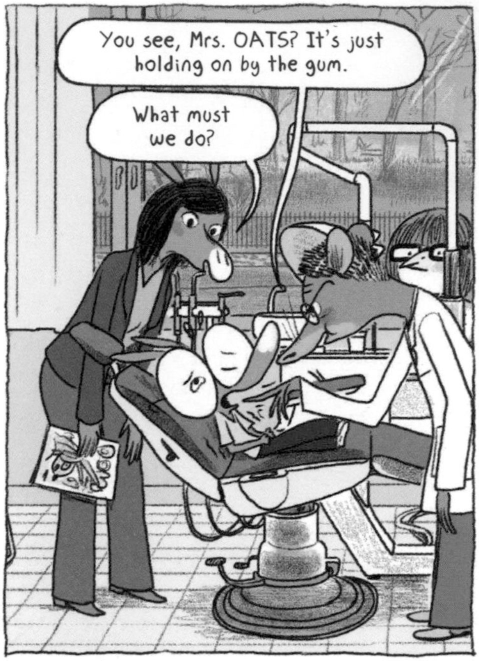

You see, Mrs. OATS? It's just holding on by the gum.
What must we do?

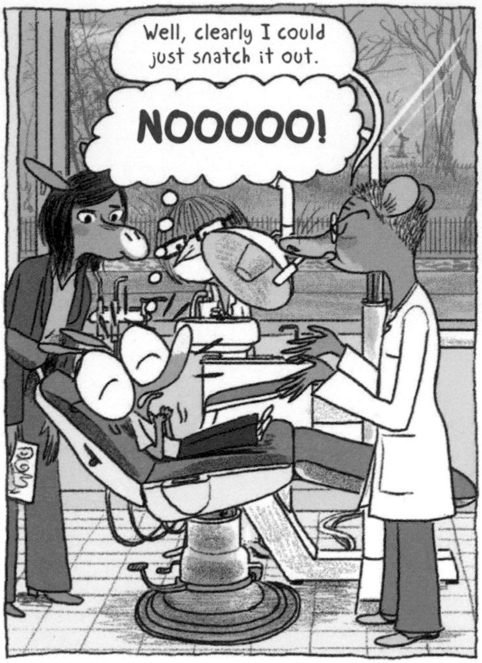

Well, clearly I could just snatch it out.
NOOOOO!

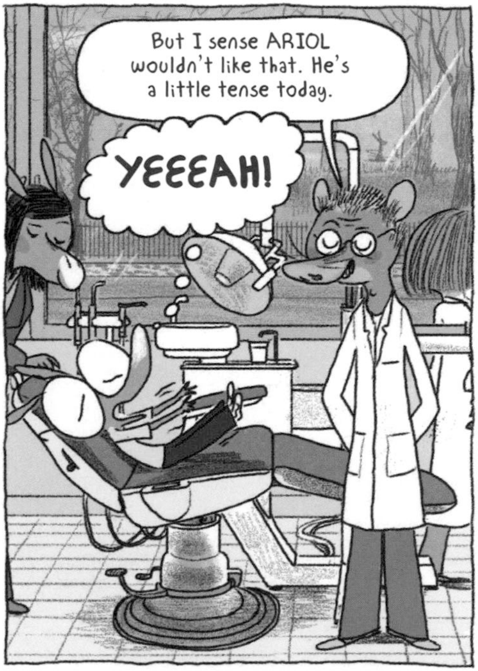

But I sense ARIOL wouldn't like that. He's a little tense today.
YEEEAH!

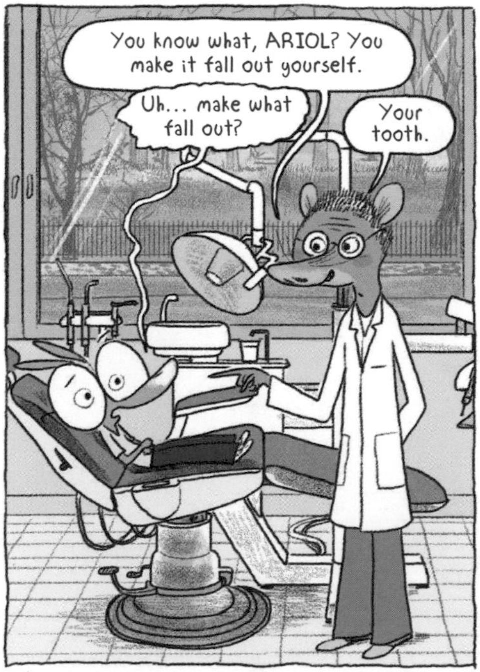

You know what, ARIOL? You make it fall out yourself.
Uh... make what fall out?
Your tooth.

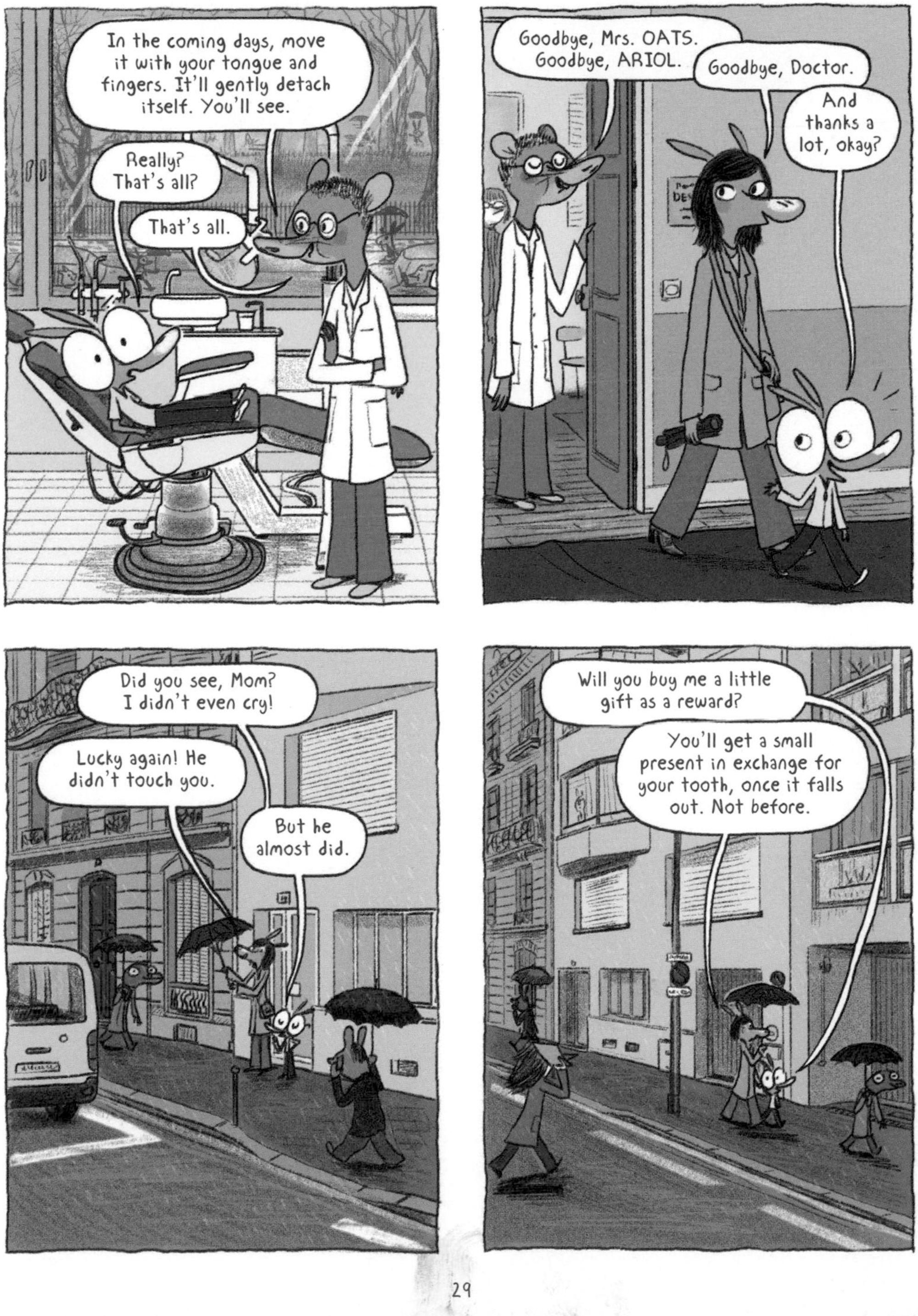
In the coming days, move it with your tongue and fingers. It'll gently detach itself. You'll see.
Really? That's all?
That's all.
Goodbye, Mrs. OATS. Goodbye, ARIOL.
Goodbye, Doctor.
And thanks a lot, okay?
Did you see, Mom? I didn't even cry!
Lucky again! He didn't touch you.
But he almost did.
Will you buy me a little gift as a reward?
You'll get a small present in exchange for your tooth, once it falls out. Not before.

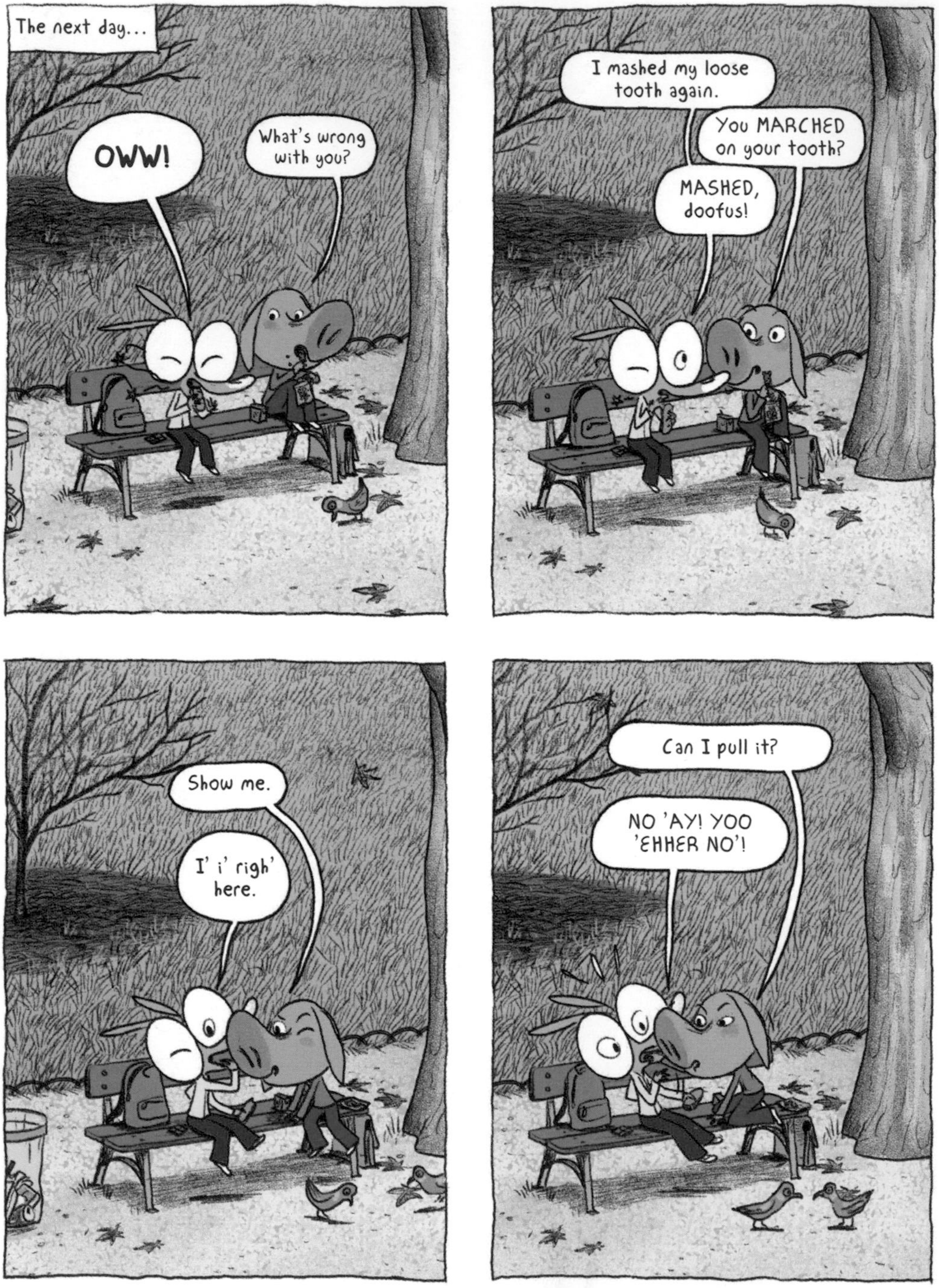
The next day...
OWW!
What's wrong with you?
I mashed my loose tooth again.
You MARCHED on your tooth?
MASHED, doofus!
Show me.
I' i' righ' here.
Can I pull it?
NO 'AY! YOO 'EHHER NO'!

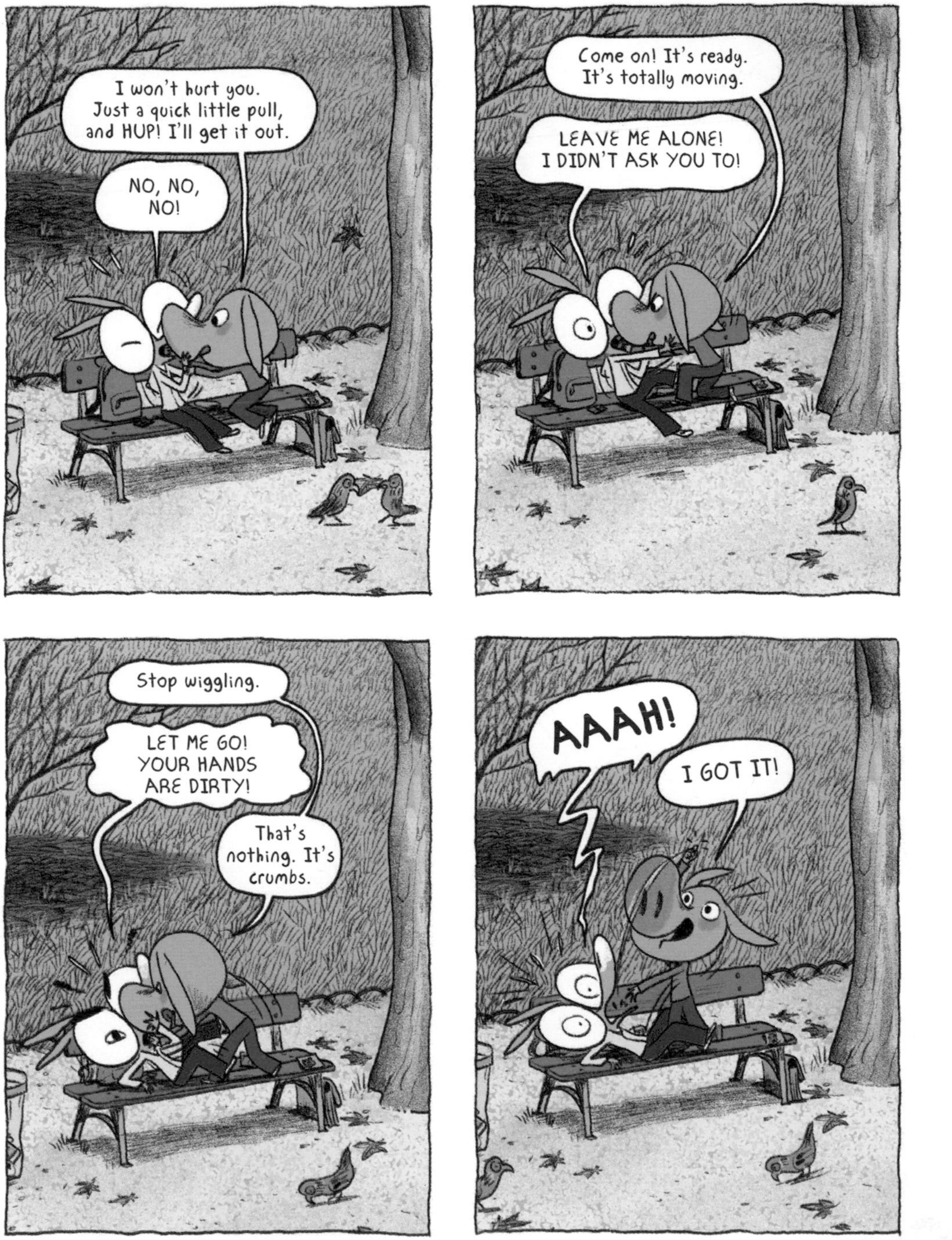
I won't hurt you. Just a quick little pull, and HUP! I'll get it out.
NO, NO, NO!
Come on! It's ready. It's totally moving.
LEAVE ME ALONE! I DIDN'T ASK YOU TO!
Stop wiggling.
LET ME GO! YOUR HANDS ARE DIRTY!
That's nothing. It's crumbs.
AAAH!
I GOT IT!

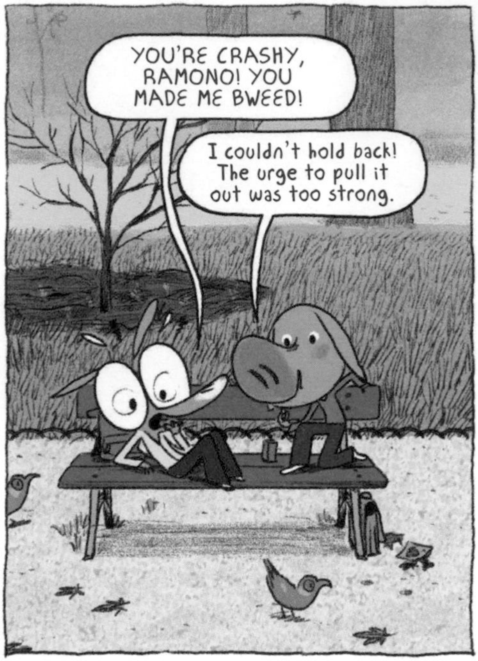
YOU'RE CRASHY, RAMONO! YOU MADE ME BWEED!
I couldn't hold back! The urge to pull it out was too strong.

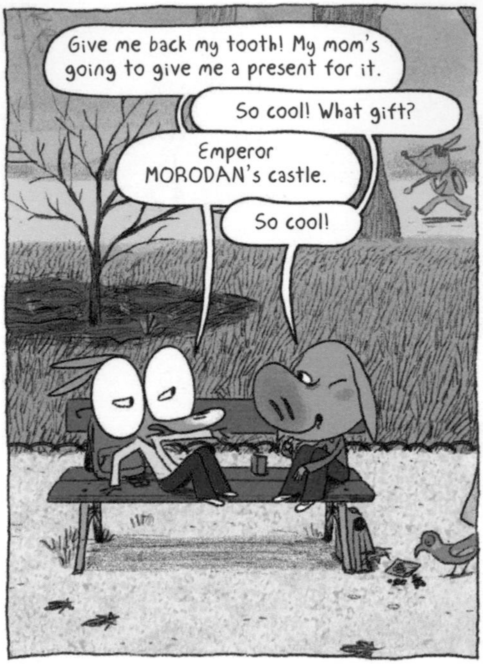
Give me back my tooth! My mom's going to give me a present for it.
So cool! What gift?
Emperor MORODAN's castle.
So cool!

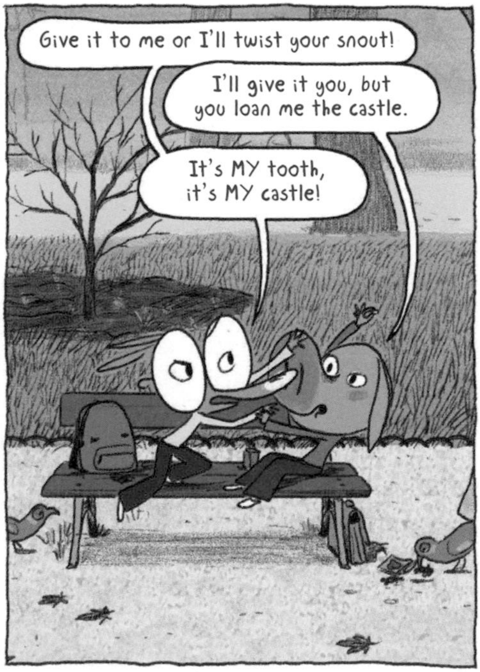
Give it to me or I'll twist your snout!
I'll give it you, but you loan me the castle.
It's MY tooth, it's MY castle!

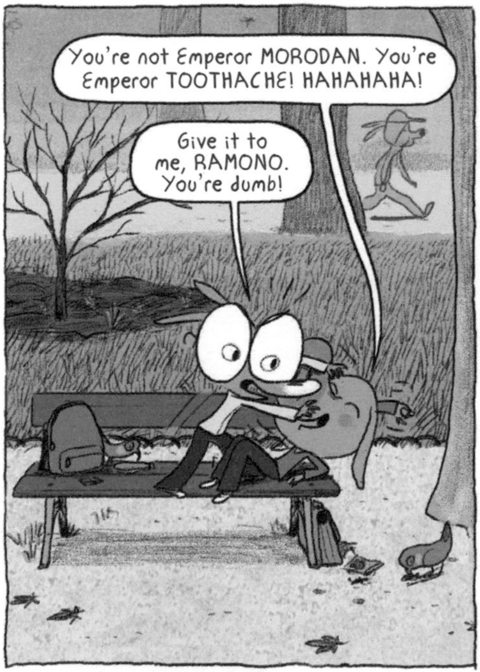
You're not Emperor MORODAN. You're Emperor TOOTHACHE! HAHAHAHA!
Give it to me, RAMONO. You're dumb!

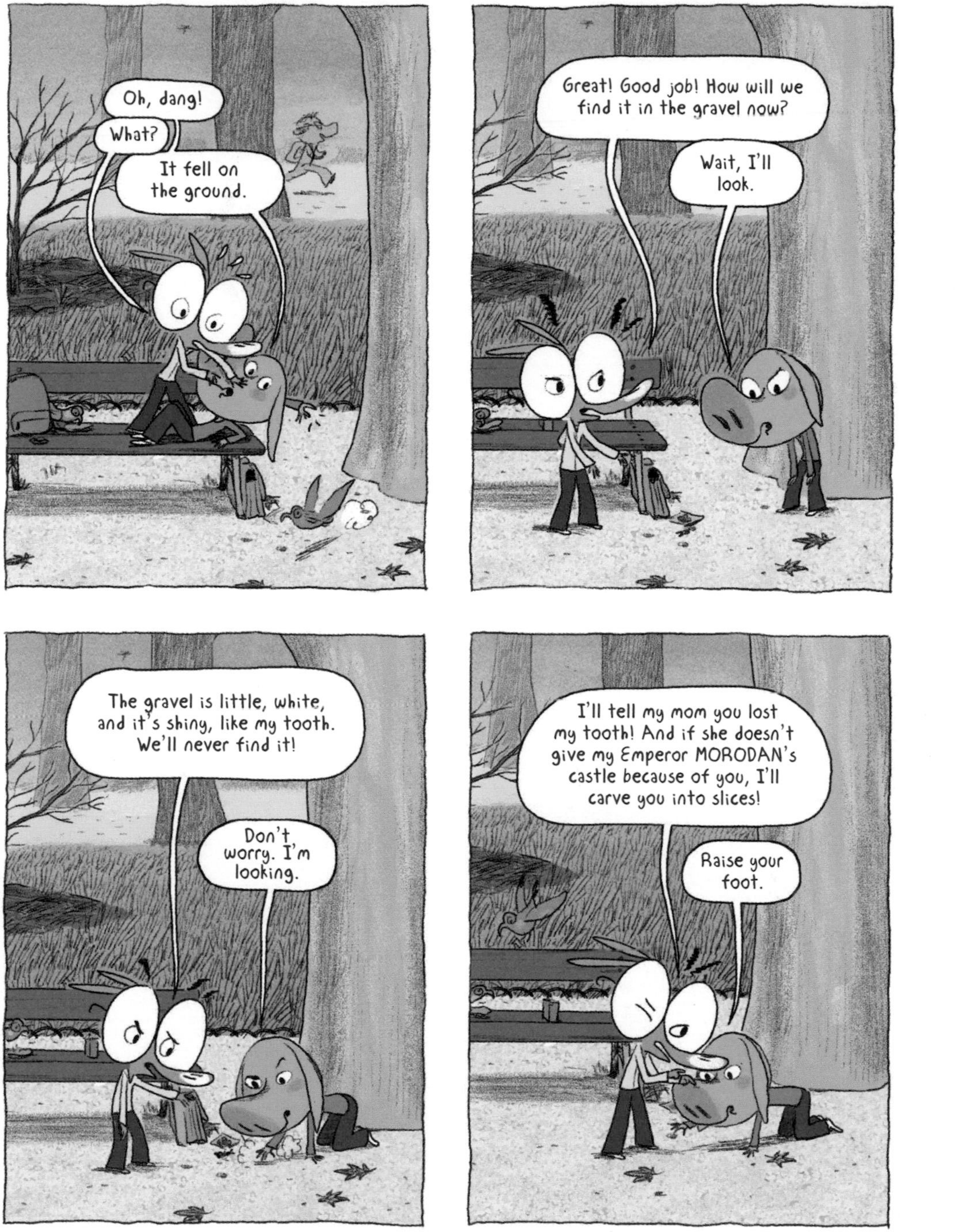
Oh, dang!
What?
It fell on the ground.
Great! Good job! How will we find it in the gravel now?
Wait, I'll look.
The gravel is little, white, and it's shiny, like my tooth. We'll never find it!
Don't worry. I'm looking.
I'll tell my mom you lost my tooth! And if she doesn't give my Emperor MORODAN's castle because of you, I'll carve you into slices!
Raise your foot.

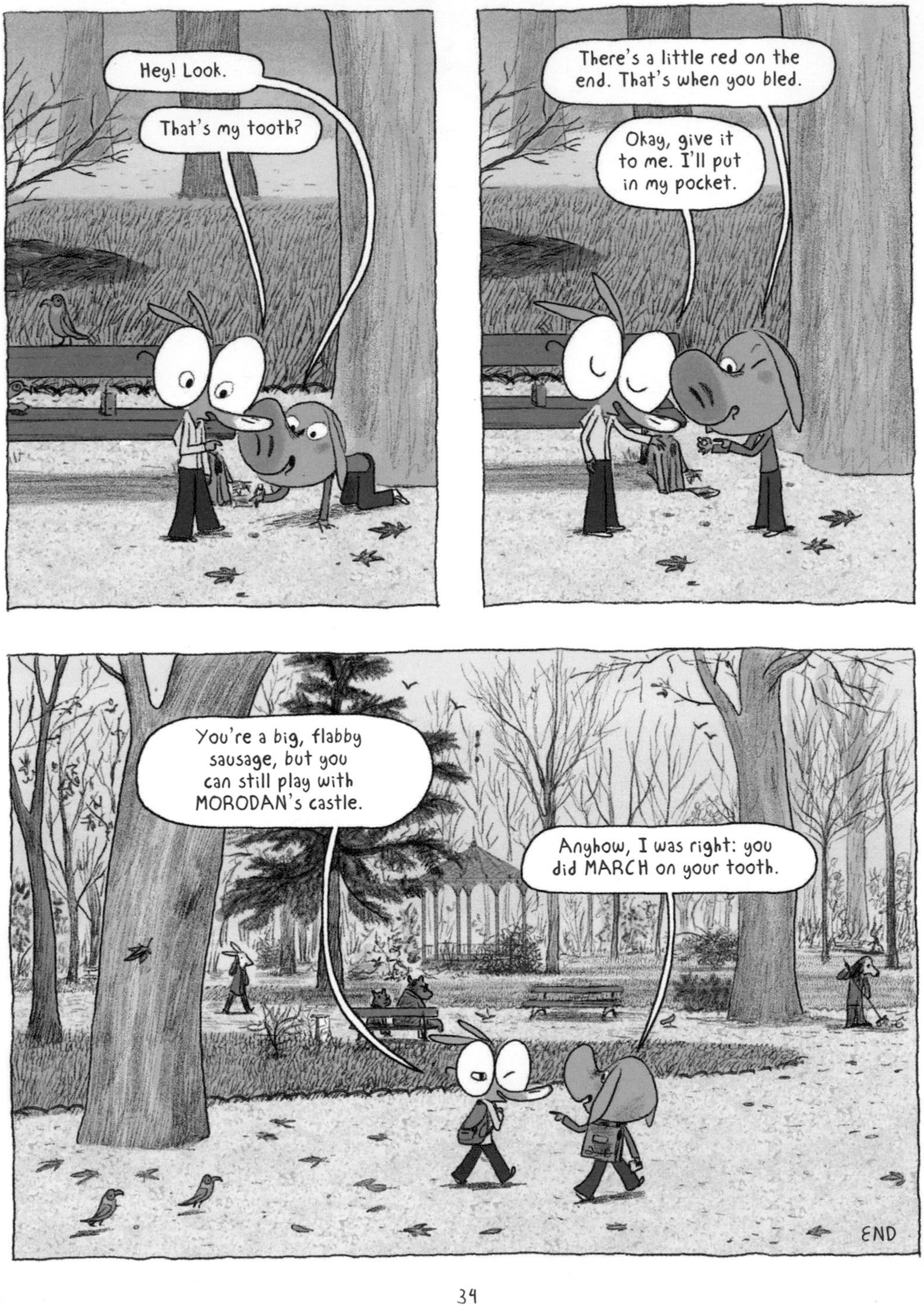
Hey! Look.
That's my tooth?
There's a little red on the end. That's when you bled.
Okay, give it to me. I'll put in my pocket.
You're a big, flabby sausage, but you can still play with MORODAN's castle.
Anyhow, I was right: you did MARCH on your tooth.
END

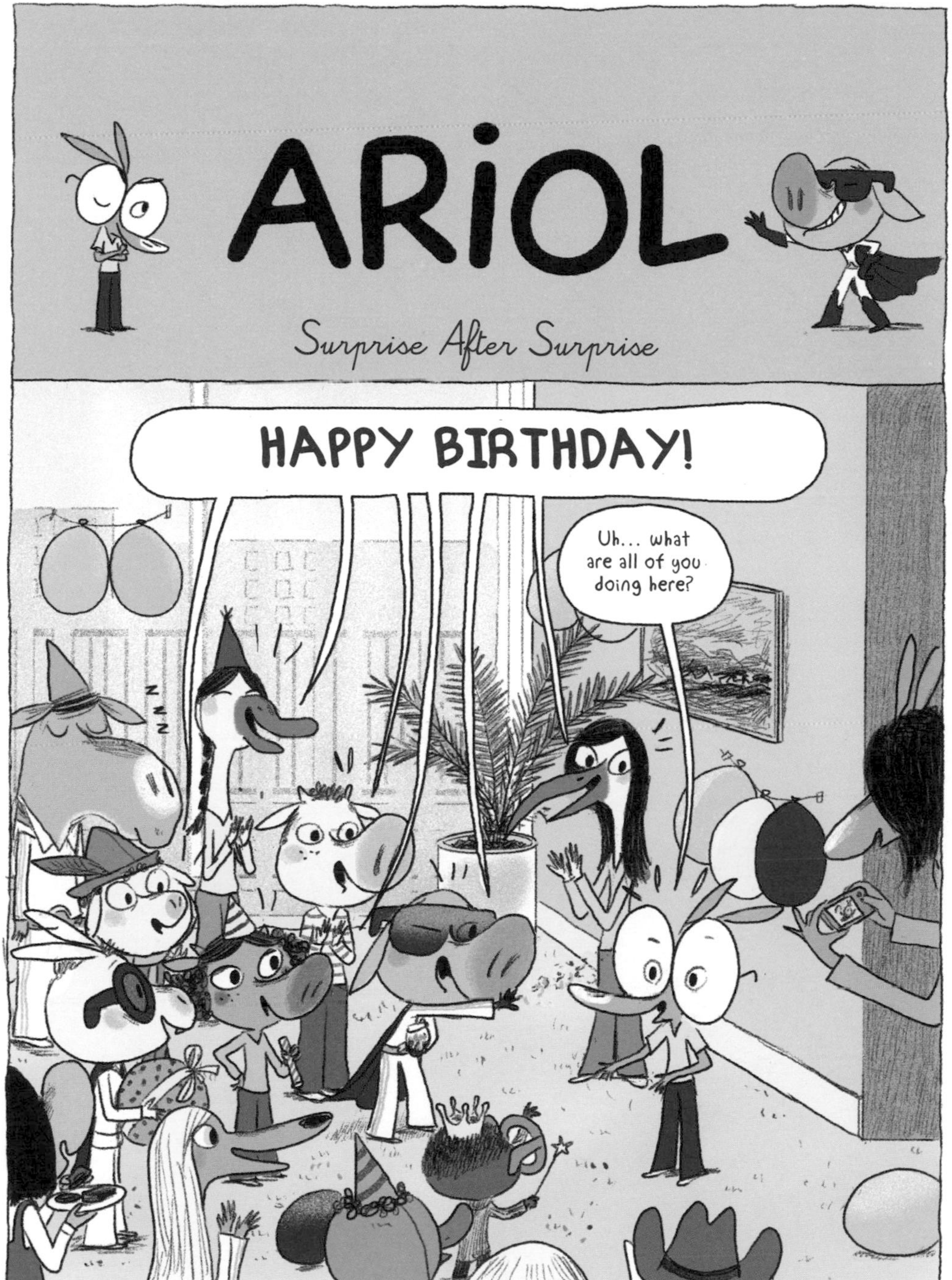
ARiOL
Surprise After Surprise
HAPPY BIRTHDAY!
Z Z Z
Uh... what are all of you doing here?

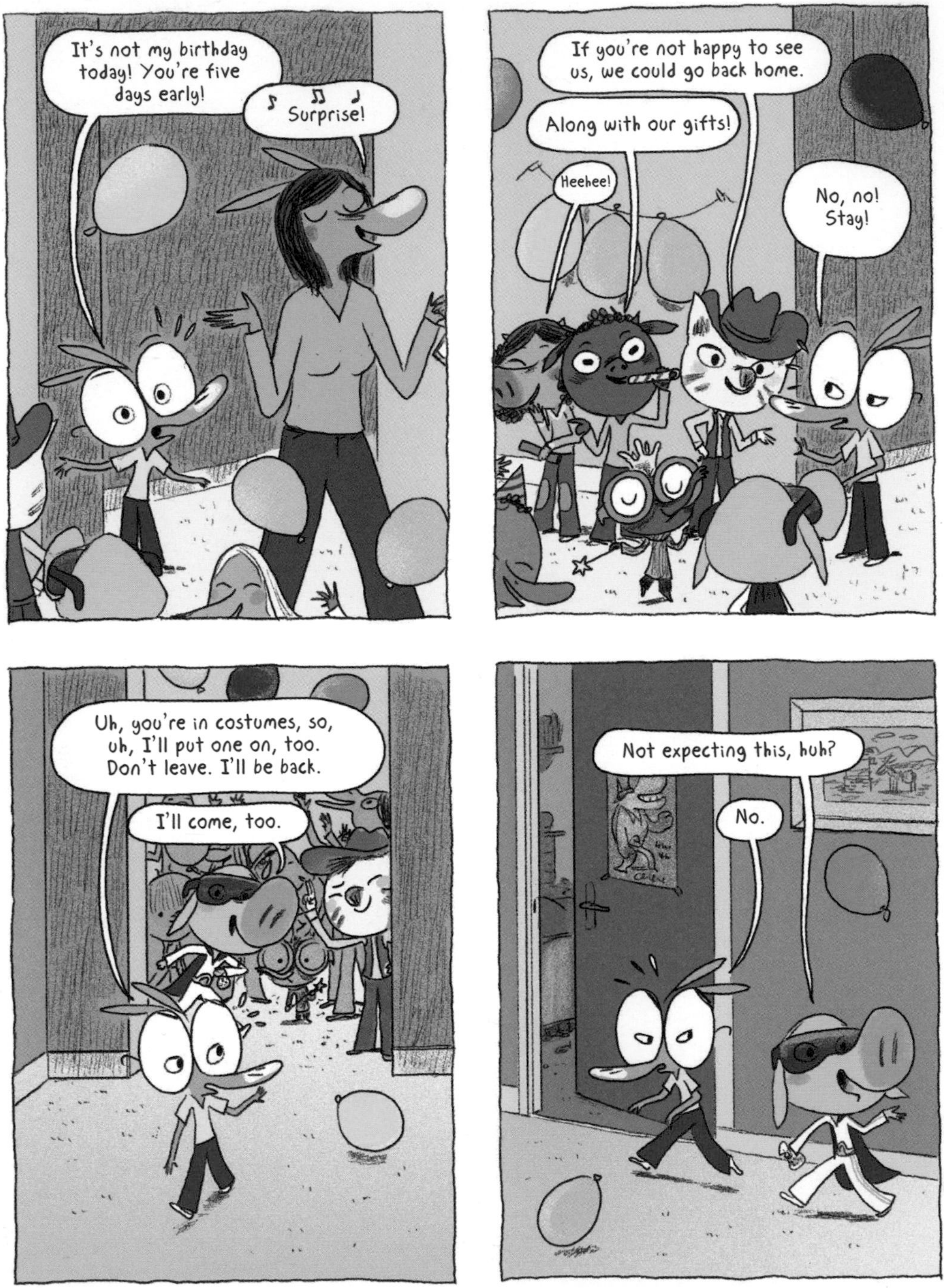
It's not my birthday today! You're five days early!
Surprise!
If you're not happy to see us, we could go back home.
Along with our gifts!
Heehee!
No, no! Stay!
Uh, you're in costumes, so, uh, I'll put one on, too. Don't leave. I'll be back.
I'll come, too.
Not expecting this, huh?
No.

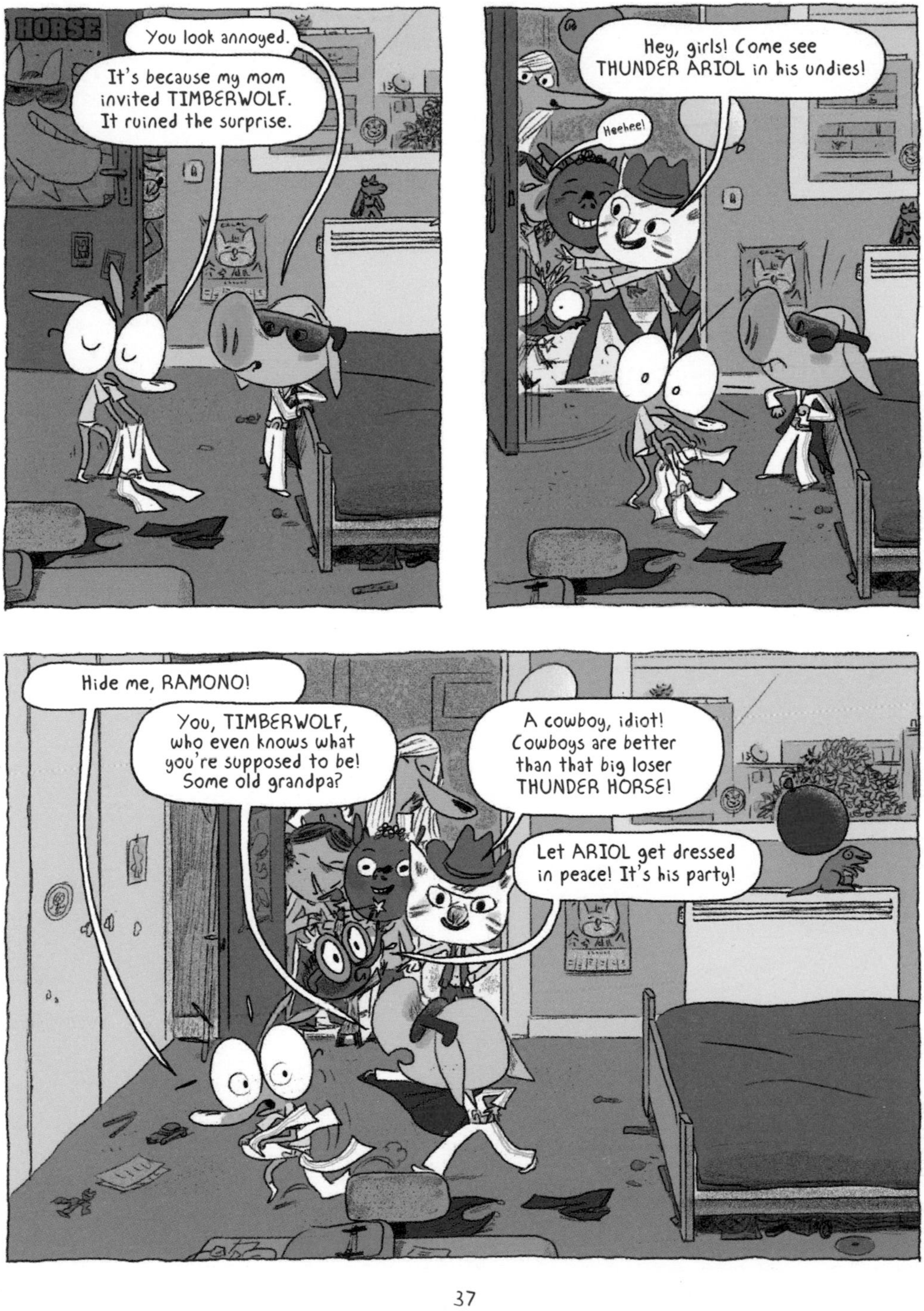
You look annoyed.
It's because my mom invited TIMBERWOLF. It ruined the surprise.
Hey, girls! Come see THUNDER ARIOL in his undies!
Heehee!
Hide me, RAMONO!
You, TIMBERWOLF, who even knows what you're supposed to be! Some old grandpa?
A cowboy, idiot! Cowboys are better than that big loser THUNDER HORSE!
Let ARIOL get dressed in peace! It's his party!

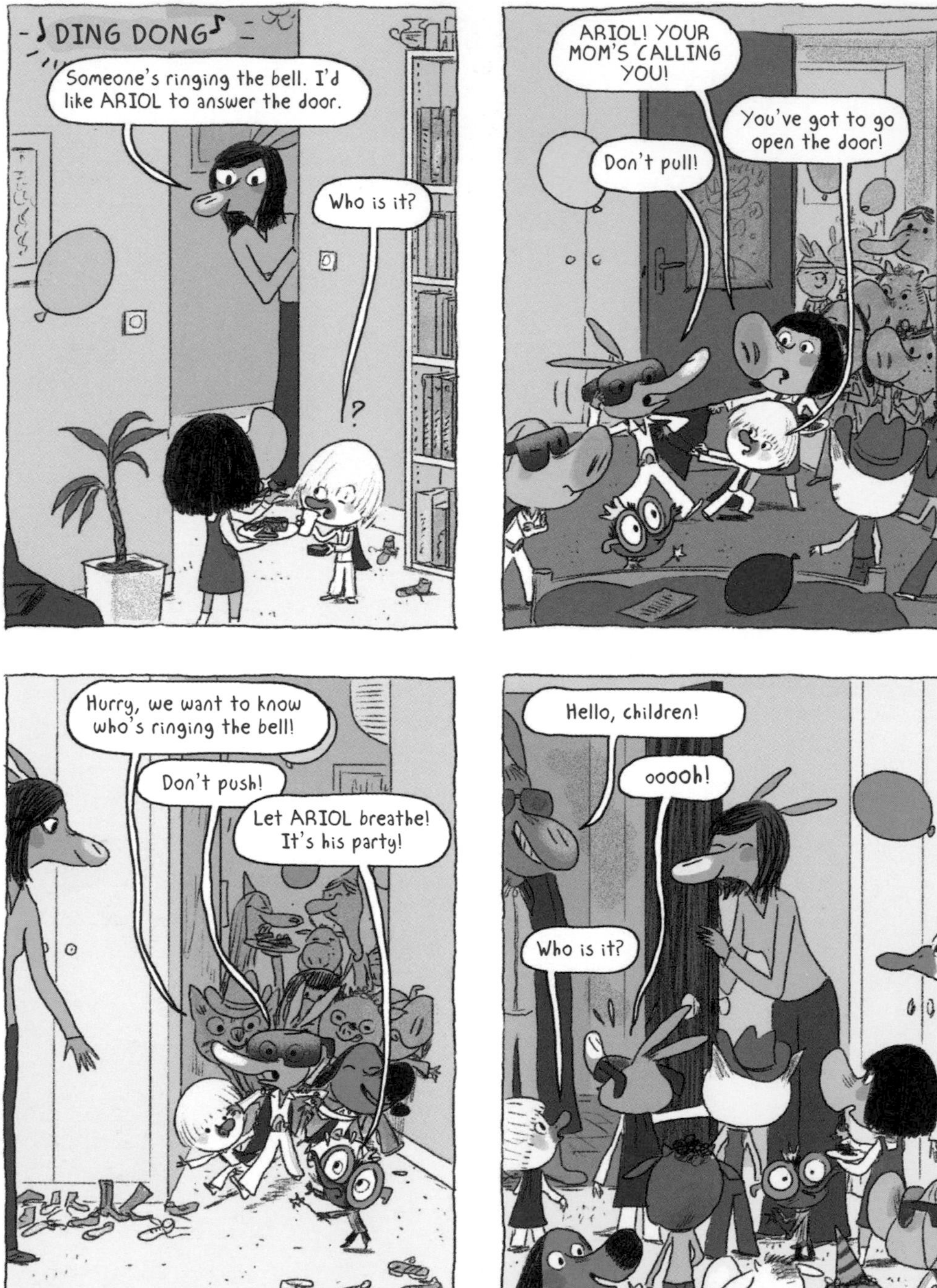
DING DONG
Someone's ringing the bell. I'd like ARIOL to answer the door.
Who is it?
?
ARIOL! YOUR MOM'S CALLING YOU!
You've got to go open the door!
Don't pull!
Hurry, we want to know who's ringing the bell!
Don't push!
Let ARIOL breathe! It's his party!
Hello, children!
ooooh!
Who is it?

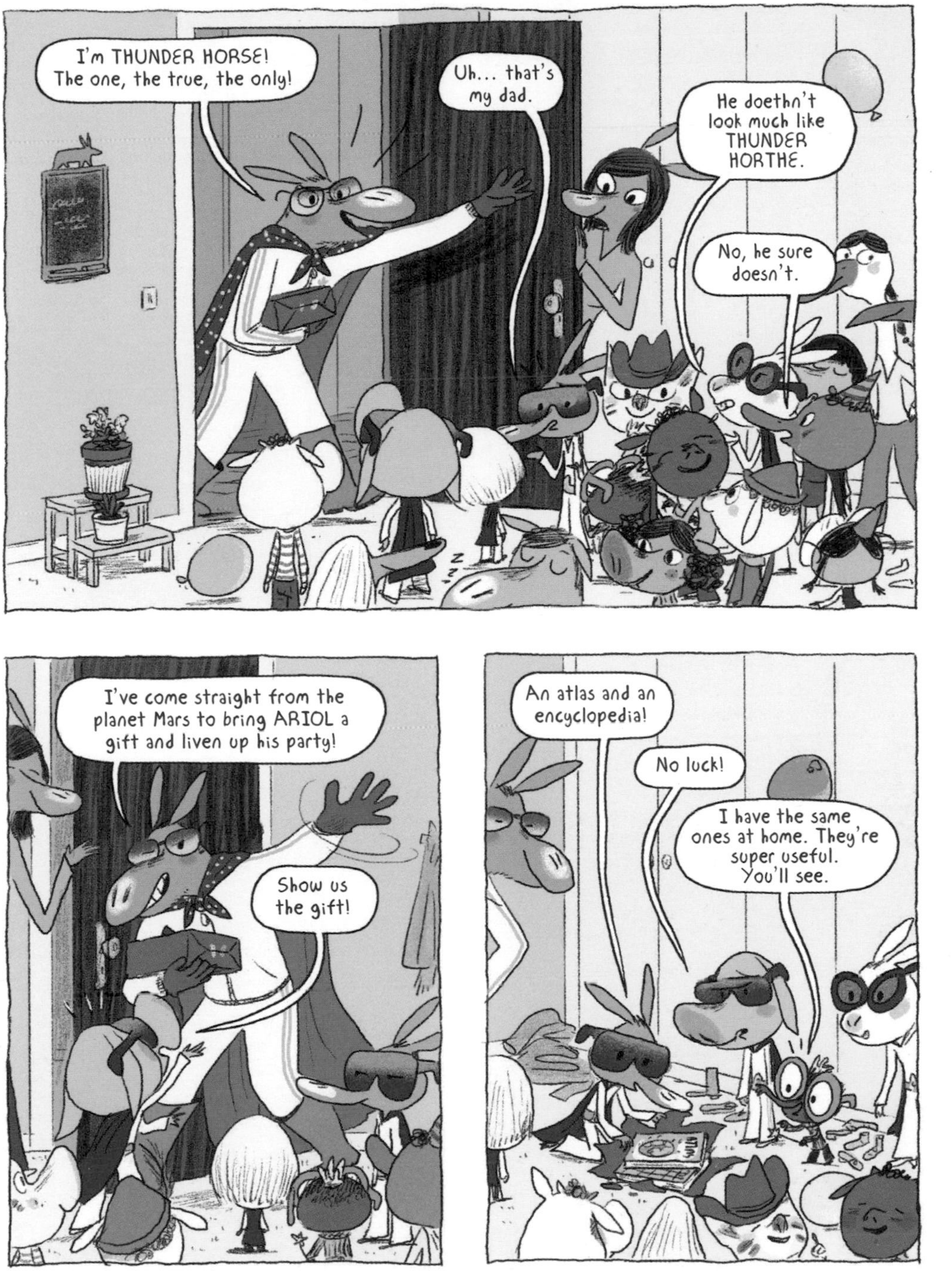
I'm THUNDER HORSE! The one, the true, the only!
Uh... that's my dad.
He doethn't look much like THUNDER HORTHE.
No, he sure doesn't.
I've come straight from the planet Mars to bring ARIOL a gift and liven up his party!
Show us the gift!
An atlas and an encyclopedia!
No luck!
I have the same ones at home. They're super useful. You'll see.

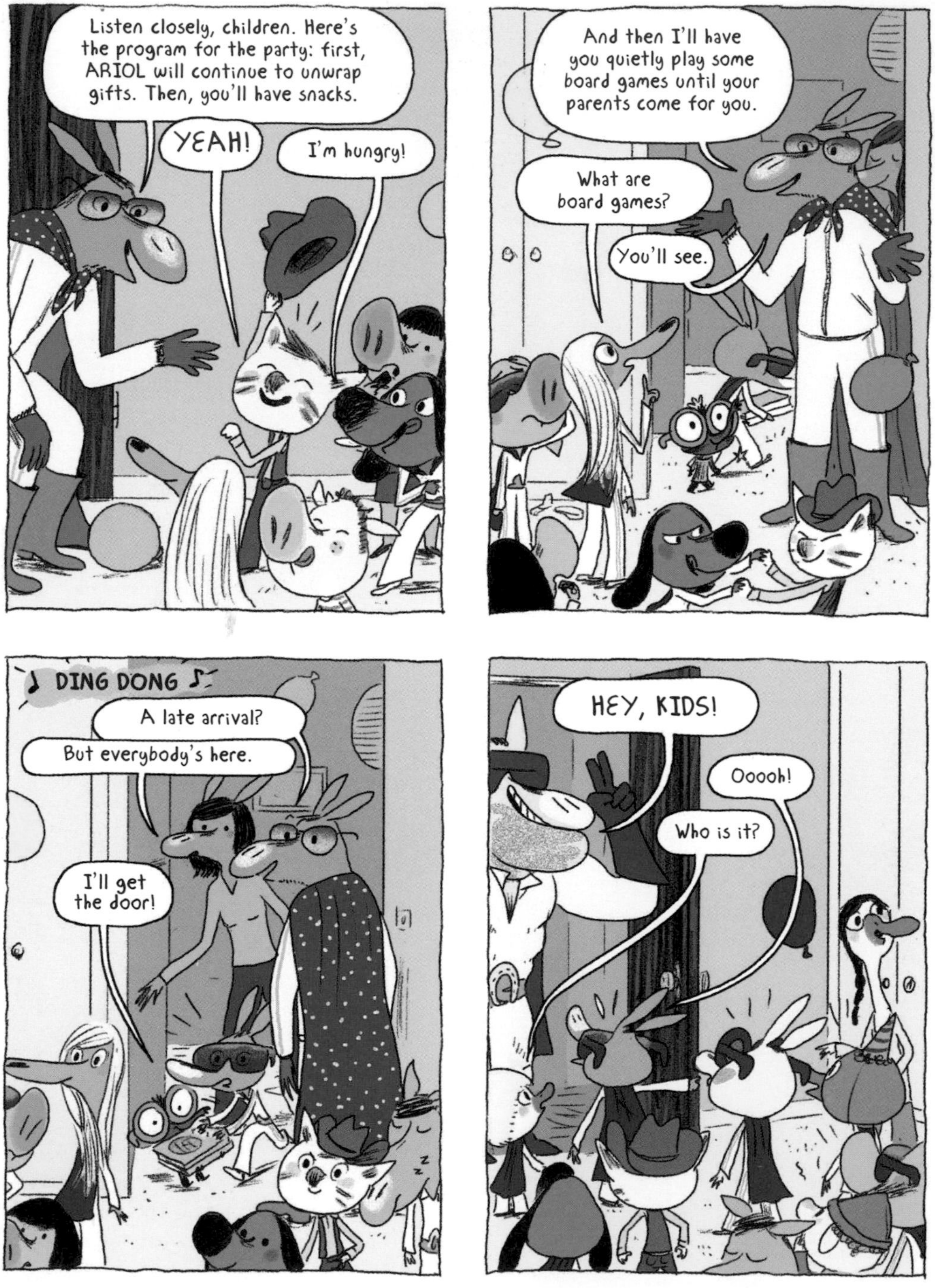
Listen closely, children. Here's the program for the party: first, ARIOL will continue to unwrap gifts. Then, you'll have snacks.
YEAH!
I'm hungry!
And then I'll have you quietly play some board games until your parents come for you.
What are board games?
You'll see.
DING DONG
A late arrival?
But everybody's here.
I'll get the door!
HEY, KIDS!
Ooooh!
Who is it?

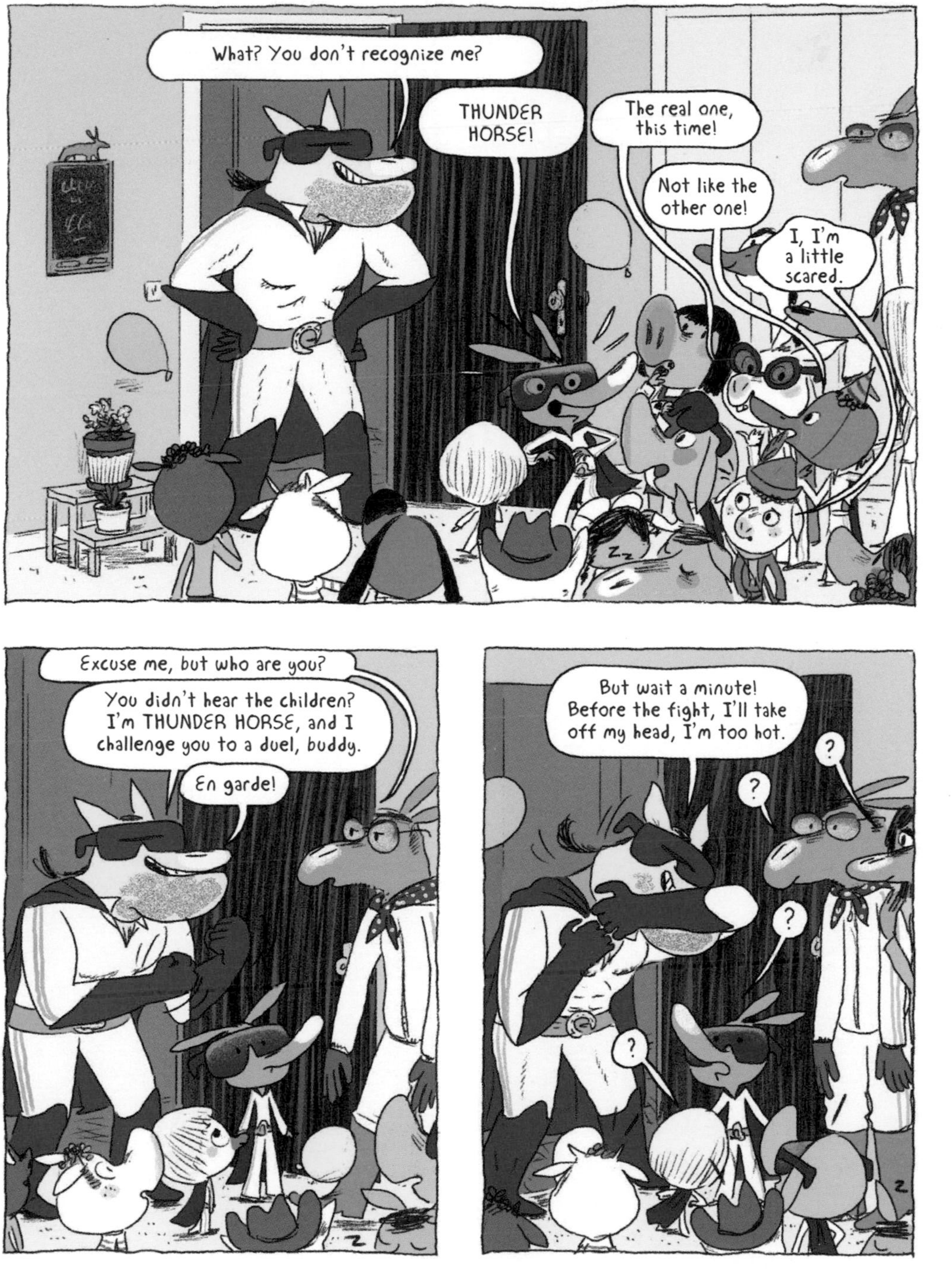
What? You don't recognize me?
THUNDER HORSE!
The real one, this time!
Not like the other one!
I, I'm a little scared.
Excuse me, but who are you?
You didn't hear the children? I'm THUNDER HORSE, and I challenge you to a duel, buddy.
En garde!
But wait a minute! Before the fight, I'll take off my head, I'm too hot.
?
?
?
?

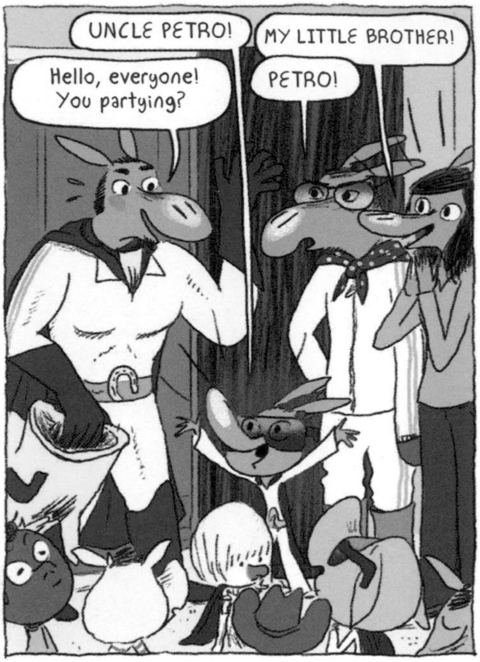
UNCLE PETRO!
MY LITTLE BROTHER!
Hello, everyone! You partying?
PETRO!

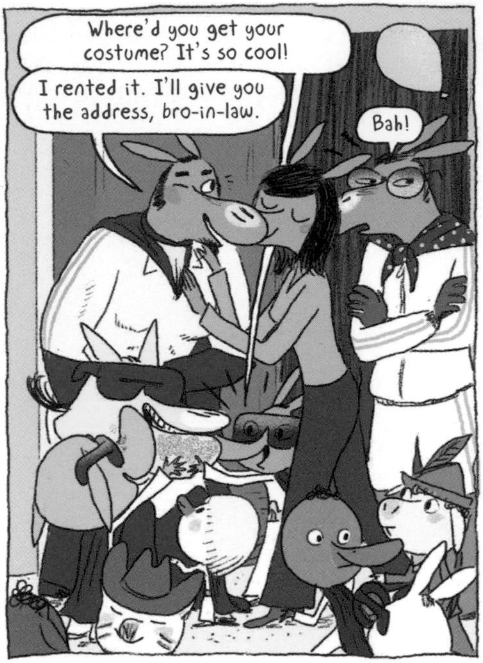
Where'd you get your costume? It's so cool!
I rented it. I'll give you the address, bro-in-law.
Bah!

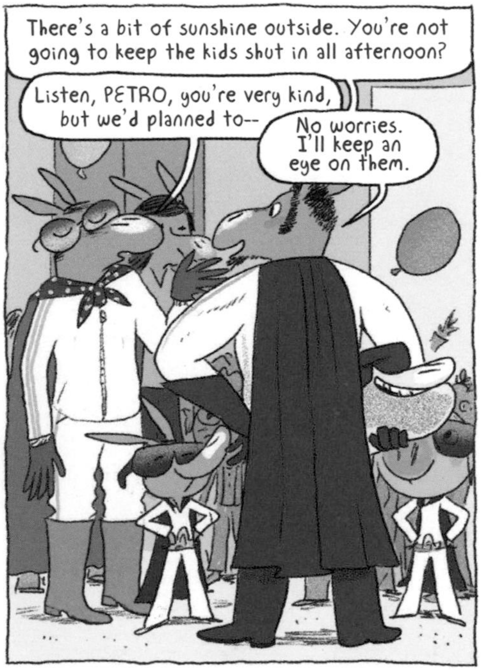
There's a bit of sunshine outside. You're not going to keep the kids shut in all afternoon?
Listen, PETRO, you're very kind, but we'd planned to--
No worries. I'll keep an eye on them.

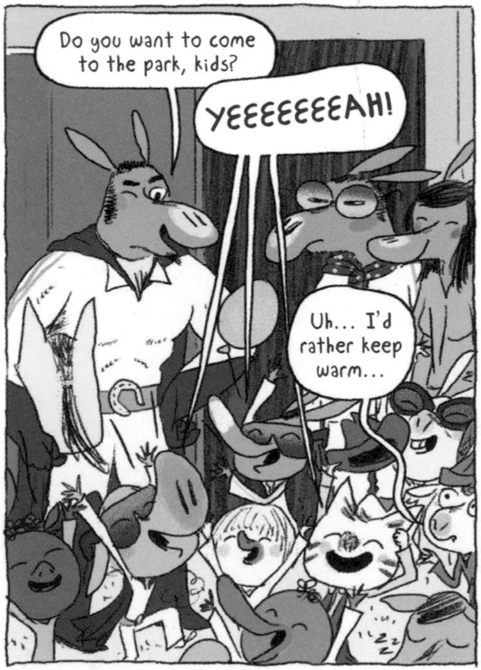
Do you want to come to the park, kids?
YEEEEEEEAH!
Uh... I'd rather keep warm...

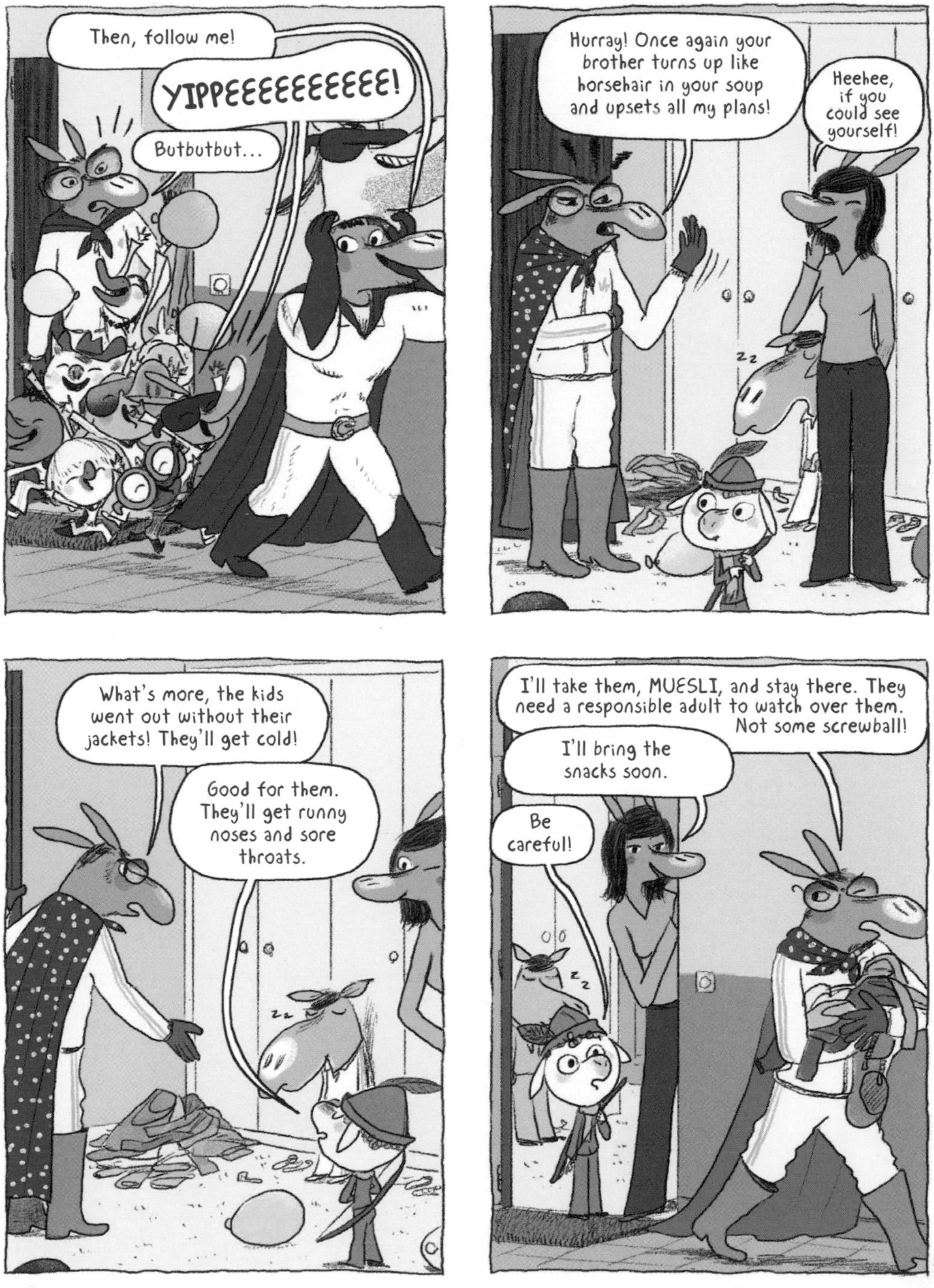

Then, follow me!
YIPPEEEEEEEEEE!
Butbutbut...
Hurray! Once again your brother turns up like horsehair in your soup and upsets all my plans!
Heehee, if you could see yourself!
What's more, the kids went out without their jackets! They'll get cold!
Good for them. They'll get runny noses and sore throats.
I'll take them, MUESLI, and stay there. They need a responsible adult to watch over them. Not some screwball!
I'll bring the snacks soon.
Be careful!

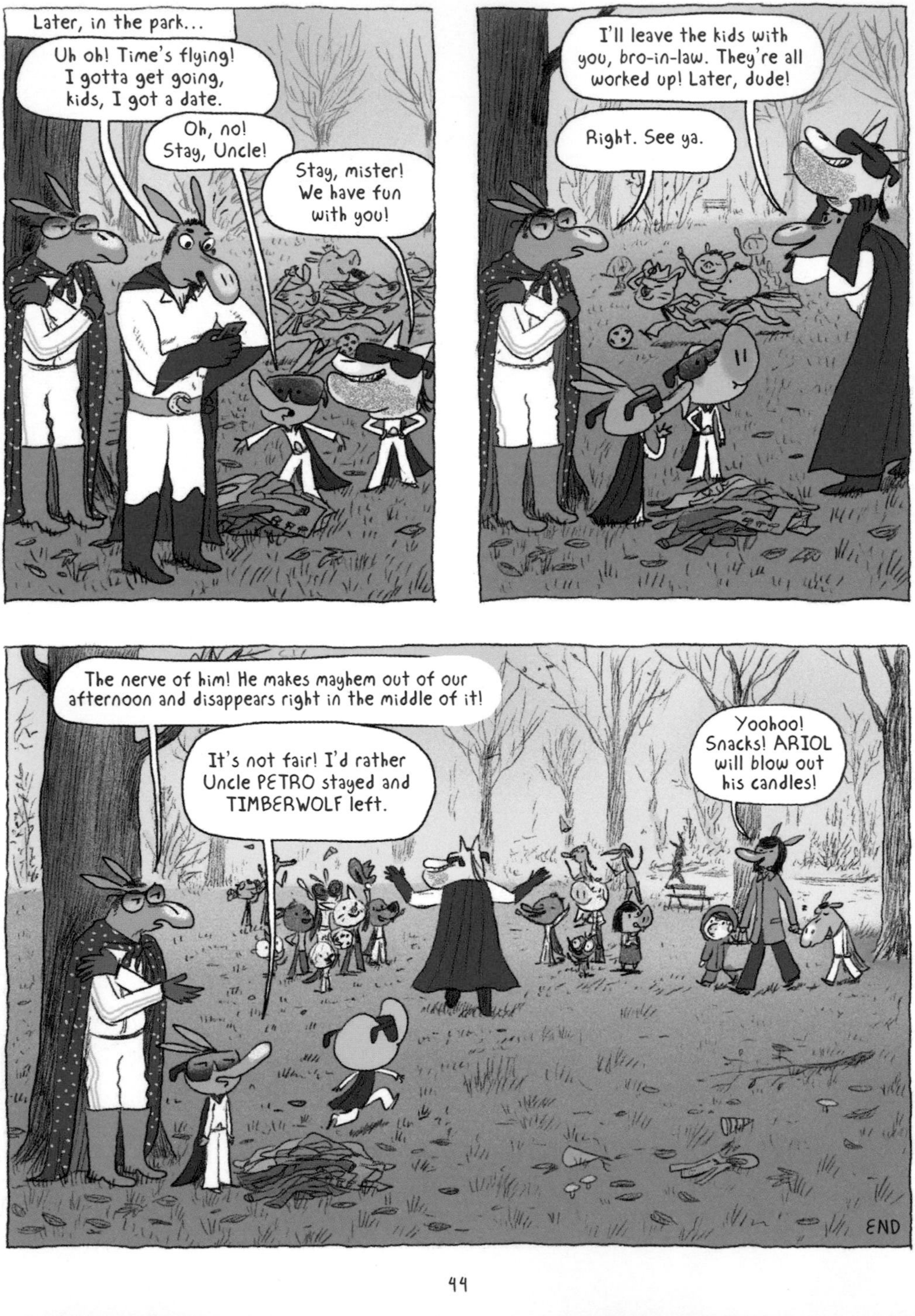

Later, in the park...
Uh oh! Time's flying! I gotta get going, kids, I got a date.
Oh, no! Stay, Uncle!
Stay, mister! We have fun with you!
I'll leave the kids with you, bro-in-law. They're all worked up! Later, dude!
Right. See ya.
The nerve of him! He makes mayhem out of our afternoon and disappears right in the middle of it!
It's not fair! I'd rather Uncle PETRO stayed and TIMBERWOLF left.
Yoohoo! Snacks! ARIOL will blow out his candles!
END

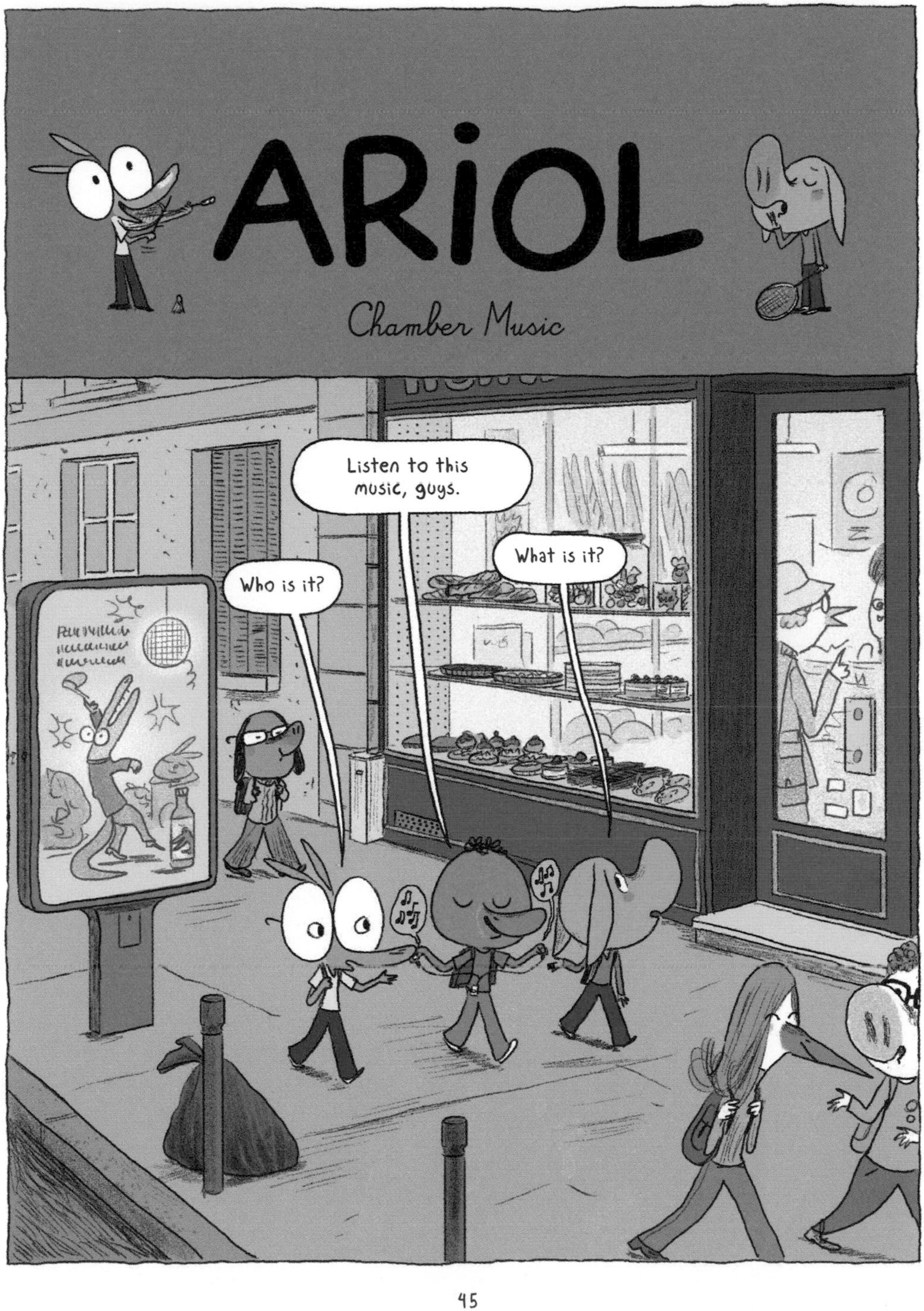
ARiOL
Chamber Music
Listen to this music, guys.
Who is it?
What is it?

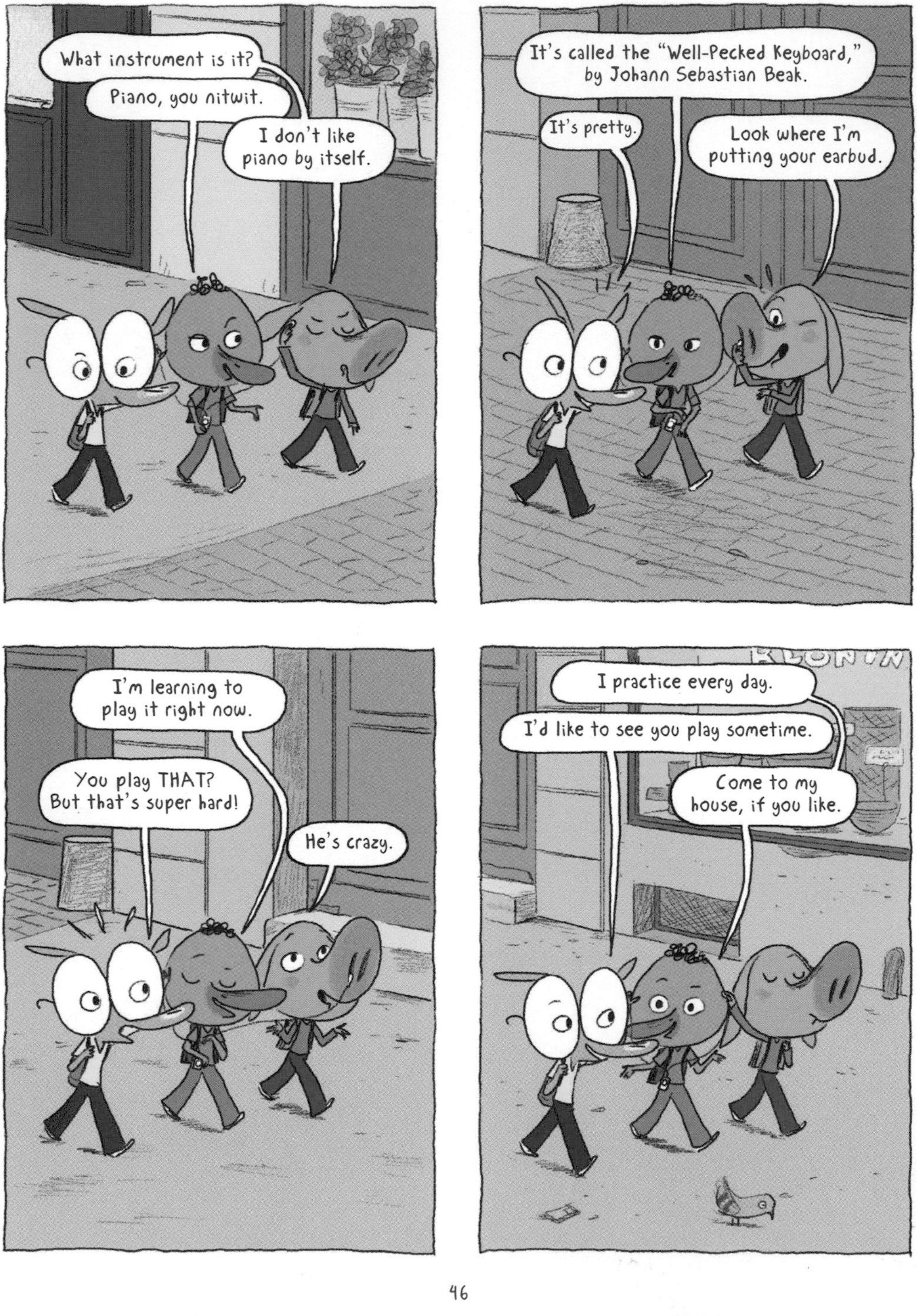
What instrument is it?
Piano, you nitwit.
I don't like piano by itself.
It's called the "Well-Pecked Keyboard," by Johann Sebastian Beak.
It's pretty.
Look where I'm putting your earbud.
I'm learning to play it right now.
You play THAT? But that's super hard!
He's crazy.
I practice every day.
I'd like to see you play sometime.
Come to my house, if you like.

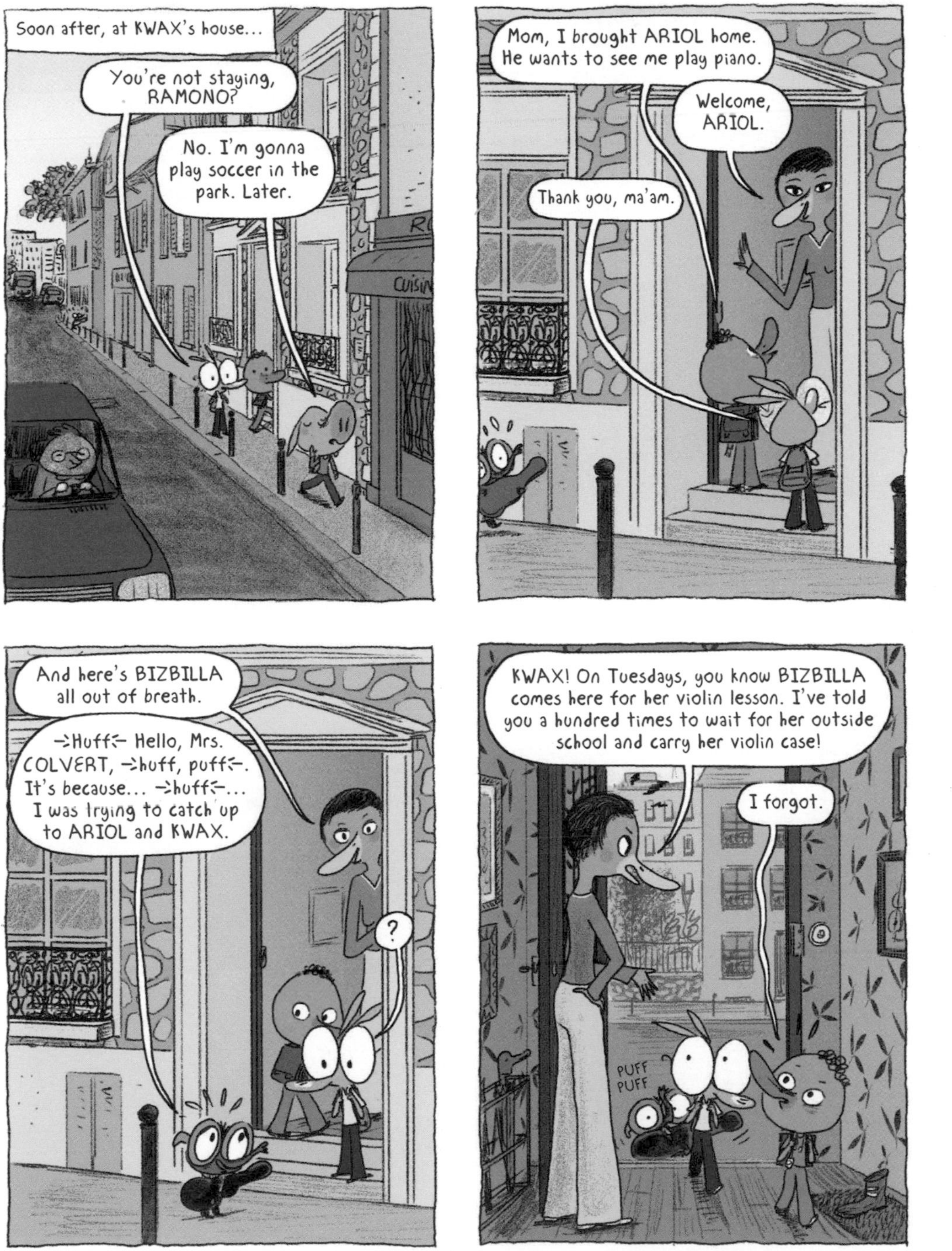

Soon after, at KWAX's house...
You're not staying, RAMONO?
No. I'm gonna play soccer in the park. Later.
Mom, I brought ARIOL home. He wants to see me play piano.
Welcome, ARIOL.
Thank you, ma'am.
And here's BIZBILLA all out of breath.
->Huff<- Hello, Mrs. COLVERT, ->huff, puff<-. It's because... ->huff<-... I was trying to catch up to ARIOL and KWAX.
?
KWAX! On Tuesdays, you know BIZBILLA comes here for her violin lesson. I've told you a hundred times to wait for her outside school and carry her violin case!
I forgot.
PUFF PUFF

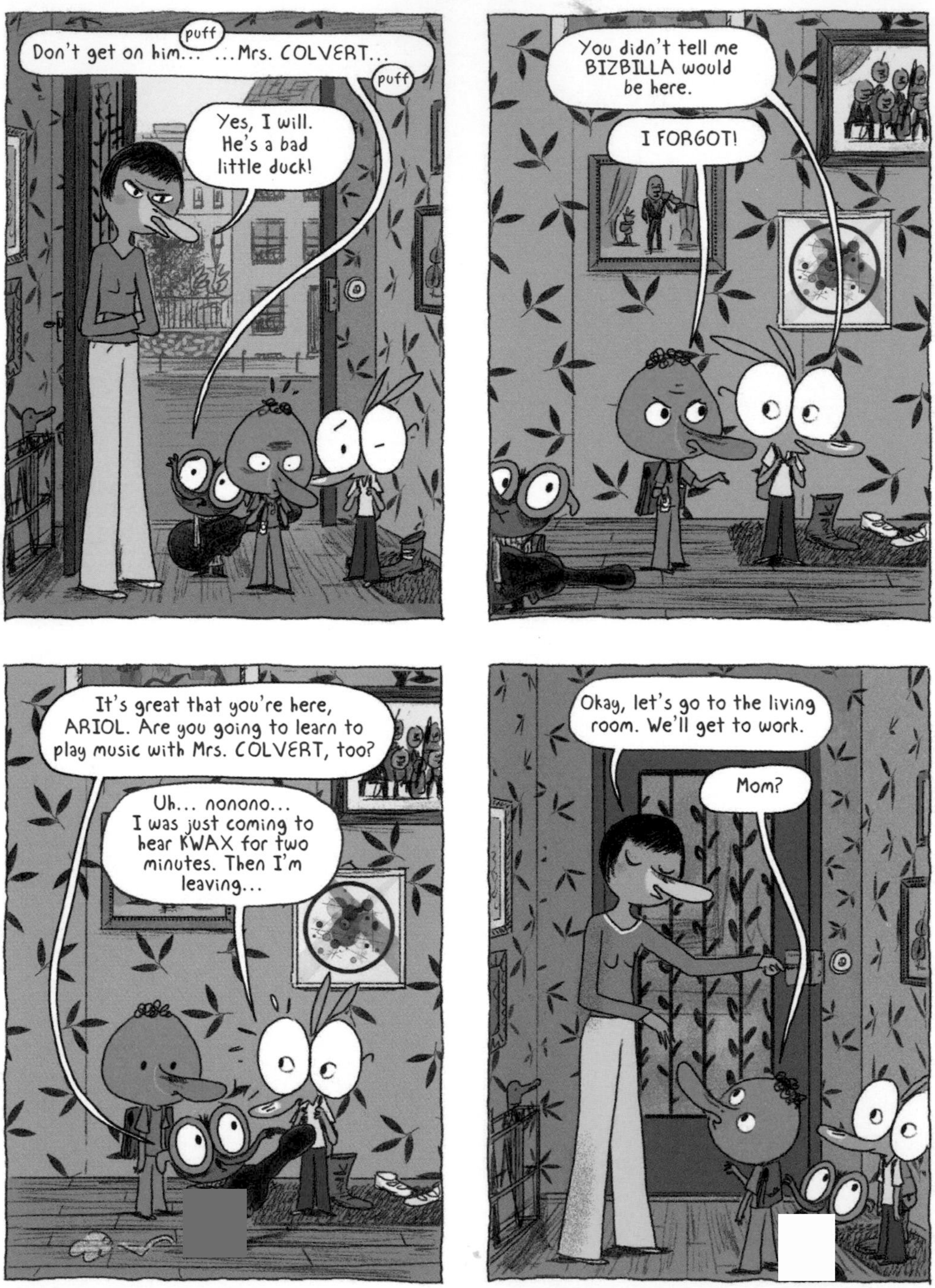

Don't get on him... puff ...Mrs. COLVERT... puff
Yes, I will. He's a bad little duck!
You didn't tell me BIZBILLA would be here.
I FORGOT!
It's great that you're here, ARIOL. Are you going to learn to play music with Mrs. COLVERT, too?
Uh... nonono... I was just coming to hear KWAX for two minutes. Then I'm leaving...
Okay, let's go to the living room. We'll get to work.
Mom?

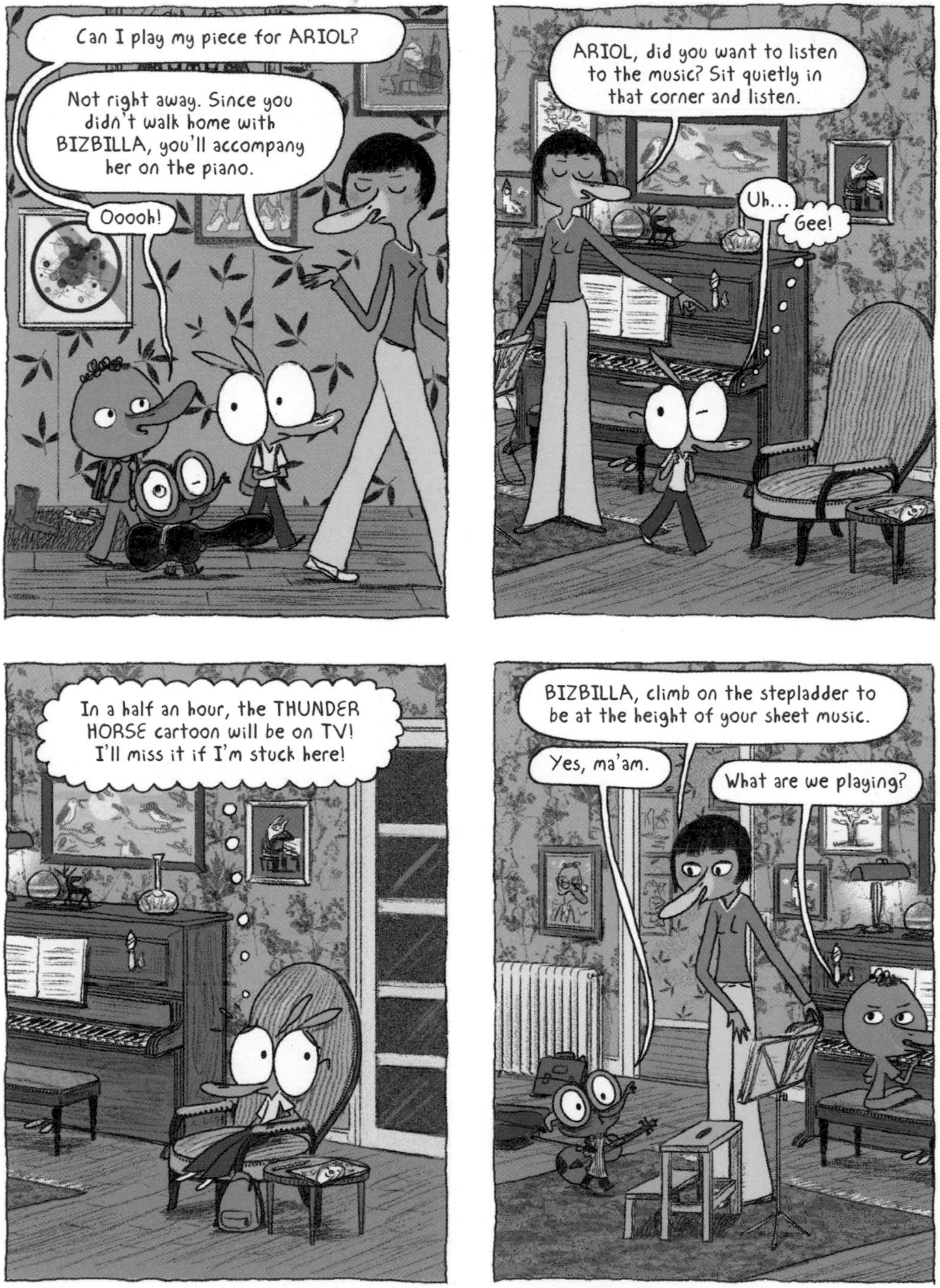

Can I play my piece for ARIOL?
Not right away. Since you didn't walk home with BIZBILLA, you'll accompany her on the piano.
Ooooh!
ARIOL, did you want to listen to the music? Sit quietly in that corner and listen.
Uh...
Gee!
In a half an hour, the THUNDER HORSE cartoon will be on TV! I'll miss it if I'm stuck here!
BIZBILLA, climb on the stepladder to be at the height of your sheet music.
Yes, ma'am.
What are we playing?

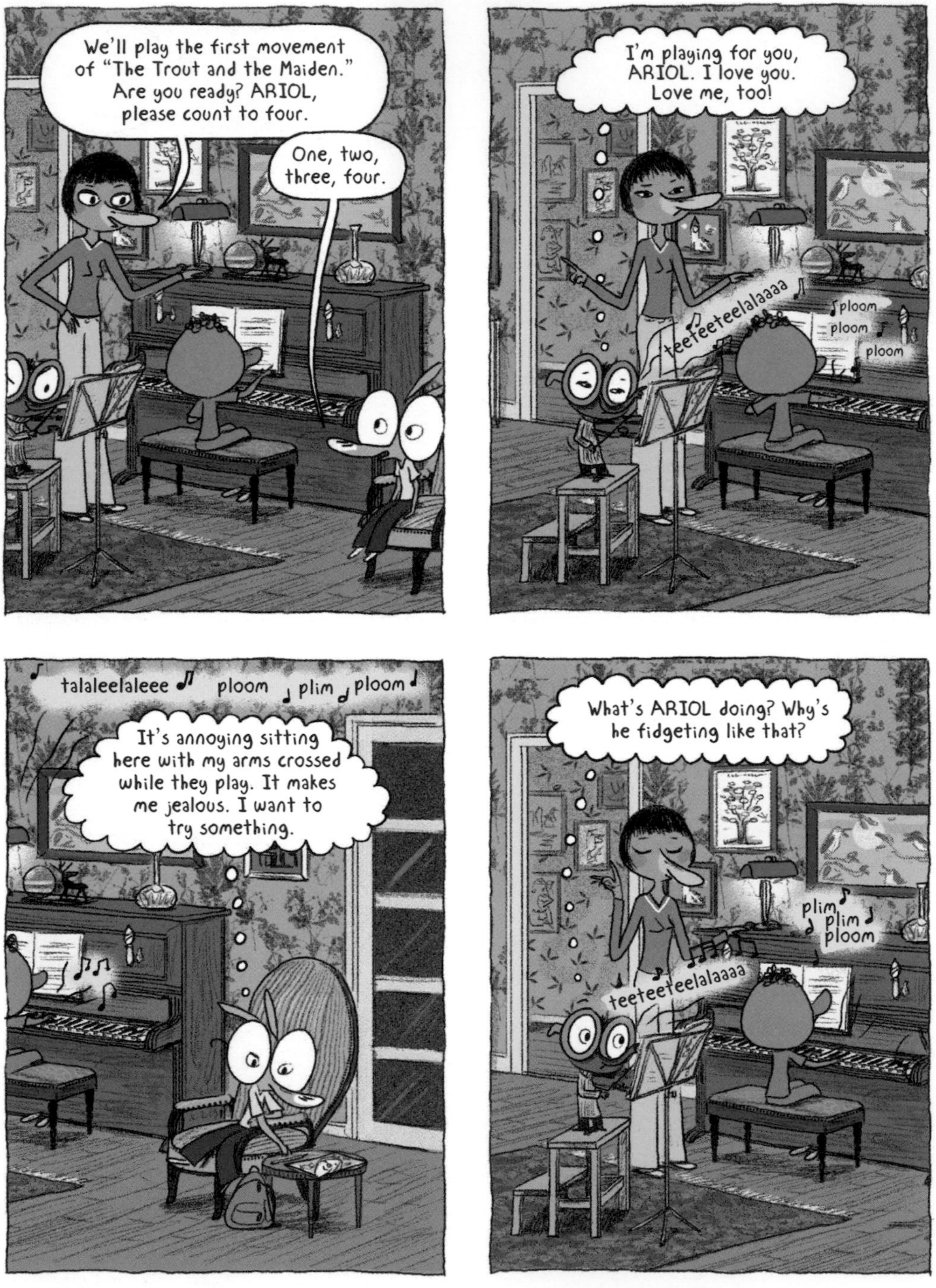
We'll play the first movement of "The Trout and the Maiden." Are you ready? ARIOL, please count to four.
One, two, three, four.
I'm playing for you, ARIOL. I love you. Love me, too!
teeteeteelalaaaa
ploom
ploom
ploom
talaleelaleee
ploom
plim
ploom
It's annoying sitting here with my arms crossed while they play. It makes me jealous. I want to try something.
What's ARIOL doing? Why's he fidgeting like that?
plim
plim
ploom
teeteeteelalaaa

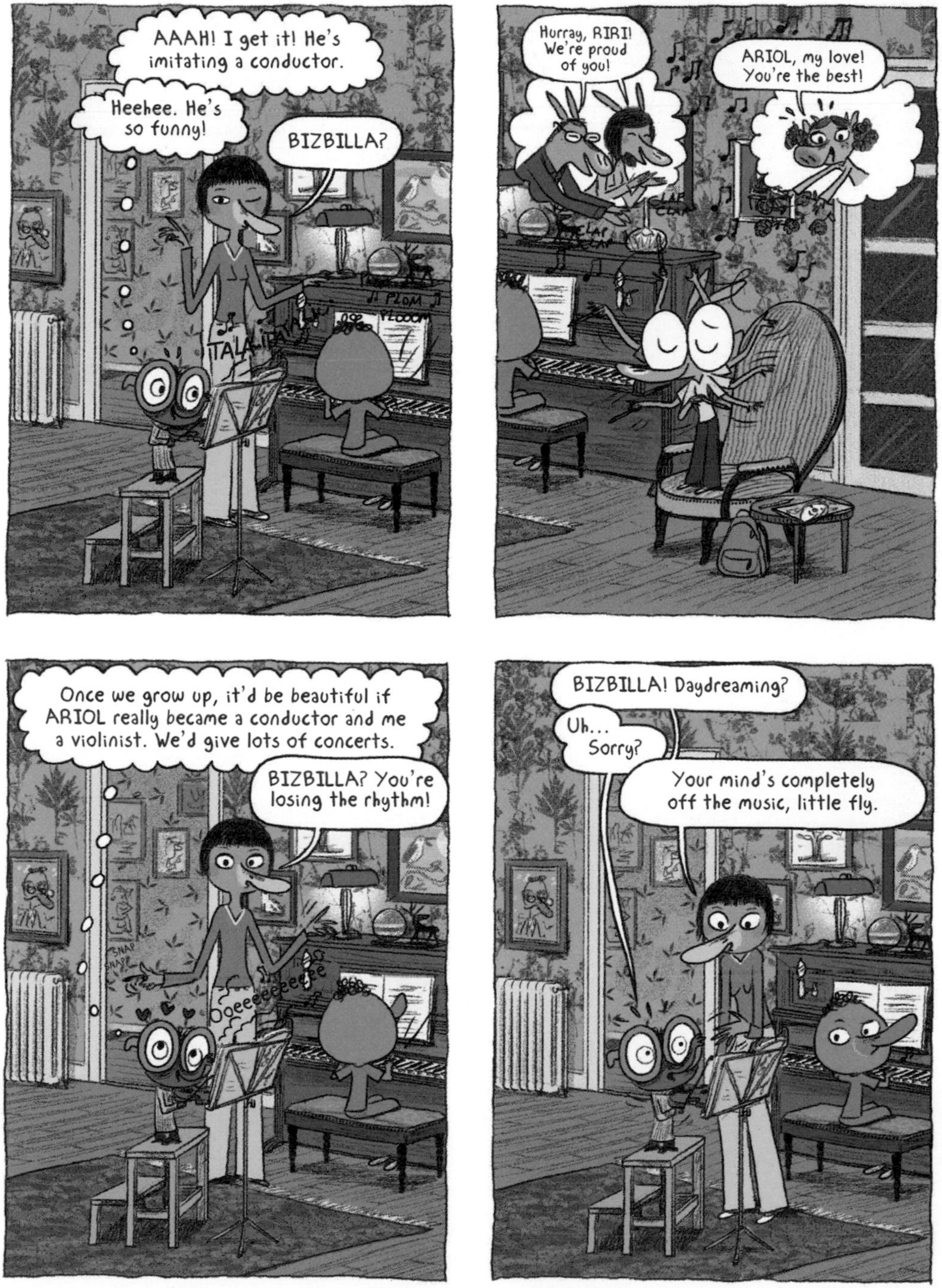
AAAH! I get it! He's imitating a conductor.
Heehee. He's so funny!
BIZBILLA?
Hurray, RIRI! We're proud of you!
ARIOL, my love! You're the best!
Once we grow up, it'd be beautiful if ARIOL really became a conductor and me a violinist. We'd give lots of concerts.
BIZBILLA? You're losing the rhythm!
BIZBILLA! Daydreaming?
Uh... Sorry?
Your mind's completely off the music, little fly.

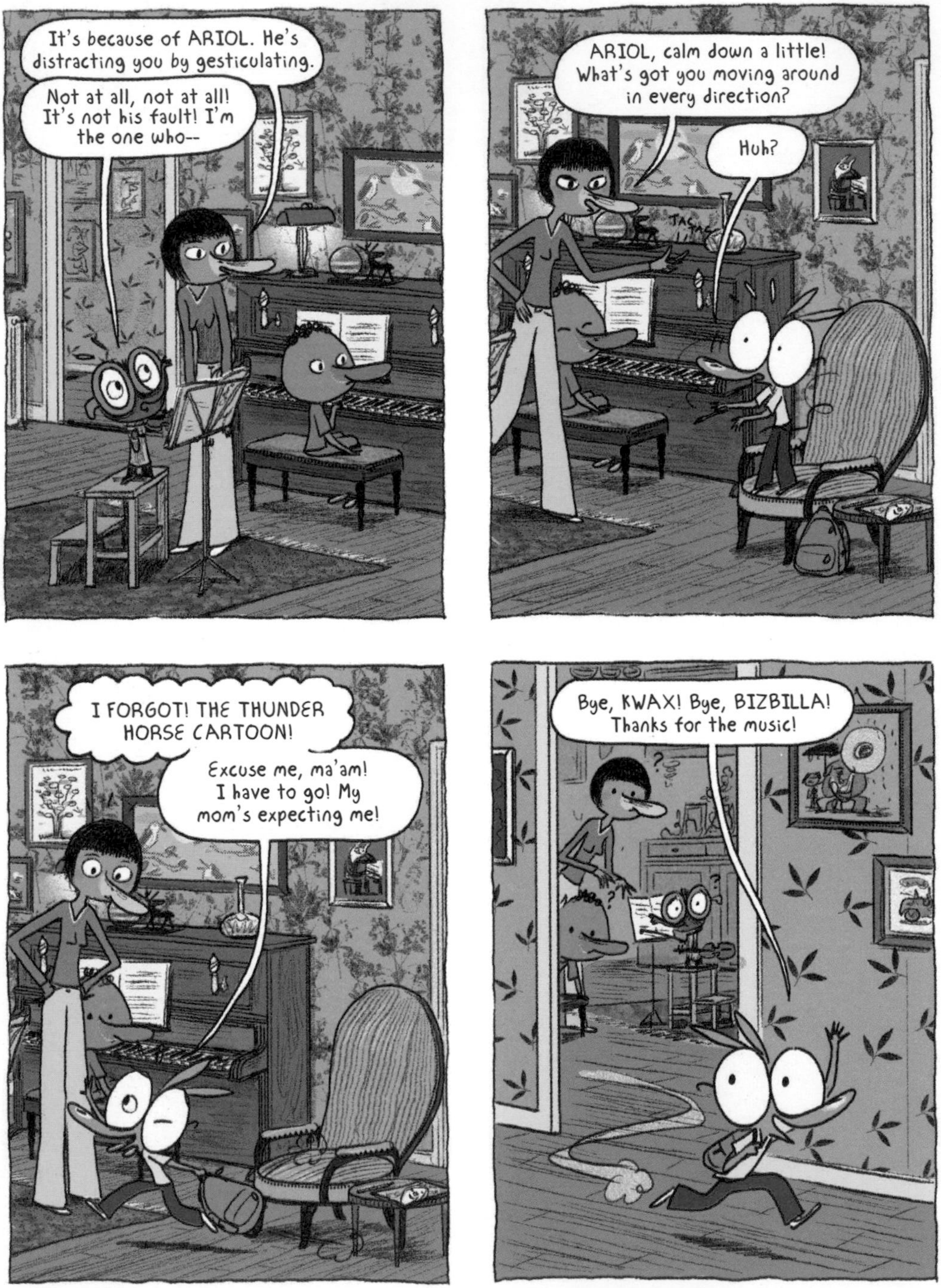
It's because of ARIOL. He's distracting you by gesticulating.
Not at all, not at all! It's not his fault! I'm the one who--
ARIOL, calm down a little! What's got you moving around in every direction?
Huh?
I FORGOT! THE THUNDER HORSE CARTOON!
Excuse me, ma'am! I have to go! My mom's expecting me!
Bye, KWAX! Bye, BIZBILLA! Thanks for the music!

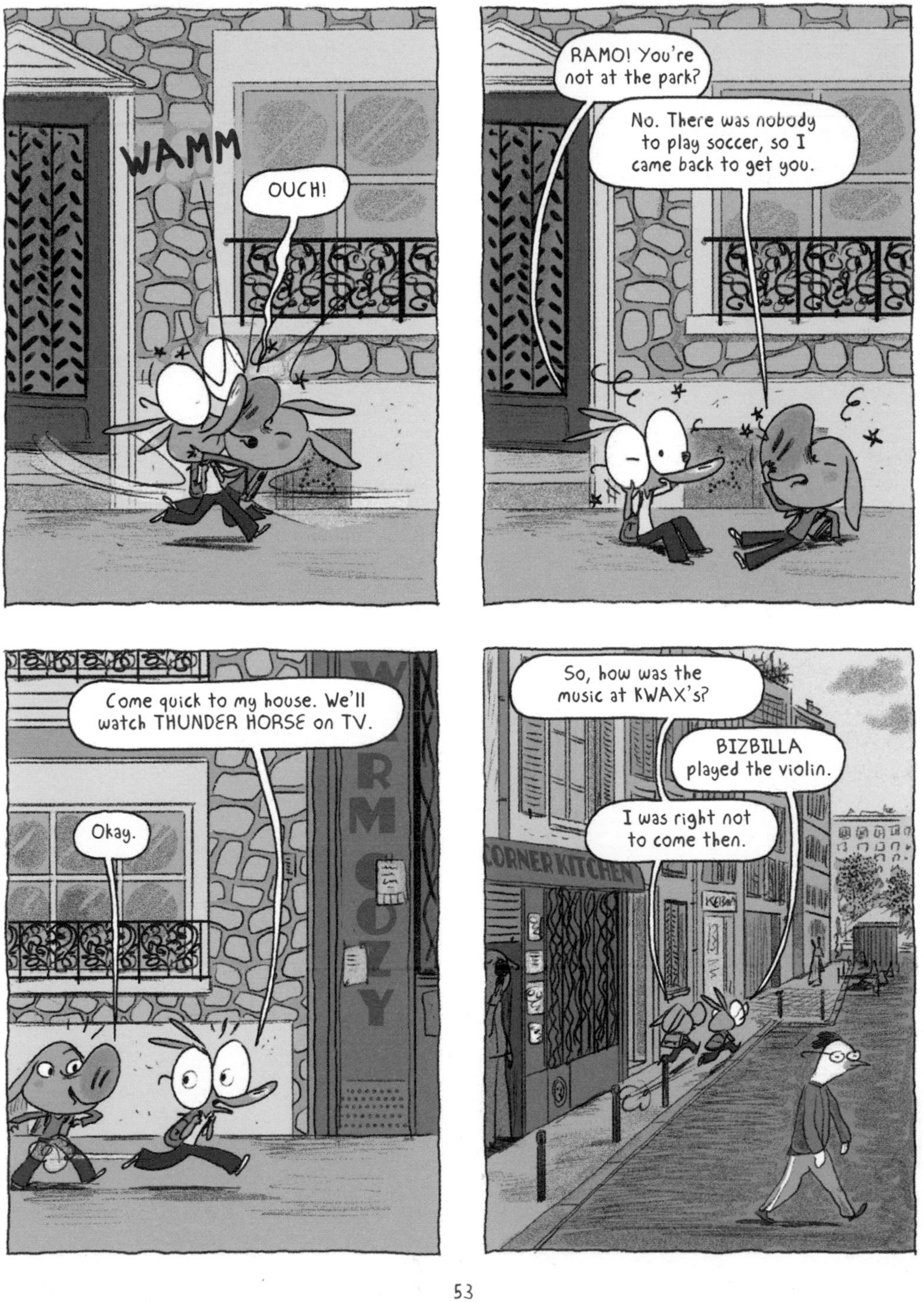
WAMM
OUCH!
RAMO! You're not at the park?
No. There was nobody to play soccer, so I came back to get you.
Come quick to my house. We'll watch THUNDER HORSE on TV.
Okay.
So, how was the music at KWAX's?
BIZBILLA played the violin.
I was right not to come then.
CORNER KITCHEN

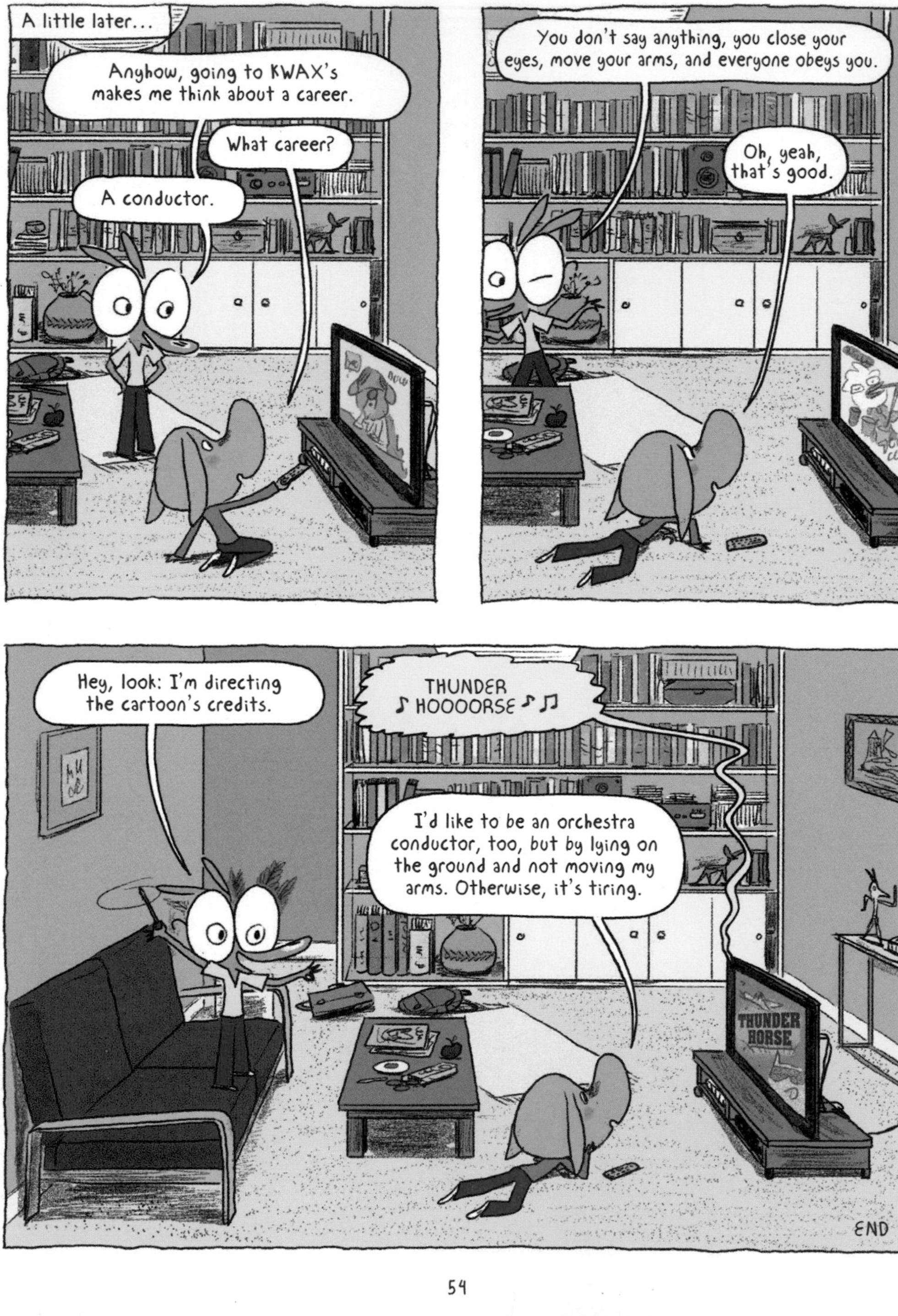

A little later...
Anyhow, going to KWAX's makes me think about a career.
What career?
A conductor.
You don't say anything, you close your eyes, move your arms, and everyone obeys you.
Oh, yeah, that's good.
Hey, look: I'm directing the cartoon's credits.
THUNDER ♪ HOOOORSE ♪ ♫
I'd like to be an orchestra conductor, too, but by lying on the ground and not moving my arms. Otherwise, it's tiring.
THUNDER HORSE
END

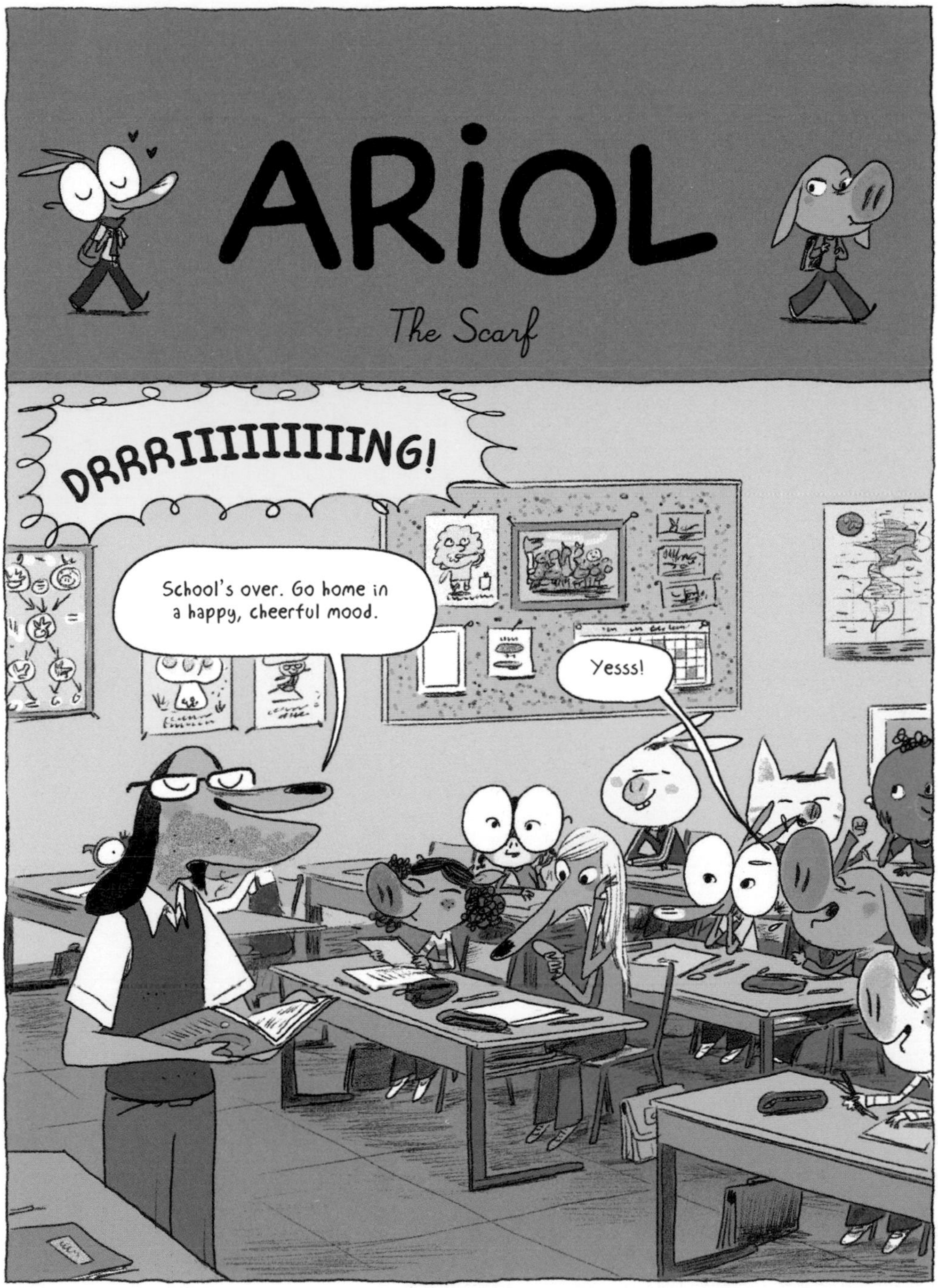
ARiOL
The Scarf
DRRRIIIIIIIIING!
School's over. Go home in a happy, cheerful mood.
Yesss!

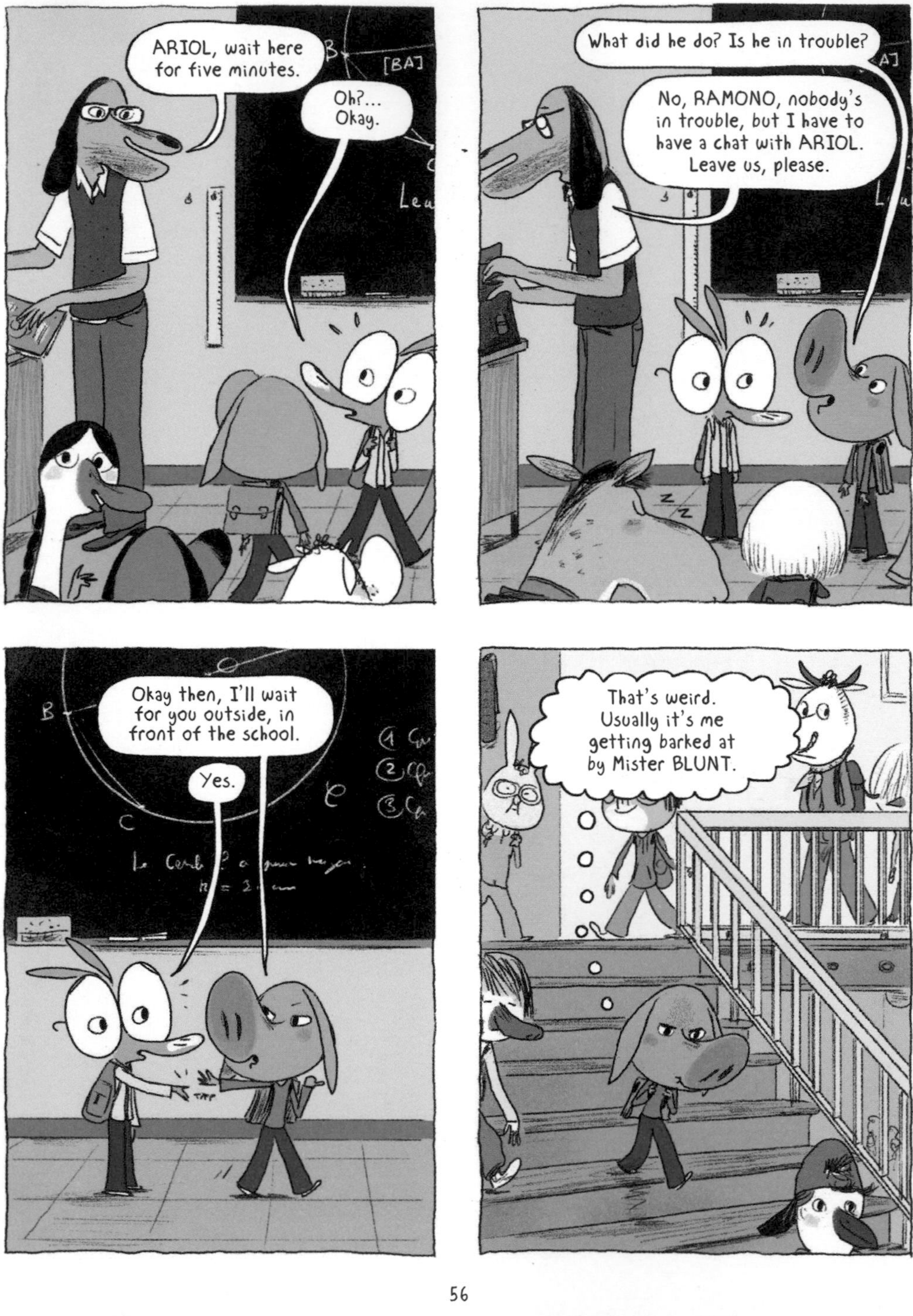
ARIOL, wait here for five minutes.
Oh?... Okay.
What did he do? Is he in trouble?
No, RAMONO, nobody's in trouble, but I have to have a chat with ARIOL. Leave us, please.
Okay then, I'll wait for you outside, in front of the school.
Yes.
That's weird. Usually it's me getting barked at by Mister BLUNT.

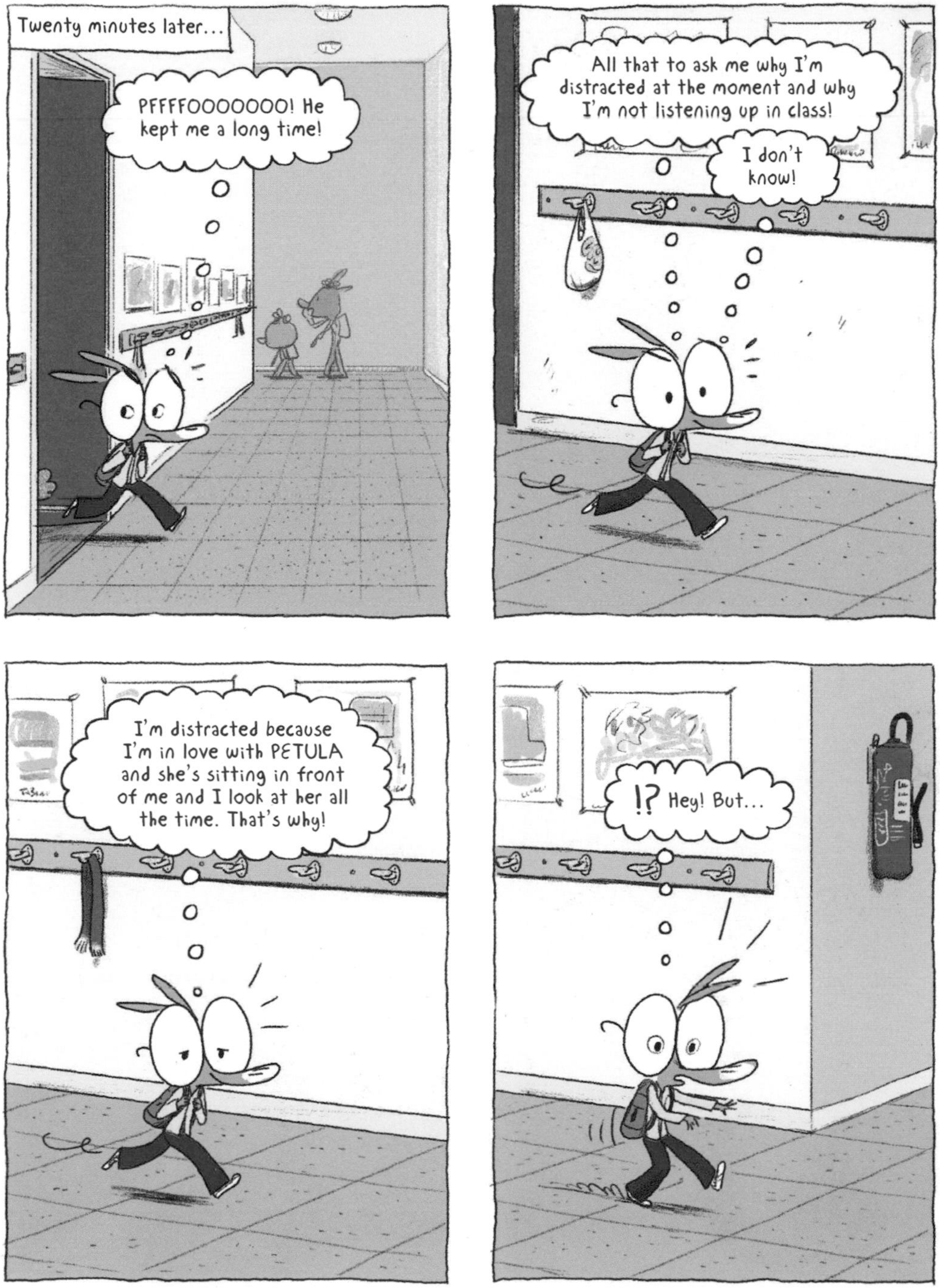
Twenty minutes later...
PFFFFOOOOOOOO! He kept me a long time!
All that to ask me why I'm distracted at the moment and why I'm not listening up in class!
I don't know!
I'm distracted because I'm in love with PETULA and she's sitting in front of me and I look at her all the time. That's why!
!? Hey! But...

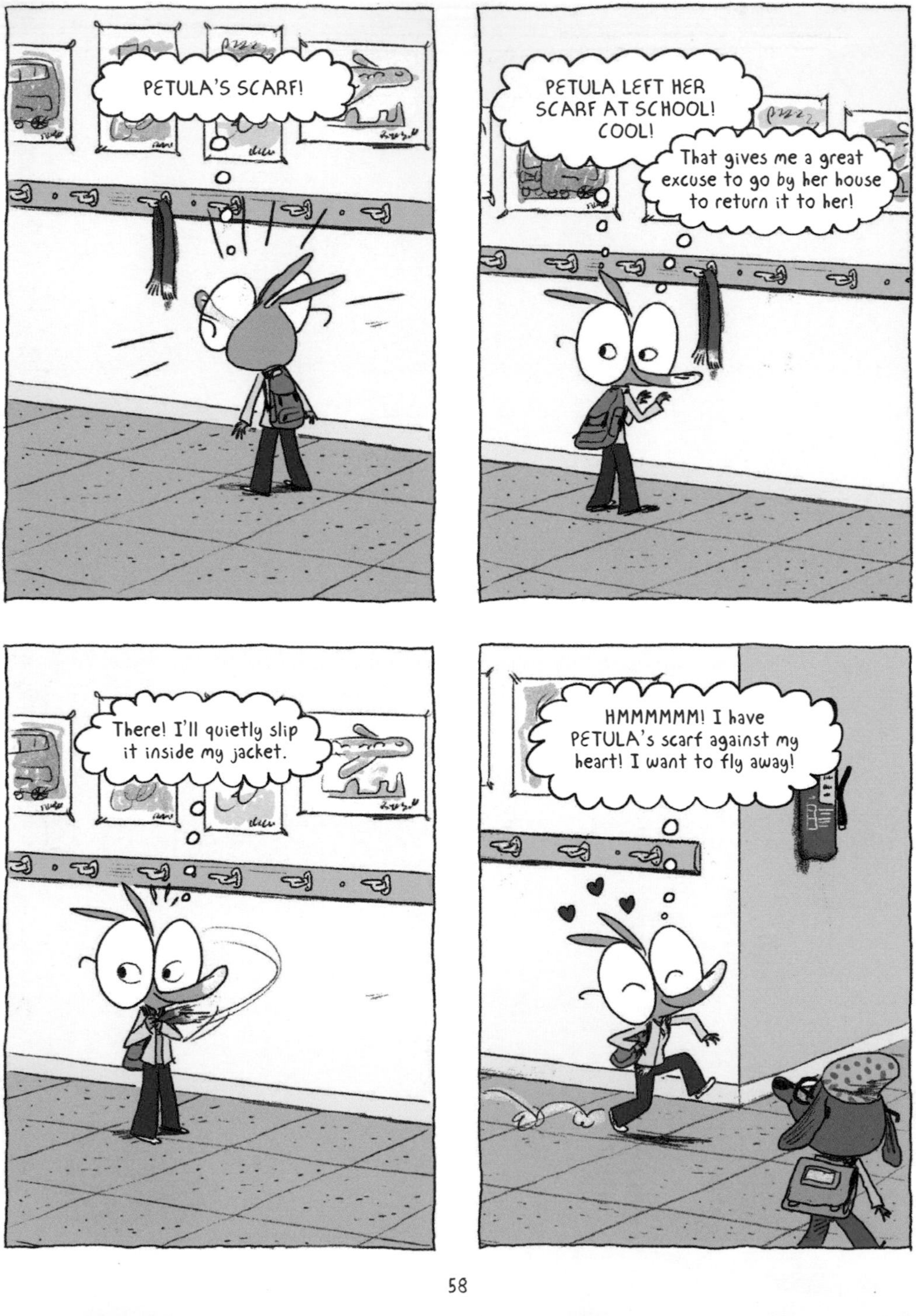
PETULA'S SCARF!
PETULA LEFT HER SCARF AT SCHOOL! COOL!
That gives me a great excuse to go by her house to return it to her!
There! I'll quietly slip it inside my jacket.
HMMMMMM! I have PETULA's scarf against my heart! I want to fly away!

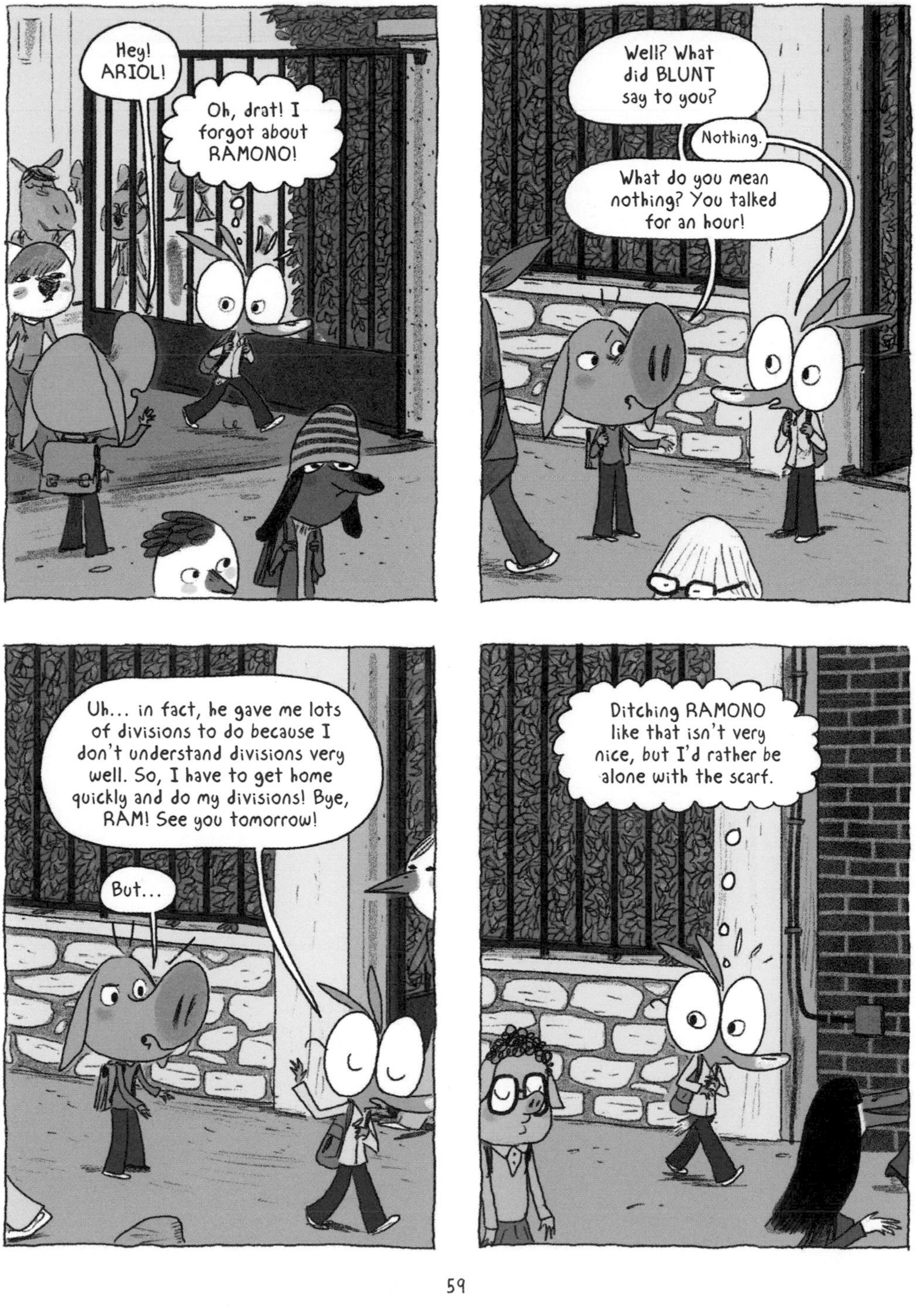
Hey! ARIOL!
Oh, drat! I forgot about RAMONO!
Well? What did BLUNT say to you?
Nothing.
What do you mean nothing? You talked for an hour!
Uh... in fact, he gave me lots of divisions to do because I don't understand divisions very well. So, I have to get home quickly and do my divisions! Bye, RAM! See you tomorrow!
But...
Ditching RAMONO like that isn't very nice, but I'd rather be alone with the scarf.

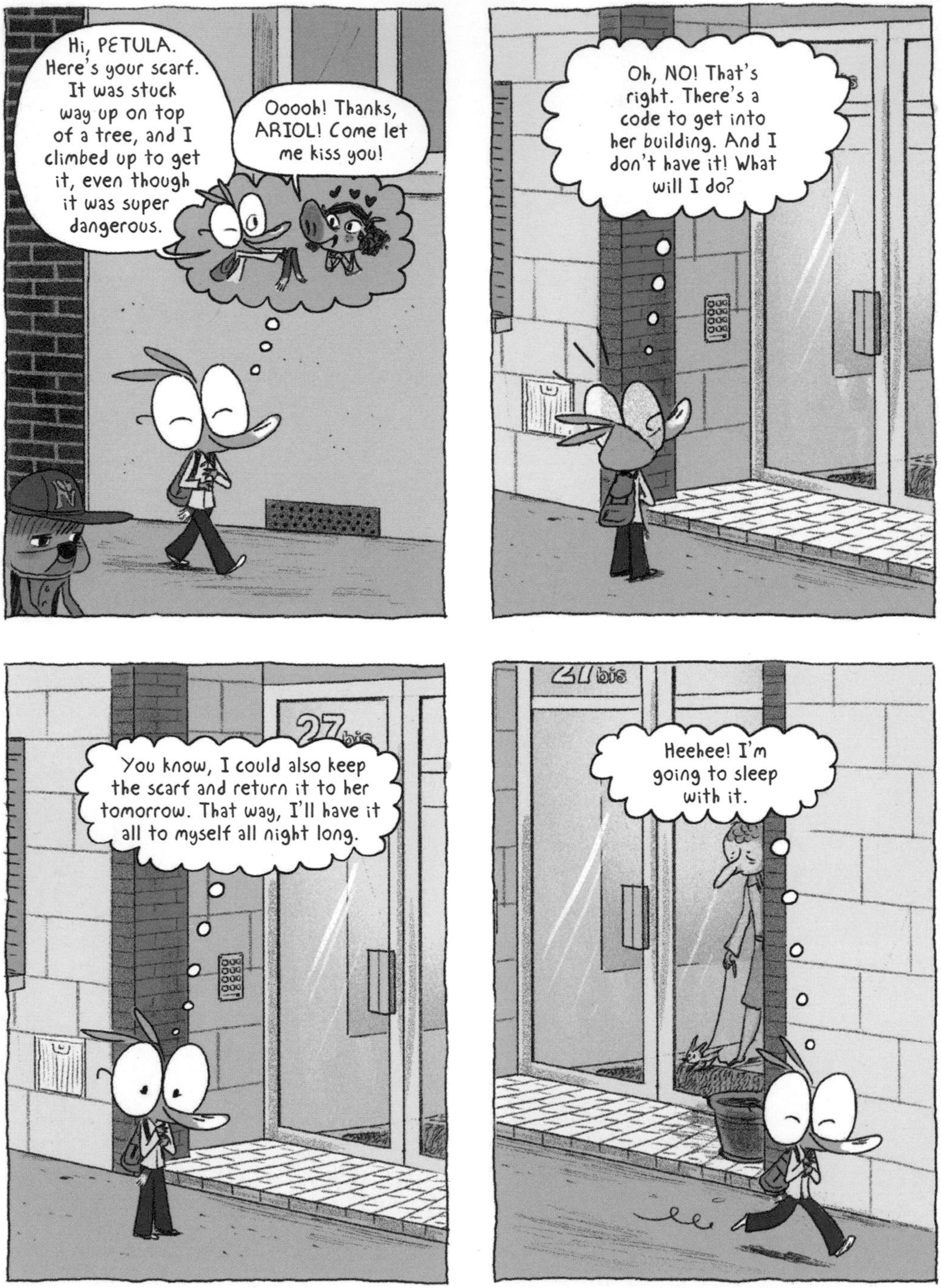
Hi, PETULA. Here's your scarf. It was stuck way up on top of a tree, and I climbed up to get it, even though it was super dangerous.
Ooooh! Thanks, ARIOL! Come let me kiss you!
Oh, NO! That's right. There's a code to get into her building. And I don't have it! What will I do?
27 bis
You know, I could also keep the scarf and return it to her tomorrow. That way, I'll have it all to myself all night long.
Heehee! I'm going to sleep with it.

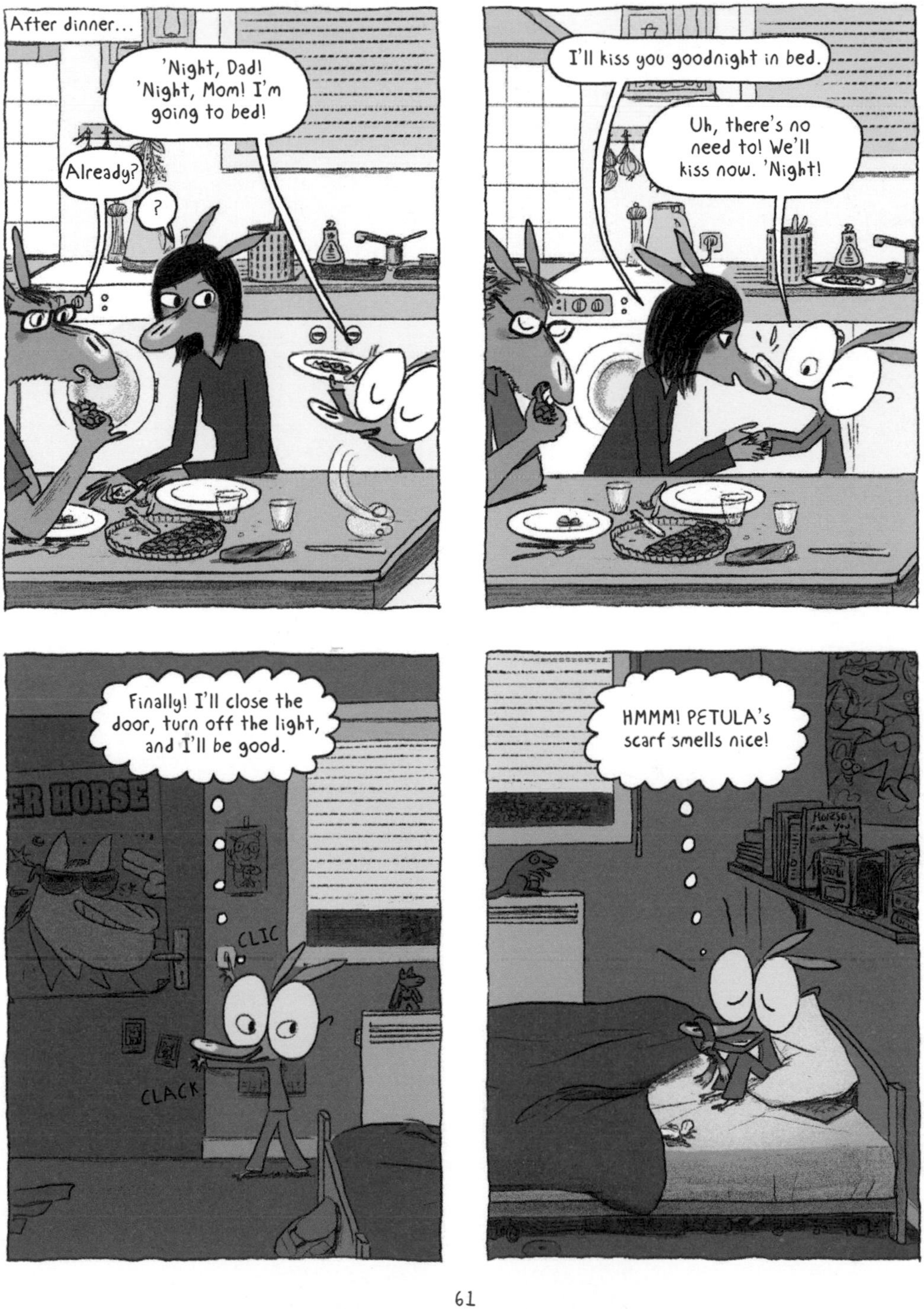
After dinner...
'Night, Dad! 'Night, Mom! I'm going to bed!
Already?
?
I'll kiss you goodnight in bed.
Uh, there's no need to! We'll kiss now. 'Night!
Finally! I'll close the door, turn off the light, and I'll be good.
CLIC
CLACK
HMMM! PETULA's scarf smells nice!

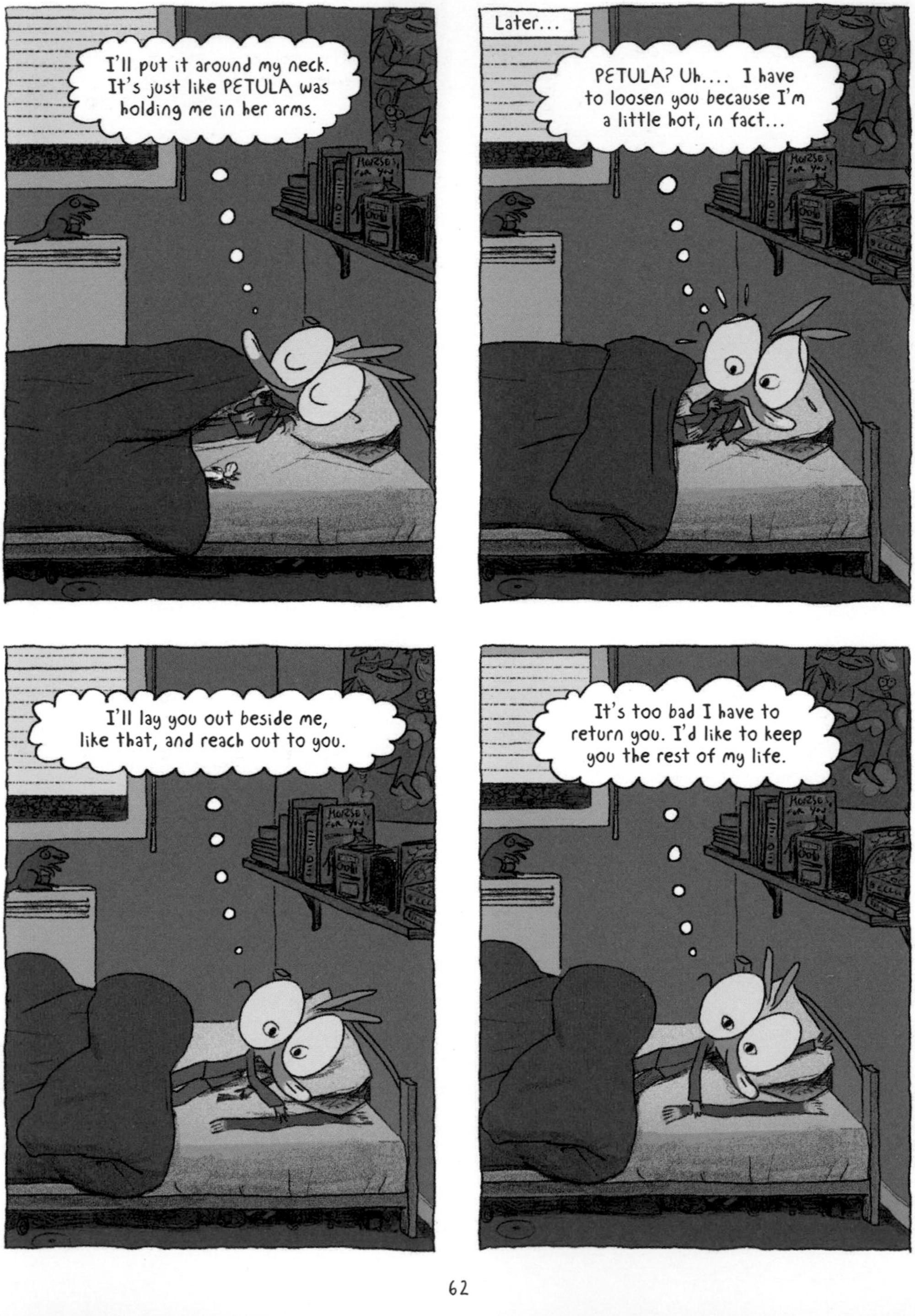
I'll put it around my neck. It's just like PETULA was holding me in her arms.
Later...
PETULA? Uh.... I have to loosen you because I'm a little hot, in fact...
I'll lay you out beside me, like that, and reach out to you.
It's too bad I have to return you. I'd like to keep you the rest of my life.

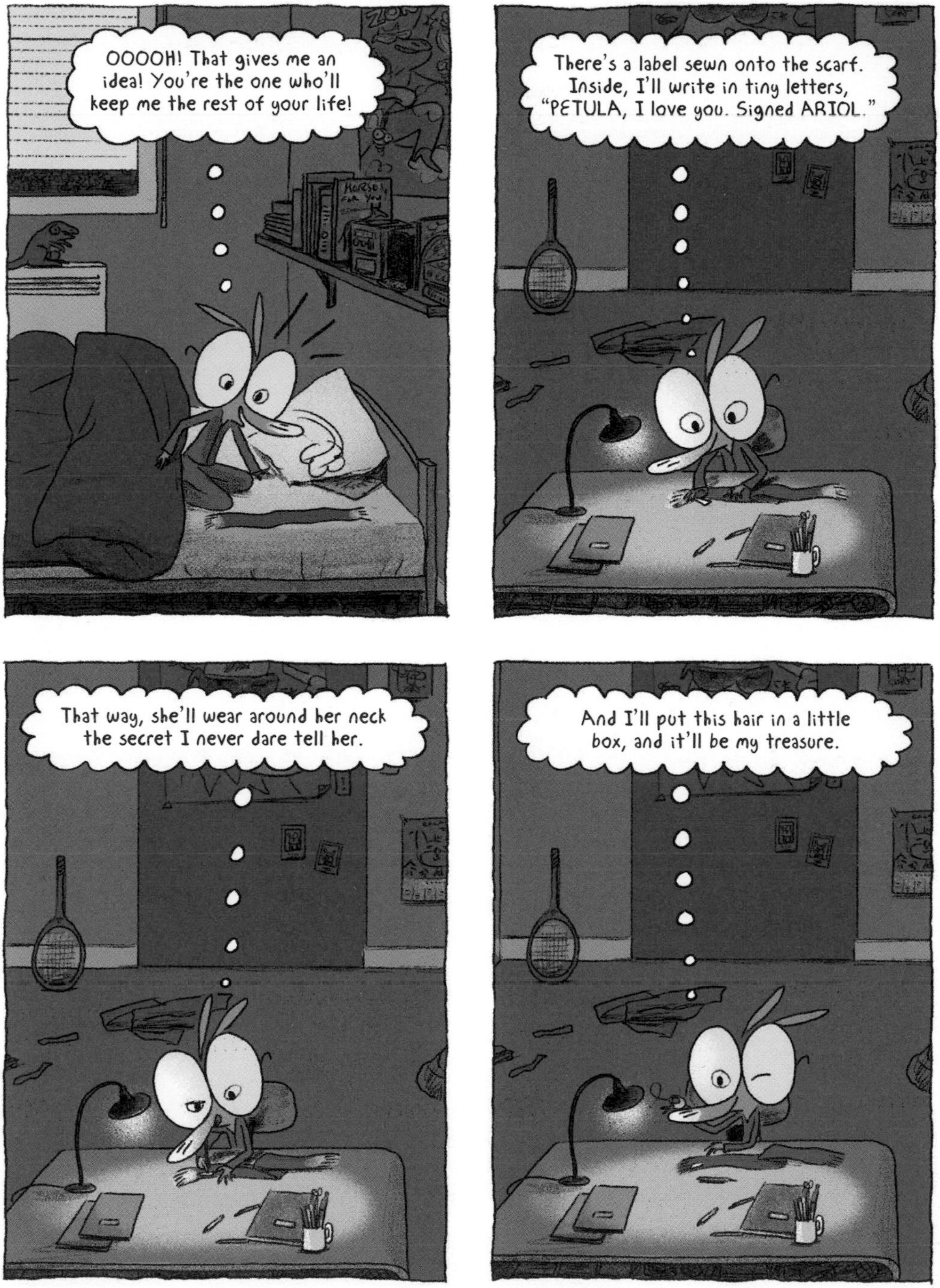
OOOOH! That gives me an idea! You're the one who'll keep me the rest of your life!
There's a label sewn onto the scarf. Inside, I'll write in tiny letters, "PETULA, I love you. Signed ARIOL."
That way, she'll wear around her neck the secret I never dare tell her.
And I'll put this hair in a little box, and it'll be my treasure.

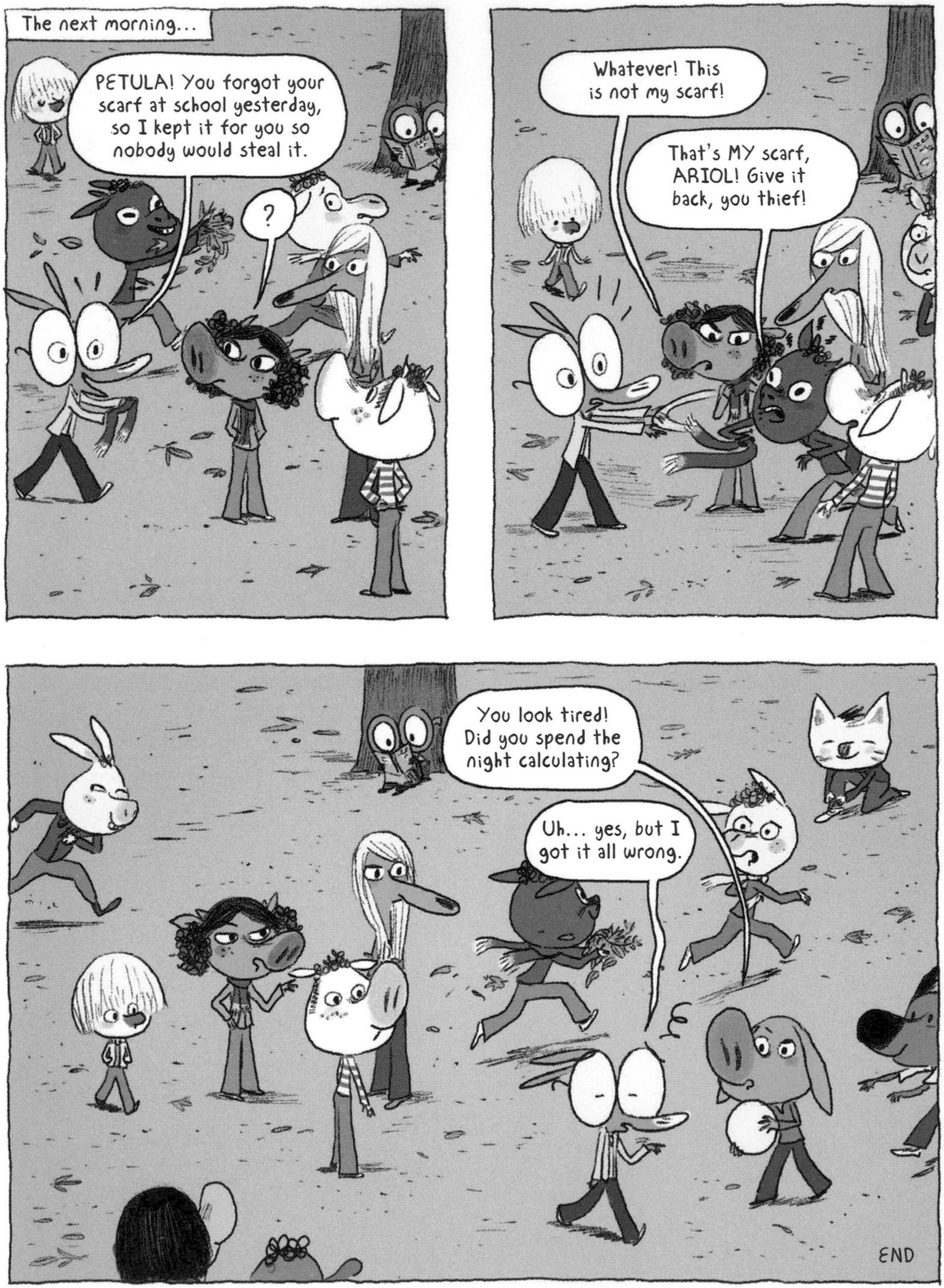
The next morning...
PETULA! You forgot your scarf at school yesterday, so I kept it for you so nobody would steal it.
?
Whatever! This is not my scarf!
That's MY scarf, ARIOL! Give it back, you thief!
You look tired! Did you spend the night calculating?
Uh... yes, but I got it all wrong.
END

ARiOL

Help, RAMONO!

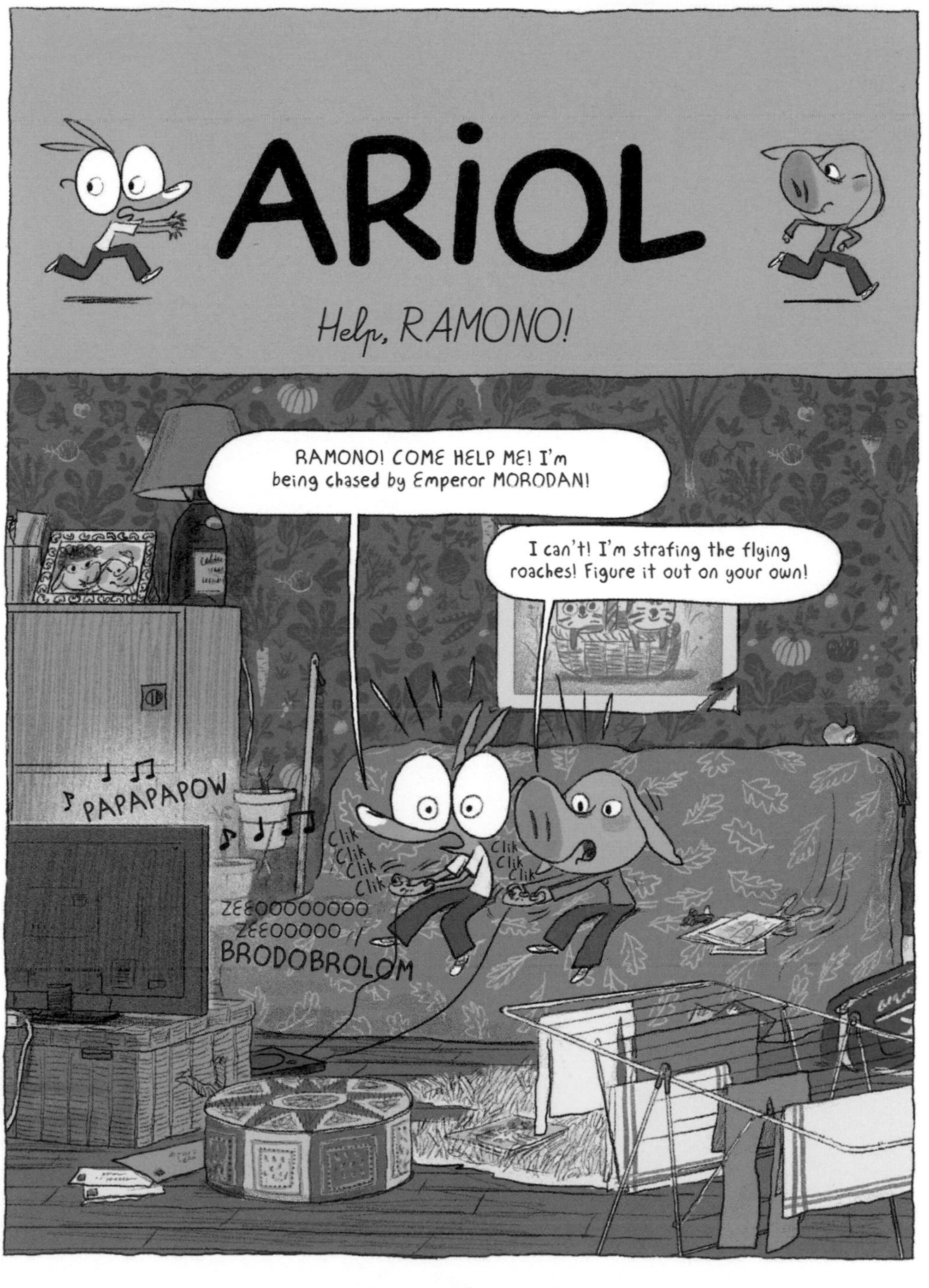
RAMONO! COME HELP ME! I'm being chased by Emperor MORODAN!
I can't! I'm strafing the flying roaches! Figure it out on your own!
PAPAPAPOW
Clik Clik Clik Clik
Clik Clik Clik
ZEEOOOOOOOO
ZEEOOOOO
BRODOBROLOM

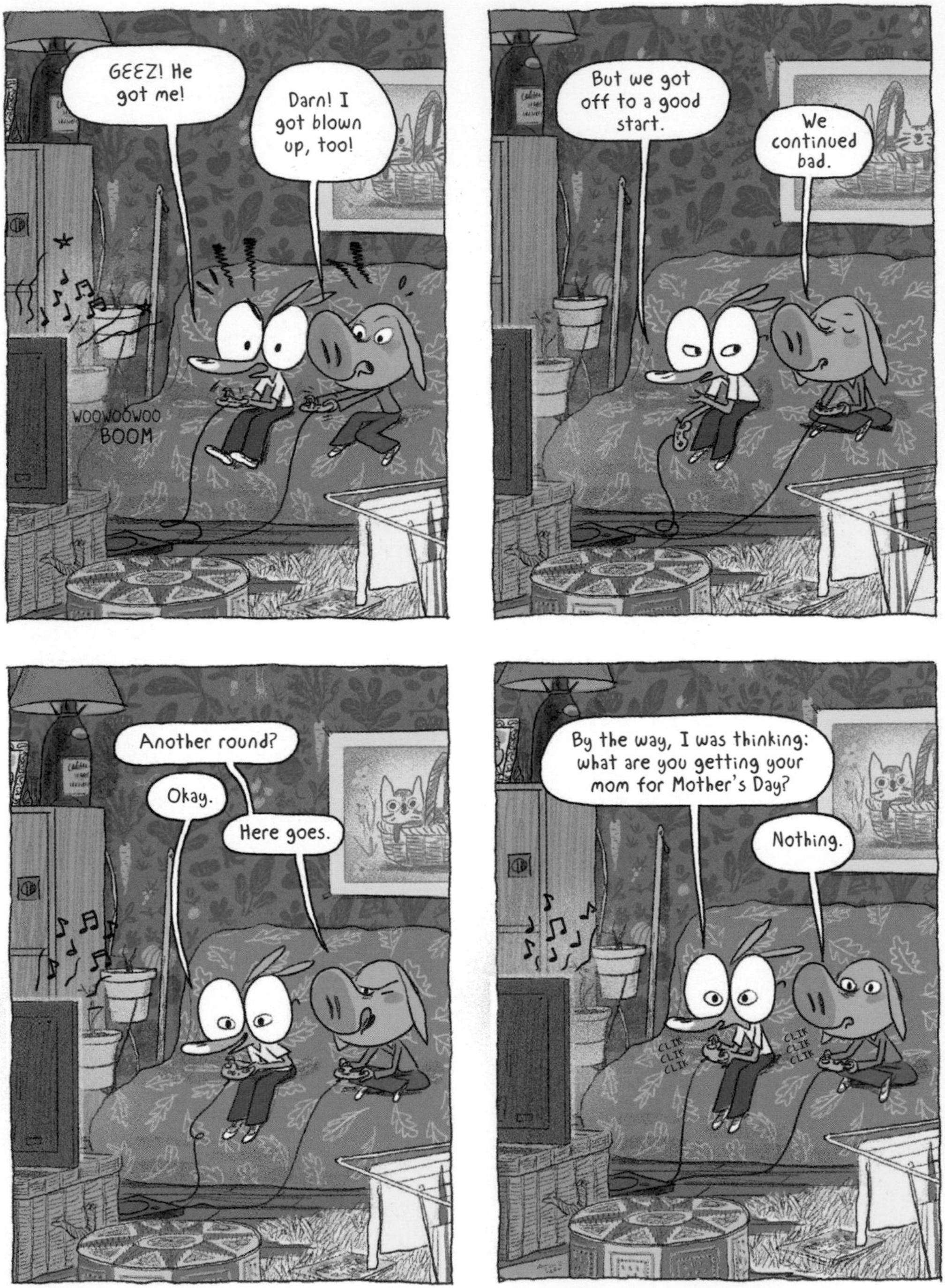
GEEZ! He got me!
Darn! I got blown up, too!
WOOWOOWOO BOOM
But we got off to a good start.
We continued bad.
Another round?
Okay.
Here goes.
By the way, I was thinking: what are you getting your mom for Mother's Day?
Nothing.
CLIK CLIK CLIK
CLIK CLIK CLIK

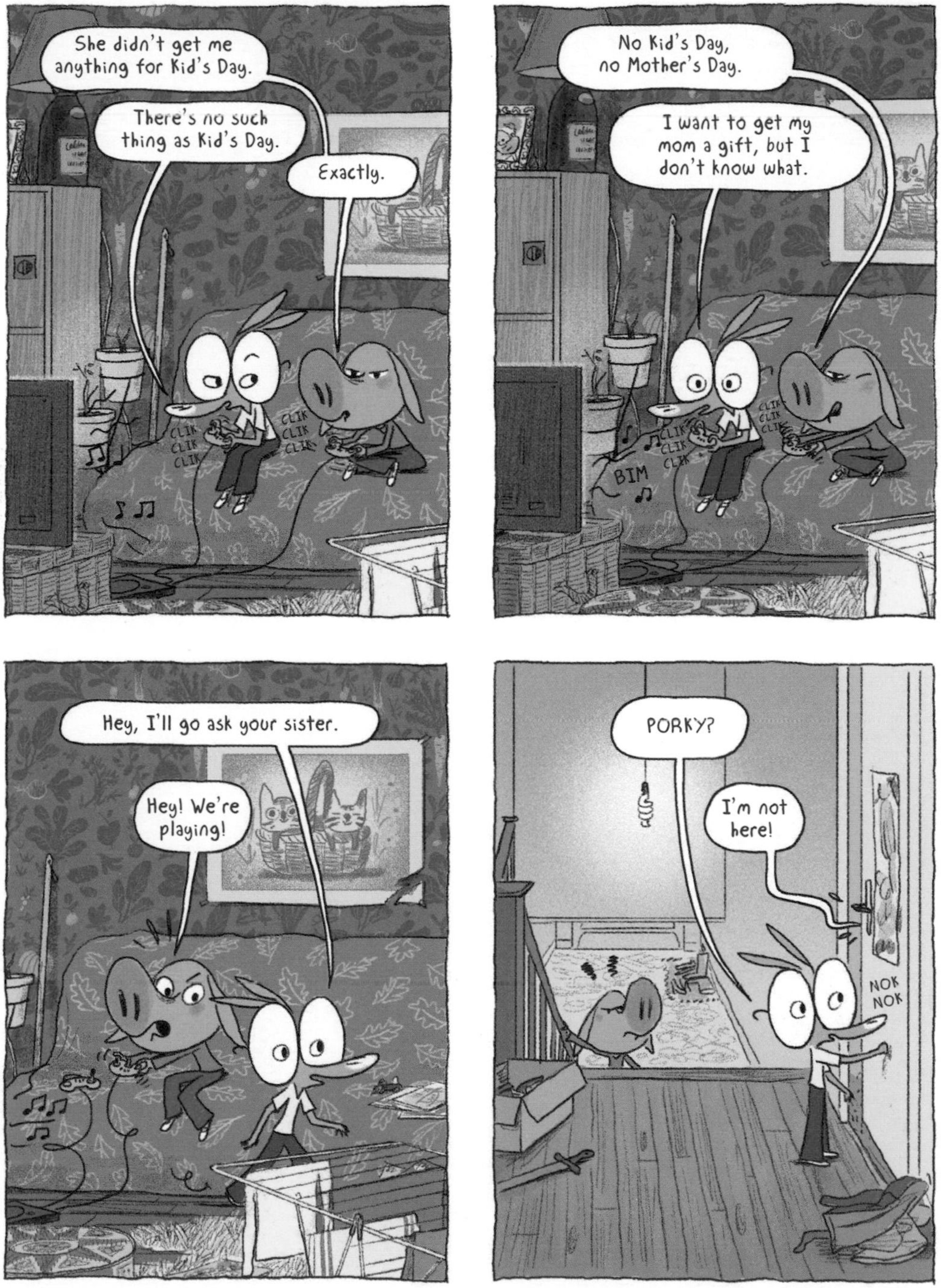
She didn't get me anything for Kid's Day.
There's no such thing as Kid's Day.
Exactly.
CLIK CLIK CLIK
CLIK CLIK CLIK
No Kid's Day, no Mother's Day.
I want to get my mom a gift, but I don't know what.
CLIK CLIK CLIK
CLIK CLIK CLIK
BIM
Hey, I'll go ask your sister.
Hey! We're playing!
PORKY?
I'm not here!
NOK NOK

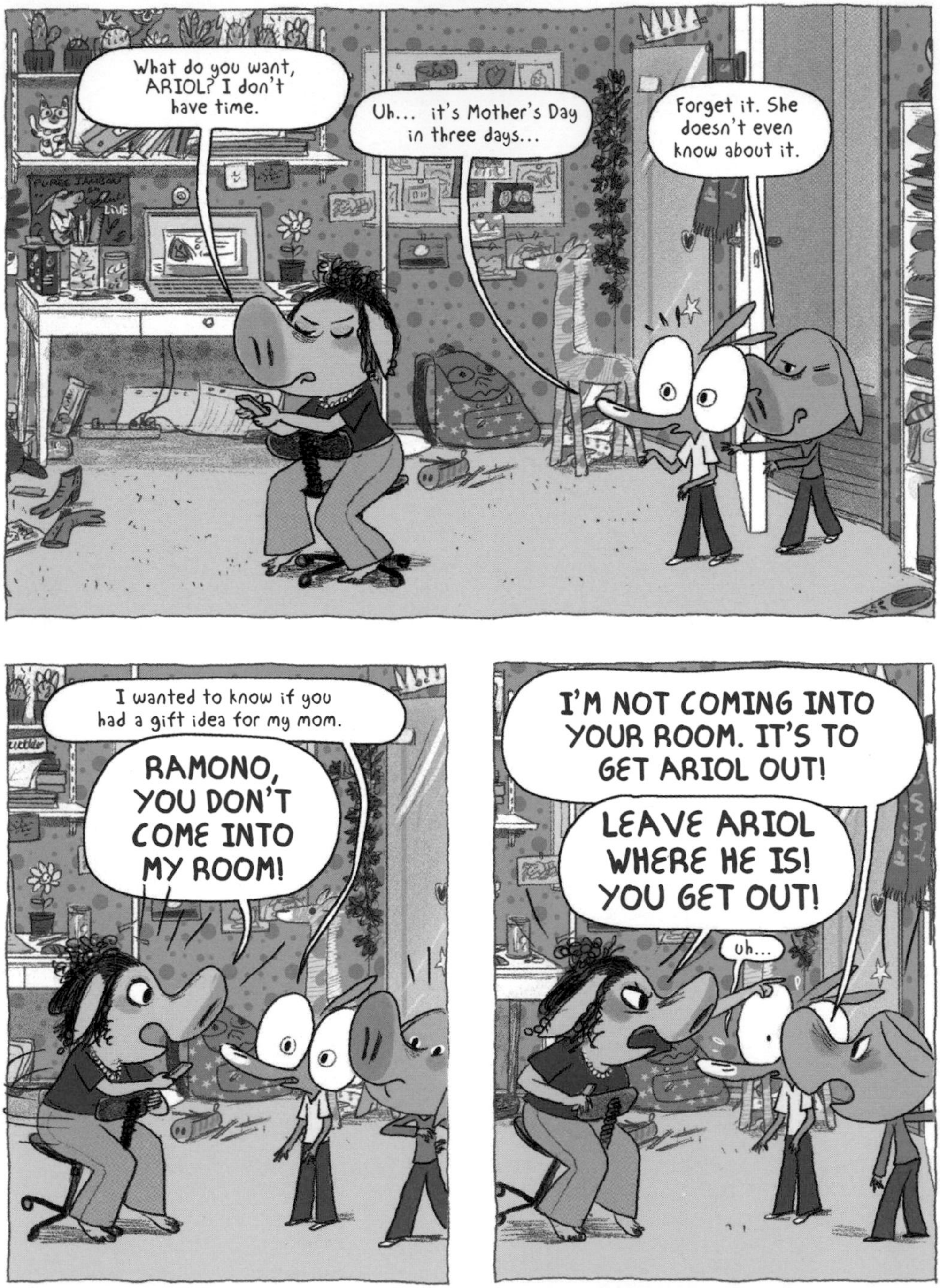
What do you want, ARIOL? I don't have time.
Uh... it's Mother's Day in three days...
Forget it. She doesn't even know about it.
I wanted to know if you had a gift idea for my mom.
RAMONO, YOU DON'T COME INTO MY ROOM!
I'M NOT COMING INTO YOUR ROOM. IT'S TO GET ARIOL OUT!
LEAVE ARIOL WHERE HE IS! YOU GET OUT!
uh...

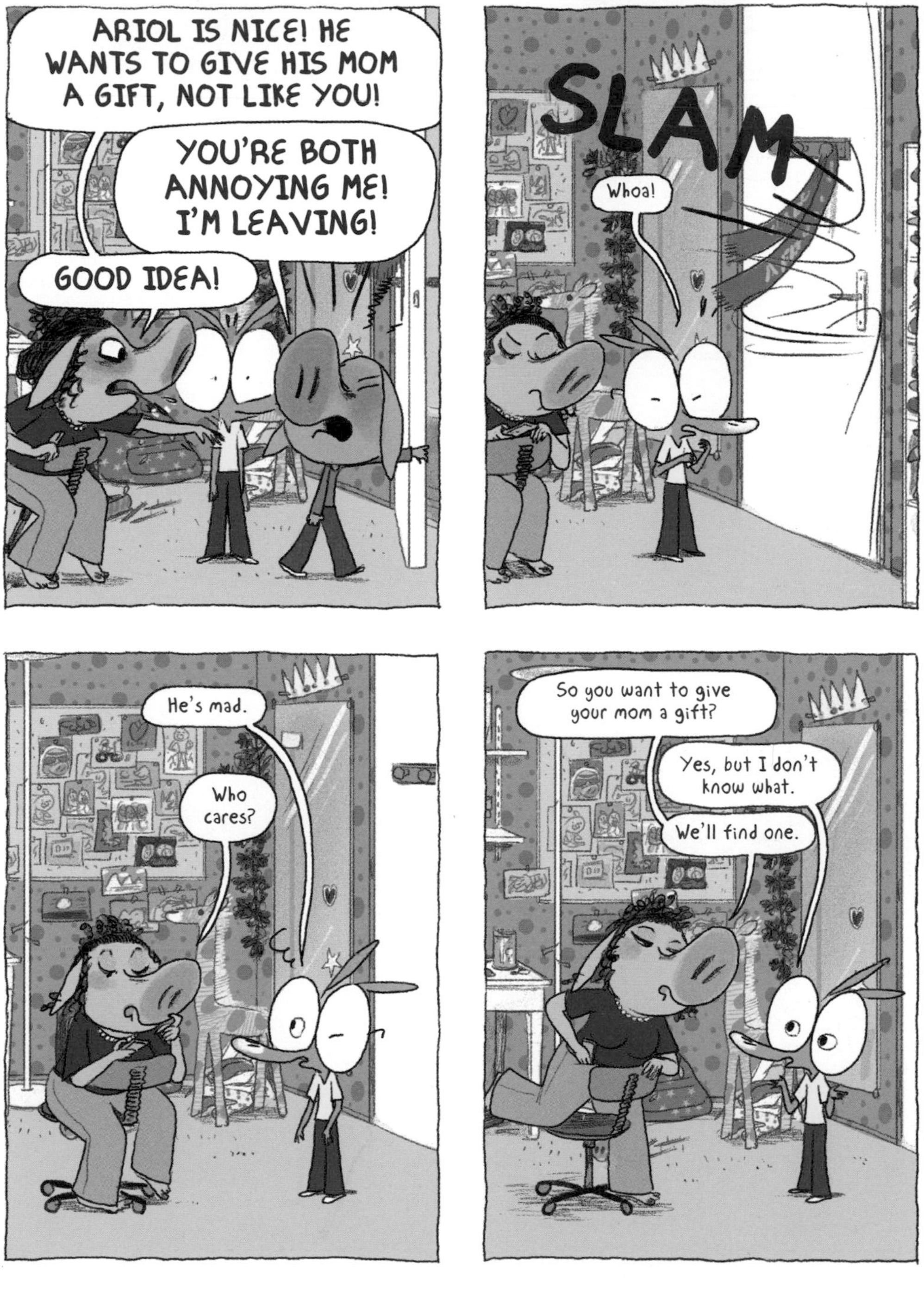
ARIOL IS NICE! HE WANTS TO GIVE HIS MOM A GIFT, NOT LIKE YOU!
YOU'RE BOTH ANNOYING ME! I'M LEAVING!
GOOD IDEA!
SLAM
Whoa!
He's mad.
Who cares?
So you want to give your mom a gift?
Yes, but I don't know what.
We'll find one.

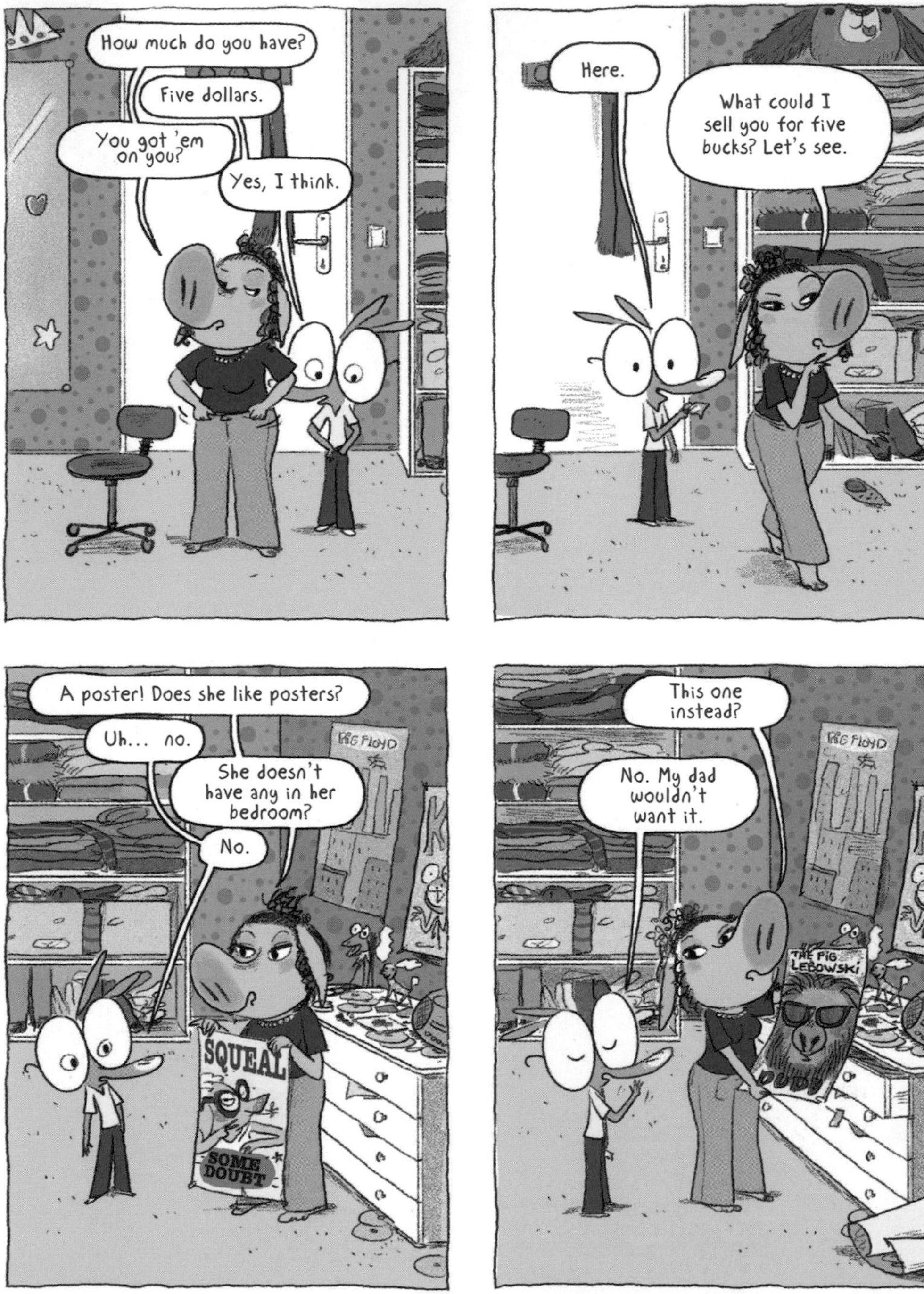
How much do you have?
Five dollars.
You got 'em on you?
Yes, I think.
Here.
What could I sell you for five bucks? Let's see.
A poster! Does she like posters?
Uh... no.
She doesn't have any in her bedroom?
No.
SQUEAL
SOME DOUBT
PIG FLOYD
This one instead?
No. My dad wouldn't want it.
THE PIG LEBOWSKI

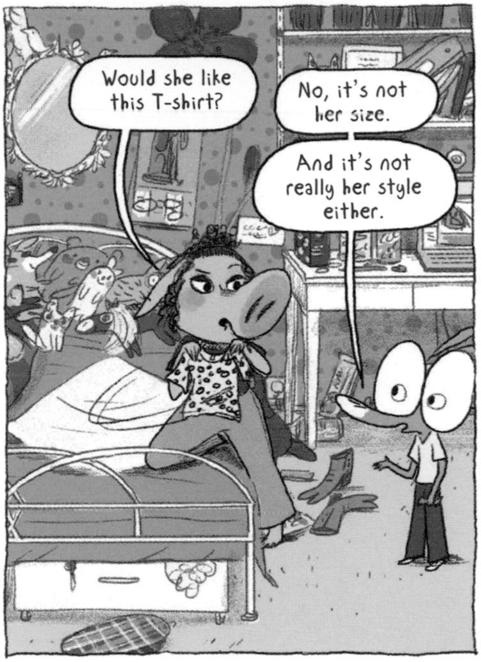
Would she like this T-shirt?
No, it's not her size.
And it's not really her style either.

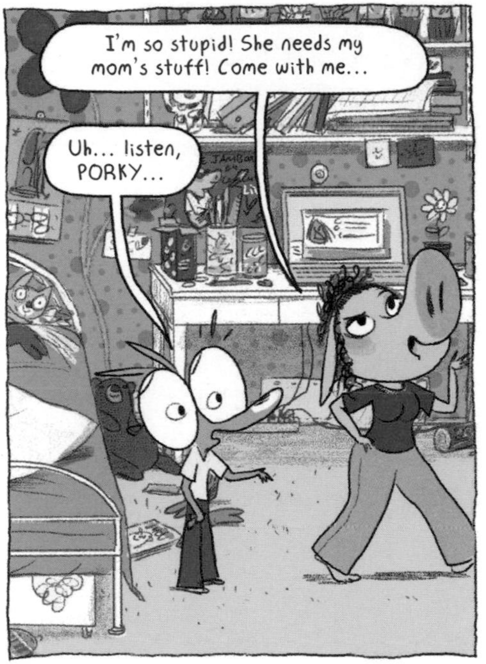
I'm so stupid! She needs my mom's stuff! Come with me...
Uh... listen, PORKY...

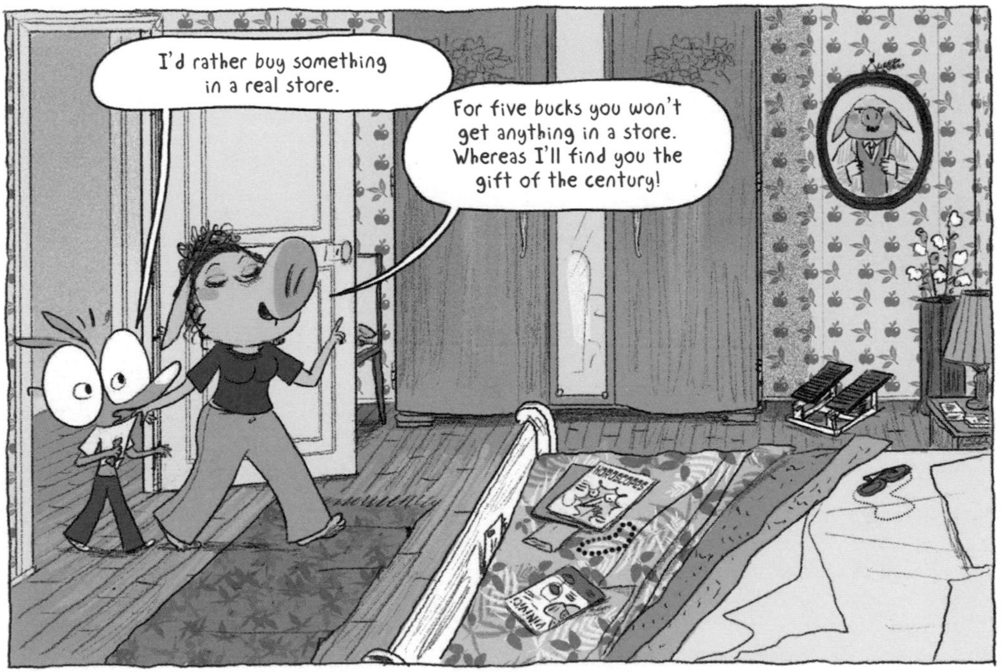
I'd rather buy something in a real store.
For five bucks you won't get anything in a store. Whereas I'll find you the gift of the century!

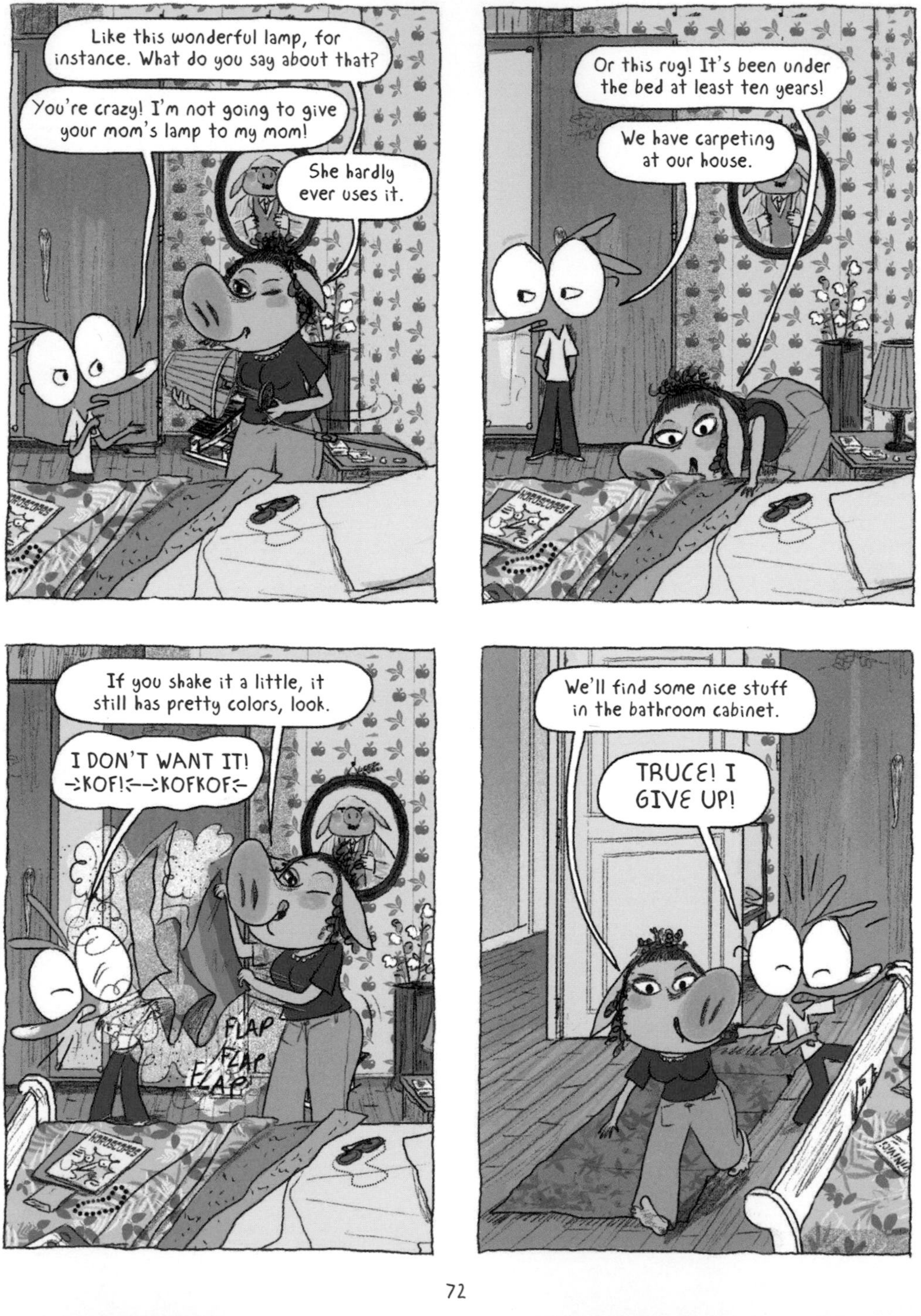
Like this wonderful lamp, for instance. What do you say about that?
You're crazy! I'm not going to give your mom's lamp to my mom!
She hardly ever uses it.
Or this rug! It's been under the bed at least ten years!
We have carpeting at our house.
If you shake it a little, it still has pretty colors, look.
I DON'T WANT IT! KOF! KOFKOF
FLAP FLAP FLAP
We'll find some nice stuff in the bathroom cabinet.
TRUCE! I GIVE UP!

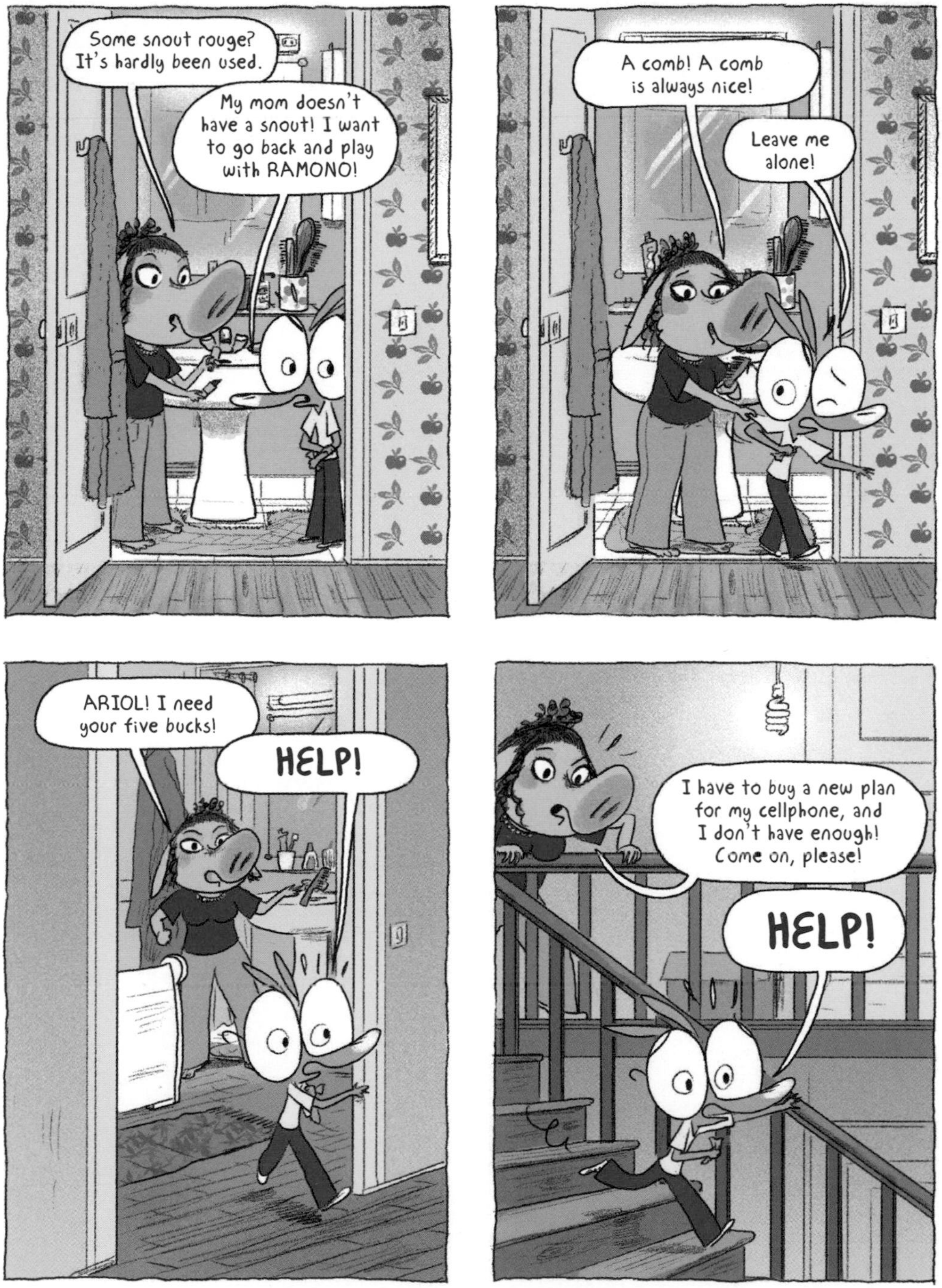
Some snout rouge? It's hardly been used.
My mom doesn't have a snout! I want to go back and play with RAMONO!
A comb! A comb is always nice!
Leave me alone!
ARIOL! I need your five bucks!
HELP!
I have to buy a new plan for my cellphone, and I don't have enough! Come on, please!
HELP!

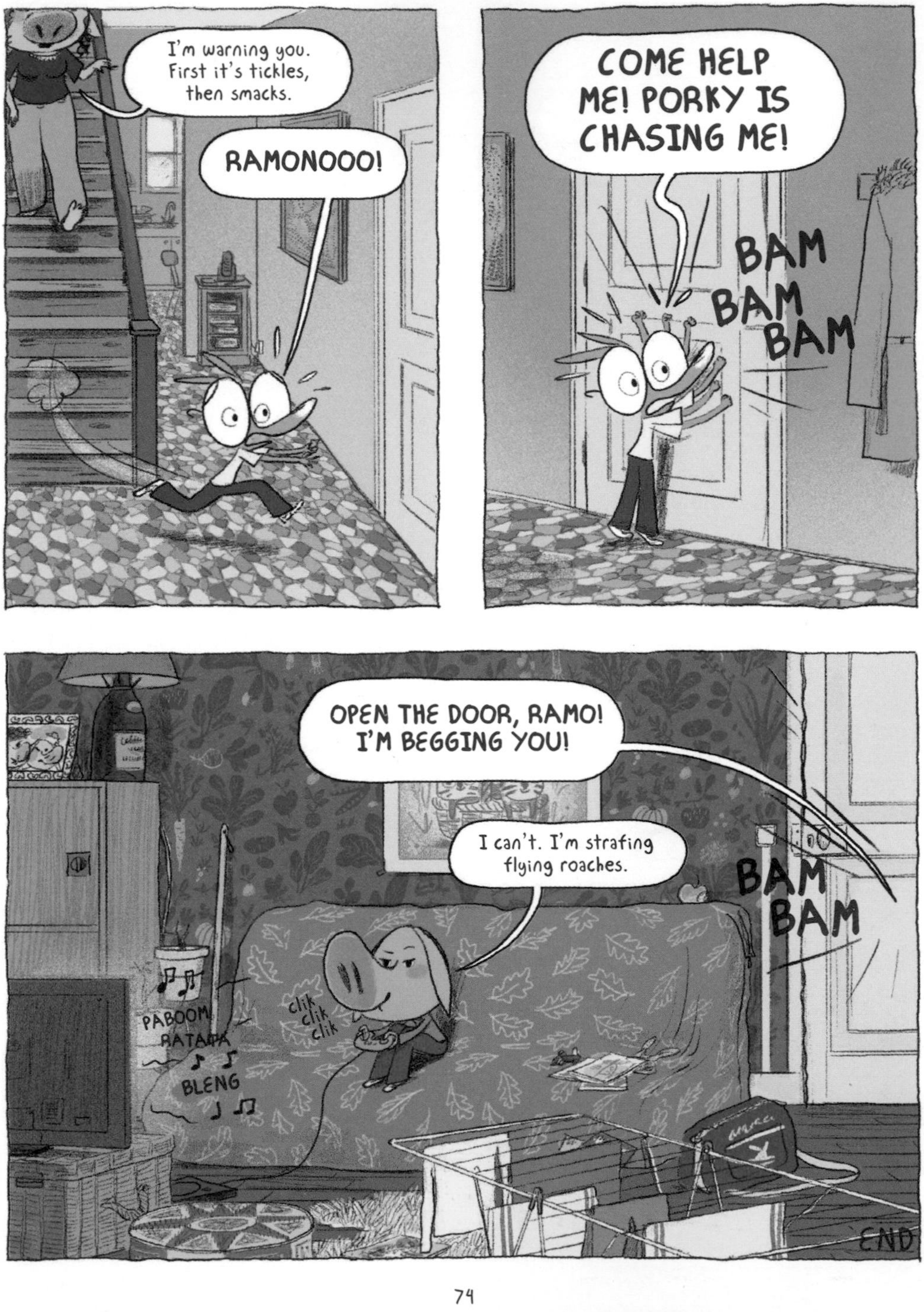
I'm warning you. First it's tickles, then smacks.
RAMONOOO!
COME HELP ME! PORKY IS CHASING ME!
BAM BAM BAM
OPEN THE DOOR, RAMO! I'M BEGGING YOU!
I can't. I'm strafing flying roaches.
BAM BAM
PABOOM RATAPA BLENG
clik clik clik
END

ARiOL

The Goddess of Love

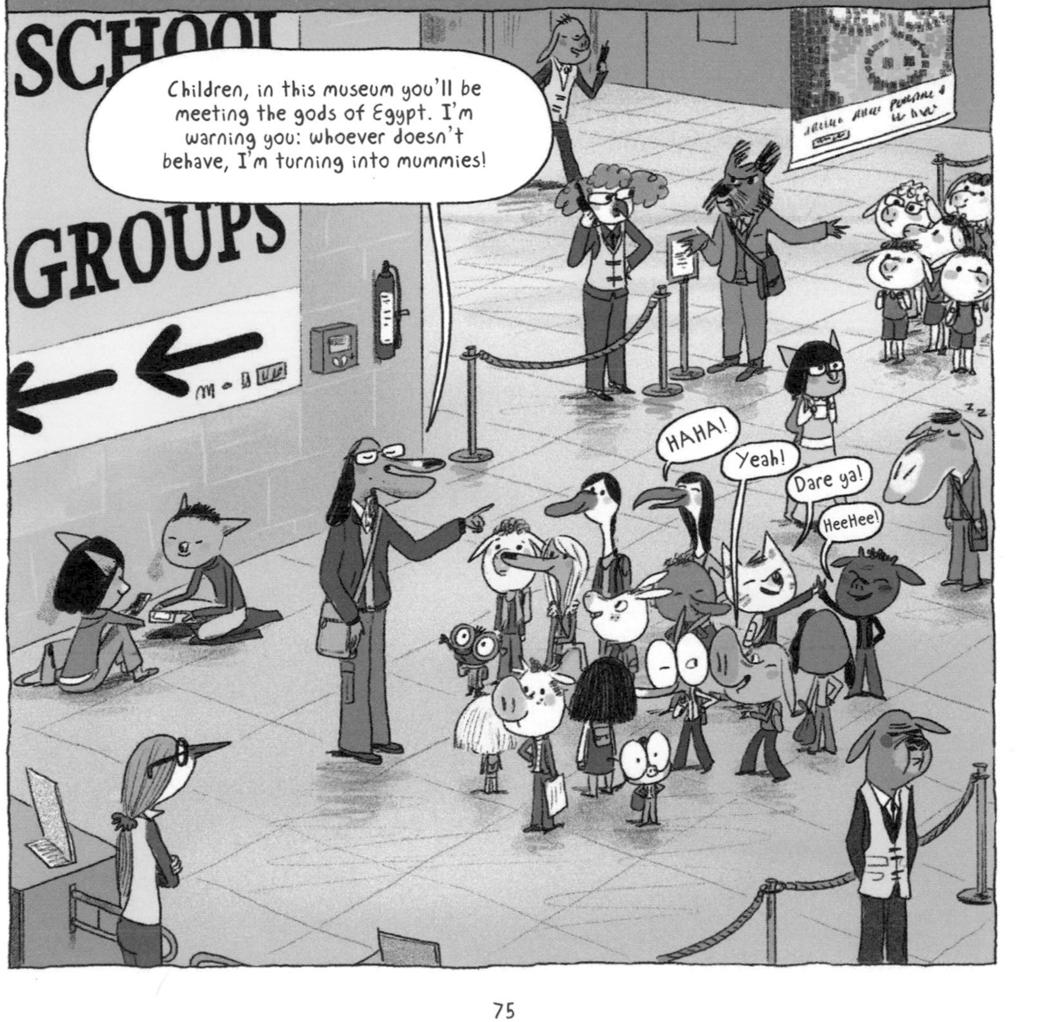
SCHOOL GROUPS
Children, in this museum you'll be meeting the gods of Egypt. I'm warning you: whoever doesn't behave, I'm turning into mummies!
HAHA!
Yeah!
Dare ya!
HeeHee!

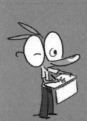

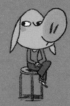

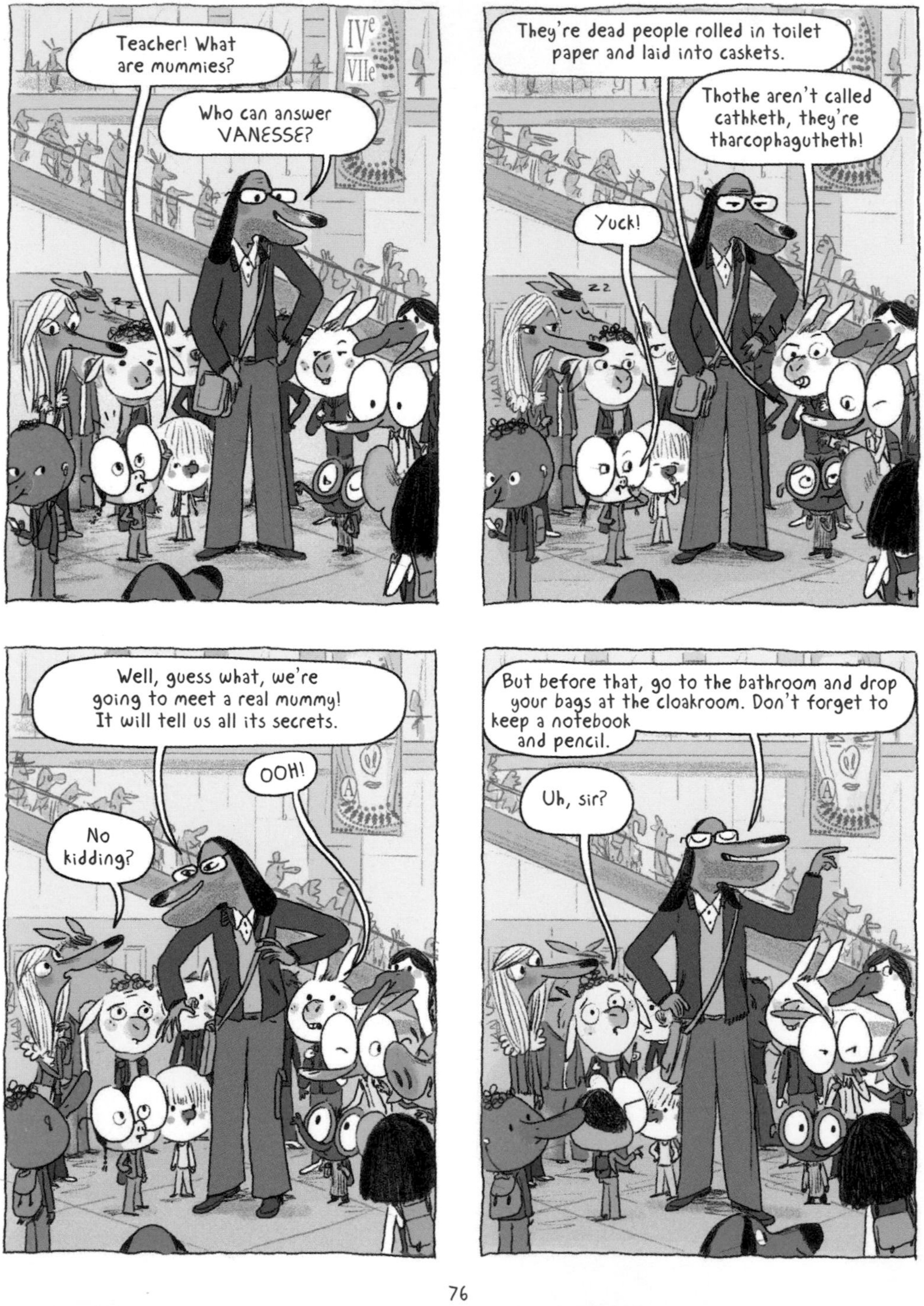
IVe VIIe
Teacher! What are mummies?
Who can answer VANESSE?
They're dead people rolled in toilet paper and laid into caskets.
Thothe aren't called cathketh, they're tharcophagutheth!
Yuck!
Well, guess what, we're going to meet a real mummy! It will tell us all its secrets.
OOH!
No kidding?
But before that, go to the bathroom and drop your bags at the cloakroom. Don't forget to keep a notebook and pencil.
Uh, sir?

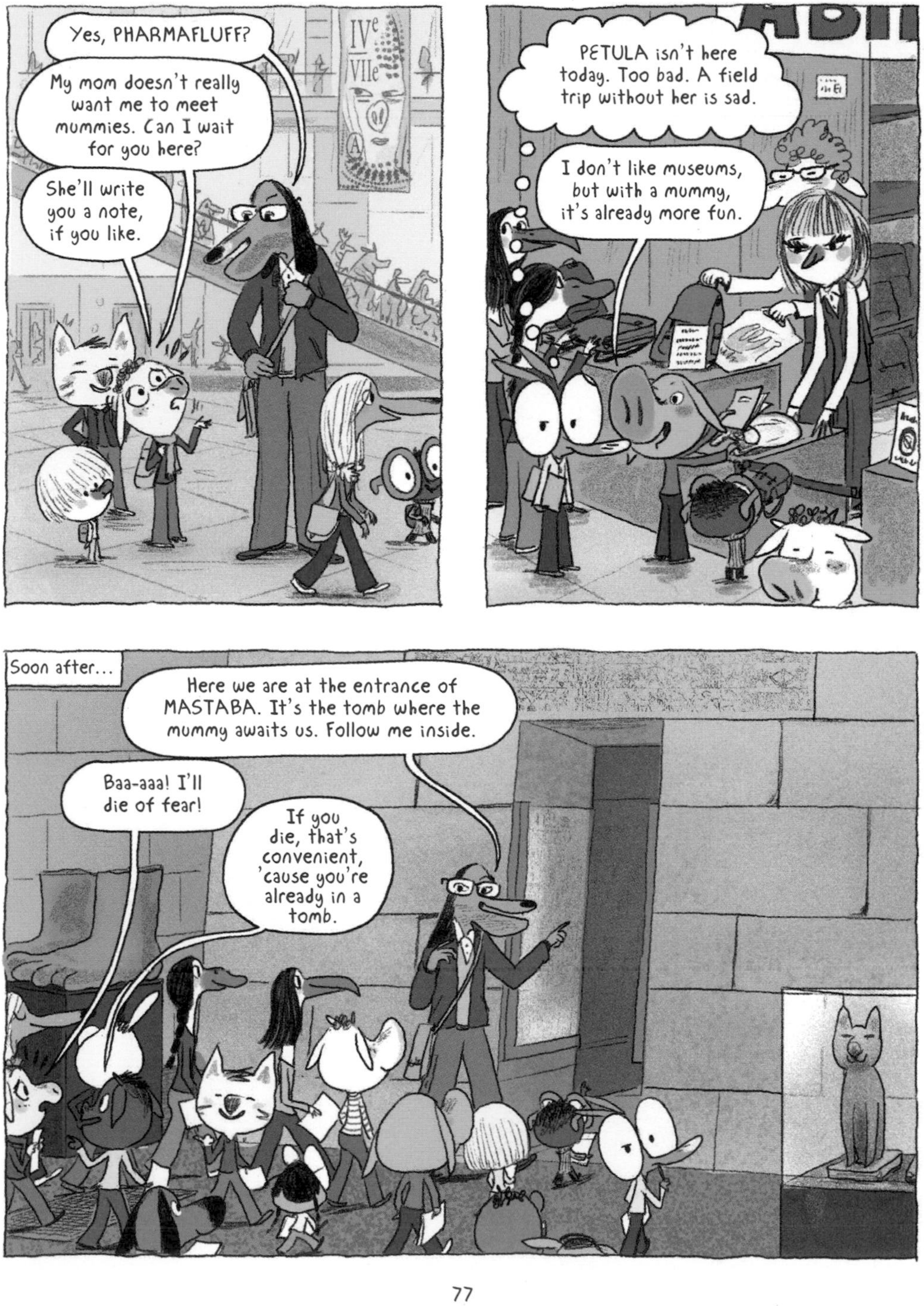
Yes, PHARMAFLUFF?
My mom doesn't really want me to meet mummies. Can I wait for you here?
She'll write you a note, if you like.
PETULA isn't here today. Too bad. A field trip without her is sad.
I don't like museums, but with a mummy, it's already more fun.
Soon after...
Here we are at the entrance of MASTABA. It's the tomb where the mummy awaits us. Follow me inside.
Baa-aaa! I'll die of fear!
If you die, that's convenient, 'cause you're already in a tomb.

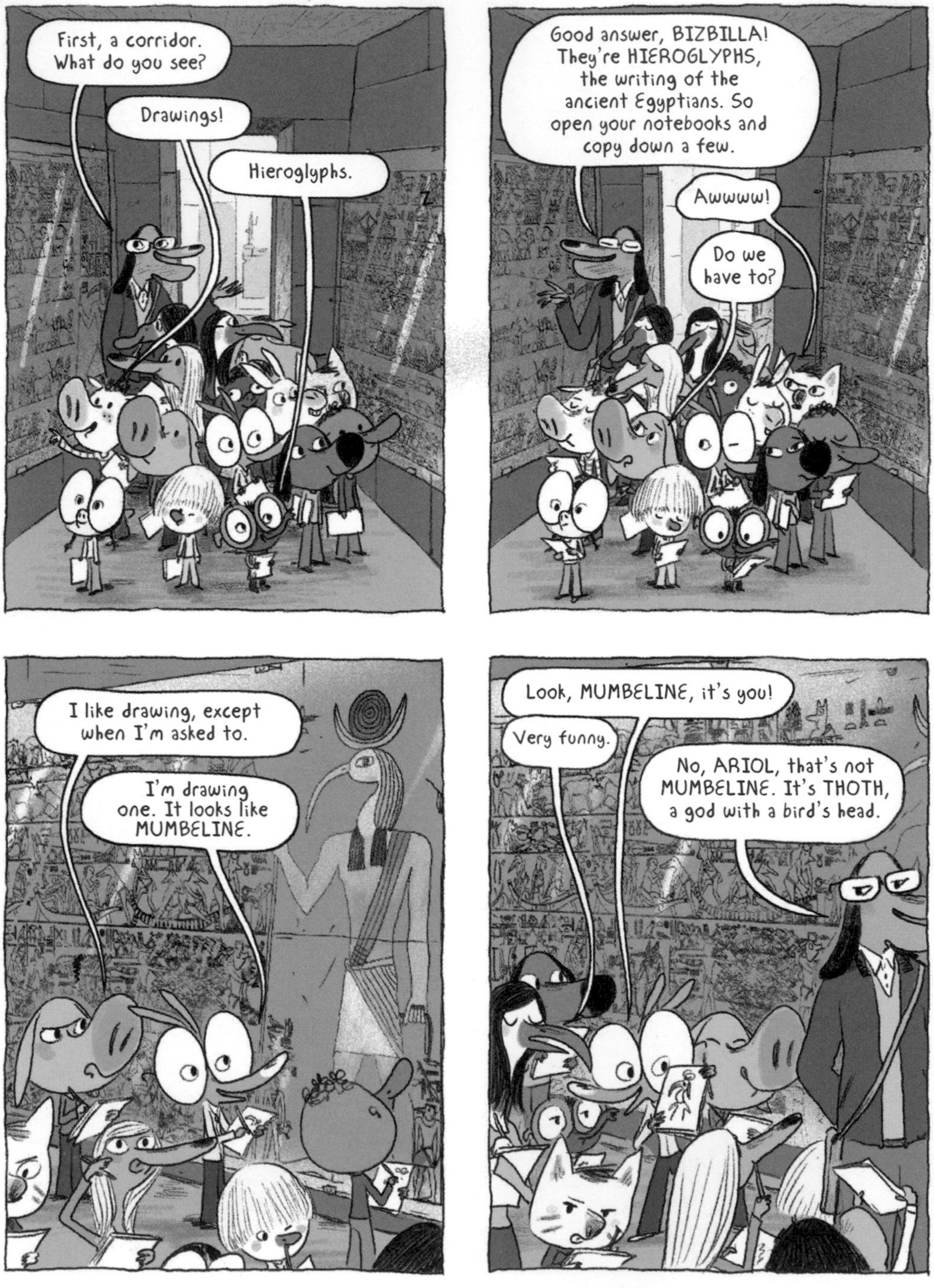
First, a corridor. What do you see?
Drawings!
Hieroglyphs.
Z
Good answer, BIZBILLA! They're HIEROGLYPHS, the writing of the ancient Egyptians. So open your notebooks and copy down a few.
Awwww!
Do we have to?
I like drawing, except when I'm asked to.
I'm drawing one. It looks like MUMBELINE.
Look, MUMBELINE, it's you!
Very funny.
No, ARIOL, that's not MUMBELINE. It's THOTH, a god with a bird's head.

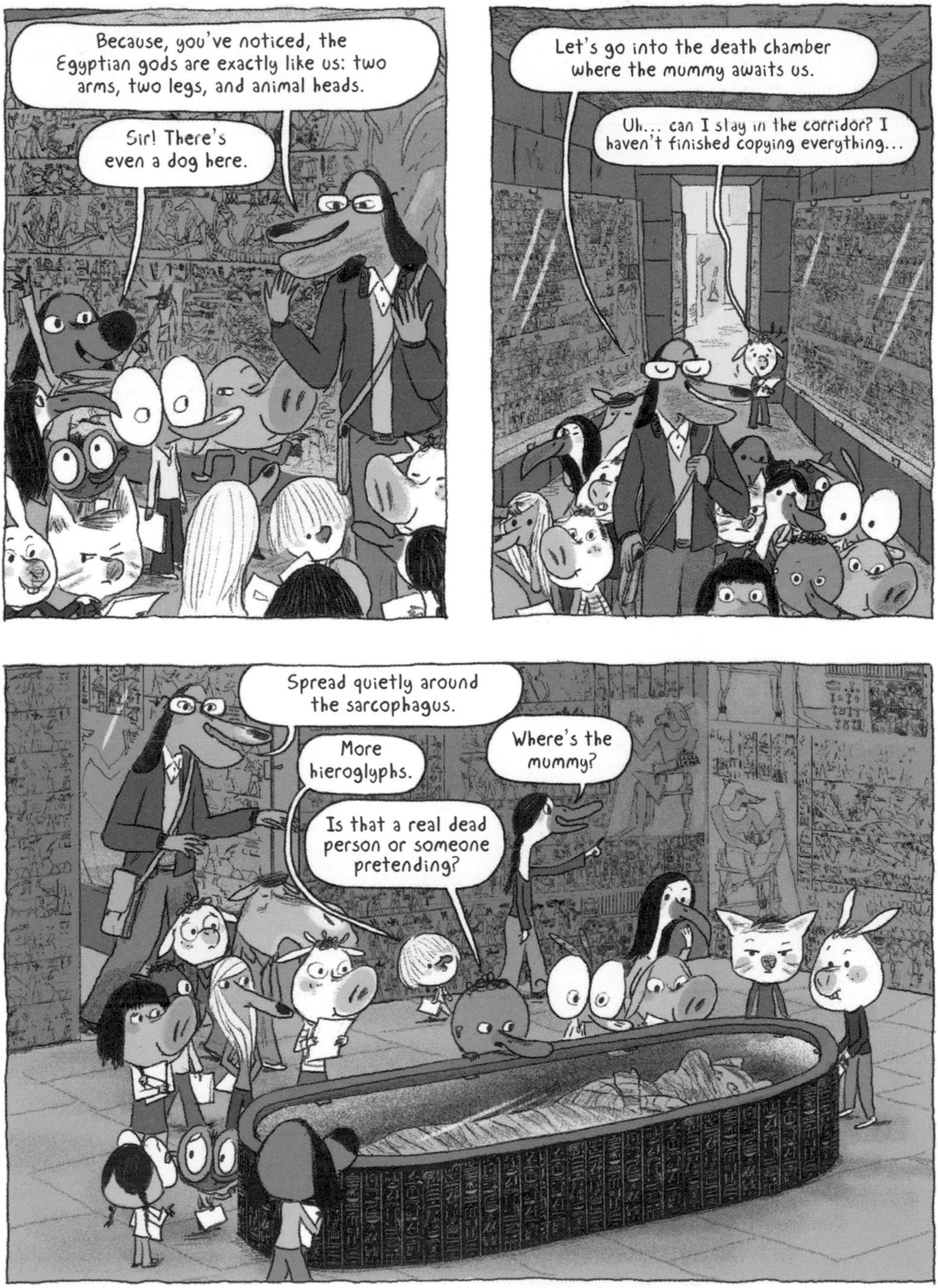
Because, you've noticed, the Egyptian gods are exactly like us: two arms, two legs, and animal heads.
Sir! There's even a dog here.
Let's go into the death chamber where the mummy awaits us.
Uh... can I stay in the corridor? I haven't finished copying everything...
Spread quietly around the sarcophagus.
More hieroglyphs.
Where's the mummy?
Is that a real dead person or someone pretending?

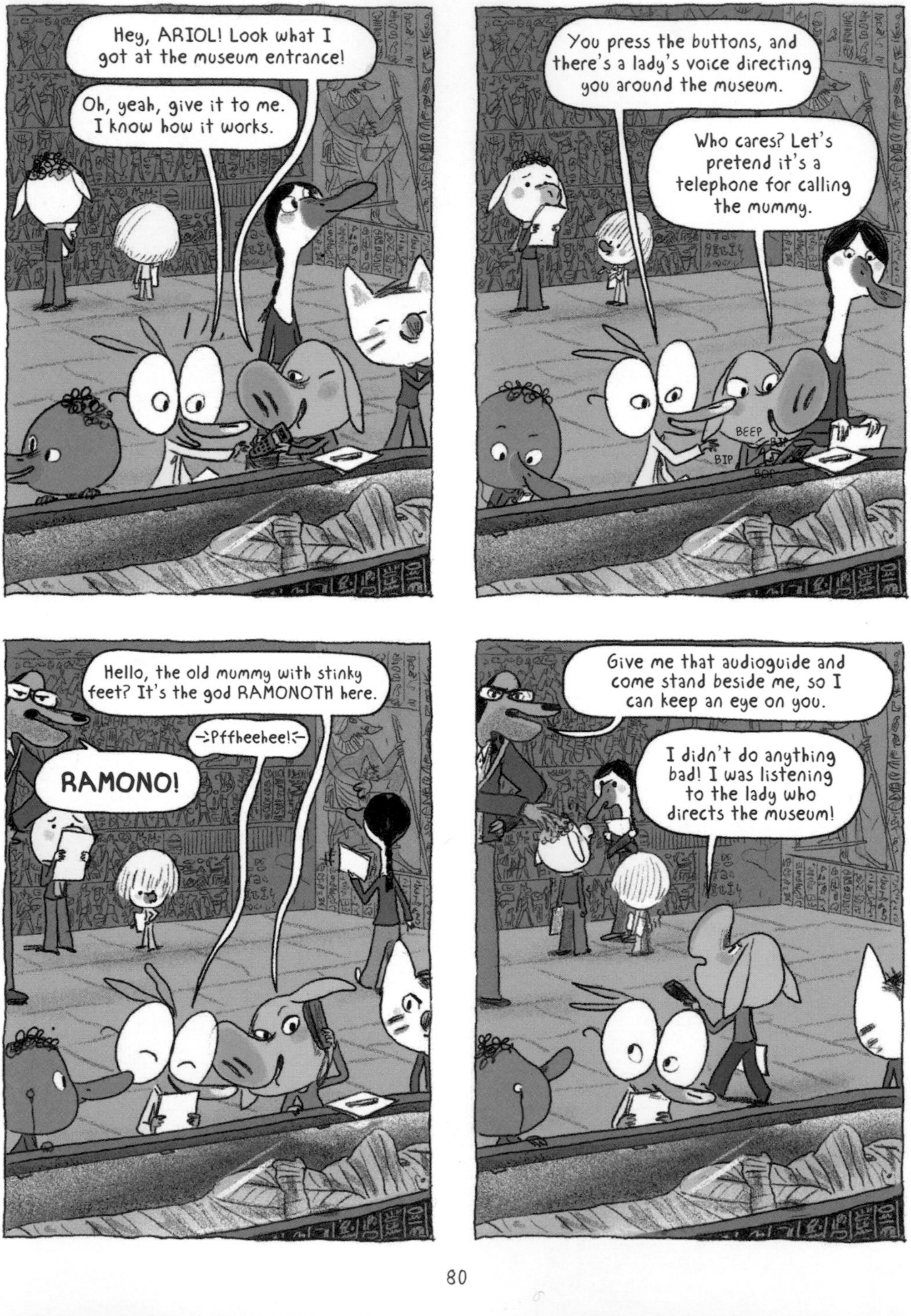

Hey, ARIOL! Look what I got at the museum entrance!
Oh, yeah, give it to me. I know how it works.
You press the buttons, and there's a lady's voice directing you around the museum.
Who cares? Let's pretend it's a telephone for calling the mummy.
BEEP
BIP
Hello, the old mummy with stinky feet? It's the god RAMONOTH here.
Pffheehee!
RAMONO!
Give me that audioguide and come stand beside me, so I can keep an eye on you.
I didn't do anything bad! I was listening to the lady who directs the museum!

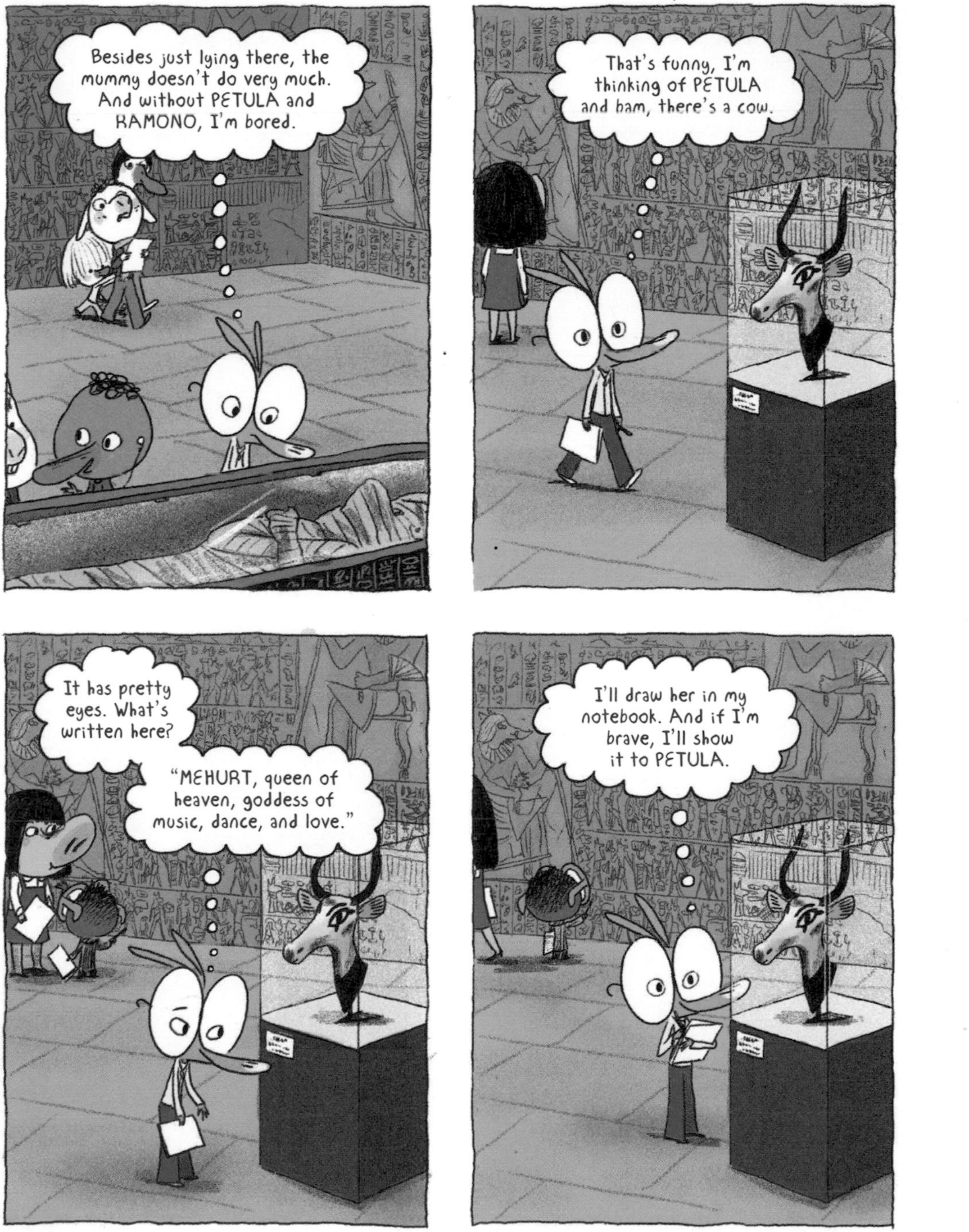
Besides just lying there, the mummy doesn't do very much. And without PETULA and RAMONO, I'm bored.
That's funny, I'm thinking of PETULA and bam, there's a cow.
It has pretty eyes. What's written here?
"MEHURT, queen of heaven, goddess of music, dance, and love."
I'll draw her in my notebook. And if I'm brave, I'll show it to PETULA.

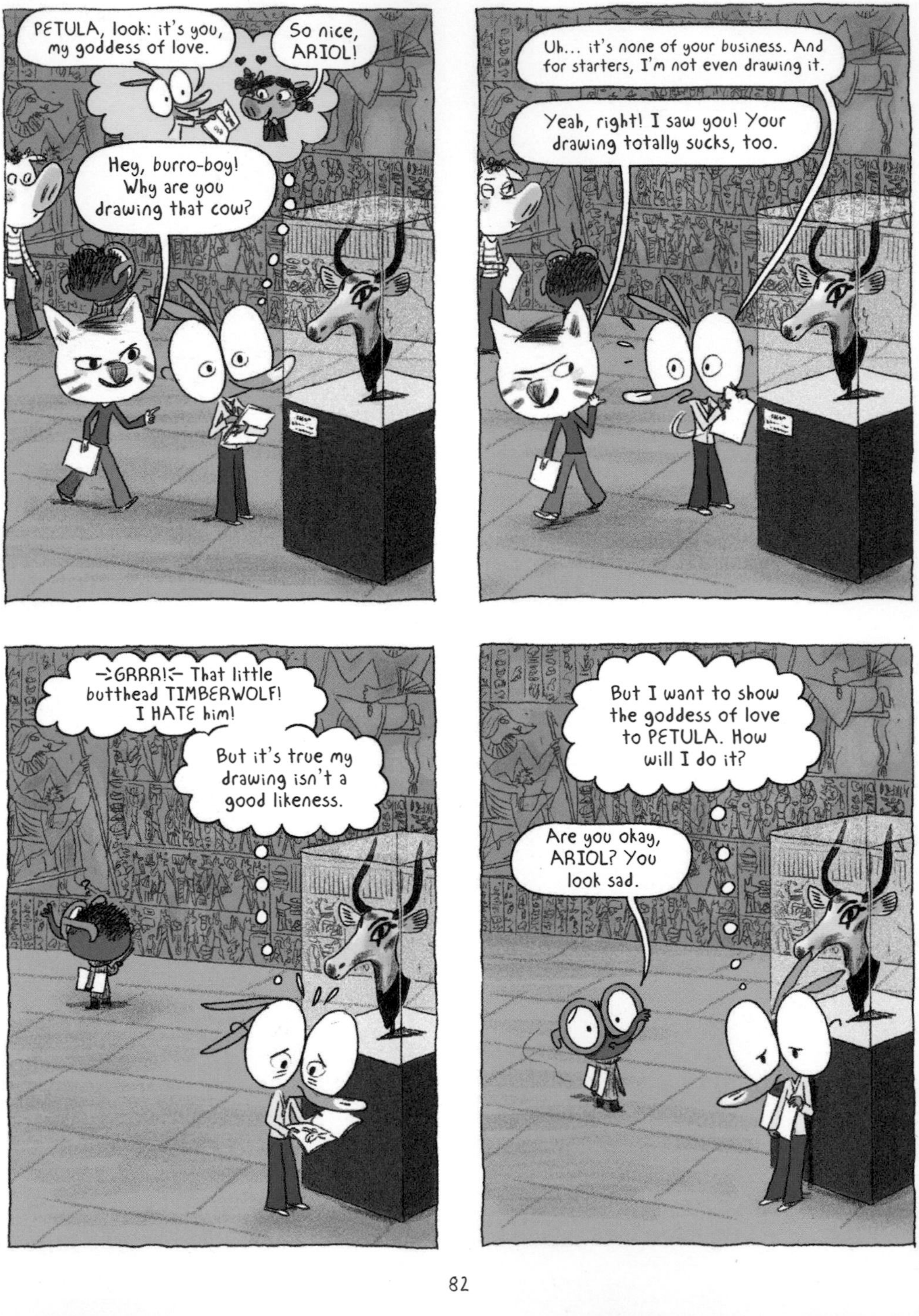
PETULA, look: it's you, my goddess of love.
So nice, ARIOL!
Hey, burro-boy! Why are you drawing that cow?
Uh... it's none of your business. And for starters, I'm not even drawing it.
Yeah, right! I saw you! Your drawing totally sucks, too.
⇝GRRR!⇜ That little butthead TIMBERWOLF! I HATE him!
But it's true my drawing isn't a good likeness.
But I want to show the goddess of love to PETULA. How will I do it?
Are you okay, ARIOL? You look sad.

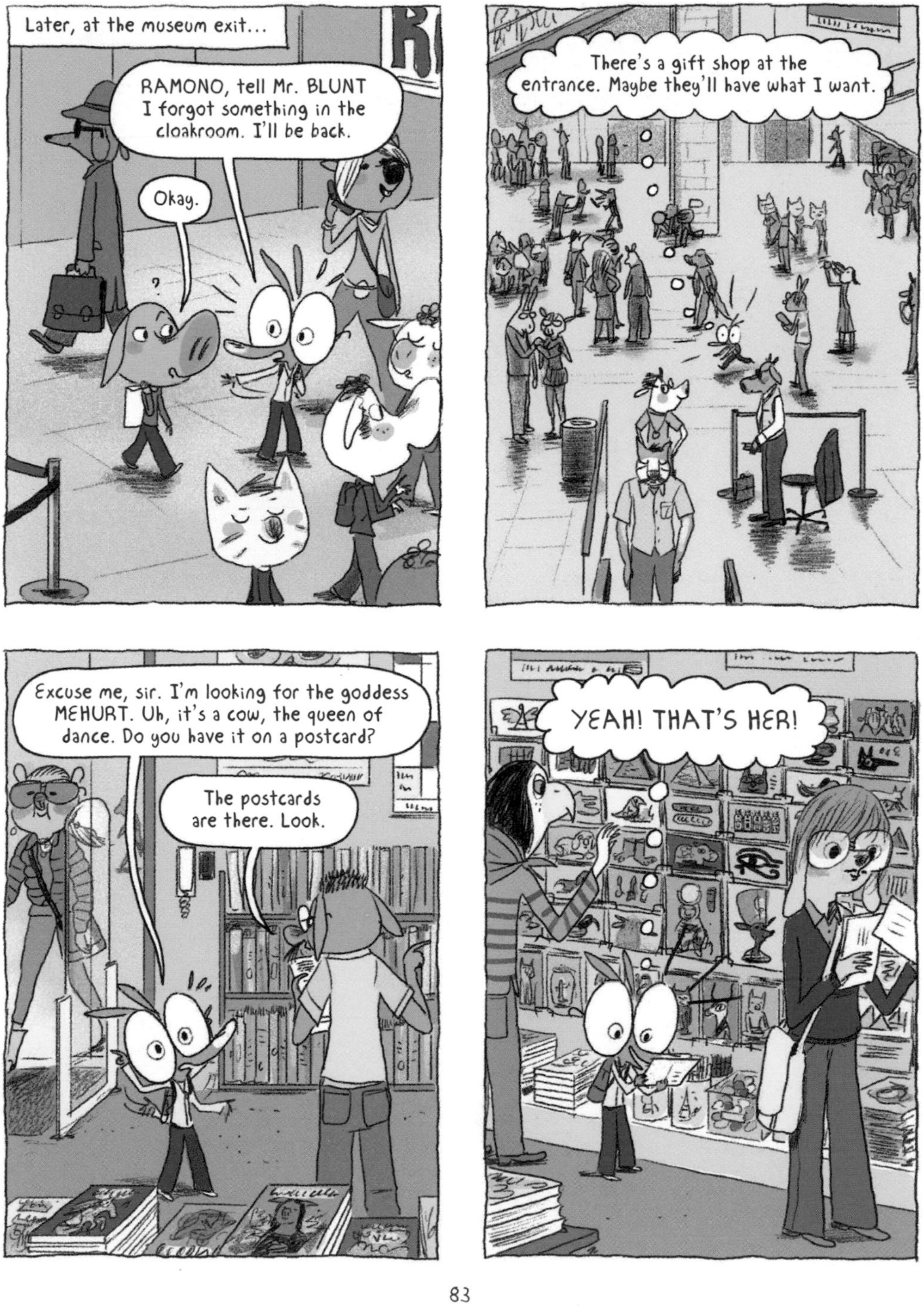
Later, at the museum exit...
RAMONO, tell Mr. BLUNT I forgot something in the cloakroom. I'll be back.
Okay.
There's a gift shop at the entrance. Maybe they'll have what I want.
Excuse me, sir. I'm looking for the goddess MEHURT. Uh, it's a cow, the queen of dance. Do you have it on a postcard?
The postcards are there. Look.
YEAH! THAT'S HER!

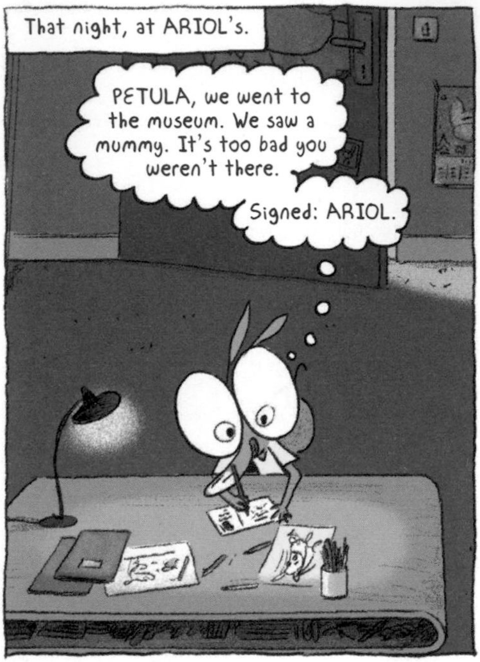
That night, at ARIOL's.
PETULA, we went to the museum. We saw a mummy. It's too bad you weren't there.
Signed: ARIOL.

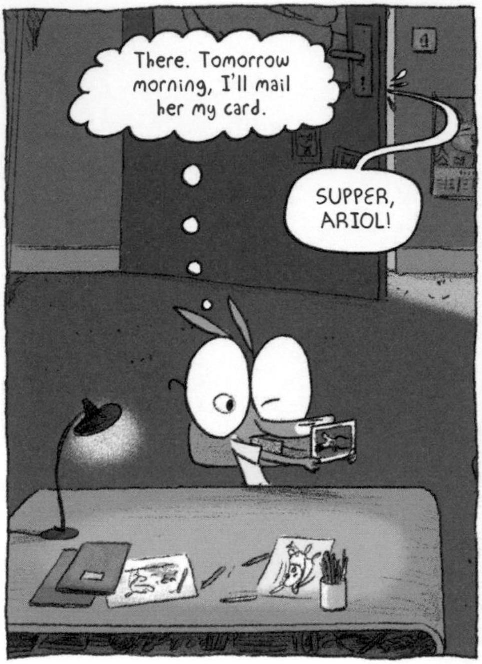
There. Tomorrow morning, I'll mail her my card.
SUPPER, ARIOL!

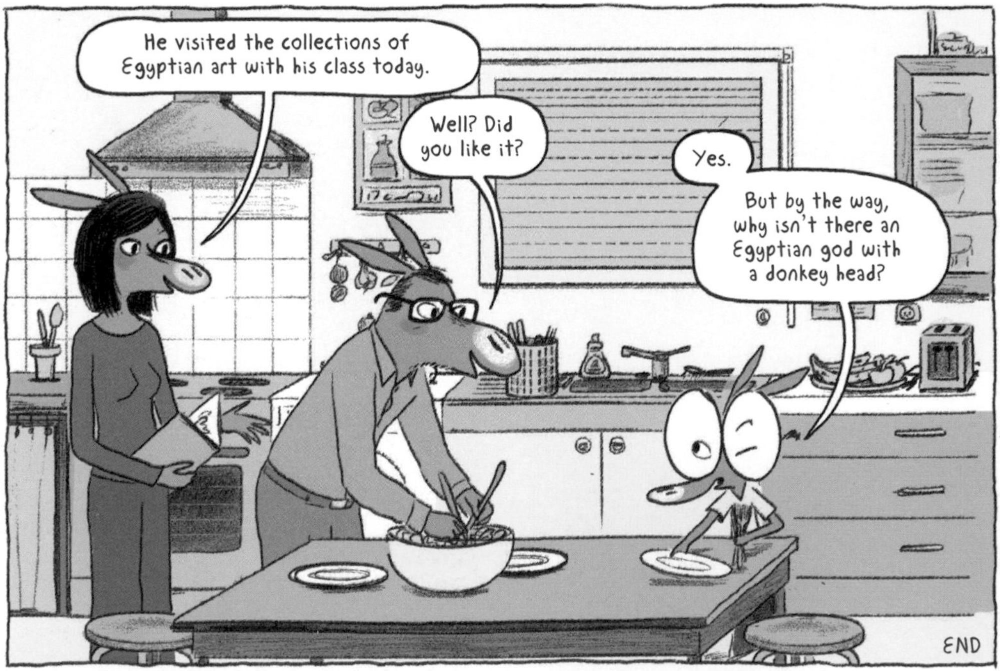
He visited the collections of Egyptian art with his class today.
Well? Did you like it?
Yes.
But by the way, why isn't there an Egyptian god with a donkey head?
END

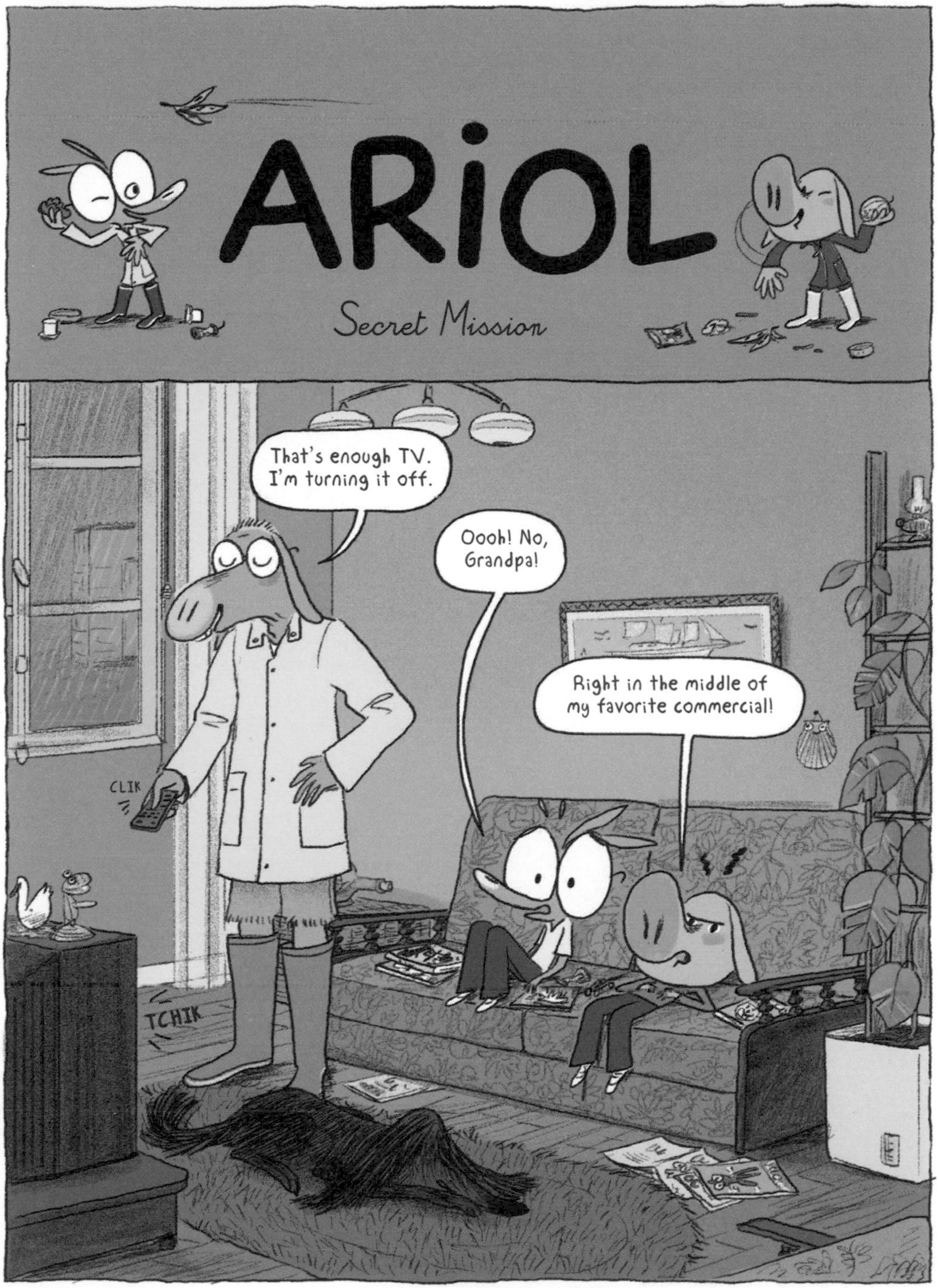
ARiOL
Secret Mission
That's enough TV. I'm turning it off.
CLIK
TCHIK
Oooh! No, Grandpa!
Right in the middle of my favorite commercial!

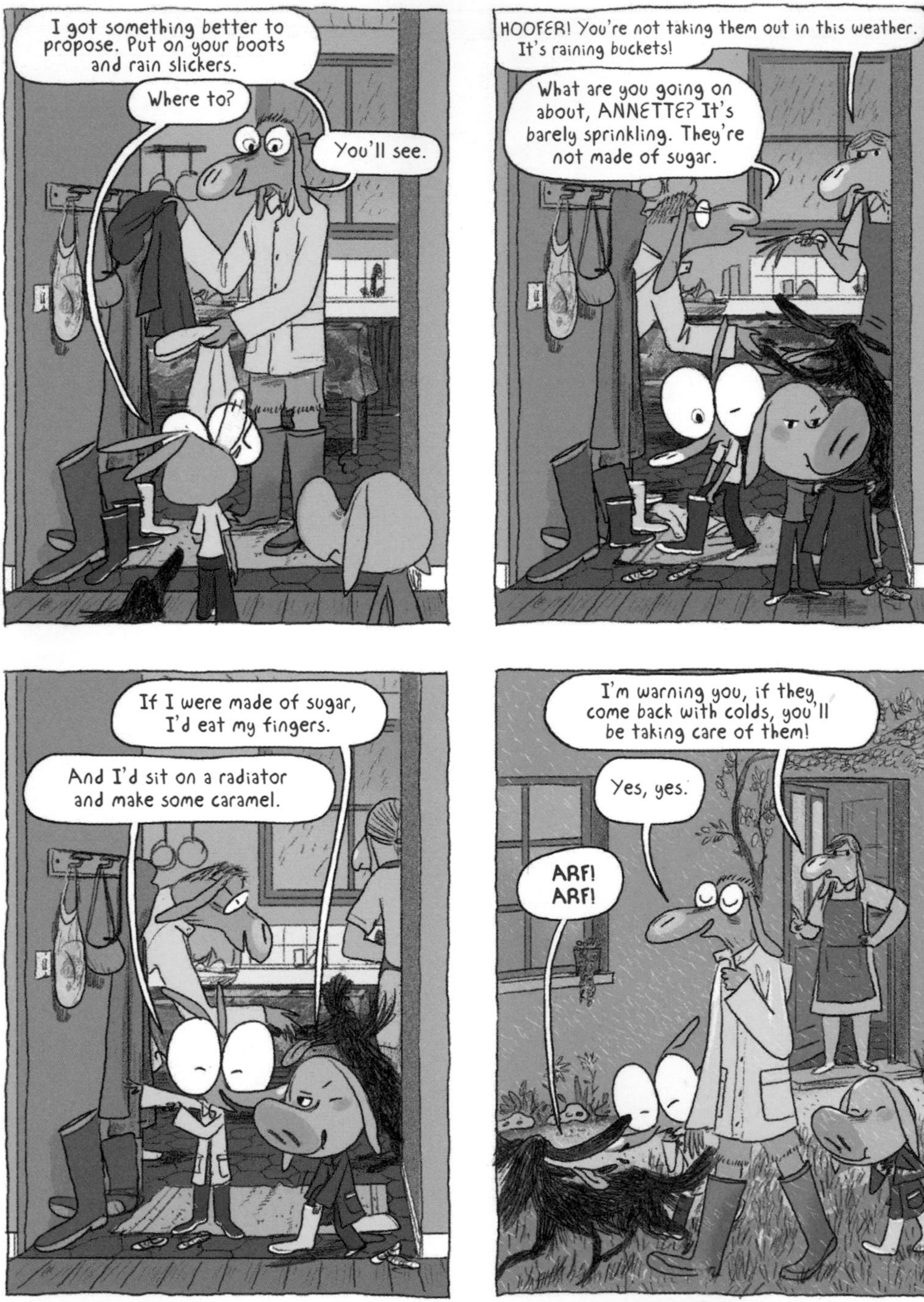
I got something better to propose. Put on your boots and rain slickers.
Where to?
You'll see.
HOOFER! You're not taking them out in this weather. It's raining buckets!
What are you going on about, ANNETTE? It's barely sprinkling. They're not made of sugar.
If I were made of sugar, I'd eat my fingers.
And I'd sit on a radiator and make some caramel.
I'm warning you, if they come back with colds, you'll be taking care of them!
Yes, yes.
ARF! ARF!

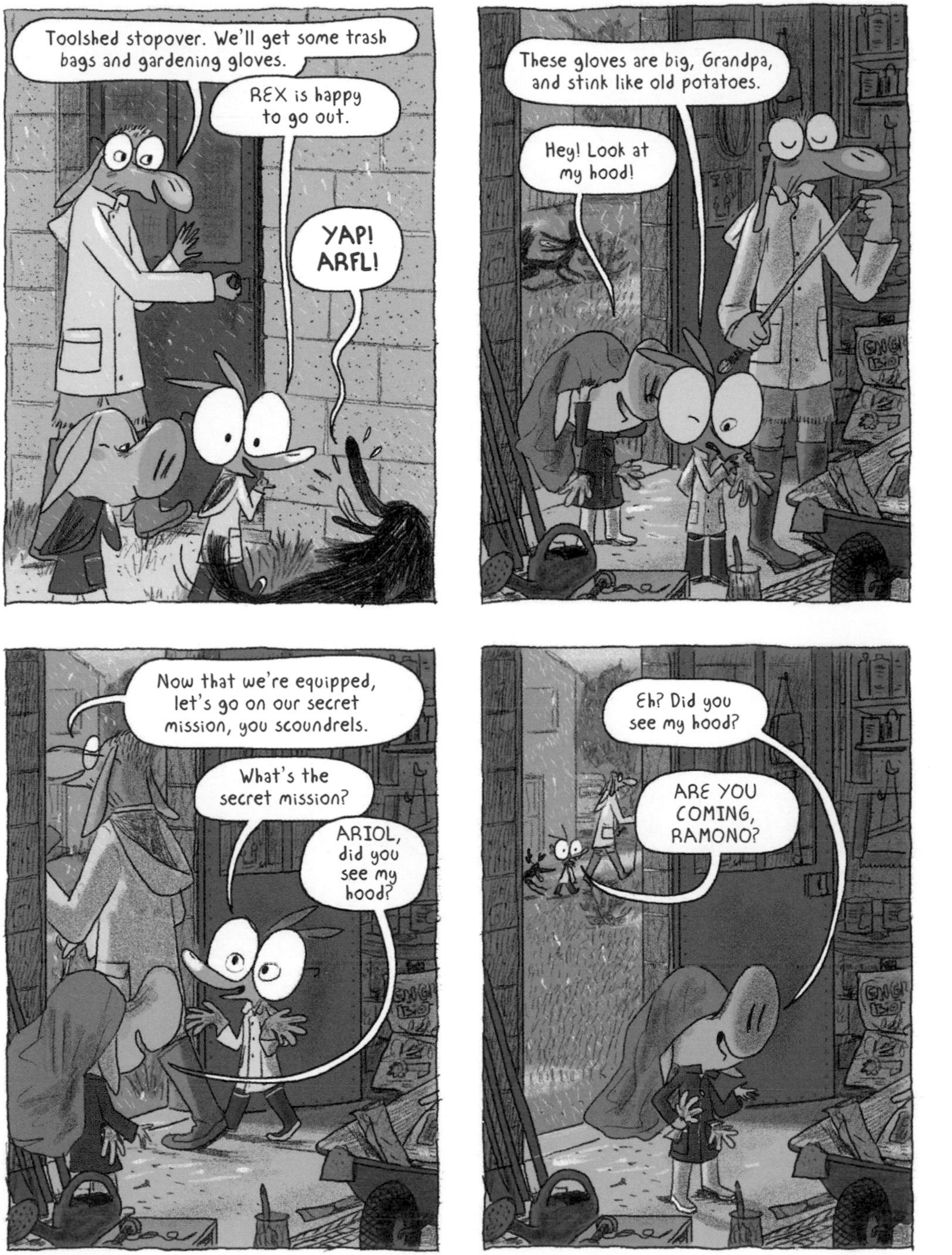
Toolshed stopover. We'll get some trash bags and gardening gloves.
REX is happy to go out.
YAP! ARFL!
These gloves are big, Grandpa, and stink like old potatoes.
Hey! Look at my hood!
Now that we're equipped, let's go on our secret mission, you scoundrels.
What's the secret mission?
ARIOL, did you see my hood?
Eh? Did you see my hood?
ARE YOU COMING, RAMONO?

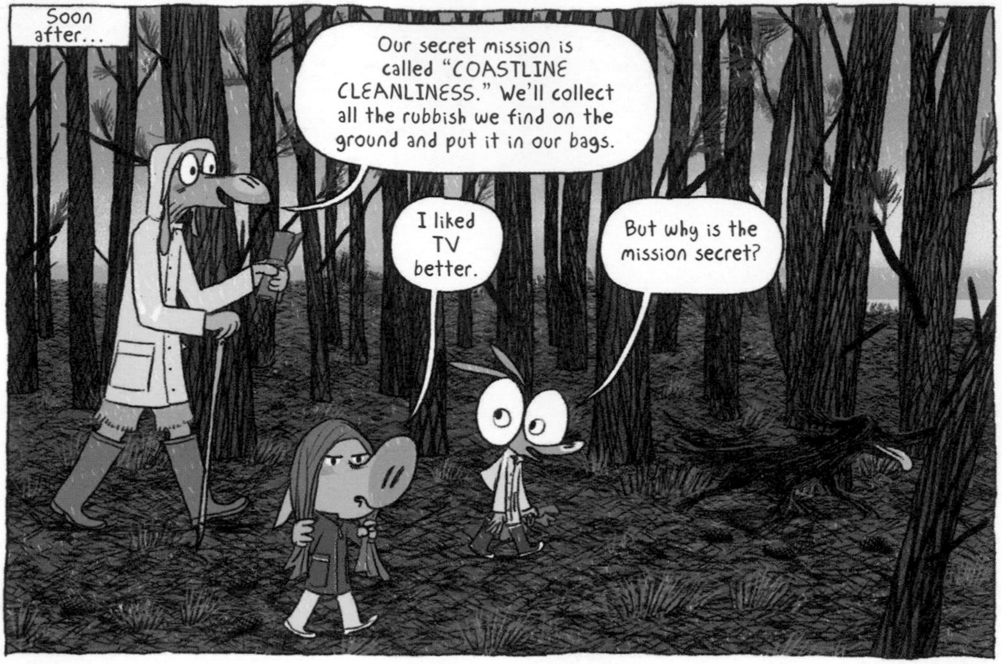

Soon after...
Our secret mission is called "COASTLINE CLEANLINESS." We'll collect all the rubbish we find on the ground and put it in our bags.
I liked TV better.
But why is the mission secret?

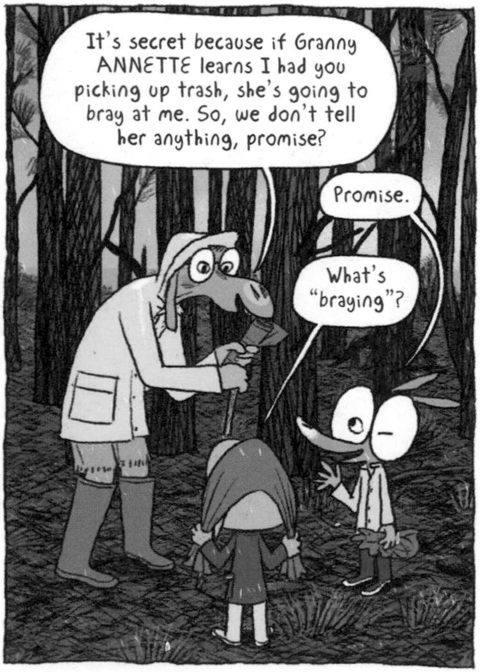

It's secret because if Granny ANNETTE learns I had you picking up trash, she's going to bray at me. So, we don't tell her anything, promise?
Promise.
What's "braying"?

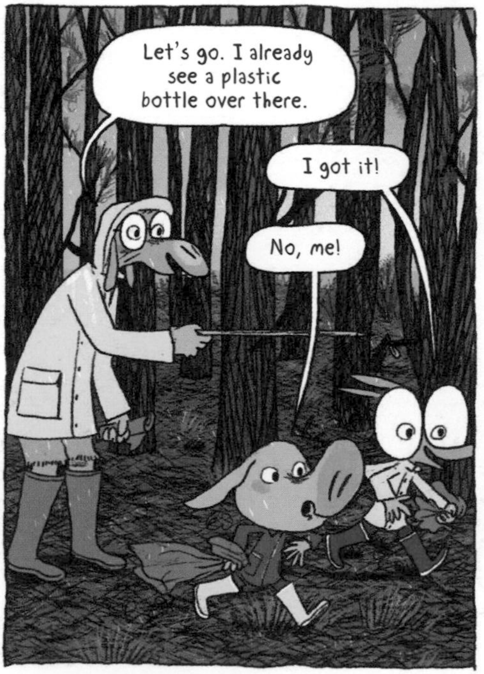

Let's go. I already see a plastic bottle over there.
I got it!
No, me!

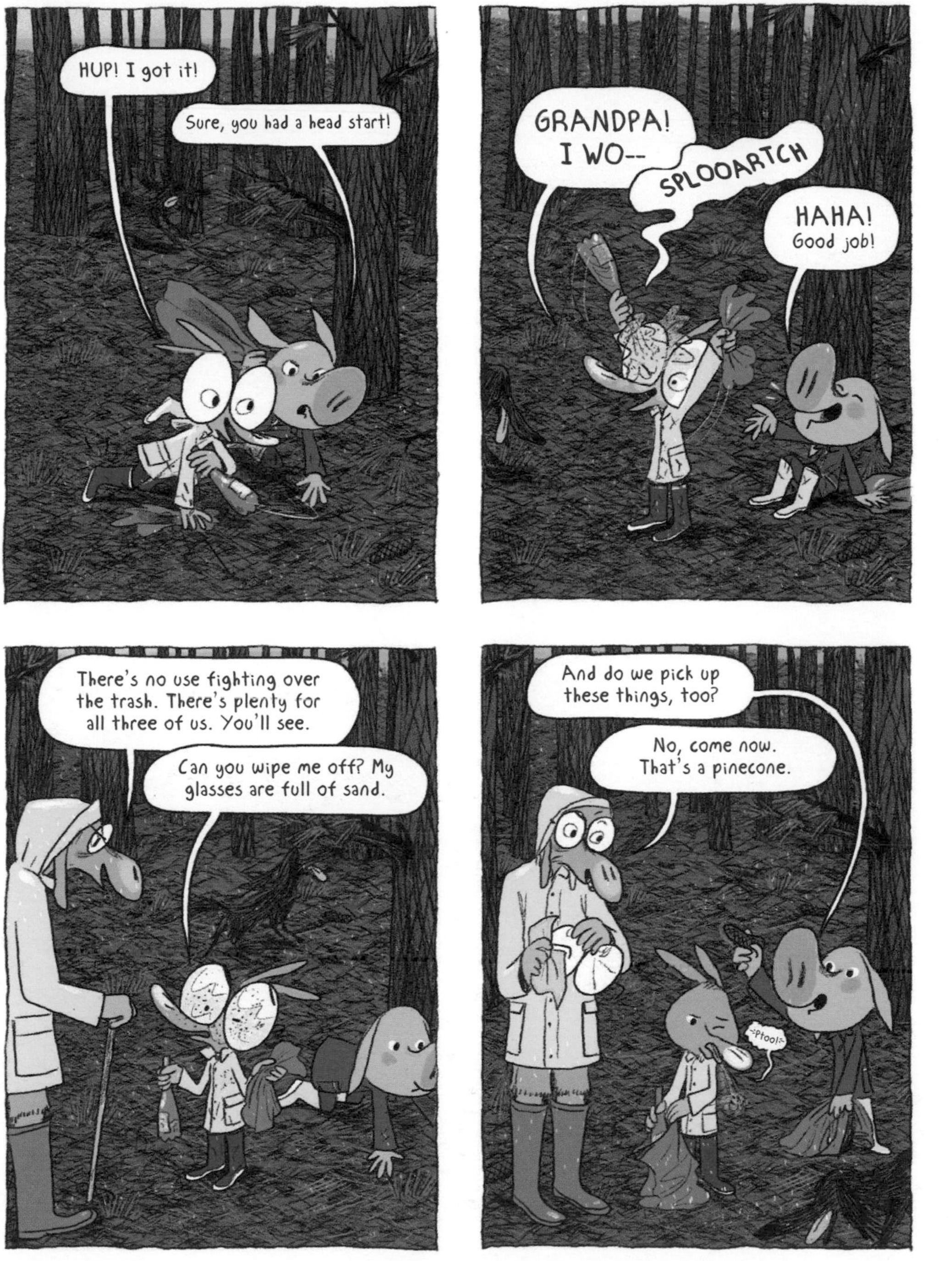
HUP! I got it!
Sure, you had a head start!
GRANDPA! I WO--
SPLOOARTCH
HAHA! Good job!
There's no use fighting over the trash. There's plenty for all three of us. You'll see.
Can you wipe me off? My glasses are full of sand.
And do we pick up these things, too?
No, come now. That's a pinecone.
Ptoo!

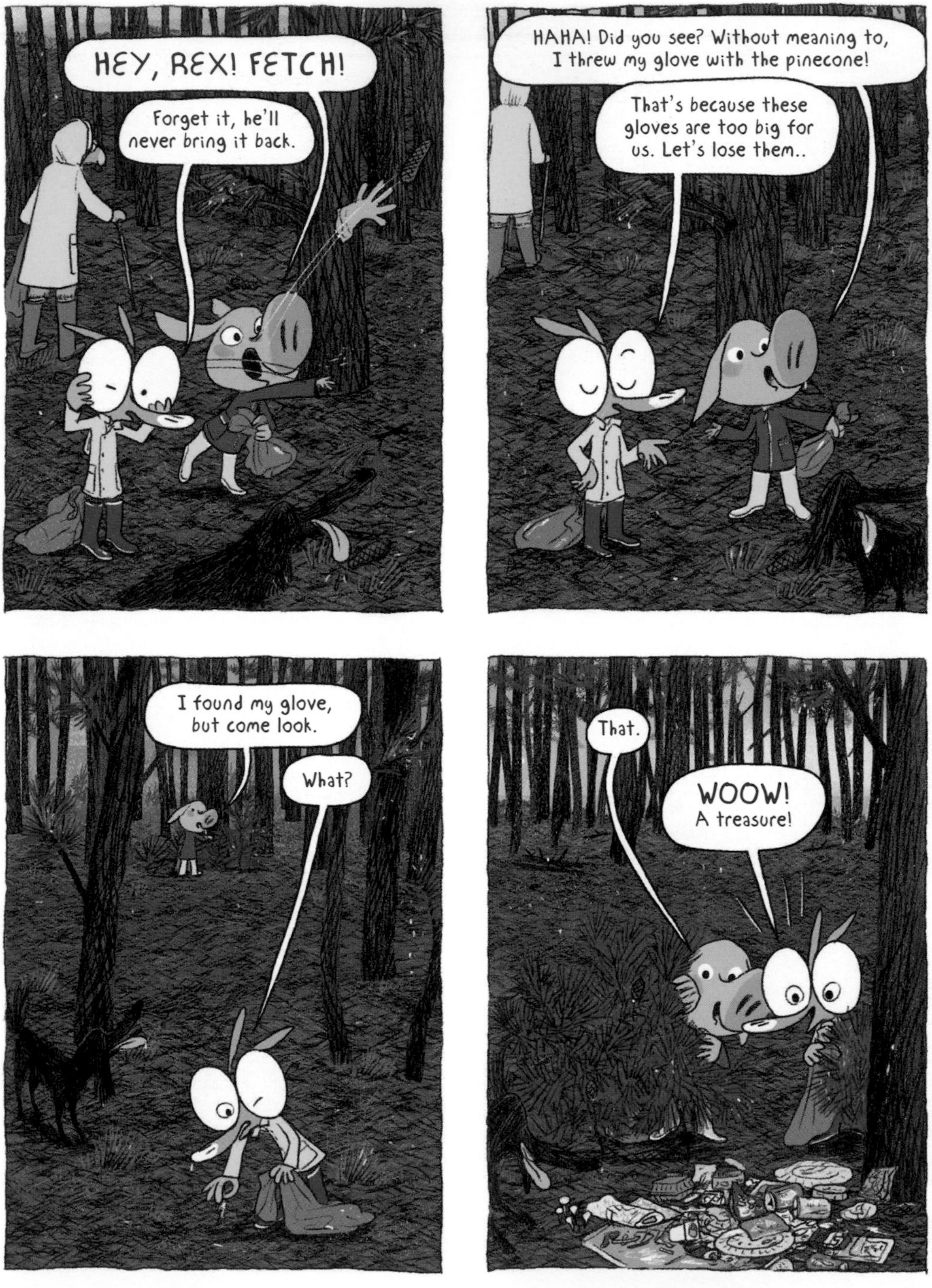
HEY, REX! FETCH!
Forget it, he'll never bring it back.
HAHA! Did you see? Without meaning to, I threw my glove with the pinecone!
That's because these gloves are too big for us. Let's lose them..
I found my glove, but come look.
What?
That.
WOOW! A treasure!

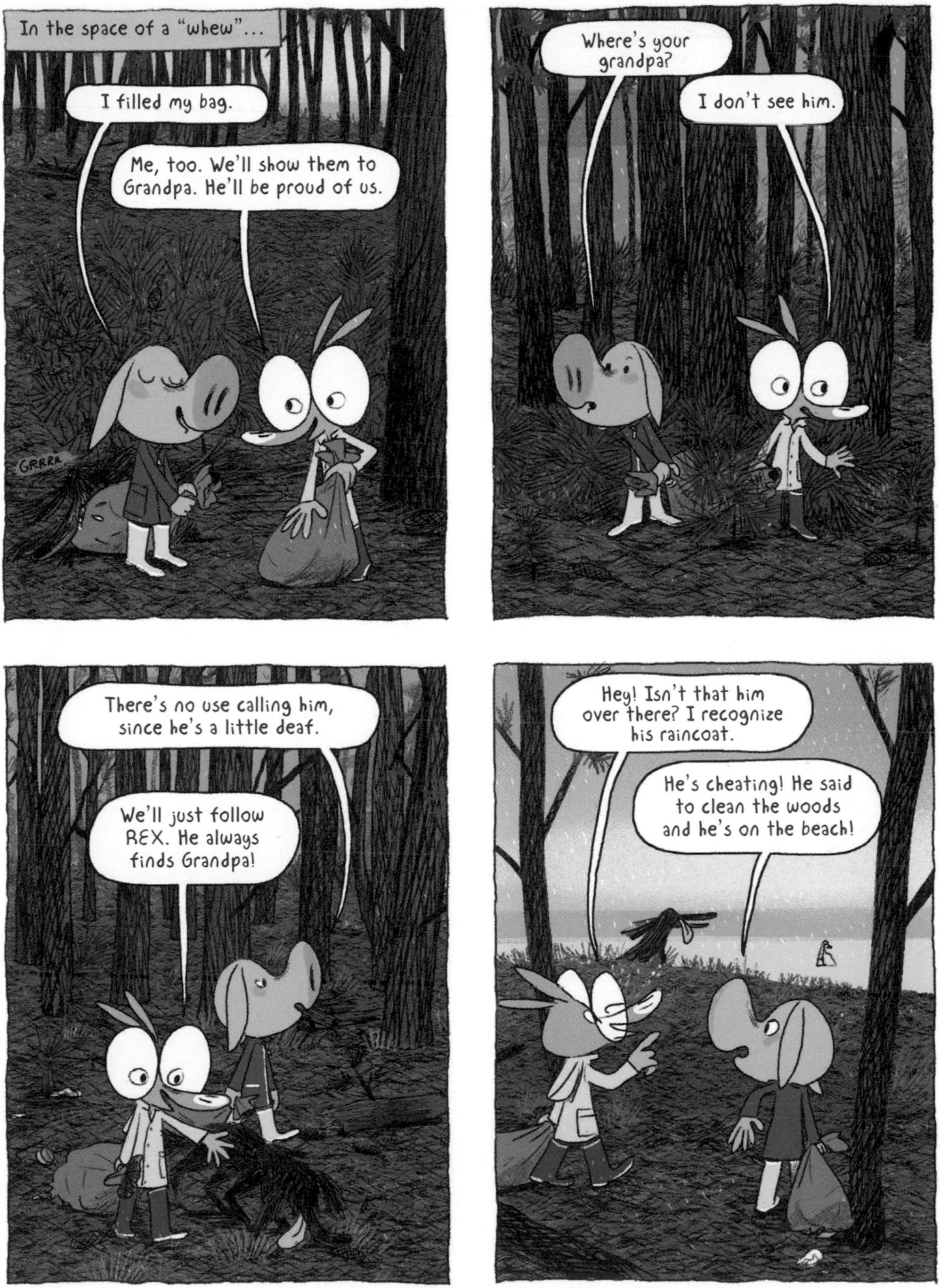
In the space of a "whew"...
I filled my bag.
Me, too. We'll show them to Grandpa. He'll be proud of us.
GRRRR
Where's your grandpa?
I don't see him.
There's no use calling him, since he's a little deaf.
We'll just follow REX. He always finds Grandpa!
Hey! Isn't that him over there? I recognize his raincoat.
He's cheating! He said to clean the woods and he's on the beach!

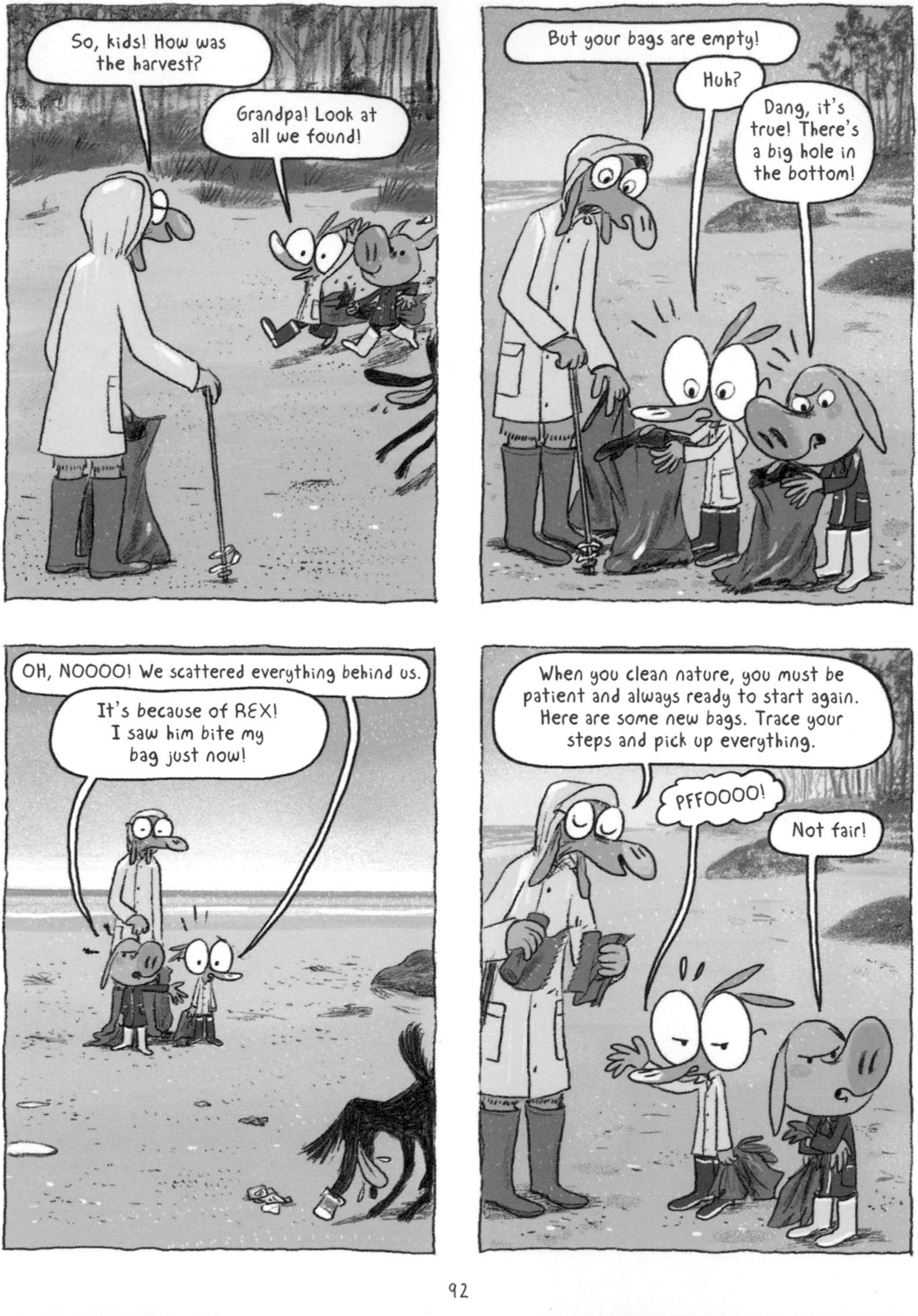

So, kids! How was the harvest?
Grandpa! Look at all we found!
But your bags are empty!
Huh?
Dang, it's true! There's a big hole in the bottom!
OH, NOOOO! We scattered everything behind us.
It's because of REX! I saw him bite my bag just now!
When you clean nature, you must be patient and always ready to start again. Here are some new bags. Trace your steps and pick up everything.
PFFOOOO!
Not fair!

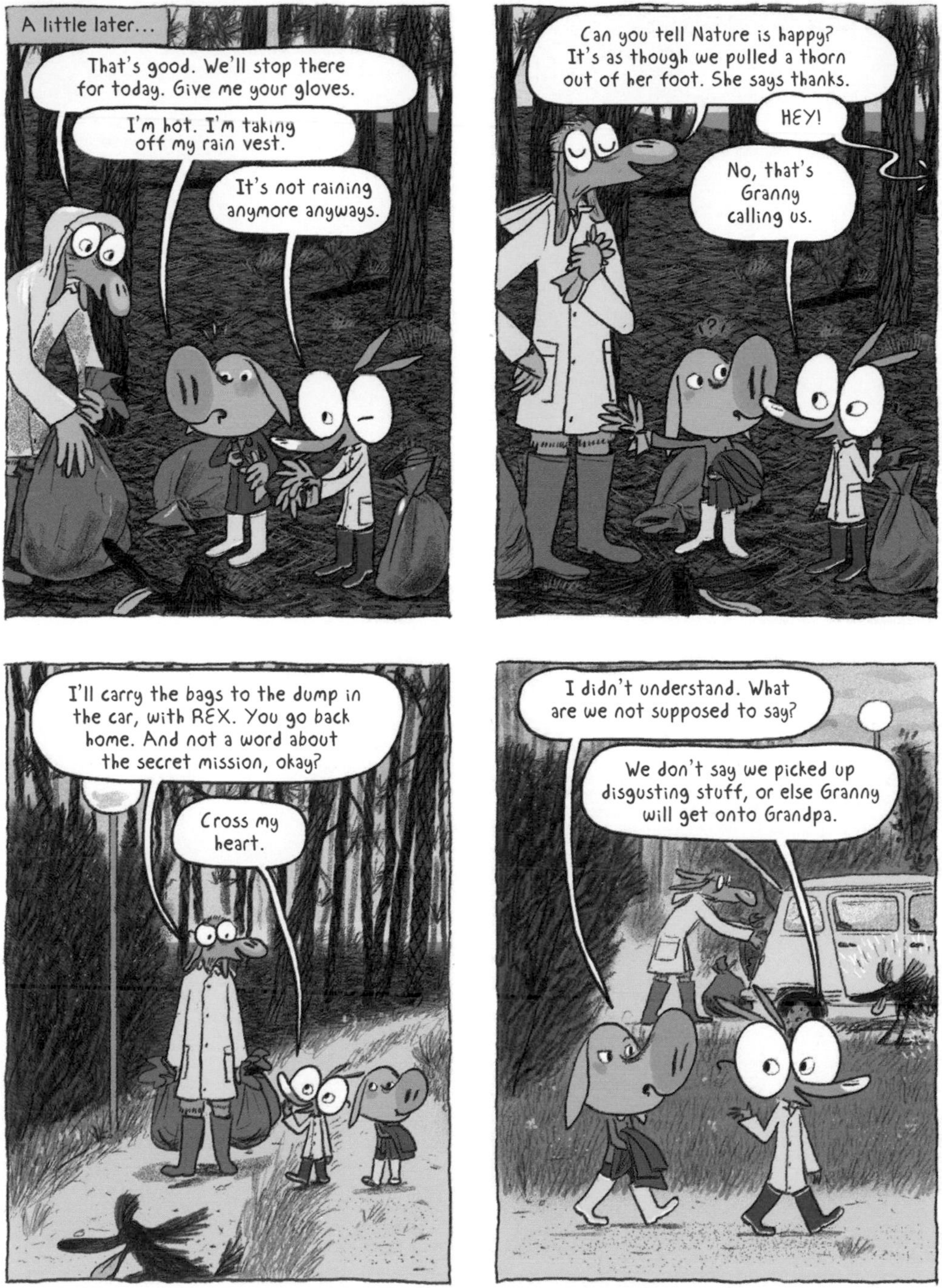
A little later...
That's good. We'll stop there for today. Give me your gloves.
I'm hot. I'm taking off my rain vest.
It's not raining anymore anyways.
Can you tell Nature is happy? It's as though we pulled a thorn out of her foot. She says thanks.
HEY!
No, that's Granny calling us.
I'll carry the bags to the dump in the car, with REX. You go back home. And not a word about the secret mission, okay?
Cross my heart.
I didn't understand. What are we not supposed to say?
We don't say we picked up disgusting stuff, or else Granny will get onto Grandpa.

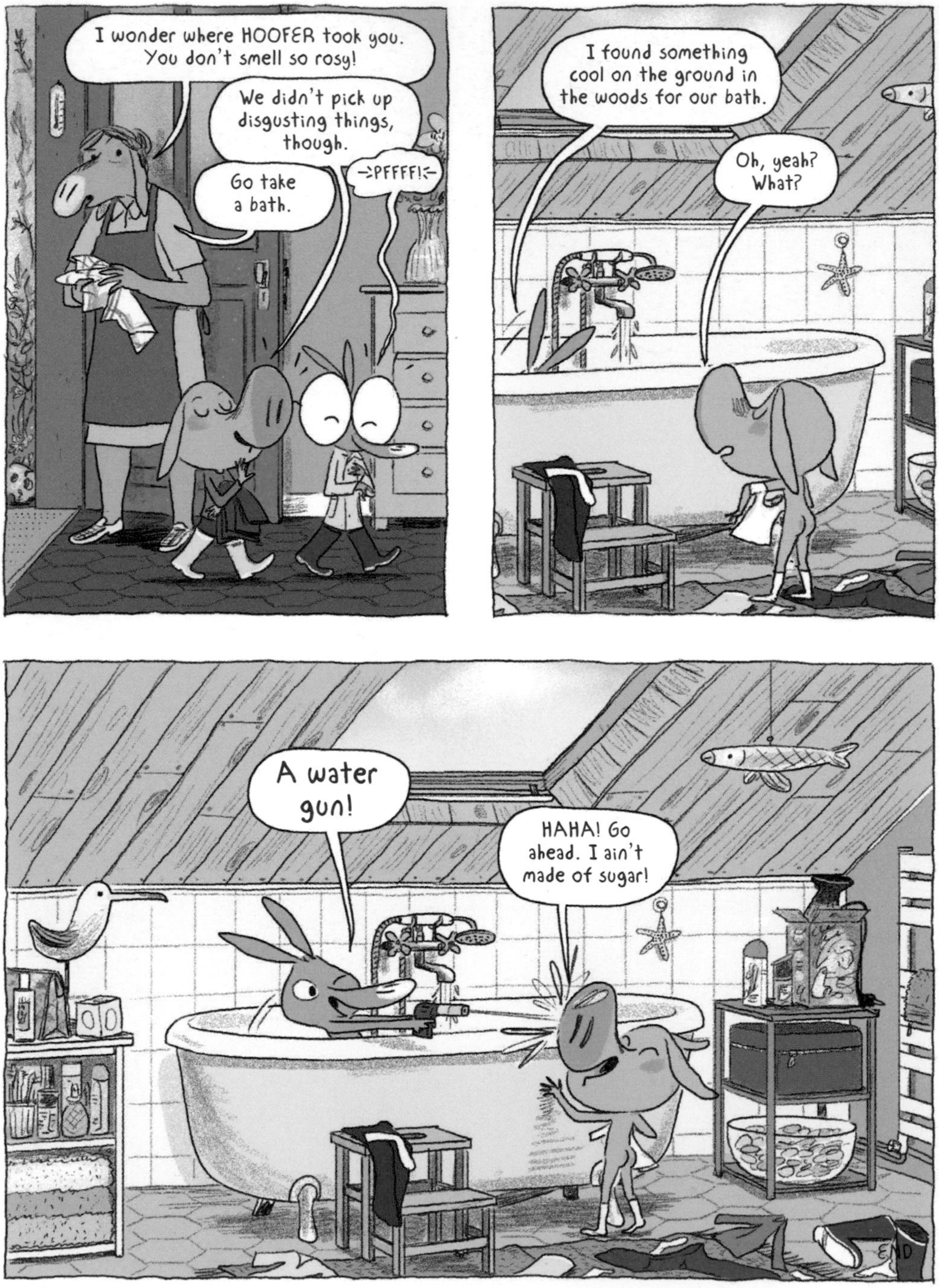
I wonder where HOOFER took you. You don't smell so rosy!
We didn't pick up disgusting things, though.
Go take a bath.
PFFFFF!
I found something cool on the ground in the woods for our bath.
Oh, yeah? What?
A water gun!
HAHA! Go ahead. I ain't made of sugar!
END

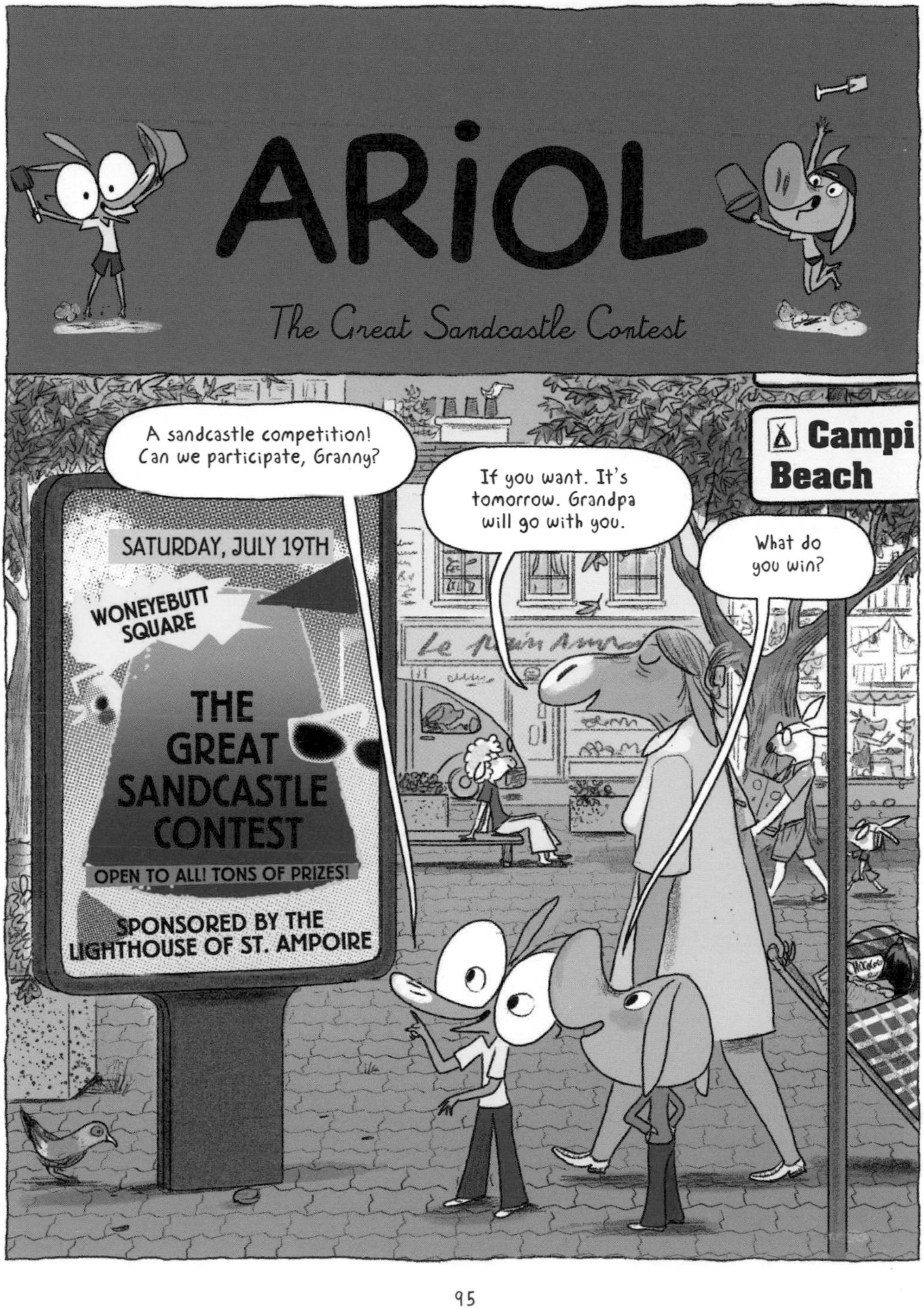
ARiOL
The Great Sandcastle Contest
A sandcastle competition! Can we participate, Granny?
SATURDAY, JULY 19TH
WONEYEBUTT SQUARE
THE GREAT SANDCASTLE CONTEST
OPEN TO ALL! TONS OF PRIZES!
SPONSORED BY THE LIGHTHOUSE OF ST. AMPOIRE
If you want. It's tomorrow. Grandpa will go with you.
Campi Beach
What do you win?

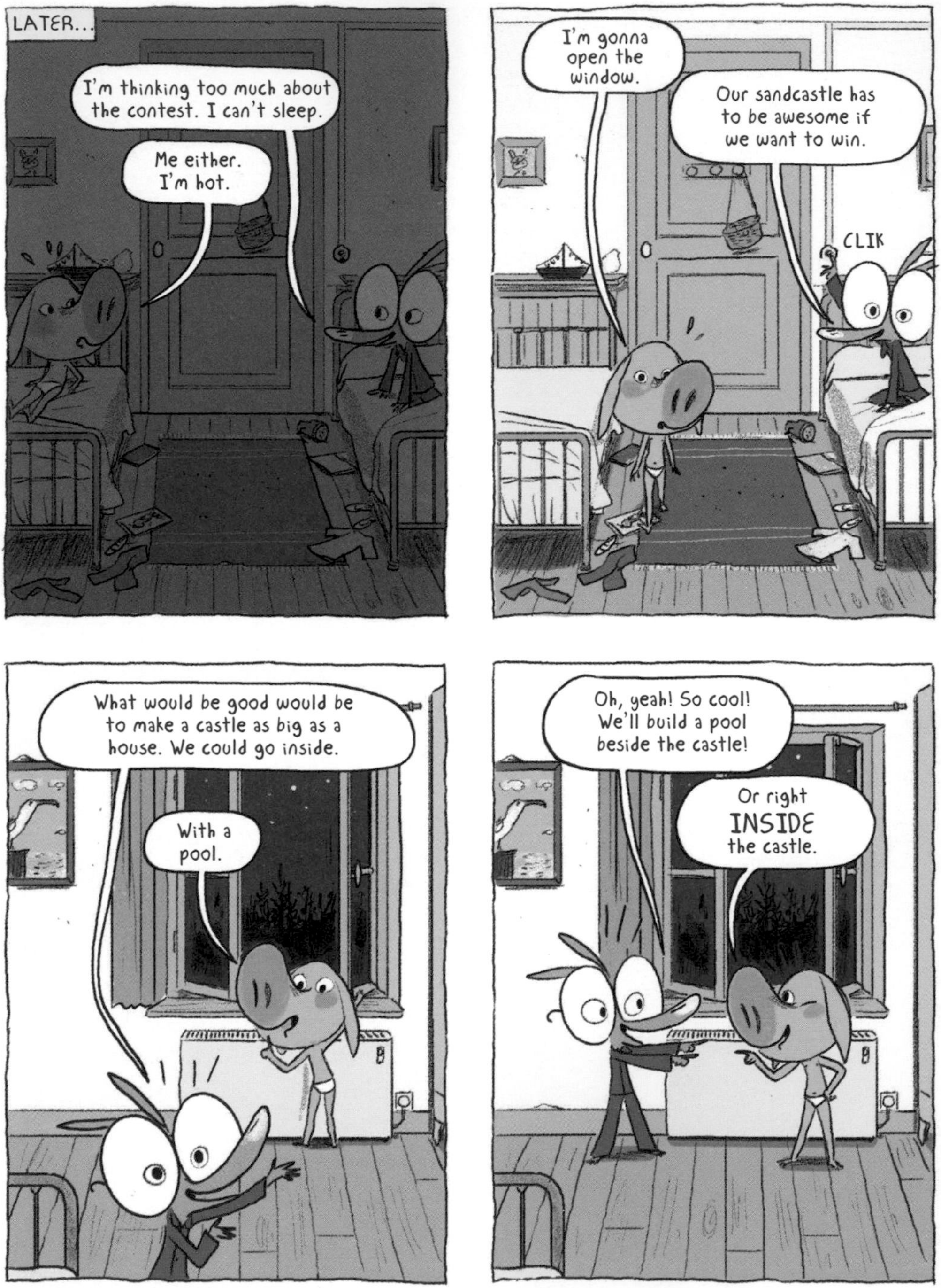
LATER...
I'm thinking too much about the contest. I can't sleep.
Me either. I'm hot.
I'm gonna open the window.
Our sandcastle has to be awesome if we want to win.
CLIK
What would be good would be to make a castle as big as a house. We could go inside.
With a pool.
Oh, yeah! So cool! We'll build a pool beside the castle!
Or right INSIDE the castle.

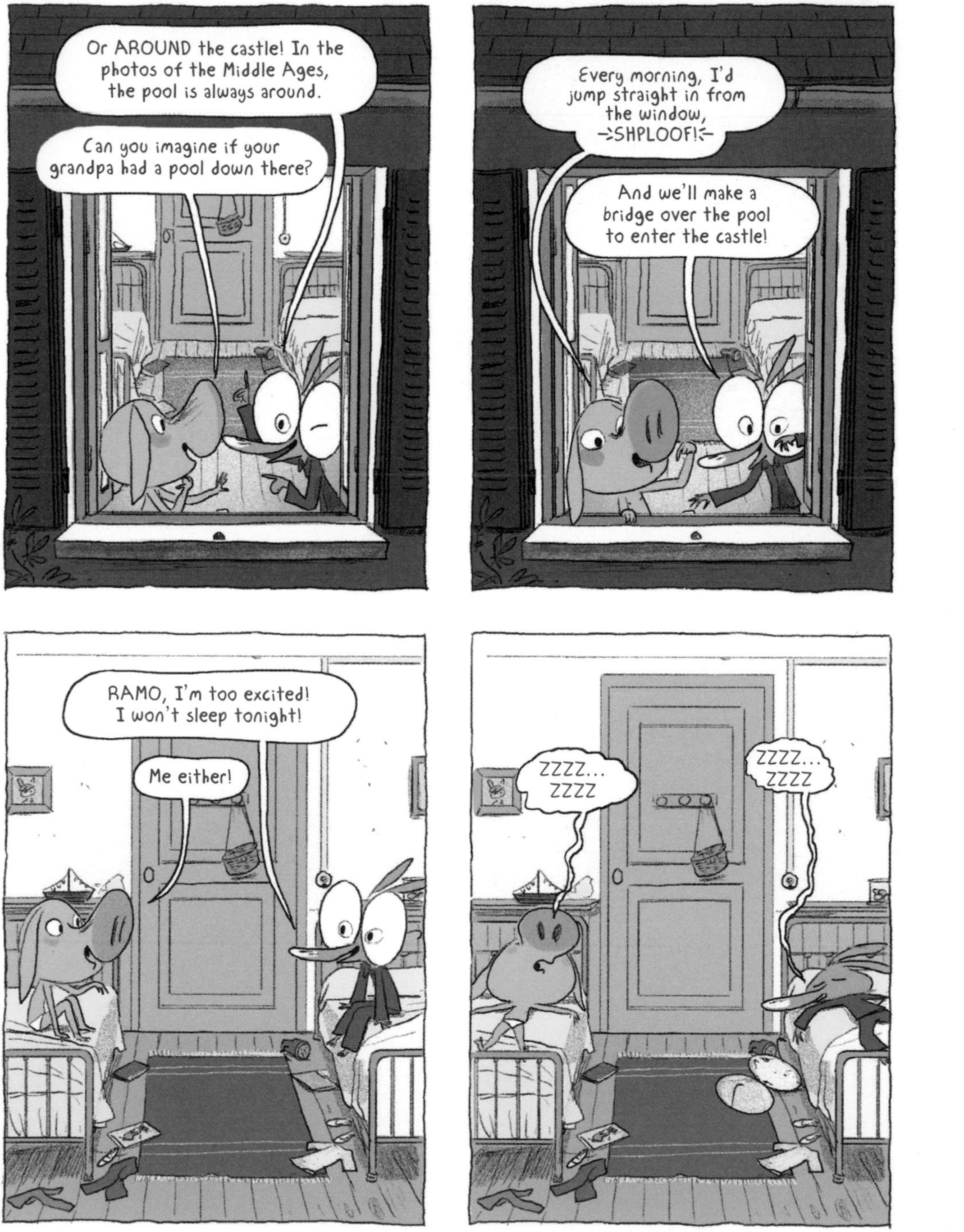
Or AROUND the castle! In the photos of the Middle Ages, the pool is always around.
Can you imagine if your grandpa had a pool down there?
Every morning, I'd jump straight in from the window, SHPLOOF!
And we'll make a bridge over the pool to enter the castle!
RAMO, I'm too excited! I won't sleep tonight!
Me either!
ZZZZ... ZZZZ
ZZZZ... ZZZZ

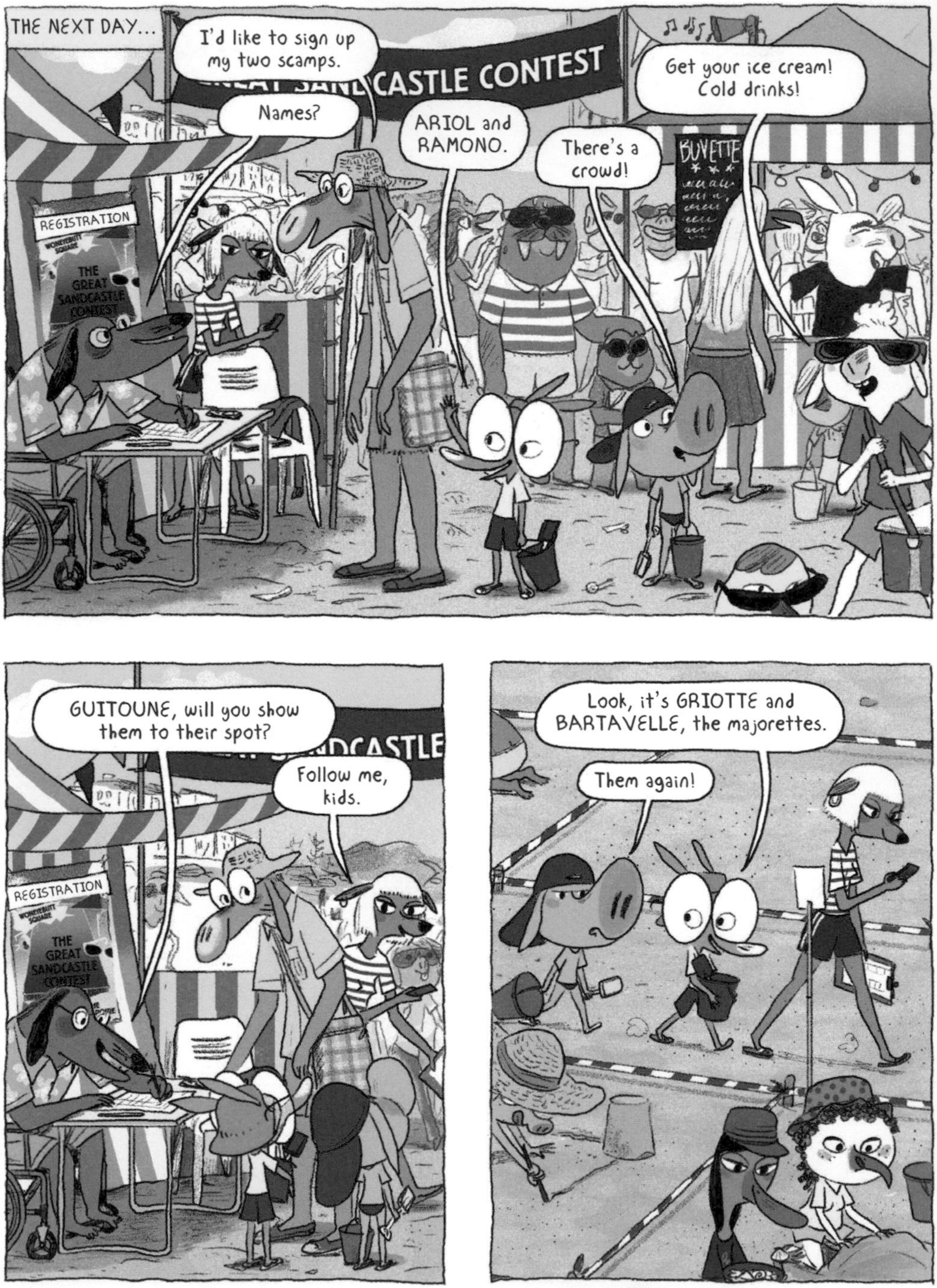
THE NEXT DAY...
I'd like to sign up my two scamps.
GREAT SANDCASTLE CONTEST
Names?
ARIOL and RAMONO.
There's a crowd!
Get your ice cream! Cold drinks!
BUVETTE
REGISTRATION
THE GREAT SANDCASTLE CONTEST
GUITOUNE, will you show them to their spot?
Follow me, kids.
Look, it's GRIOTTE and BARTAVELLE, the majorettes.
Them again!

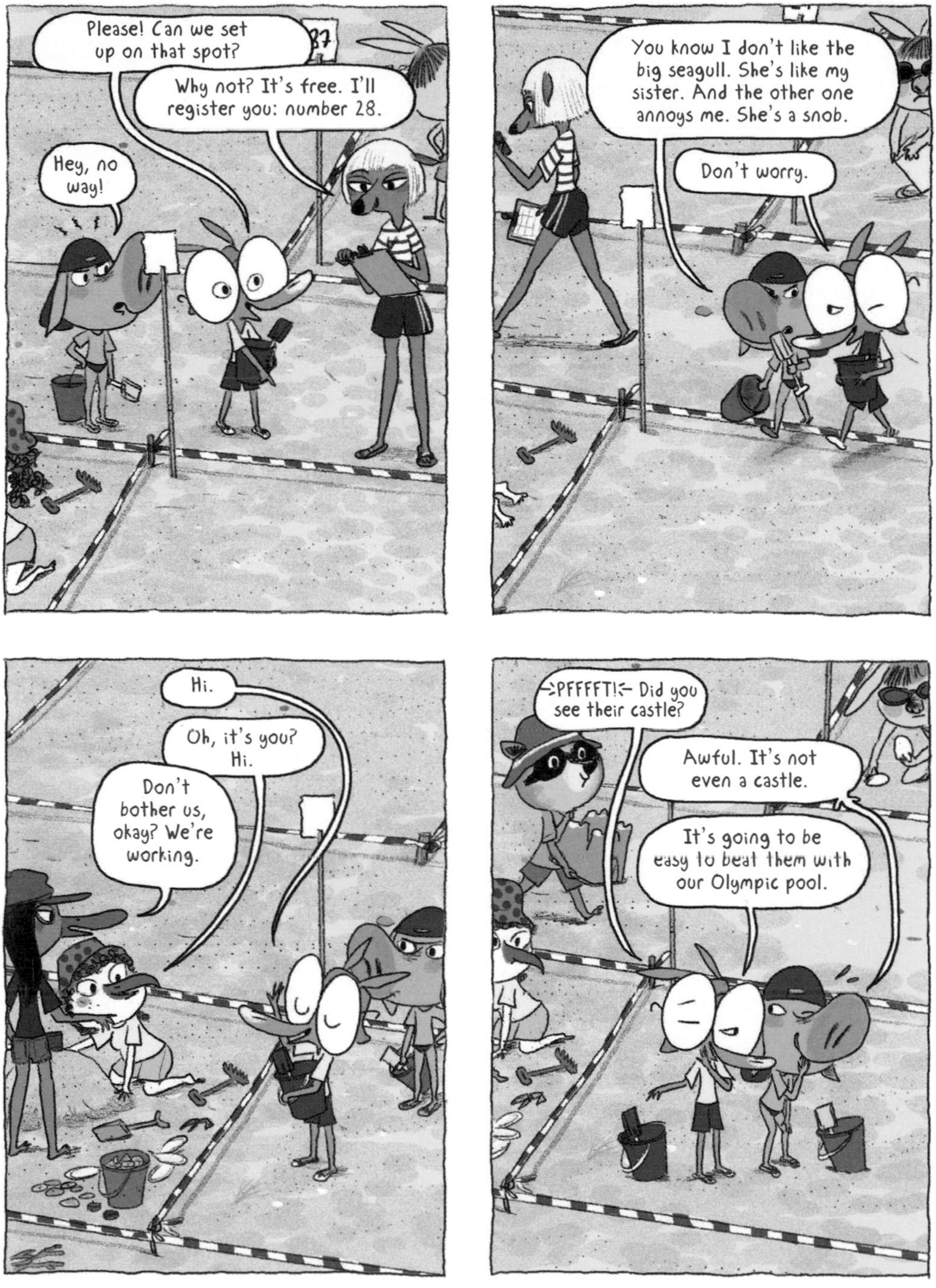
Please! Can we set up on that spot?
Why not? It's free. I'll register you: number 28.
Hey, no way!
You know I don't like the big seagull. She's like my sister. And the other one annoys me. She's a snob.
Don't worry.
Hi.
Oh, it's you? Hi.
Don't bother us, okay? We're working.
PFFFFT! Did you see their castle?
Awful. It's not even a castle.
It's going to be easy to beat them with our Olympic pool.

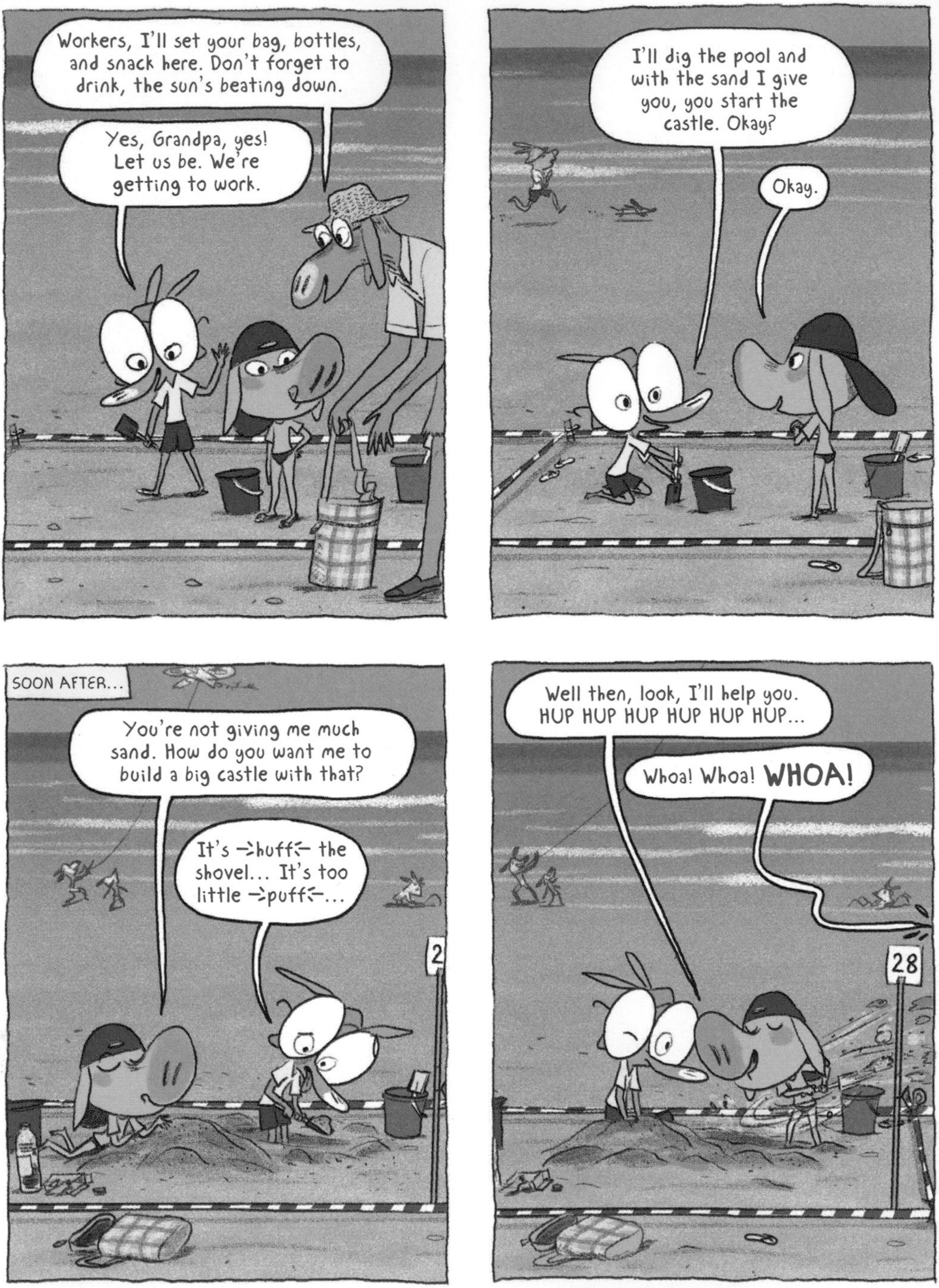
Workers, I'll set your bag, bottles, and snack here. Don't forget to drink, the sun's beating down.
Yes, Grandpa, yes! Let us be. We're getting to work.
I'll dig the pool and with the sand I give you, you start the castle. Okay?
Okay.
SOON AFTER...
You're not giving me much sand. How do you want me to build a big castle with that?
It's →huff← the shovel... It's too little →puff←...
Well then, look, I'll help you. HUP HUP HUP HUP HUP HUP...
Whoa! Whoa! WHOA!
28

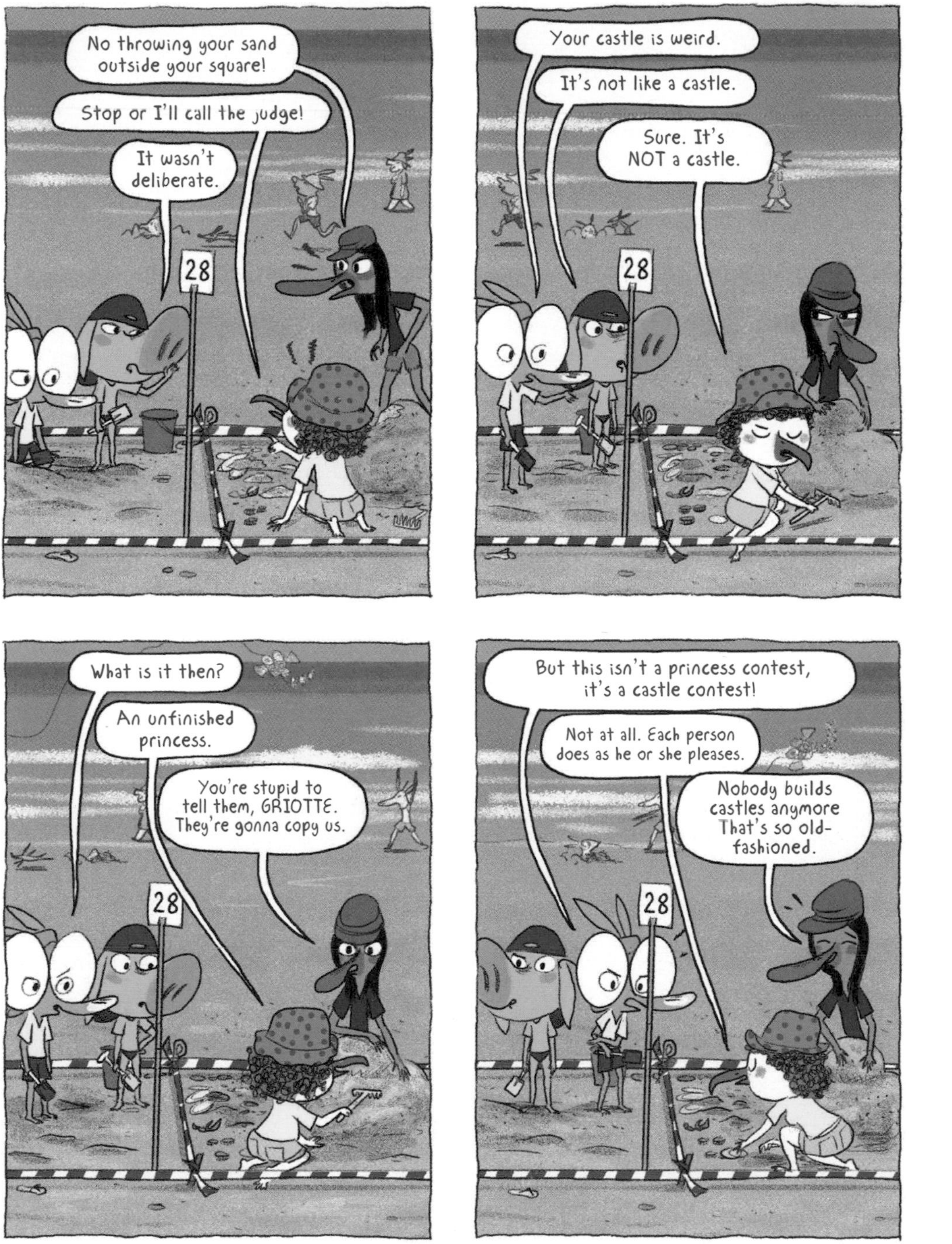
No throwing your sand outside your square!
Stop or I'll call the judge!
It wasn't deliberate.
28
Your castle is weird.
It's not like a castle.
Sure. It's NOT a castle.
28
What is it then?
An unfinished princess.
You're stupid to tell them, GRIOTTE. They're gonna copy us.
28
But this isn't a princess contest, it's a castle contest!
Not at all. Each person does as he or she pleases.
Nobody builds castles anymore That's so old-fashioned.
28

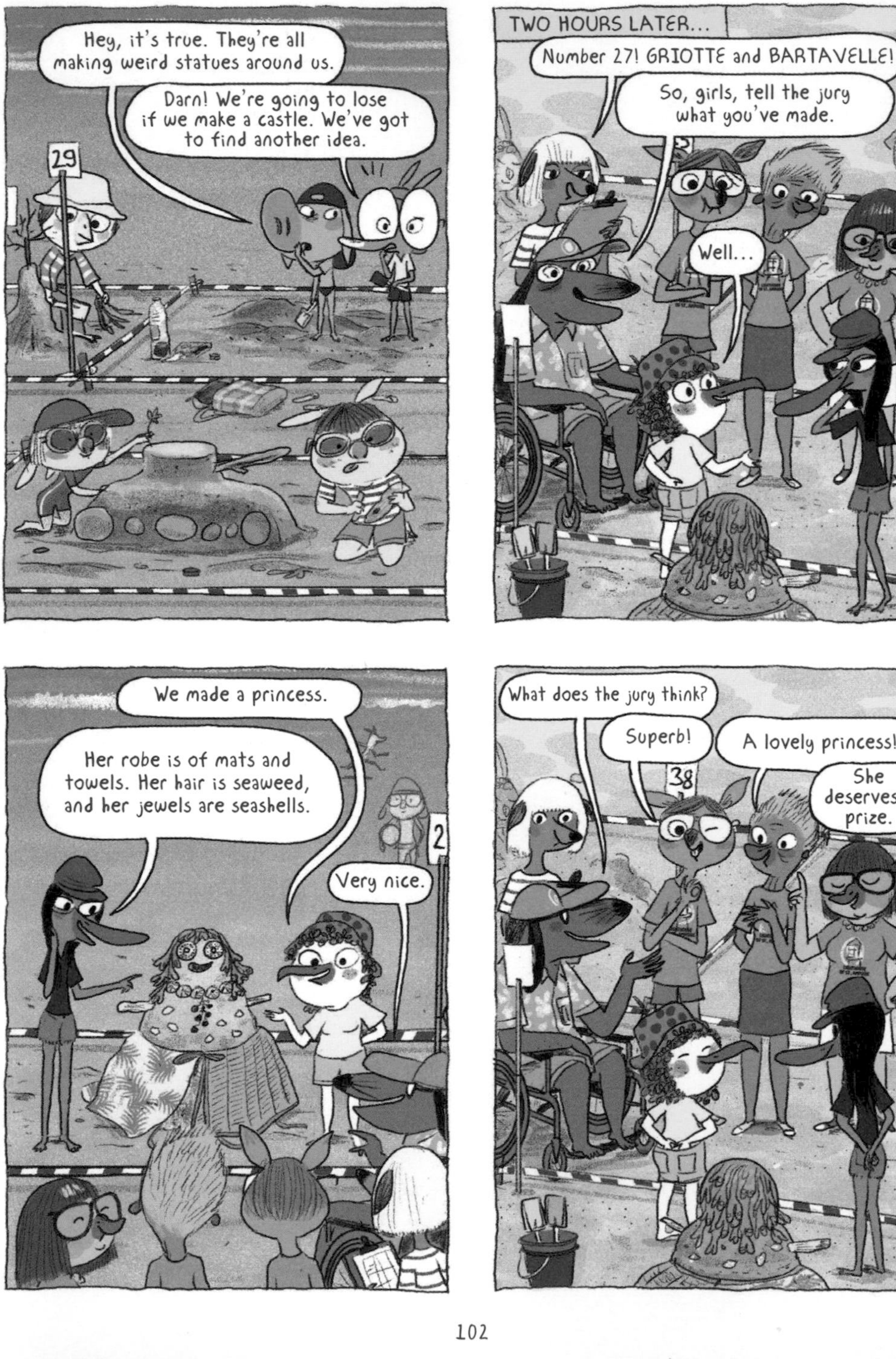
Hey, it's true. They're all making weird statues around us.
Darn! We're going to lose if we make a castle. We've got to find another idea.
29
TWO HOURS LATER...
Number 27! GRIOTTE and BARTAVELLE!
So, girls, tell the jury what you've made.
Well...
We made a princess.
Her robe is of mats and towels. Her hair is seaweed, and her jewels are seashells.
Very nice.
What does the jury think?
Superb!
A lovely princess!
She deserves a prize.
38

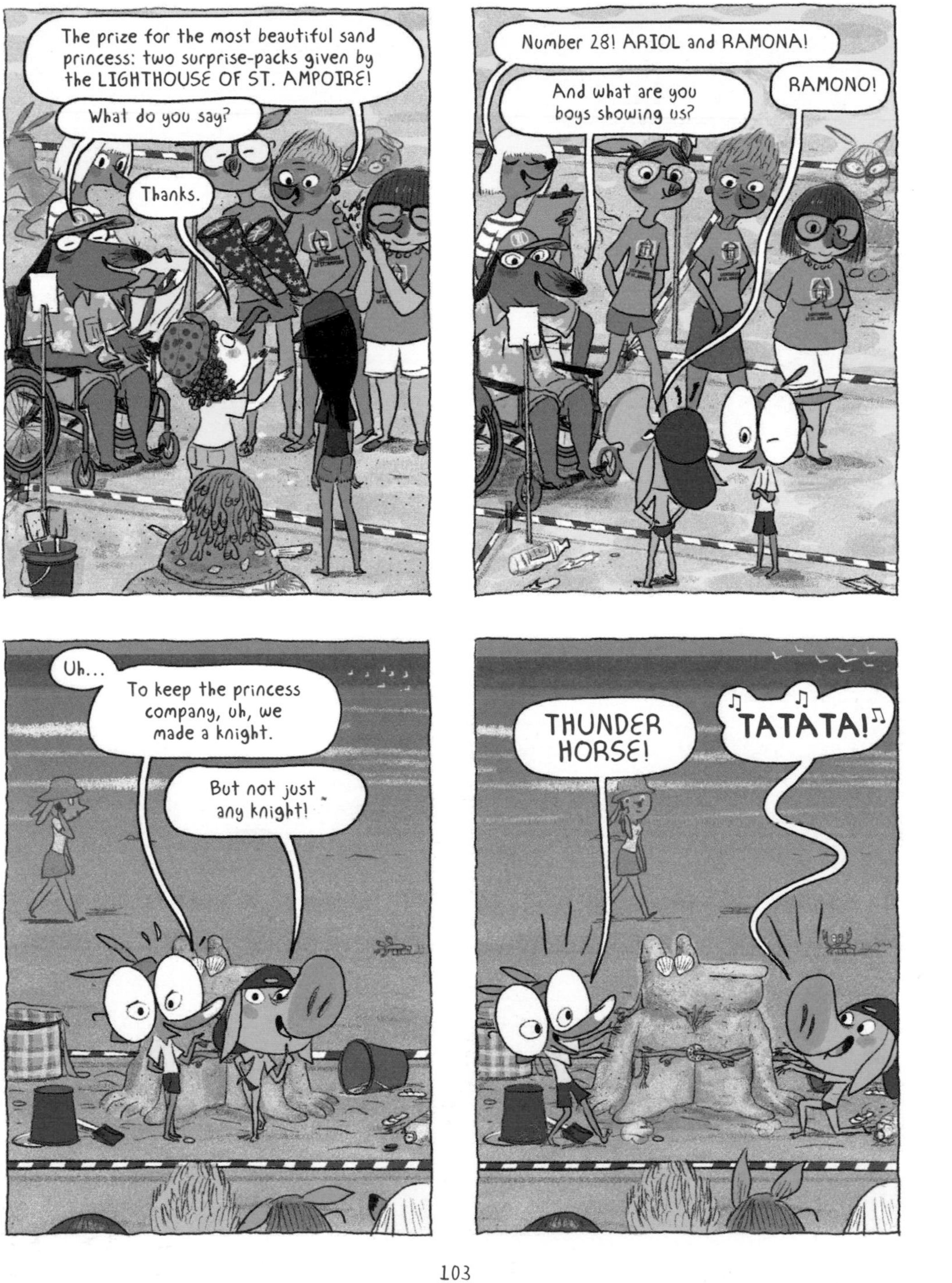
The prize for the most beautiful sand princess: two surprise-packs given by the LIGHTHOUSE OF ST. AMPOIRE!
What do you say?
Thanks.
Number 28! ARIOL and RAMONA!
And what are you boys showing us?
RAMONO!
Uh...
To keep the princess company, uh, we made a knight.
But not just any knight!
THUNDER HORSE!
TATATA!

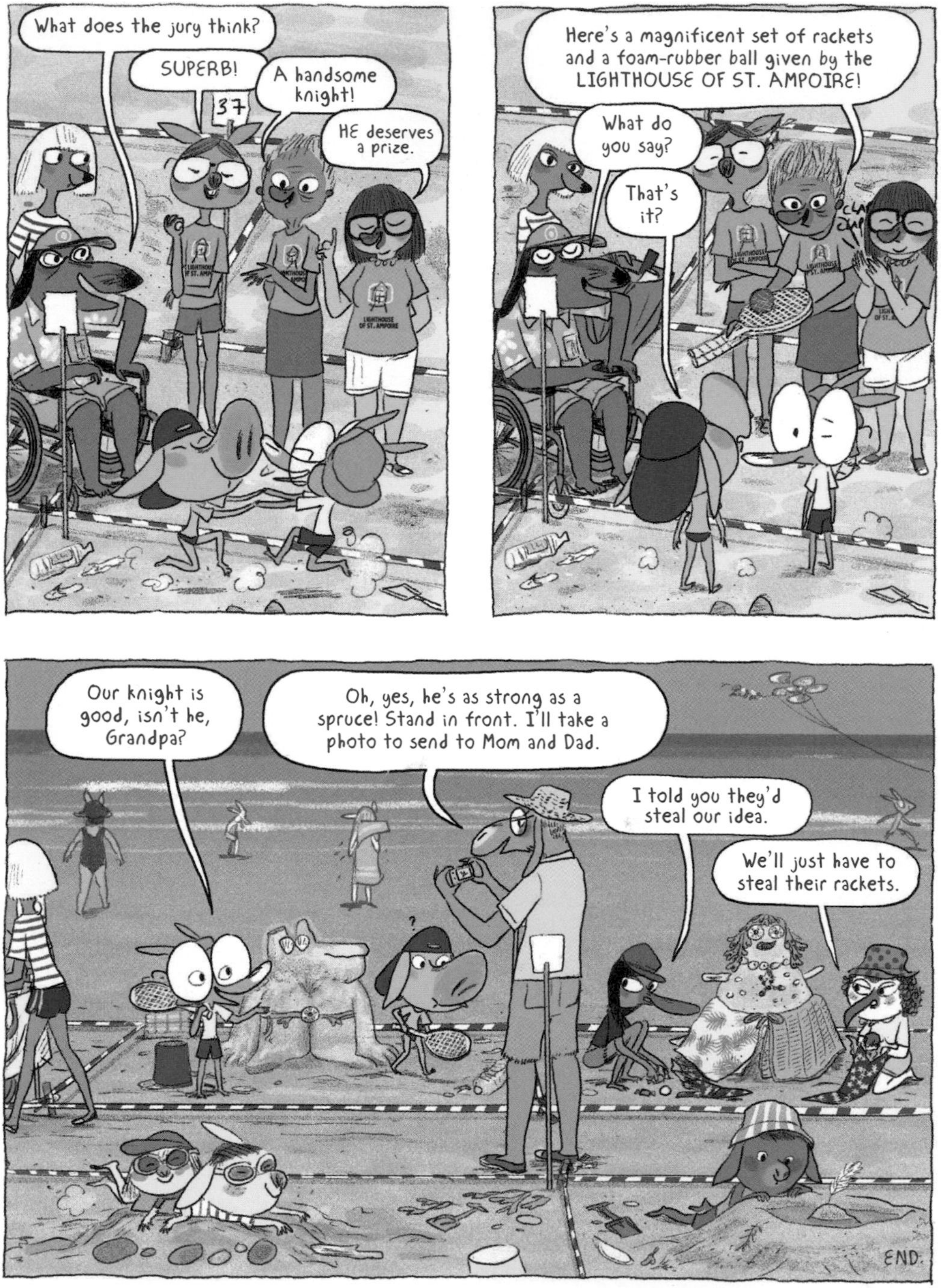
What does the jury think?
SUPERB!
37
A handsome knight!
HE deserves a prize.
LIGHTHOUSE OF ST. AMPOIRE
Here's a magnificent set of rackets and a foam-rubber ball given by the LIGHTHOUSE OF ST. AMPOIRE!
What do you say?
That's it?
Our knight is good, isn't he, Grandpa?
Oh, yes, he's as strong as a spruce! Stand in front. I'll take a photo to send to Mom and Dad.
I told you they'd steal our idea.
We'll just have to steal their rackets.
END.

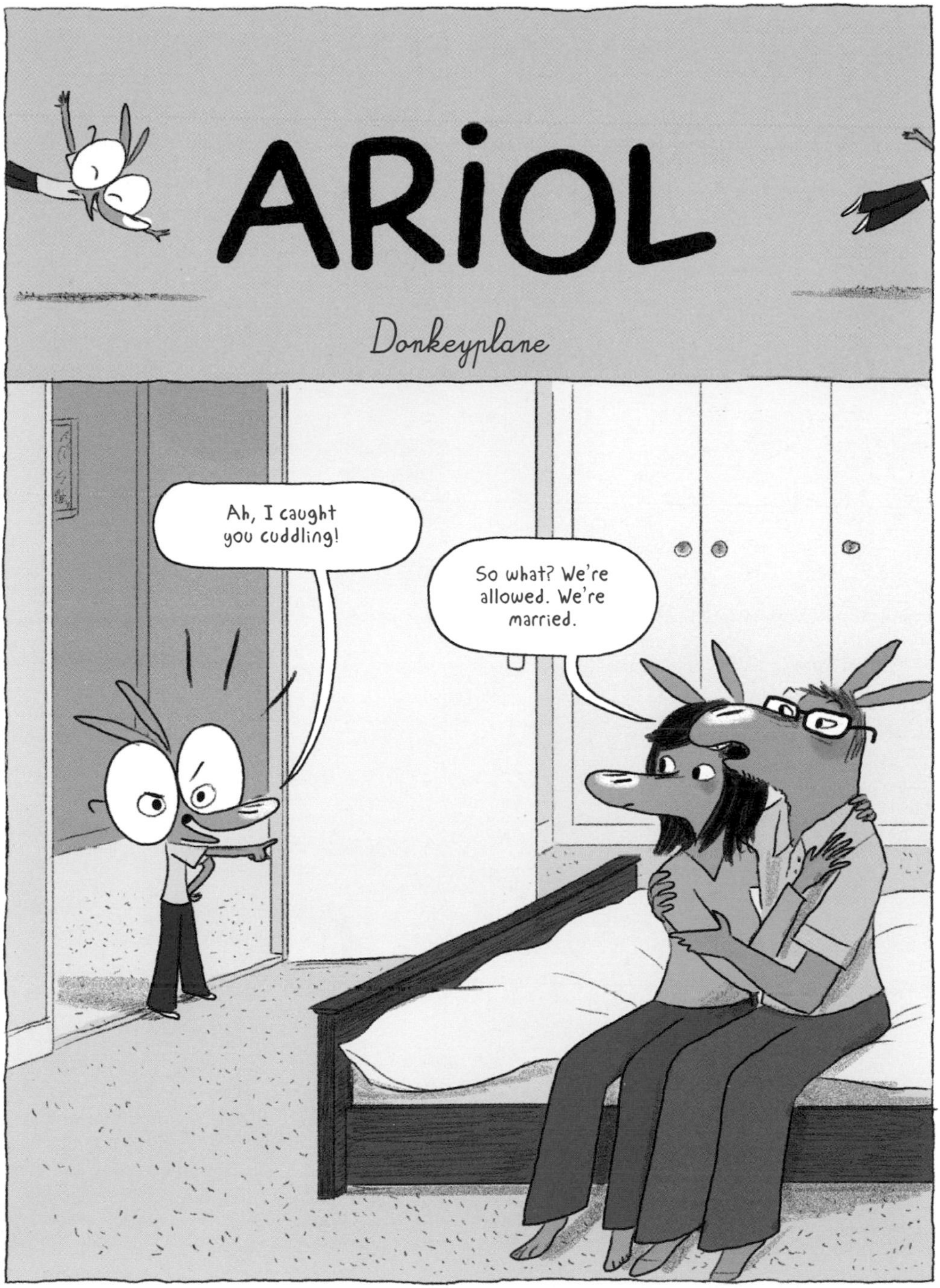
ARiOL
Donkeyplane
Ah, I caught you cuddling!
So what? We're allowed. We're married.

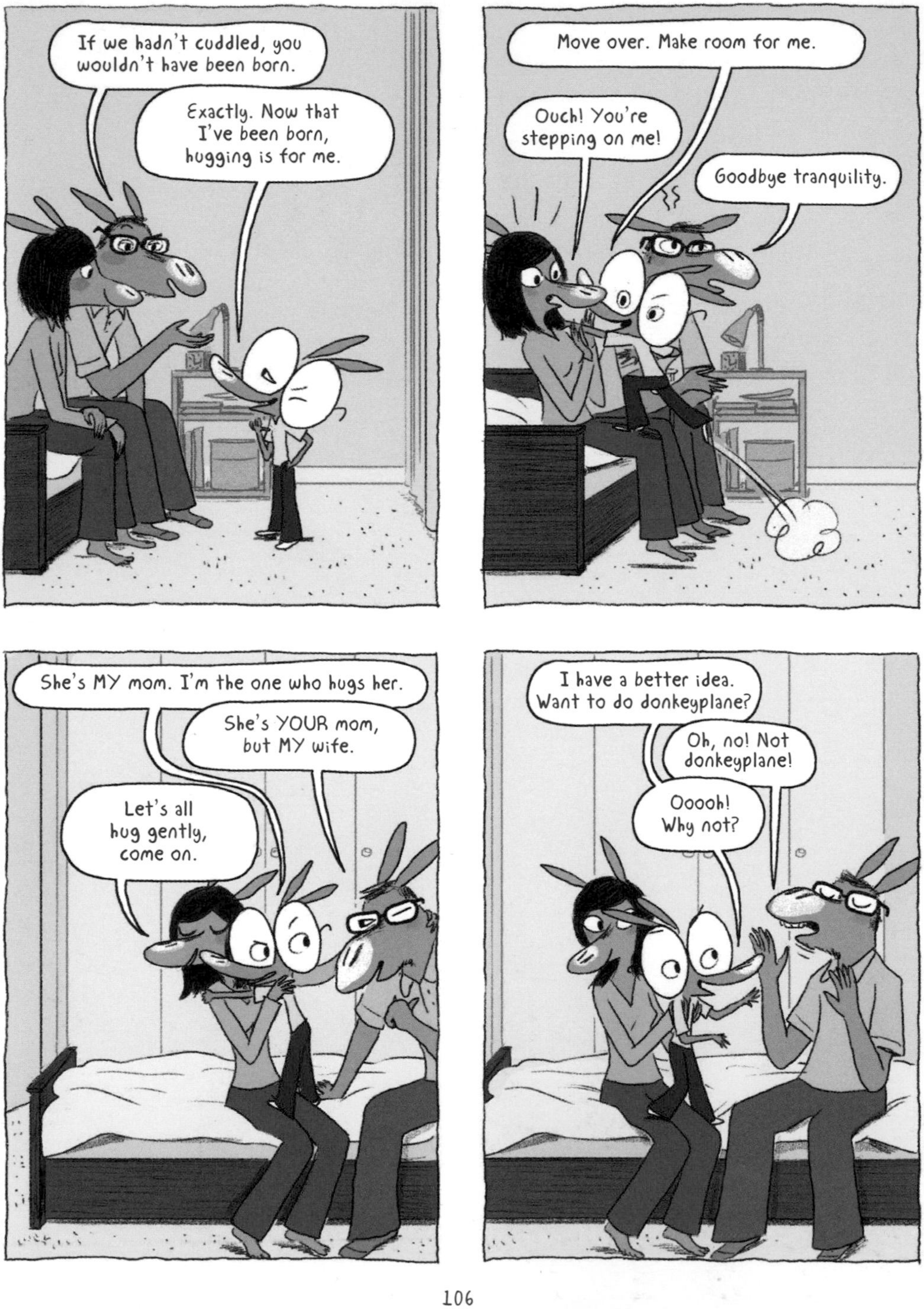
If we hadn't cuddled, you wouldn't have been born.
Exactly. Now that I've been born, hugging is for me.
Move over. Make room for me.
Ouch! You're stepping on me!
Goodbye tranquility.
She's MY mom. I'm the one who hugs her.
She's YOUR mom, but MY wife.
Let's all hug gently, come on.
I have a better idea. Want to do donkeyplane?
Oh, no! Not donkeyplane!
Ooooh! Why not?

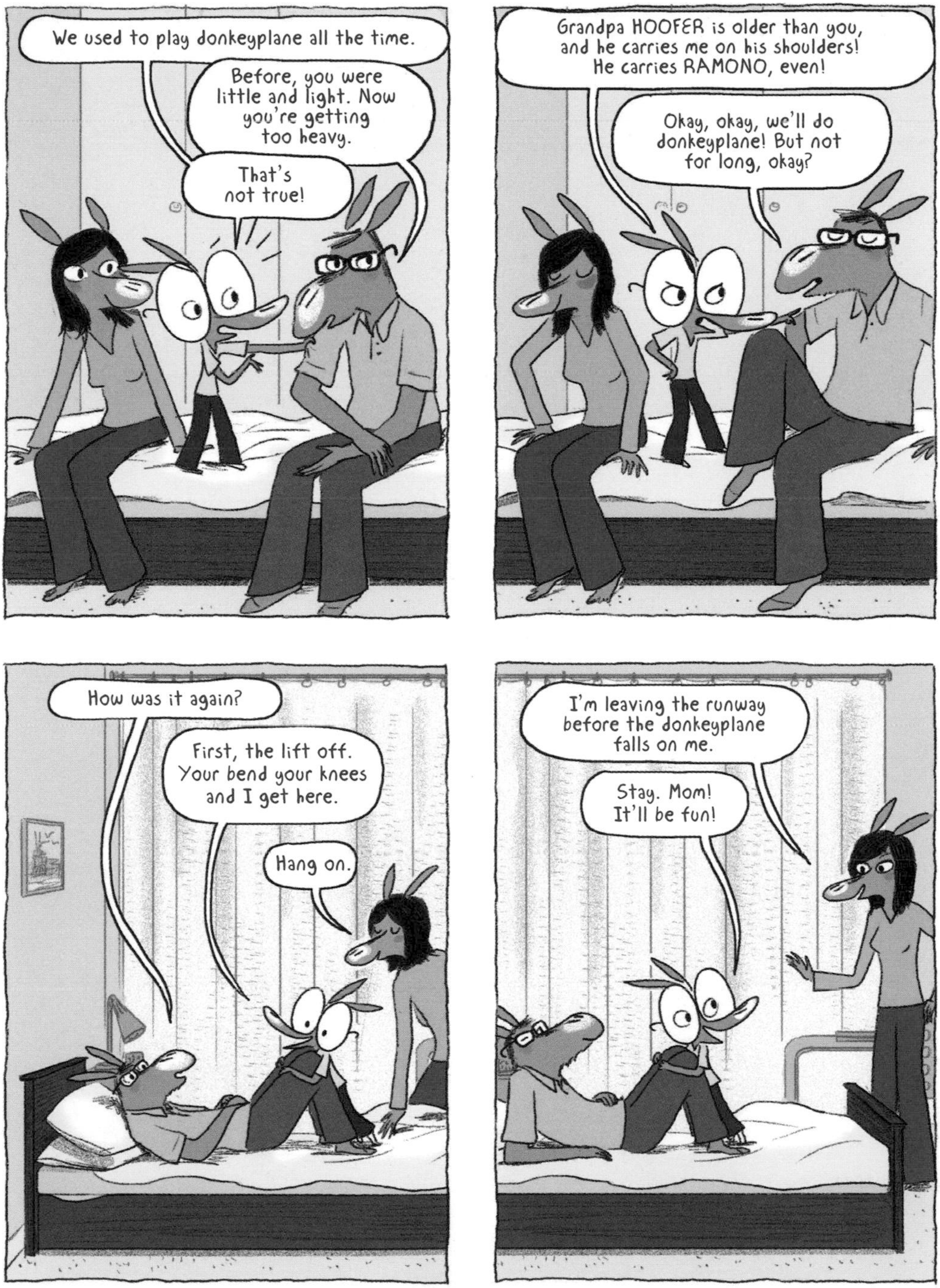
We used to play donkeyplane all the time.
Before, you were little and light. Now you're getting too heavy.
That's not true!
Grandpa HOOFER is older than you, and he carries me on his shoulders! He carries RAMONO, even!
Okay, okay, we'll do donkeyplane! But not for long, okay?
How was it again?
First, the lift off. Your bend your knees and I get here.
Hang on.
I'm leaving the runway before the donkeyplane falls on me.
Stay. Mom! It'll be fun!

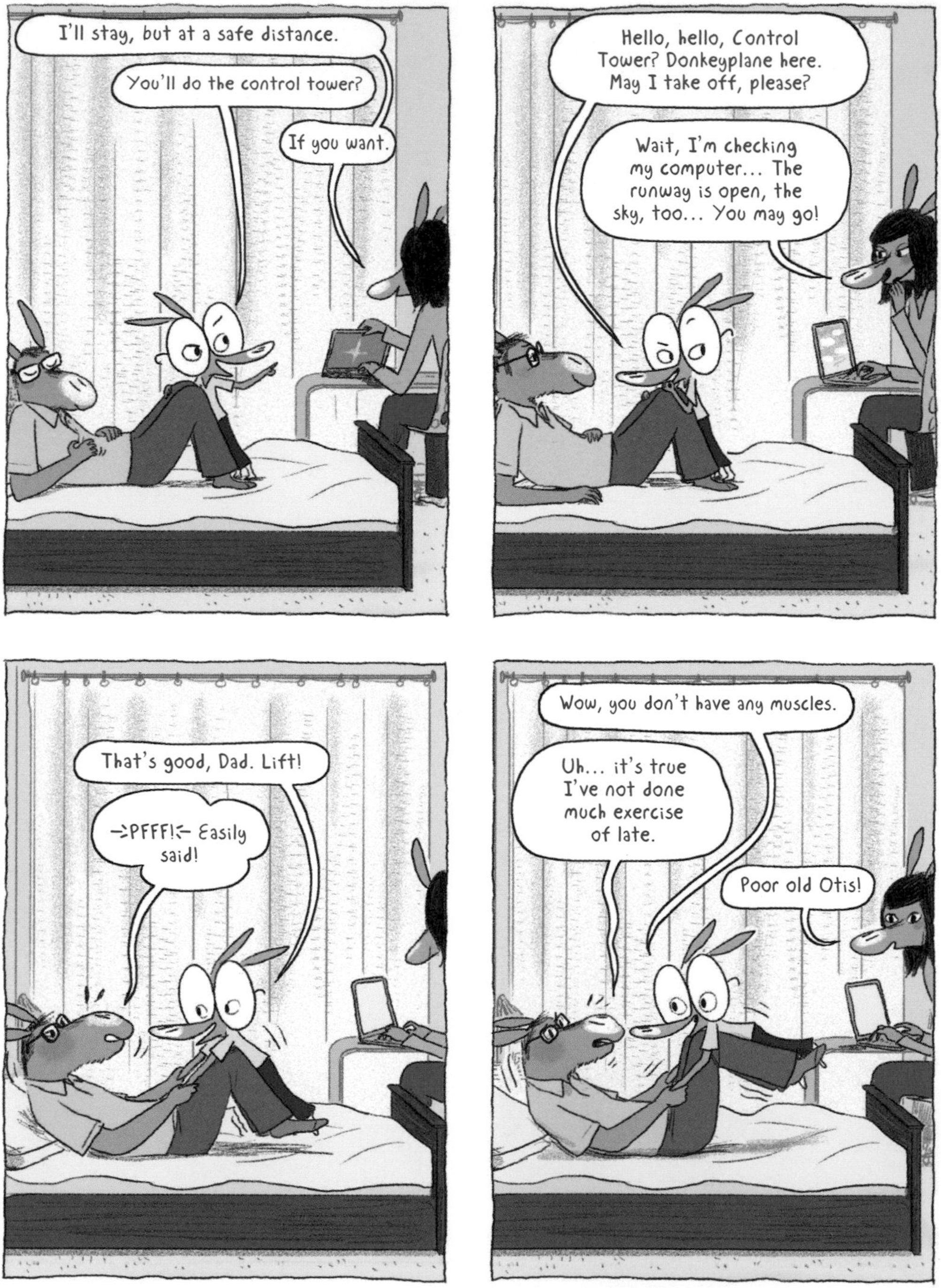
I'll stay, but at a safe distance.
You'll do the control tower?
If you want.
Hello, hello, Control Tower? Donkeyplane here. May I take off, please?
Wait, I'm checking my computer... The runway is open, the sky, too... You may go!
That's good, Dad. Lift!
⇒PFFF!⇐ Easily said!
Wow, you don't have any muscles.
Uh... it's true I've not done much exercise of late.
Poor old Otis!

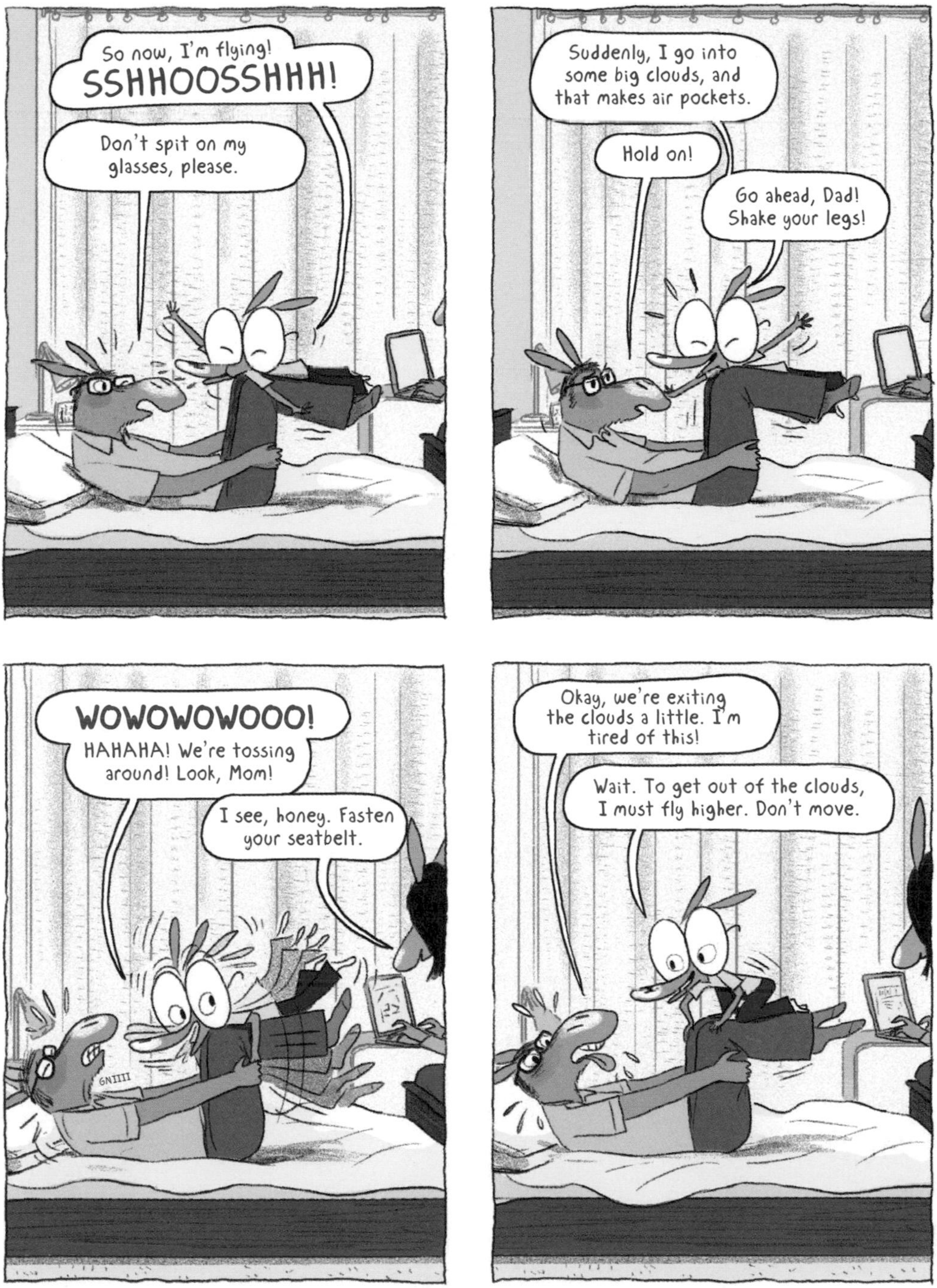

So now, I'm flying! SSHHOOSSHHH!
Don't spit on my glasses, please.
Suddenly, I go into some big clouds, and that makes air pockets.
Hold on!
Go ahead, Dad! Shake your legs!
WOWOWOWOOO! HAHAHA! We're tossing around! Look, Mom!
I see, honey. Fasten your seatbelt.
GNIIII
Okay, we're exiting the clouds a little. I'm tired of this!
Wait. To get out of the clouds, I must fly higher. Don't move.

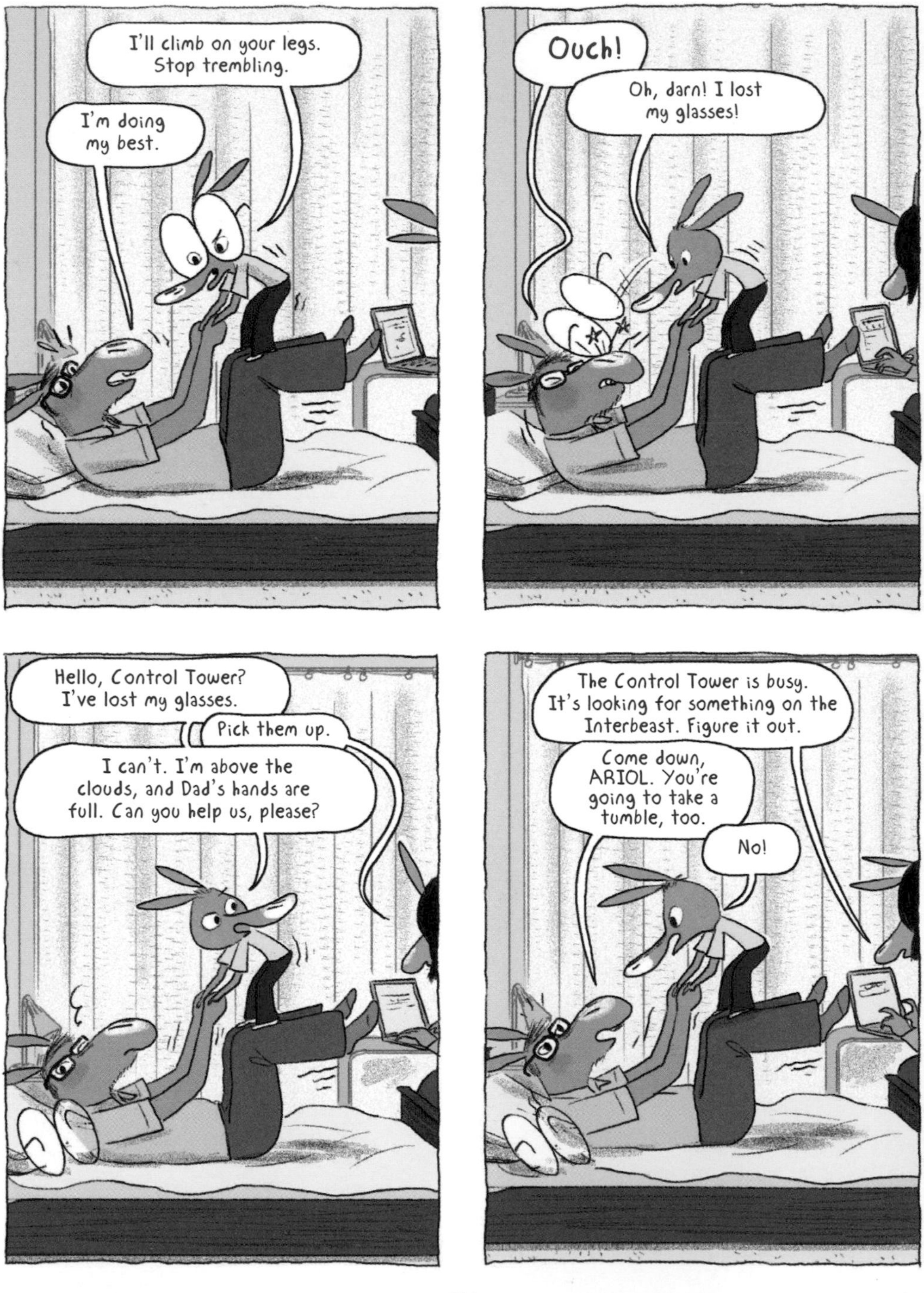
I'm doing my best.
I'll climb on your legs. Stop trembling.
Ouch!
Oh, darn! I lost my glasses!
Hello, Control Tower? I've lost my glasses.
Pick them up.
I can't. I'm above the clouds, and Dad's hands are full. Can you help us, please?
The Control Tower is busy. It's looking for something on the Interbeast. Figure it out.
Come down, ARIOL. You're going to take a tumble, too.
No!

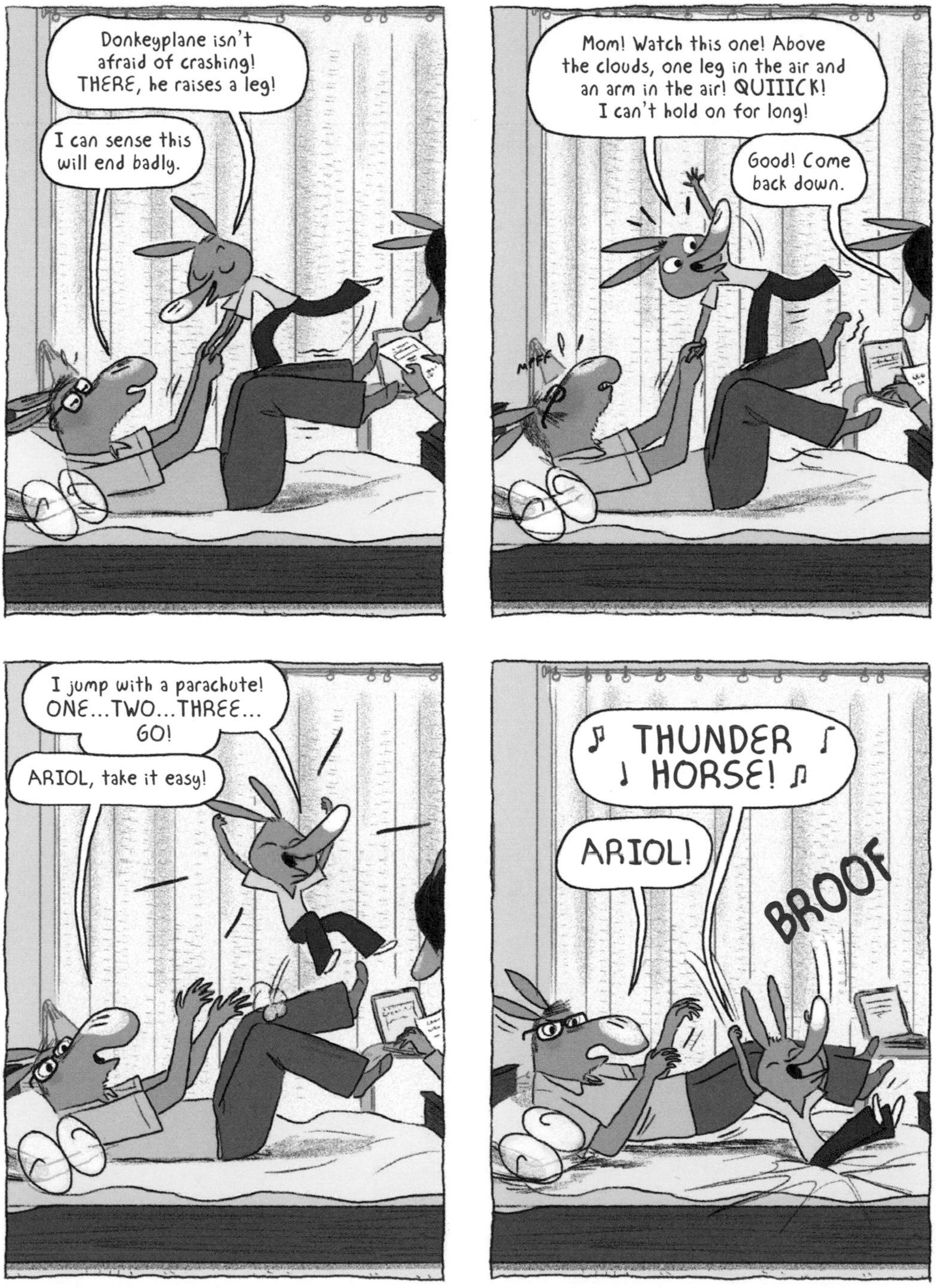

Donkeyplane isn't afraid of crashing! THERE, he raises a leg!
I can sense this will end badly.
Mom! Watch this one! Above the clouds, one leg in the air and an arm in the air! QUIIICK! I can't hold on for long!
MPFF
Good! Come back down.
I jump with a parachute! ONE...TWO...THREE... GO!
ARIOL, take it easy!
♪ THUNDER HORSE! ♫
ARIOL!
BROOF

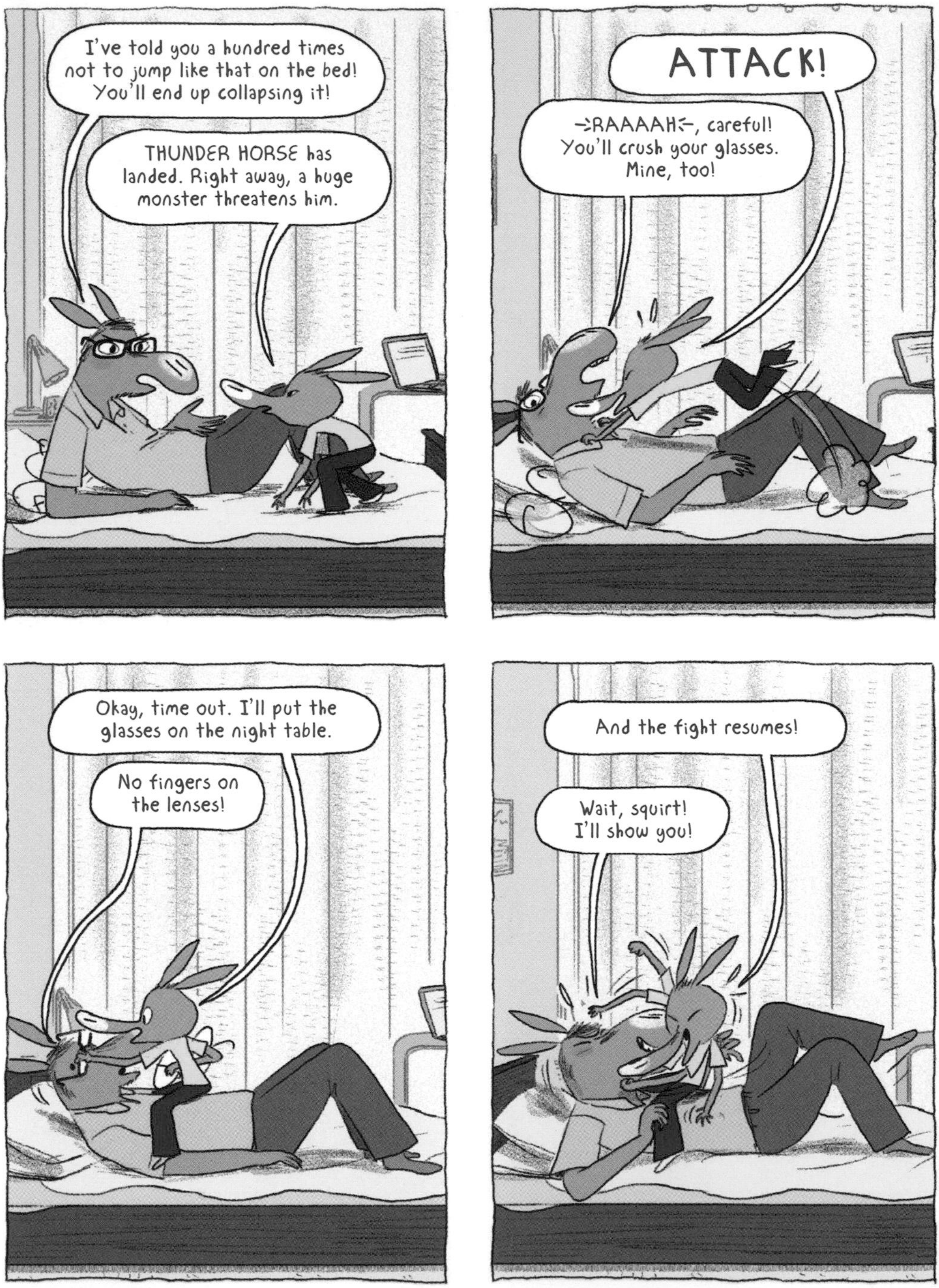
I've told you a hundred times not to jump like that on the bed! You'll end up collapsing it!
THUNDER HORSE has landed. Right away, a huge monster threatens him.
ATTACK!
⇝RAAAAH⇜, careful! You'll crush your glasses. Mine, too!
Okay, time out. I'll put the glasses on the night table.
No fingers on the lenses!
And the fight resumes!
Wait, squirt! I'll show you!

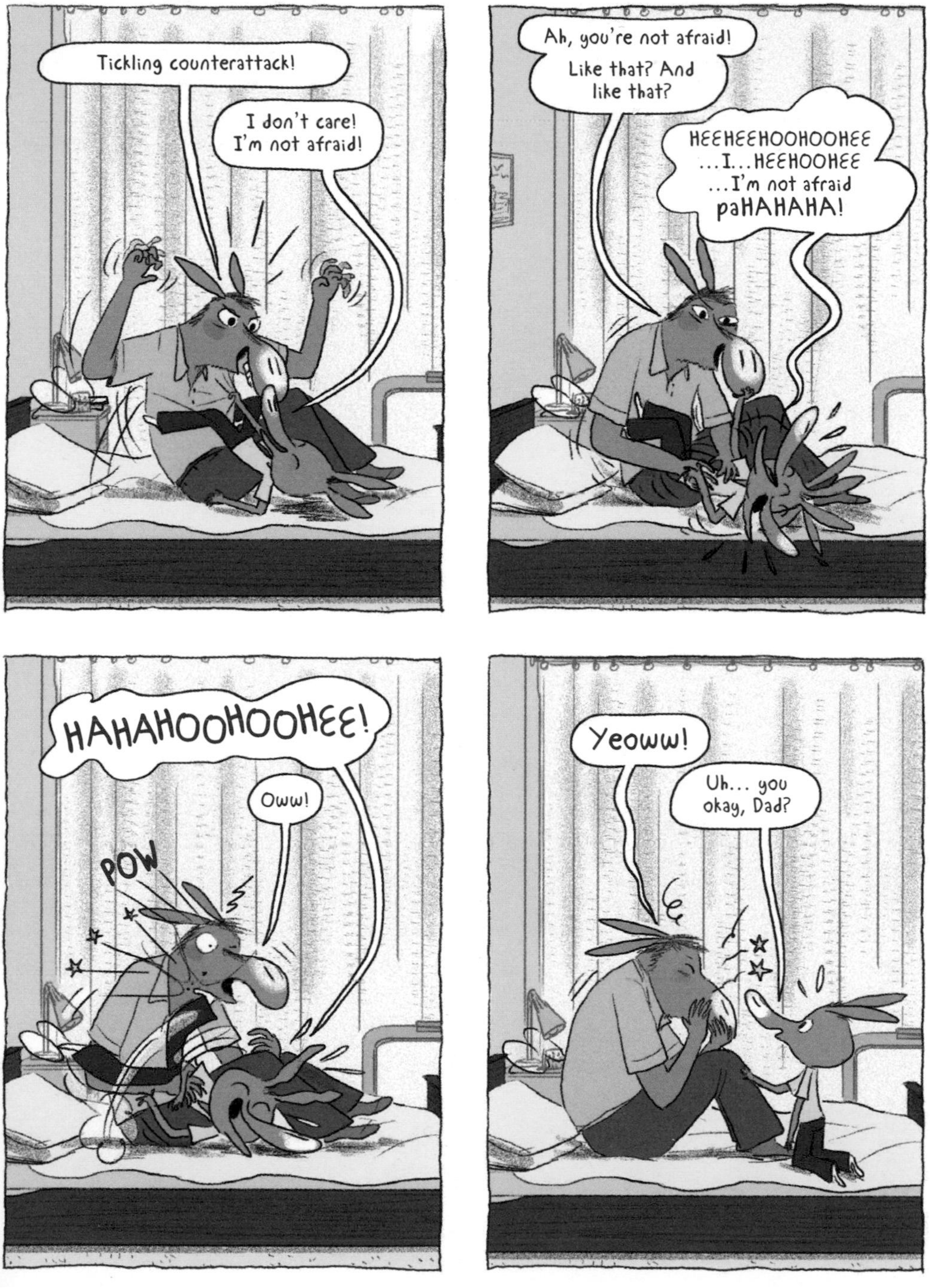
Tickling counterattack!
I don't care! I'm not afraid!
Ah, you're not afraid!
Like that? And like that?
HEEHEEHOOHOOHEE ...I...HEEHOOHEE ...I'm not afraid paHAHAHA!
HAHAHOOHOOHEE!
Oww!
POW
Yeoww!
Uh... you okay, Dad?

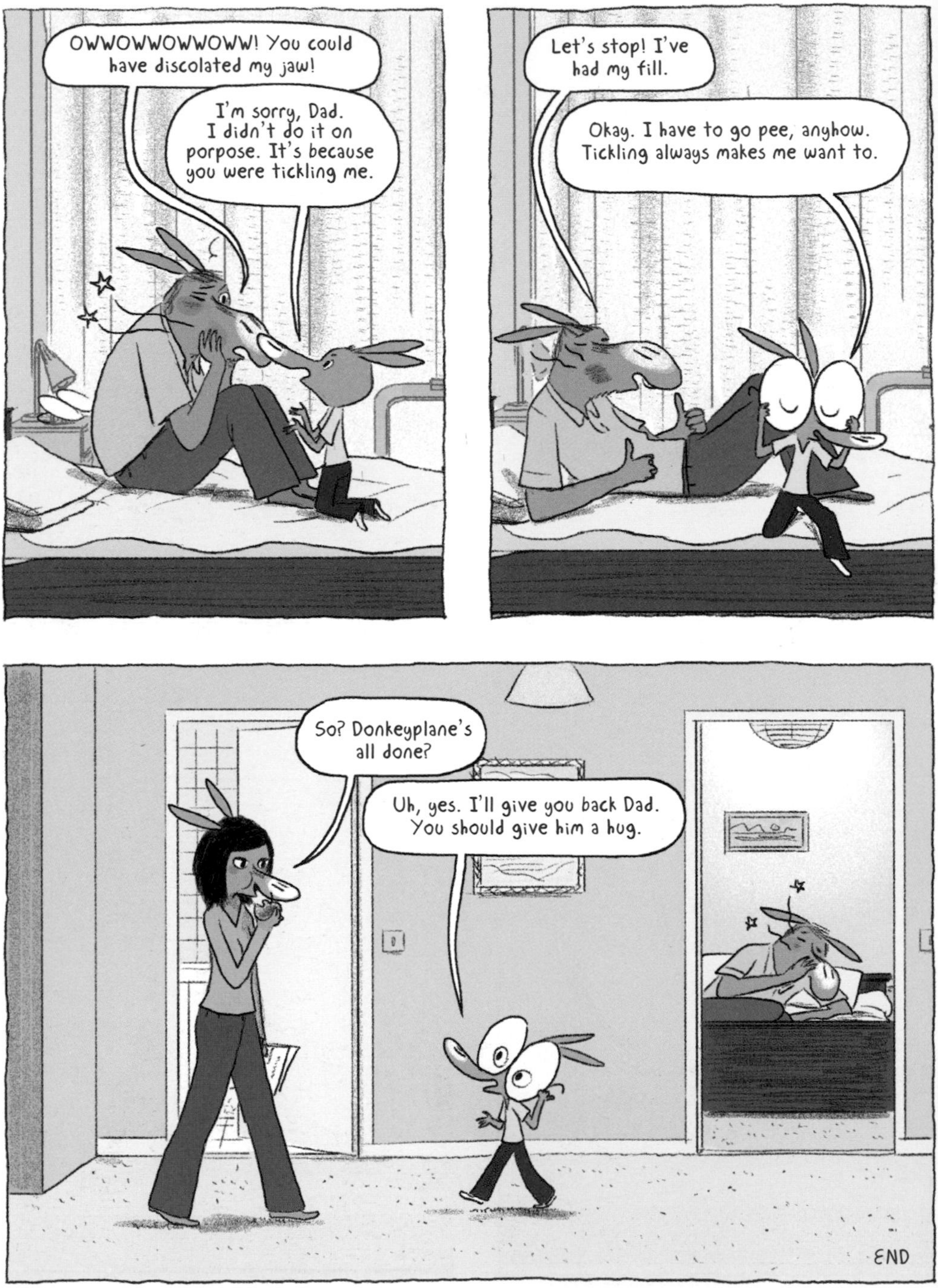

OWWOWWOWWOWW! You could have discolated my jaw!
I'm sorry, Dad. I didn't do it on porpose. It's because you were tickling me.
Let's stop! I've had my fill.
Okay. I have to go pee, anyhow. Tickling always makes me want to.
So? Donkeyplane's all done?
Uh, yes. I'll give you back Dad. You should give him a hug.
END

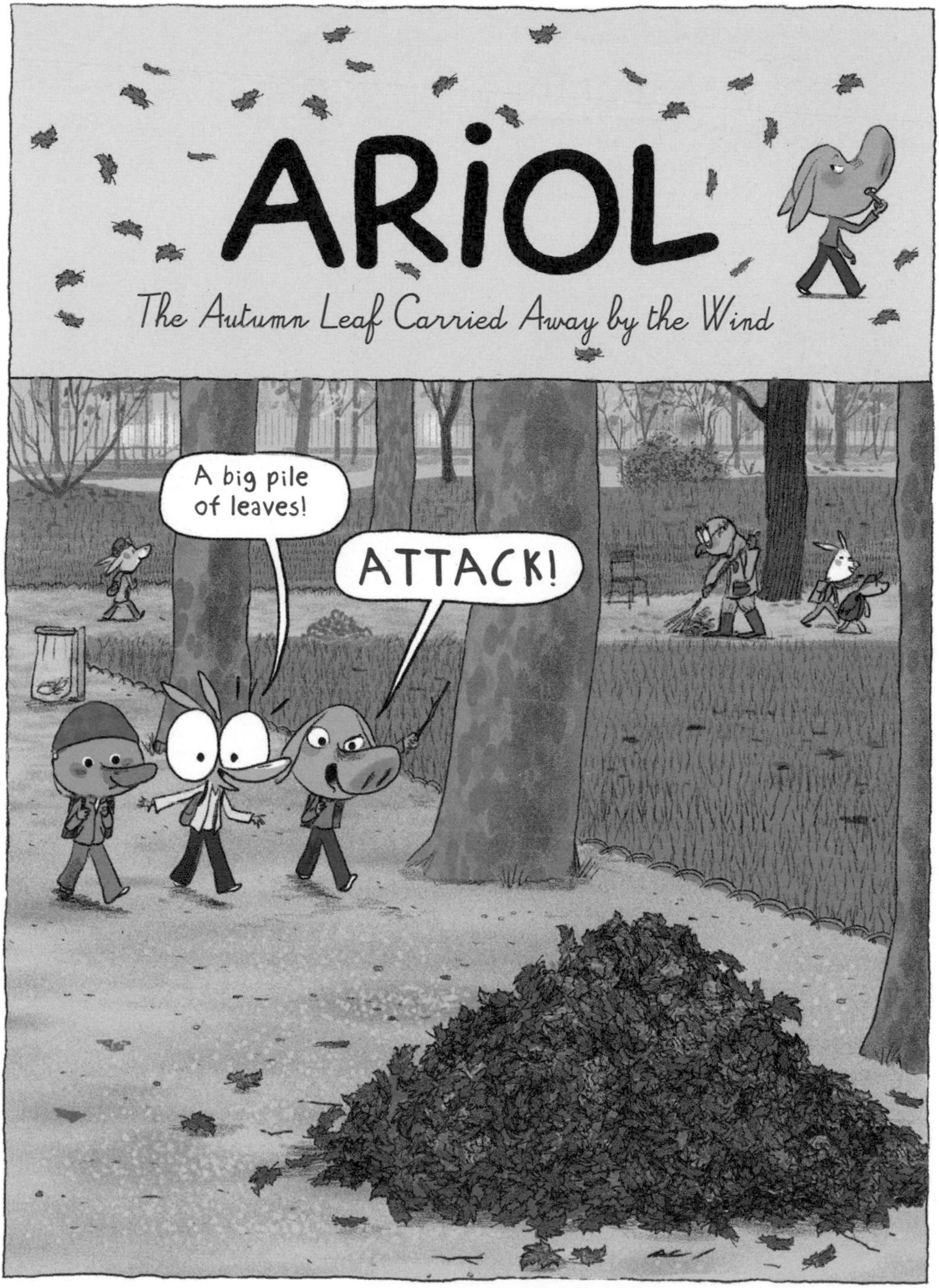
ARiOL
The Autumn Leaf Carried Away by the Wind
A big pile of leaves!
ATTACK!

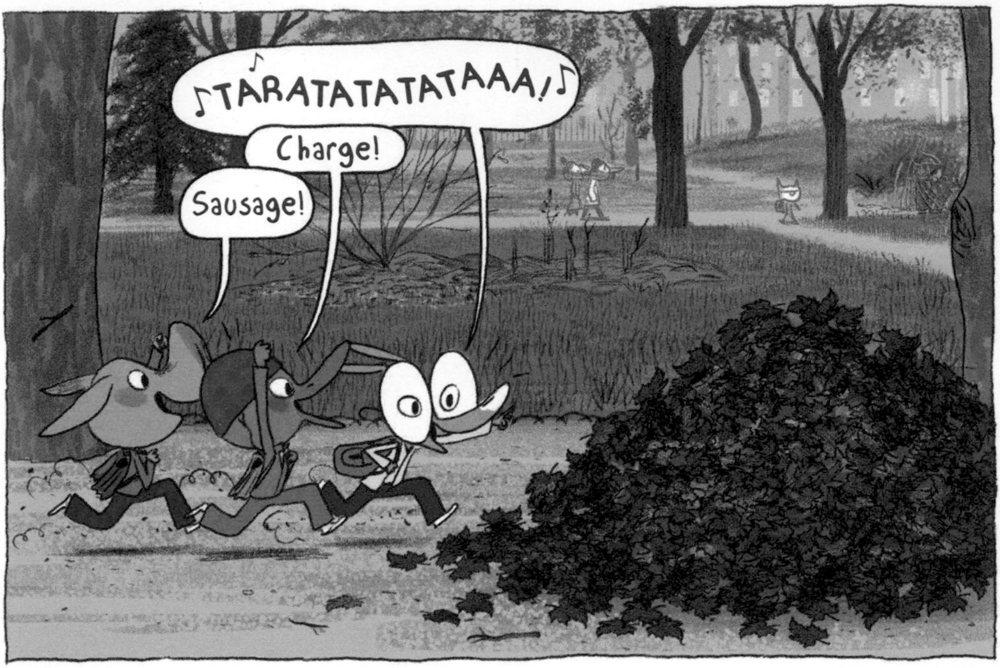
♪TARATATATATAAA!♪
Charge!
Sausage!

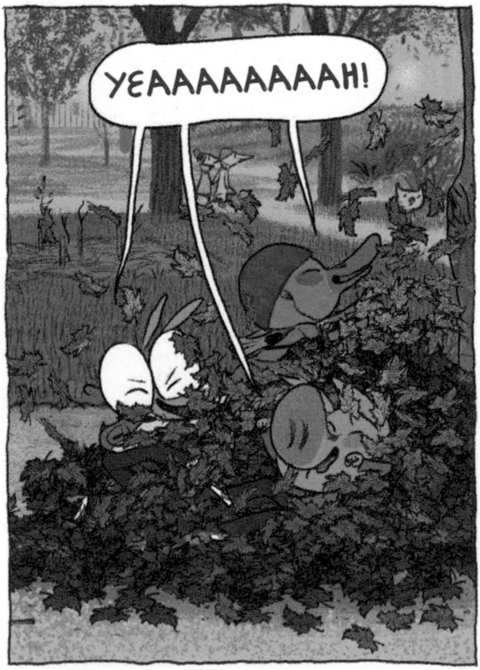
YEAAAAAAAAH!

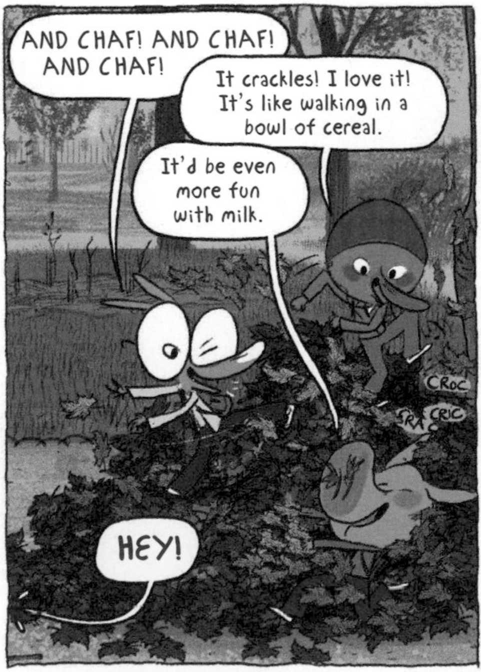
AND CHAF! AND CHAF! AND CHAF!
It crackles! I love it! It's like walking in a bowl of cereal.
It'd be even more fun with milk.
CROC
CRIC
HEY!

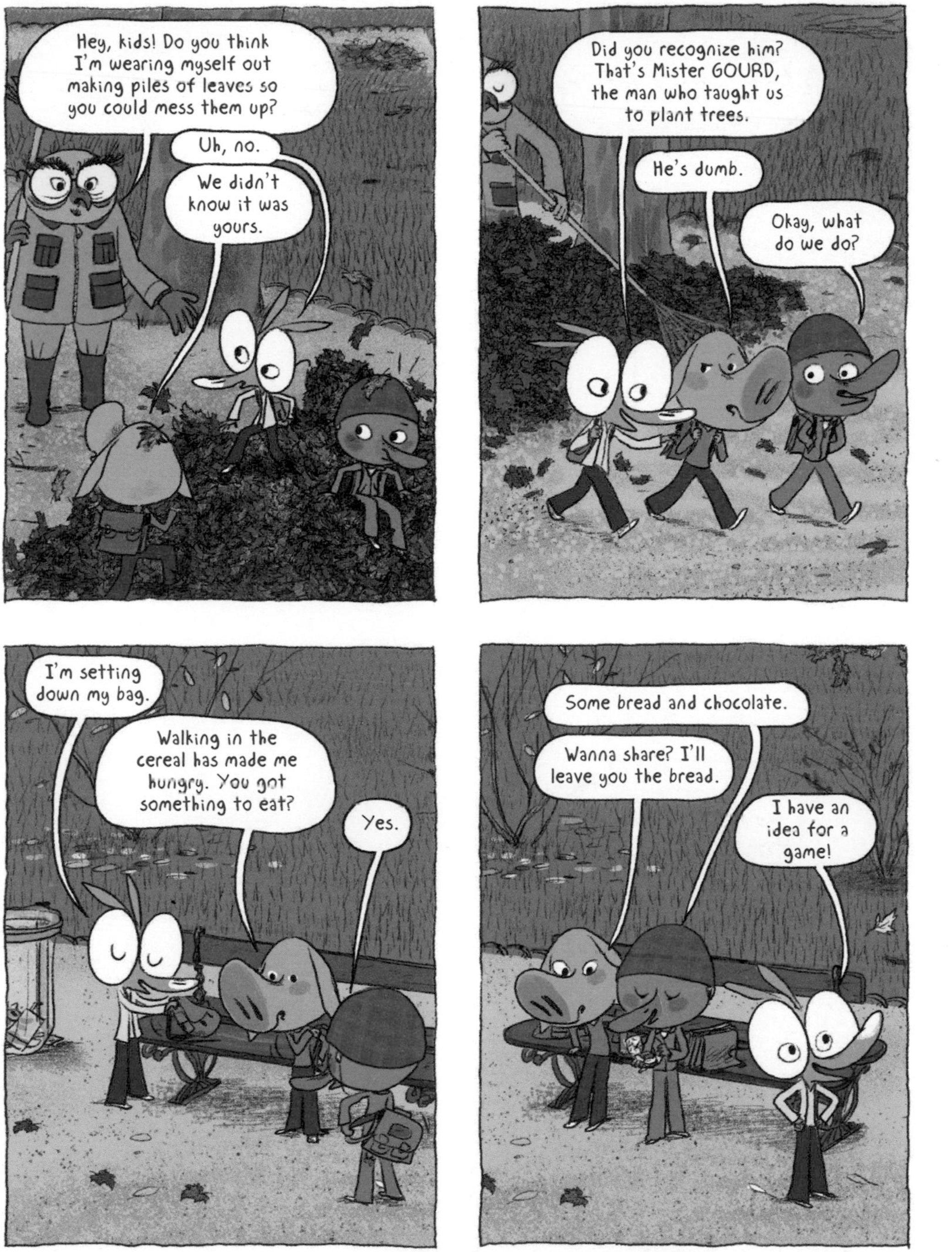
Hey, kids! Do you think I'm wearing myself out making piles of leaves so you could mess them up?
Uh, no.
We didn't know it was yours.
Did you recognize him? That's Mister GOURD, the man who taught us to plant trees.
He's dumb.
Okay, what do we do?
I'm setting down my bag.
Walking in the cereal has made me hungry. You got something to eat?
Yes.
Some bread and chocolate.
Wanna share? I'll leave you the bread.
I have an idea for a game!

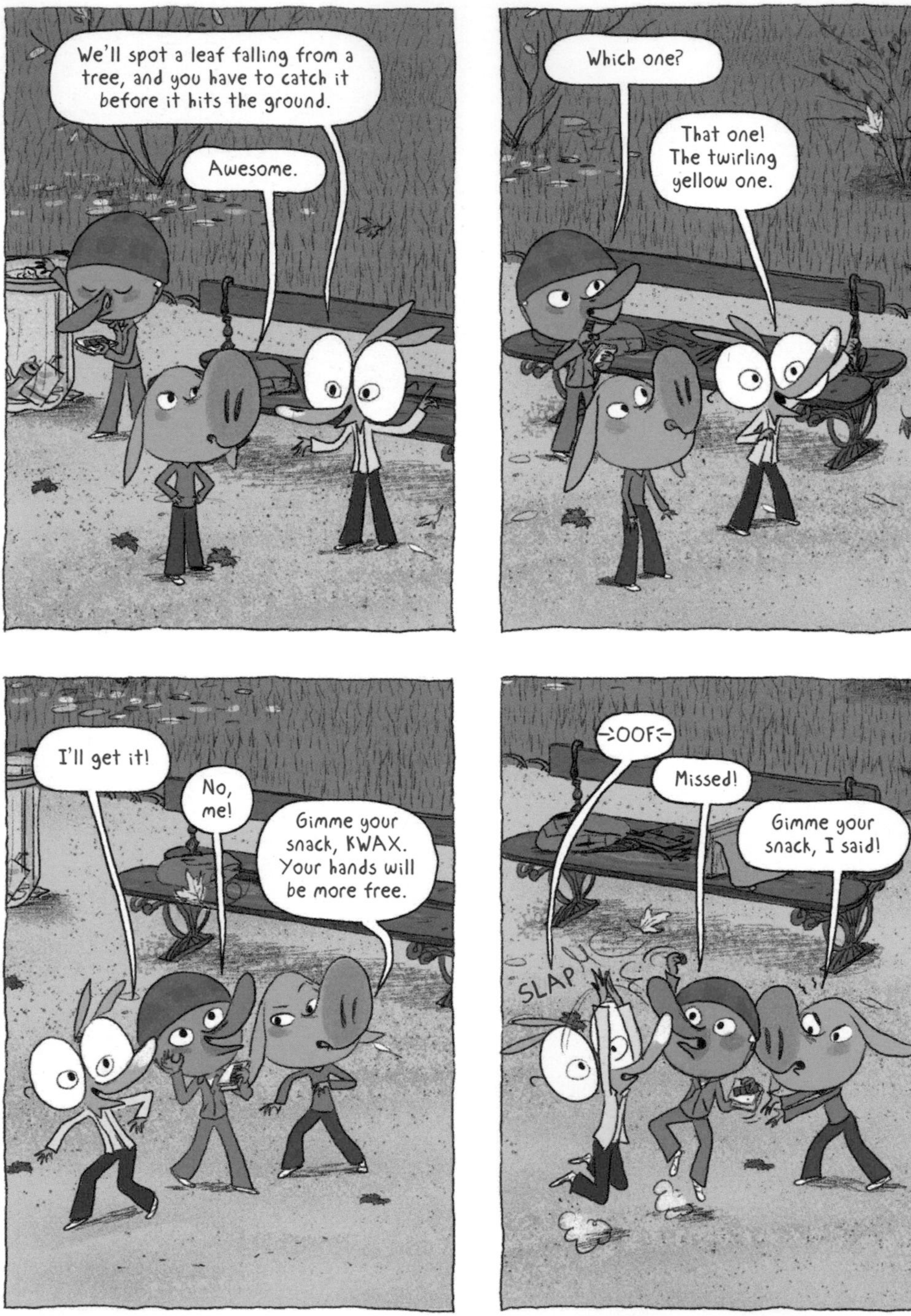
We'll spot a leaf falling from a tree, and you have to catch it before it hits the ground.
Awesome.
Which one?
That one! The twirling yellow one.
I'll get it!
No, me!
Gimme your snack, KWAX. Your hands will be more free.
OOF
Missed!
Gimme your snack, I said!
SLAP

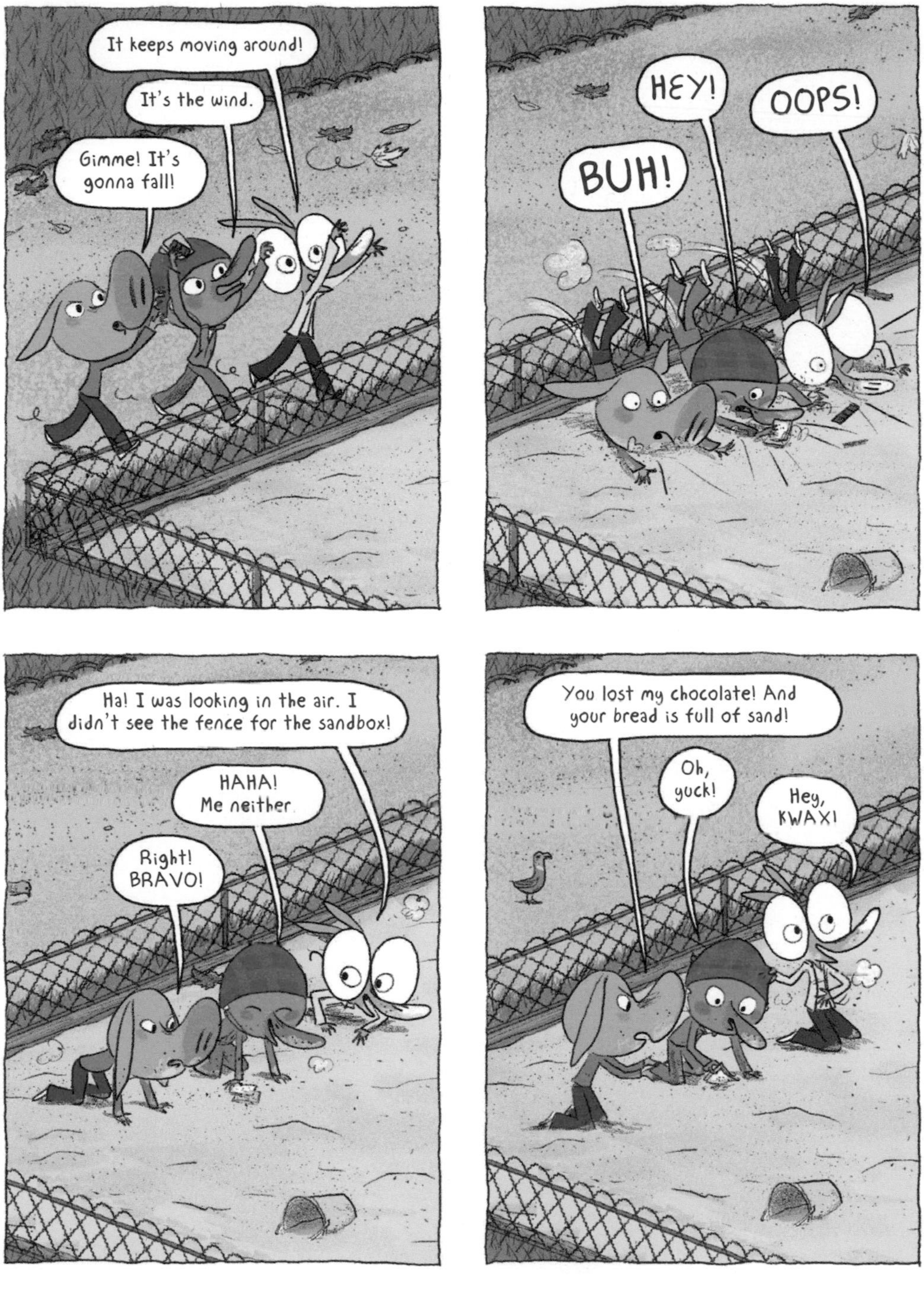

It keeps moving around!
It's the wind.
Gimme! It's gonna fall!
HEY!
OOPS!
BUH!
Ha! I was looking in the air. I didn't see the fence for the sandbox!
HAHA! Me neither.
Right! BRAVO!
You lost my chocolate! And your bread is full of sand!
Oh, yuck!
Hey, KWAX!

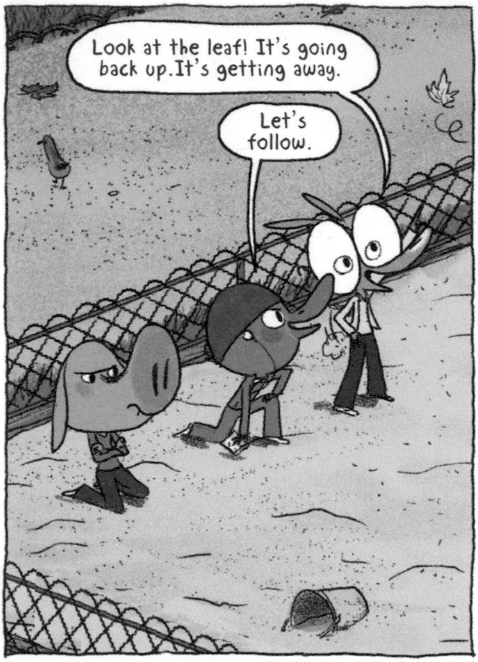
Look at the leaf! It's going back up.It's getting away.
Let's follow.

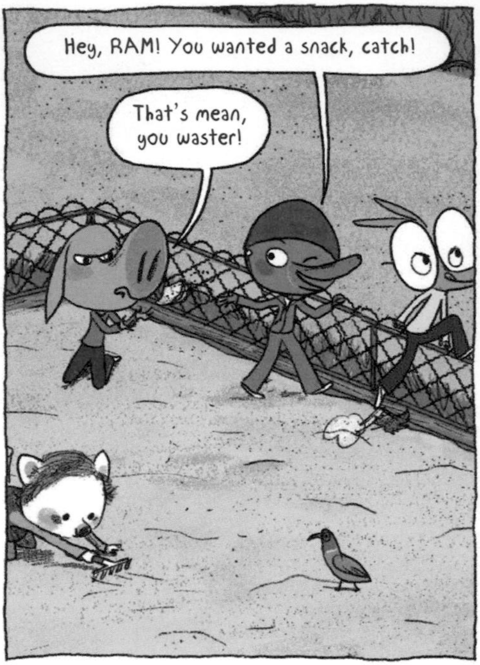
Hey, RAM! You wanted a snack, catch!
That's mean, you waster!

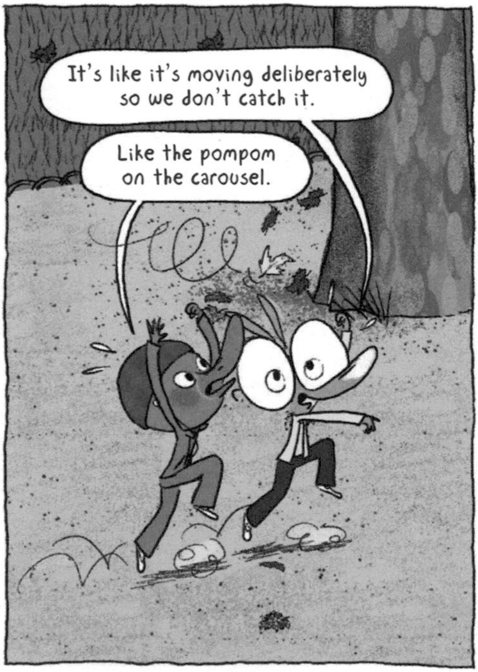
It's like it's moving deliberately so we don't catch it.
Like the pompom on the carousel.

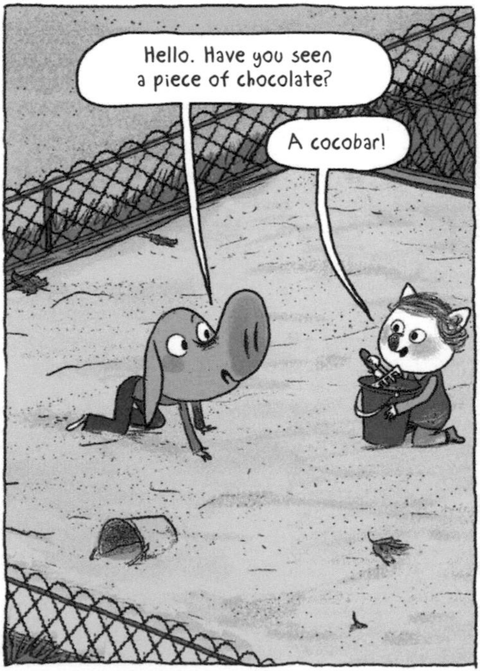
Hello. Have you seen a piece of chocolate?
A cocobar!

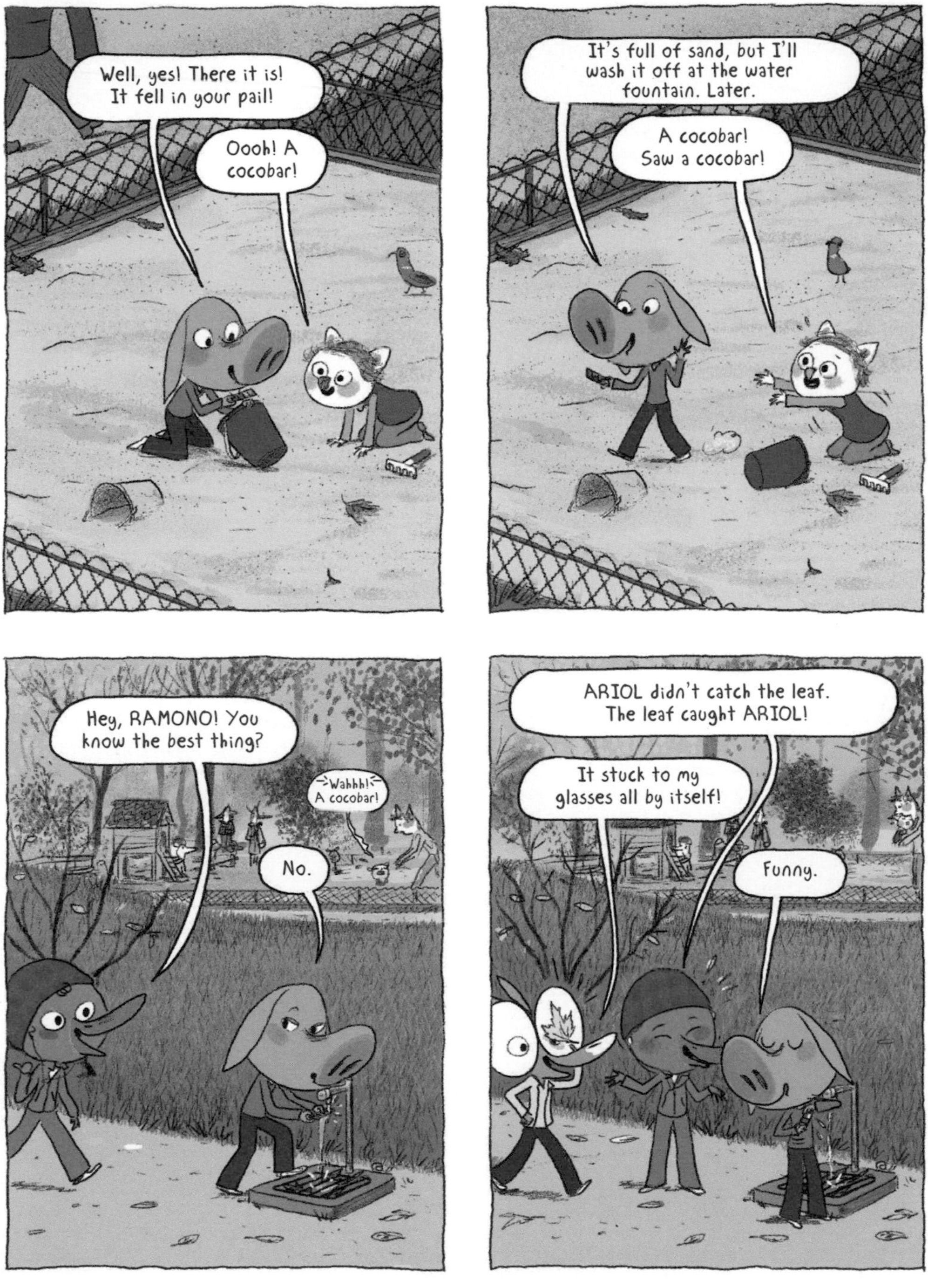

Well, yes! There it is! It fell in your pail!
Oooh! A cocobar!
It's full of sand, but I'll wash it off at the water fountain. Later.
A cocobar! Saw a cocobar!
Hey, RAMONO! You know the best thing?
Wahhh! A cocobar!
No.
ARIOL didn't catch the leaf. The leaf caught ARIOL!
It stuck to my glasses all by itself!
Funny.

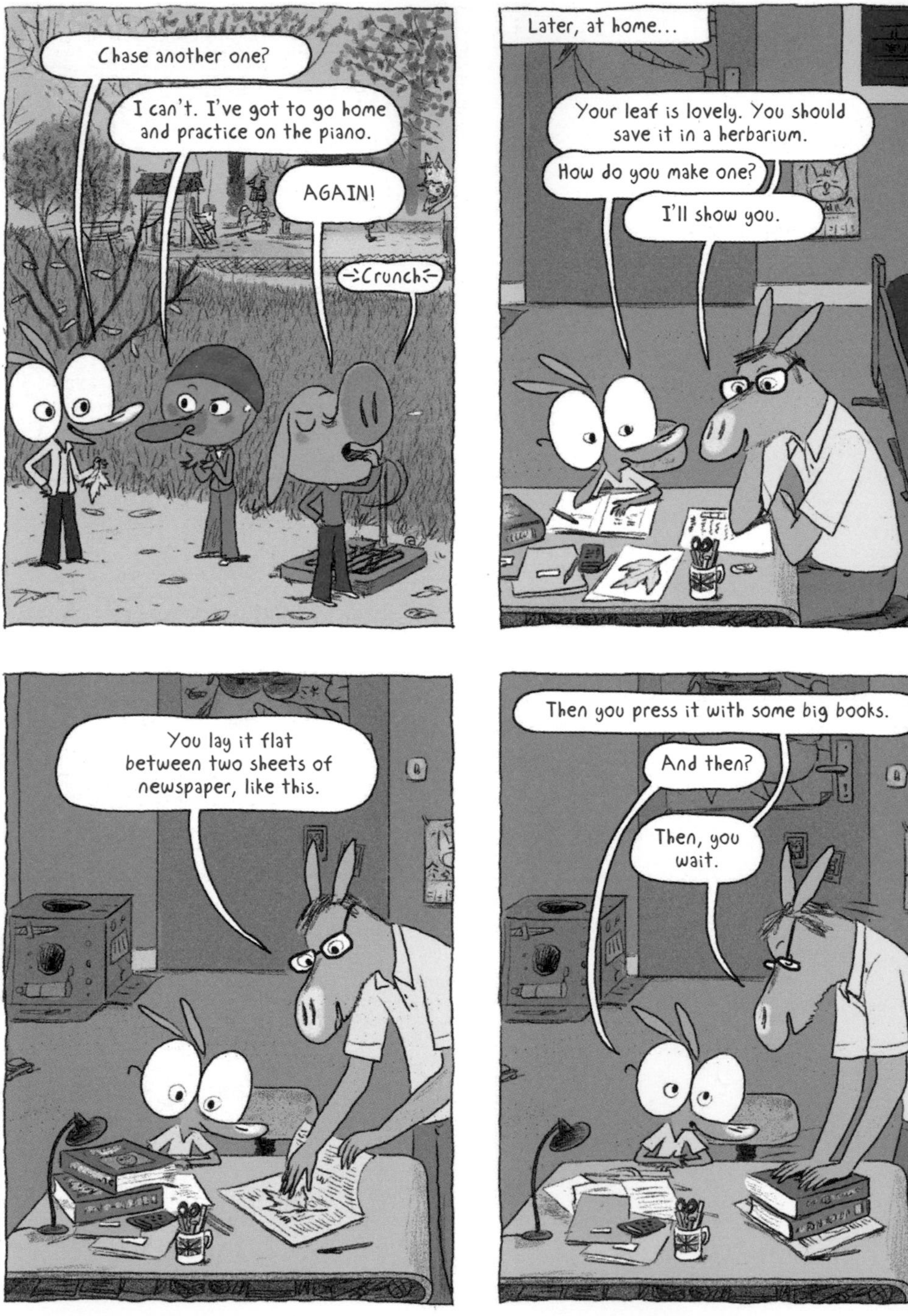
Chase another one?
I can't. I've got to go home and practice on the piano.
AGAIN!
Crunch
Later, at home...
Your leaf is lovely. You should save it in a herbarium.
How do you make one?
I'll show you.
You lay it flat between two sheets of newspaper, like this.
Then you press it with some big books.
And then?
Then, you wait.

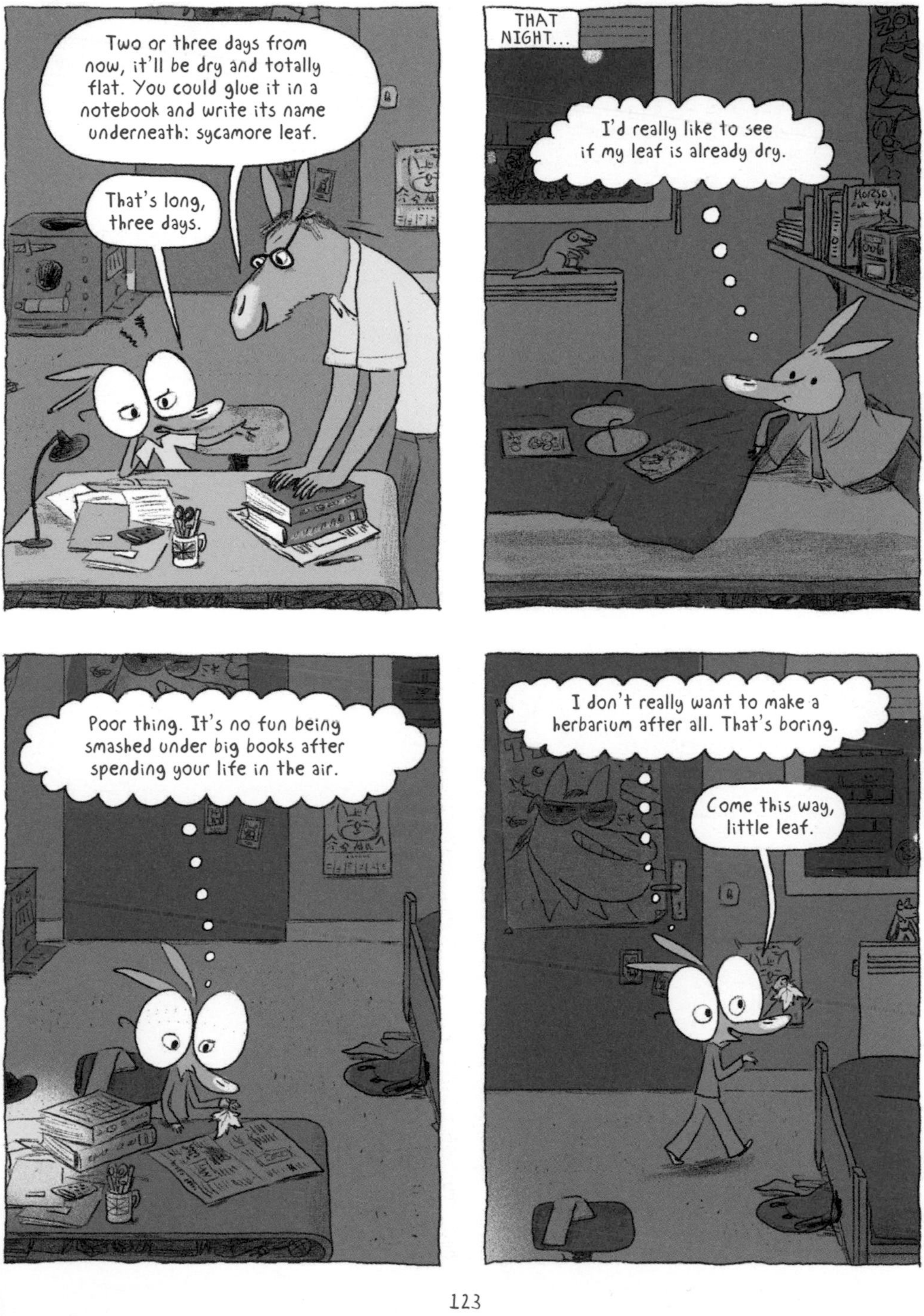
Two or three days from now, it'll be dry and totally flat. You could glue it in a notebook and write its name underneath: sycamore leaf.
That's long, three days.
THAT NIGHT...
I'd really like to see if my leaf is already dry.
Poor thing. It's no fun being smashed under big books after spending your life in the air.
I don't really want to make a herbarium after all. That's boring.
Come this way, little leaf.

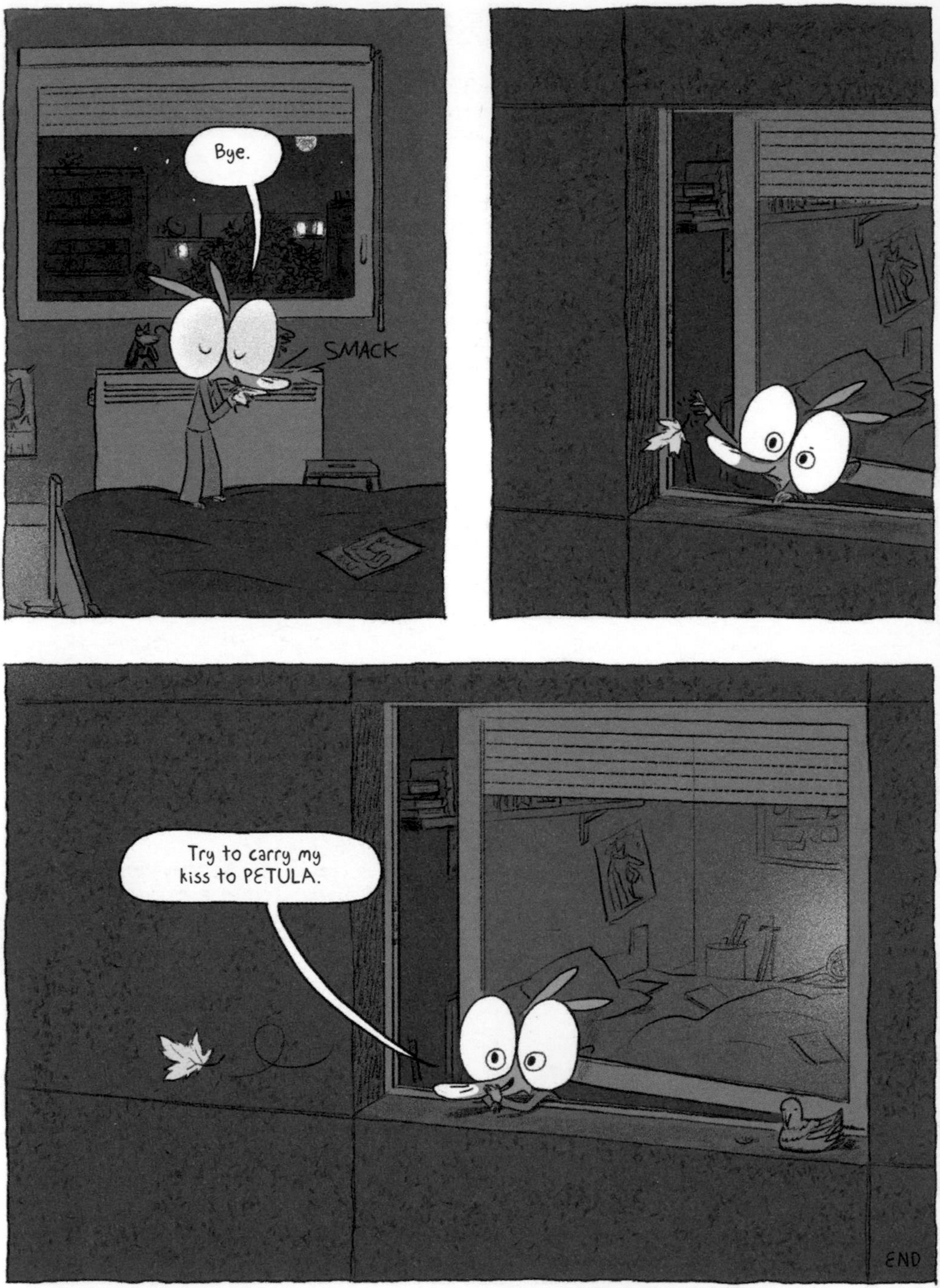

Bye.
SMACK
Try to carry my kiss to PETULA.
END

WATCH OUT FOR PAPERCUTZ™

Welcome to the enjoyable, enlightening eighth ARIOL graphic novel by the award-winning team of Emmanuel Guibert and Marc Boutavant, from Papercutz, those human-headed humans dedicated to publishing great graphic novels for all ages. I'm Jim Salicrup, the Editor-in-Chief and a donkey just like you (and Ariol).

If this is your very first ARIOL graphic novel, then you don't need me to tell you how wonderful these comics are, and if you've experienced ARIOL before, you definitely appreciate how great these comics are. So, instead of telling you what you already know, let me tip you off to an exciting comics project you may not be aware of... NICKELODEON MAGAZINE!

NICKELODEON MAGAZINE is mostly filled with all-new comics based on the latest and greatest Nickelodeon shows, such as...

SANJAY AND CRAIG, the story about a young boy, Sanjay Patel, and his talking snake, Craig. Like in ARIOL, there's quite a large cast of characters-- Sanjay's parents, friends, and Sanjay's idol-- his Thunder Horse-- Remington Tufflips, a B-movie action star.

BREADWINNERS-- the story of two odd ducks named SwaySway and Buhdeuce, who deliver all kinds of bread in their rocket van on the planet Pondgea.

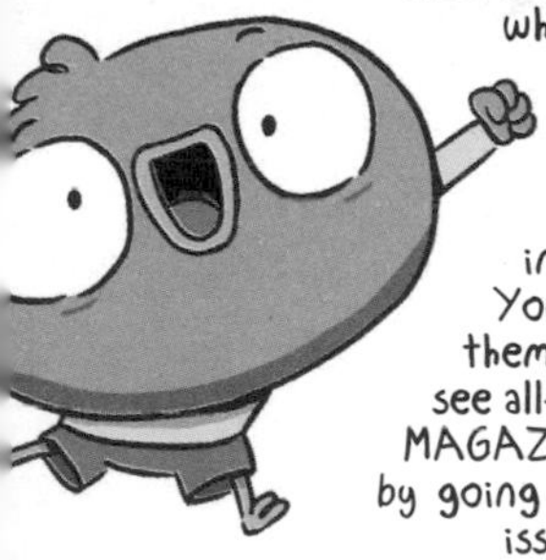

HARVEY BEAKS is also somewhat similar to ARIOL, except it's set in a wonderful wooded area. Harvey wishes he could be as wild and crazy as his two best friends Fee and Foo, and it's a lot of fun seeing him try.

PIG GOAT BANANA CRICKET is about four friends who happen to live in a world where almost anything is possible. Especially pranks.

You can check out all of the above shows on Nickelodeon, and if you enjoy them-- and we suspect you'll find at least one show to love-- you'll get to see all-new stories in NICKELODEON MAGAZINE every month. NICKELODEON MAGAZINE is available wherever magazines are sold, and you can subscribe too by going to papercutz.com. And if you're concerned that you missed the early issues of the mag-- don't worry! The Sanjay and Craig stories are collected in SANJAY AND CRAIG graphic novels, the Breadwinners stories are collected in BREADWINNERS graphic novels, the Harvey Beaks stories are collected in HARVEY BEAKS graphic novels, and surprisingly, the Pig Goat Banana Cricket stories are collected in PIG GOAT BANANA CRICKET graphic novels.

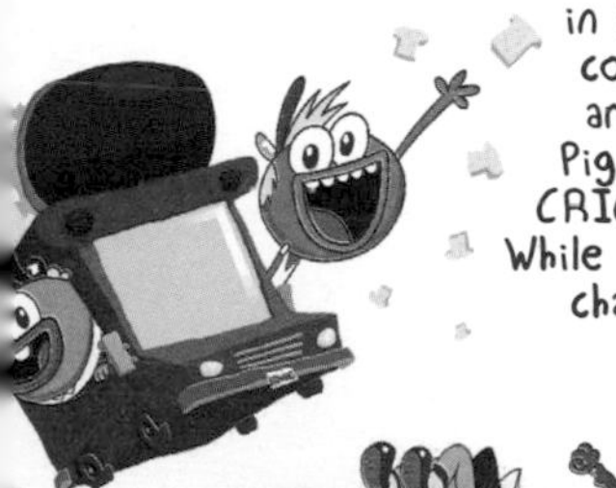

While NICKELODEON MAGAZINE is all about comics starring cartoon characters, did you know there are cartoons based on ARIOL? They were created in France, but you may find some of them on YouTube. They're very faithful to the comics. In fact, our translations of the original ARIOL comics use the character names (with the exception of Thunder Horse) created for the animated series.

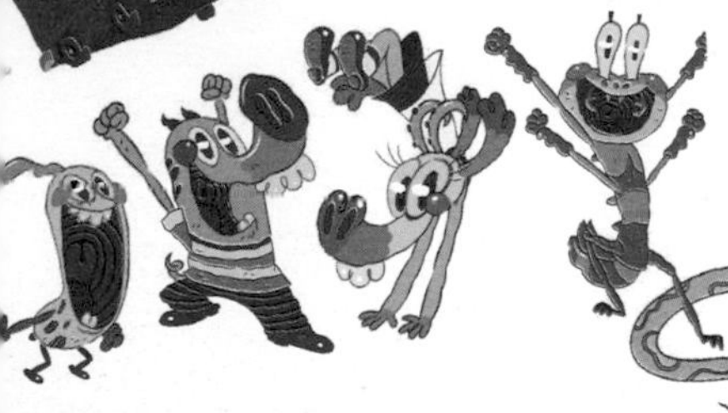

So, there you go! You now have plenty of other great comics and cartoons to check out until ARIOL #9 "The Teeth of the Rabbit."

And if that wasn't enough, go to papercutz.com for even more great graphic novels we're sure you'll love!

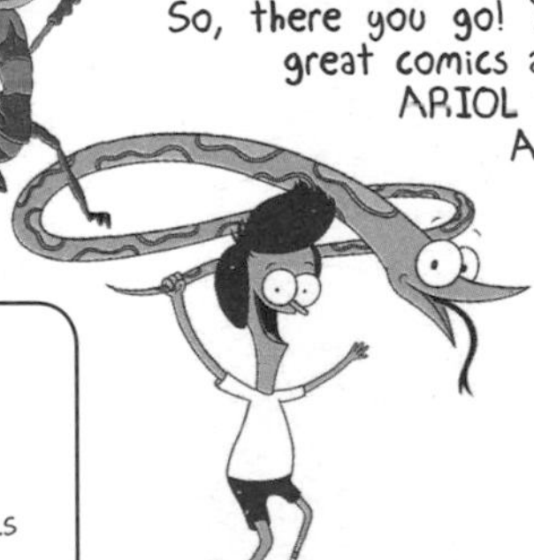

Thanks,

Jim

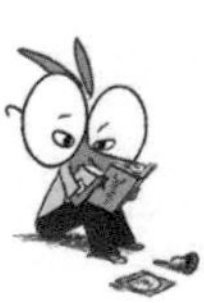

STAY IN TOUCH!

EMAIL:	salicrup@papercutz.com
WEB:	papercutz.com
TWITTER:	@papercutzgn
FACEBOOK:	PAPERCUTZGRAPHICNOVELS
REGULAR MAIL:	Papercutz, 160 Broadway, Suite 700, East Wing, New York, NY 10038

Other Great Titles From PAPERCUTZ™

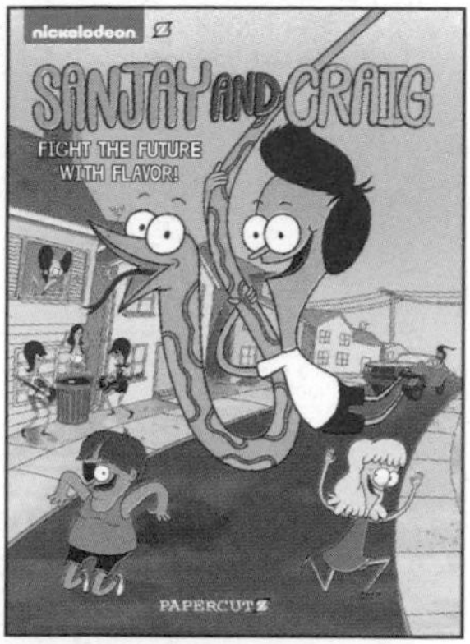
nickelodeon
SANJAY AND CRAIG
FIGHT THE FUTURE WITH FLAVOR!
PAPERCUTZ

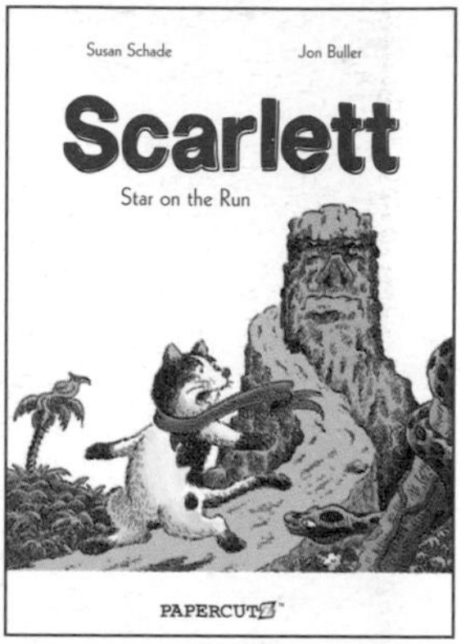
Susan Schade
Jon Buller
Scarlett
Star on the Run
PAPERCUTZ

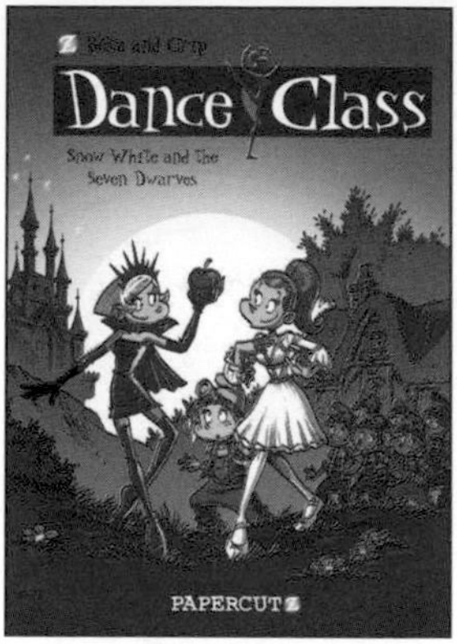
Dance Class
Snow White and The Seven Dwarves
PAPERCUTZ

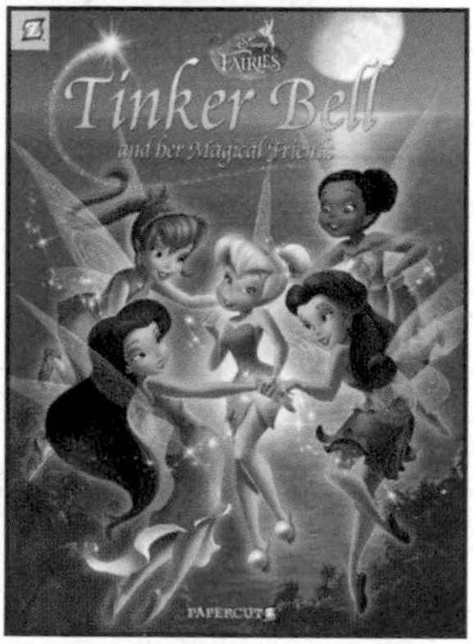
Tinker Bell
PAPERCUTZ

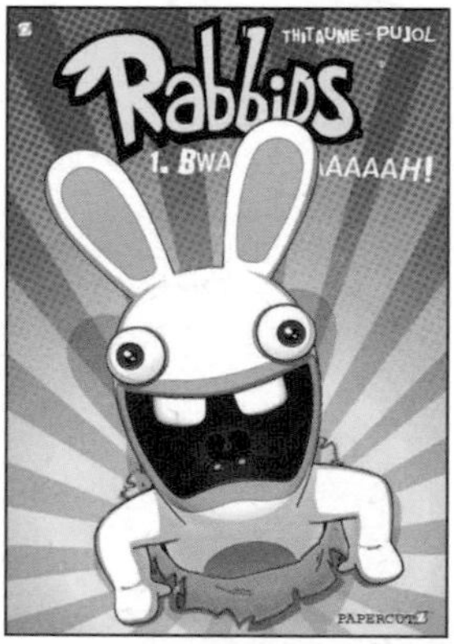
THITAUME - PUJOL
Rabbids
PAPERCUTZ

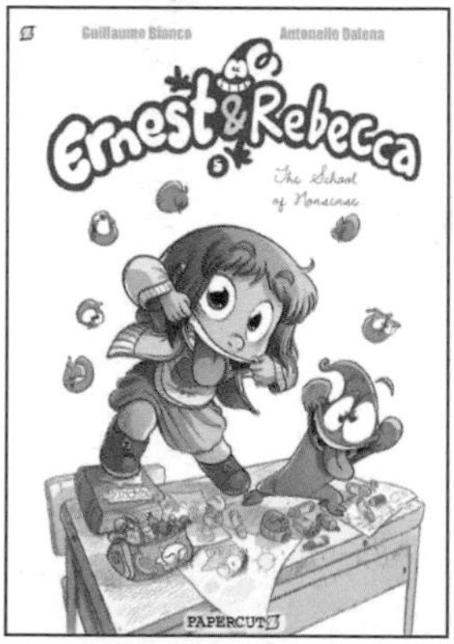
Ernest & Rebecca
PAPERCUTZ

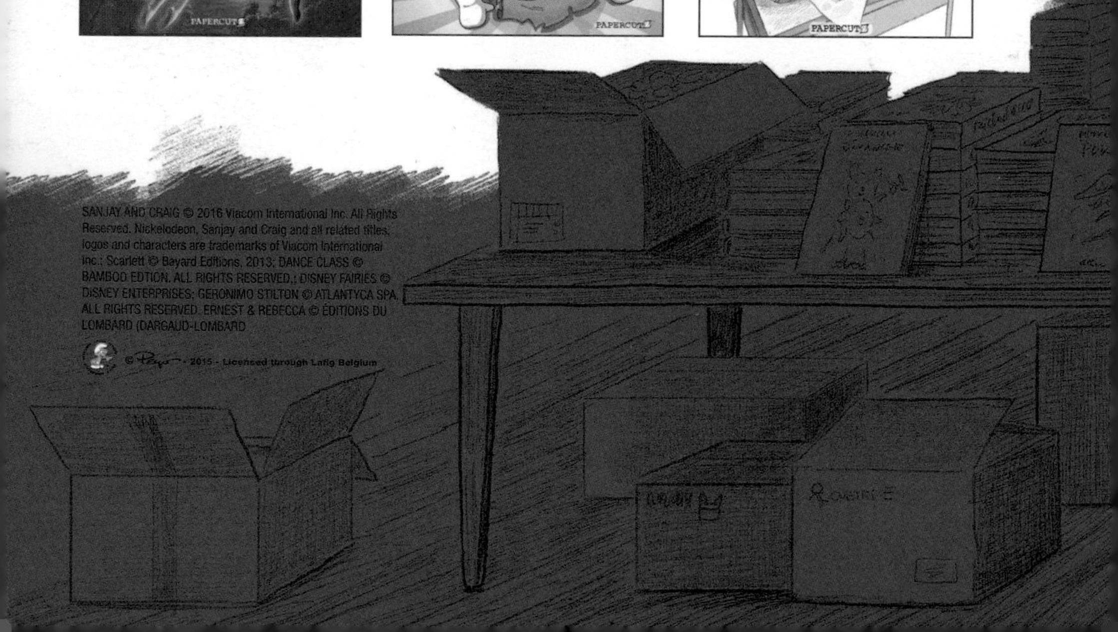

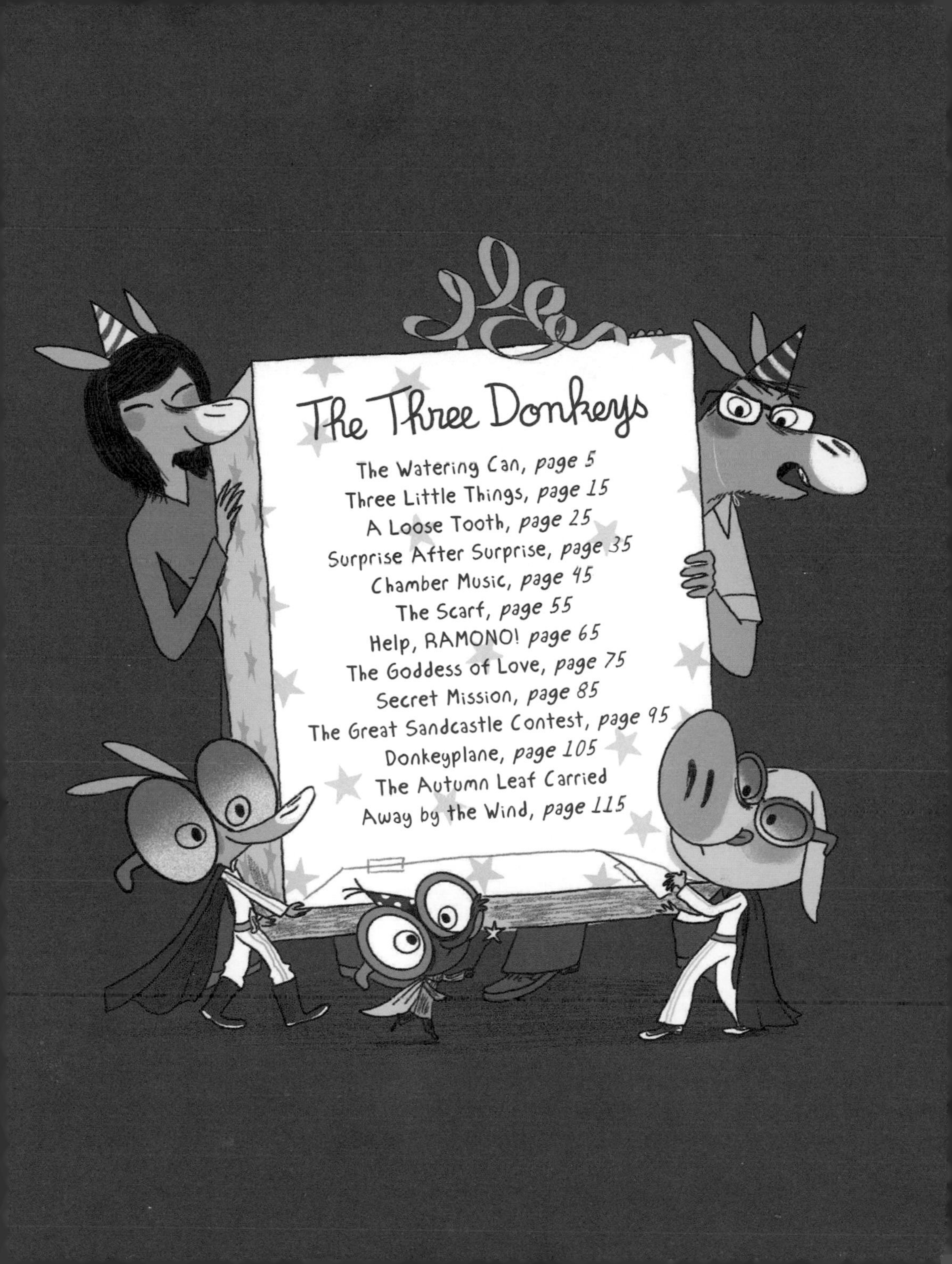
The Three Donkeys
The Watering Can, page 5
Three Little Things, page 15
A Loose Tooth, page 25
Surprise After Surprise, page 35
Chamber Music, page 45
The Scarf, page 55
Help, RAMONO! page 65
The Goddess of Love, page 75
Secret Mission, page 85
The Great Sandcastle Contest, page 95
Donkeyplane, page 105
The Autumn Leaf Carried
Away by the Wind, page 115

To Madame Machu,
— Emmanuel Guibert

ARIOL
#8 "The Three Donkeys"

Emmanuel Guibert — Writer
Marc Boutavant — Artist
Rémi Chaurand — Colorist
Joe Johnson — Translation
Big Bird Zatryb — Letterer
Jeff Whitman — Production Coordinator
Bethany Bryan — Associate Editor
Jim Salicrup
Editor-in-Chief

Volume 8: Les trois baudets © Bayard Editions, 2013

ISBN: 978-1-62991-439-8

Printed in China
Manufactured by Regent Publishing Services, Hong Kong,
Printed February 2016 in Shenzhen, Guangdong, China

Papercutz books may be purchased for business or promotional use. For information on bulk purchases
please contact Macmillan Corporate and Premium Sales Department at (800) 221-7945 x5442.

Distributed by Macmillan
First Papercutz Printing